THE
WARRIOR
MIDWIFE

This first edition published in 2022 by
Blue Moon Rising Publishing
www.ektaabali.com

ISBN ebook: 978-0-6452939-8-2
Paperback: 978-0-6452939-9-9
Hardcover: 978-0-6489830-8-8
Paperback (Pastel Edition): 978-0-6454650-3-7
Hardcover (Pastel Edition): 978-0-6454650-4-4

Illustrated Cover design by Carly Diep
Naked Hardcover by Jessica Lowdell
Map artwork by Najlakay
Chapter Header by Jessica Lowdell
Book Formatting by E.P. Bali with Vellum

The author acknowledges the Traditional Custodians of the land where this book was written. We acknowledge their connections to land, sea and community. We pay our respects to their Elders past and present and extend that respect to all Aboriginal and Torres Strait Islander Peoples today.

A NOTE ON THE CONTENT

I care about the mental health of my readers.
This book contains some themes you might want to know
about before you read.
They are listed at www.ektaabali.com/themes

E. P. BALI

THE WARRIOR MIDWIFE

BOOK ONE

KUSHA

SAMPATI CITY

TRAENARA

SHOBNA CITY

WAELAN

BALNOR CITY

QUARTZ

LOBRA

THE TEMARI FOREST

TEMPLE RUINS

ELLYTHIA

LOTA

THE LOTUS SEA

THE JUNGLE ACADEMY

ECLIPSE

HUMAN REALM

FARLOUGH CITY

ERUS

PEACH TREE CITY

KAALON

FAE WARRIOR ACADEMY

BLACK COURT

OBSIDIAN COURT

REALM OF THE DARK FAE

MIDNIGHT COURT

TWILIGHT COURT   SOLAR FAE REALMS

Midwives are rare and precious souls, and I have been lucky enough to work with many. This book is for them.

1

SARAYA

The princess sat in a whorehouse all night, the door barred with a wardrobe.

I almost snorted at the thought of the report my stepmother would receive from her spies before turning my concentration to the patient lying before me. Chirra had laboured all day and then late into the night, and when Agatha had summoned me, I knew there would be trouble.

Chirra groaned, sweat gleaming on her forehead, raven hair plastered to her beautiful but now pale face. Her labour was obstructing, and as I trained my magical eye into her body, I could see waves of uterine contractions trying to unsuccessfully push her baby boy out. Although she was fully dilated, the babe's head was ever so slightly unflexed. He should have had his chin tucked tightly to his chest, allowing the back portion of his head, the narrowest part, to come first. Instead, the crown of his head was attempting to lead.

Babies can't be born that way. The diameter is too wide for the bones of a woman's pelvis.

I gritted my teeth. This wasn't going to be easy. An obstructed birth was one of the hardest things a mother could go through during labour. Without intervention, this baby would die.

I glanced up at Agatha, standing hunched and beady-eyed next to the bed. In my ancient midwife mentor's face, I saw the wisdom and wariness of over sixty years of watching over women's labour. She already knew what I was going to say. She gave me a curt nod of permission.

"He's stuck, Chirra," I spoke plainly. That was how the hard-eyed women of Madame Yolande's brothel preferred it. "His head isn't at the right angle. I need to shift it if he's to come out alive. Have I your permission?"

At the end of yet another gruelling contraction, Chirra gave me a watery, long-suffering look. "Yeah, you got my permission, Princess Saraya. Do it, please."

I nodded and glanced at Agatha, who grabbed the girl's hand. Chirra clasped Agatha's hand back, and I saw the muscle in her jaw tick as she clenched her teeth.

Closing my eyes, I reached into Chirra's uterus with my mind and felt for her baby's head. In the bright lines of his rapidly beating heart, I could see a great tiredness. This needed to be done. I grasped the babe's head on both sides with my magic, pushed him a little out of Chirra's pelvis, and gently tucked his chin in.

Chirra swallowed her own scream. I opened my eyes to look upon her with admiration. She was a strong woman. The women of the Sticks always were.

"It's done."

Chirra groaned deep in her throat, her body signalling her to push.

Half an hour later, the baby was born, screaming bloody

murder, his head deeply moulded and swollen. We assured a worried Chirra his head would normalise in a few days, but Agatha and I exchanged a look. She would have to keep an eye on this baby and enlist a wet nurse right away, as a labour this long meant this baby had little to no reserves of energy left.

The room took on the ethereal hush that I had learned, long ago, came after the birth of a baby. A silent shiver slipped through my being, and I found myself turning to look behind me. But of course, by the soft orange glow of the luminous quartz crystal bulb, I could see the room was empty except for the wardrobe barring the door. The distant sound of pub conversation and chink of glasses that came from the drinking room on the ground floor of the brothel, filtered through.

Agatha helped Chirra latch her baby to her breast while I kept a fixed magical eye on Chirra's uterus, as she was at high risk of haemorrhaging. After her placenta was born a little while later, I assisted her tired uterus to contract and control its bleeding while Agatha fed Chirra a tonic of ergot to help prevent excessive blood loss after I left.

I sighed in relief. Picking up the wooden bowl with the dinner plate-sized placenta within, I wiped my own sweaty brow with my wrist and took the placenta over to the door so that Agatha could bury it later, as was Lobrathian custom.

I washed my hands thoroughly using the pitcher of water and soap in the small basin Agatha had brought in. When I finished, I turned and caught Chirra's dark eye, her babe snuggled and suckling by her side. We smiled tiredly at each other.

"Thank you, Princess." Her voice was barely a dry rasp.

"My pleasure. You'll take some time off, please?"

Chirra grimaced. "I'll try, Princess."

Agatha, watching over the babe, grumbled under her breath. We both knew Chirra would wait a week maximum, plugging her bleeding with the special sea moss dubbed 'the whore's best friend' and pass the baby off to a wet nurse for the evenings. There was no way for Chirra to know who the father was, so she was on her own. And even in the shining capital of Quartz, where the luminous quartz quarry brought plenty of money into the city, you only got paid if you worked.

It had been better when my mother was alive. In the five years of her absence, the city's poor had burgeoned, and once again, as before her arrival, the slums took back their name, 'the Sticks,' for the Stickly tree branches they used to thatch their leaking rooves.

I went over to the door of Chirra's room and proceeded to shove my weight against the wardrobe, pushing it back into place against the wall.

Abilities like mine had long since disappeared from the human realm for reasons unknown. Although it was common knowledge that I 'helped' childbearing women, most commonfolk didn't really understand how I did it, even if they saw it with their bare eyes. And in a brothel like this, locks on doors were not approved of, but I still needed to work undisturbed.

Agatha beckoned to me, and we left Chirra to doze with her new baby in peace, which was likely one of the few free evenings she would get. Yolande Tully was a fair and hard-working Madame, but she expected no less from her girls. We walked down the creaking, wooden corridor, ignoring the various sounds coming from the rooms we passed, and headed to the small balcony the girls used to smoke or get fresh air.

The night was cool, and I appreciated its caress on my hot skin, the air smelling of the sweet magnolias that Yolande had planted around her establishment in an attempt to make it look more pleasant. The city lay before us, illuminated by the multi-coloured luminous quartz crystals that our city was known for. Mined in the great quarry just outside the city gates, we traded the valuable crystals with our neighbouring human kingdoms. It was the only known mine on the continent, and it made us a valuable ally.

A crescent moon sat queen-like high in the western sky, and I knew that meant I should be hurrying back to the palace within the hour.

Agatha took a hand-rolled cigarette out of one of the many pockets in her patchwork cardigan and lit it up, inhaling deeply. She exhaled blue smoke, and we watched it coil in the breeze like something from a dream.

Blue ganja was the popular relaxant amongst both nobility and commonfolk and, I supposed, the only way Agatha could unwind after decades of midwifery.

"I need you alert for Bluebell," she croaked, eyeing me with piercing blue eyes that missed nothing. "Those twins will come any day now. The last time was bad enough."

I cringed inwardly. Bluebell was only a girl of seventeen, and this was her second pregnancy. I'd been at her first birth two years ago and hadn't gotten there in time to be of any use. The baby had been stillborn, and I don't think she ever fully mentally recovered from it.

"I know," I said. "At this point, it'll take the goddess herself to keep me away. She has a purple candle."

5

"I'll light it myself. Visit her beforehand if you can. She's an anxious little thing."

I nodded and took a moment to centre myself, looking out at the bright city of my home.

There were hidden, multicoloured candles in my room given to me by my mother before she passed. I had a whole stack of them lined up in a neat row, and Agatha and I gave them out to the pregnant mothers in case of emergency. Each candle came as a pair, and when one was lit, its twin would light up too. So if one of the many midwives in the city needed help, she'd light a candle, I'd see its twin light up in my room, and I'd head out into the city.

Attending every birth was impossible, of course. The many midwives of the city were far too competent under Agatha's watchful eye, but when there was an issue that couldn't be solved with herbs and brains, they'd call for me, and I'd come running every time.

I bade Agatha goodbye and trudged through the long corridor of pleasure rooms and down the winding stairs into the drinking room.

I was a usual presence in the city at night. Though the women never batted an eyelid at me, men never neglected to make sure I knew they were watching. But drunk men were always quick to notice a lone woman, especially a half-Ellythian with skin noticeably darker than the pale-skinned Lobrathian natives.

"Is it that princess again?" came a gruff slur from a table to my right.

Shooting a droll look at the group of men sitting at the table closest to the stair, I paused. They were labourers from the quarry by the dirt and dust on their clothes. And by the lilt in his accent, I guessed they'd come from Kaalon, our neighbouring Kingdom, to seek work. I tried my best to ignore blonde-haired Genevieve, grinding against a man in the corner of the room, her skirts hitched high around her waist. All in another night's work.

"*That princess,*" I said loftily, "is pleased to tell you that Chirra has birthed a bouncing baby boy. Both are alive and well."

"That means she's out of business for how long?" whined a younger man with barely a wisp of hair on his upper lip. The others grumbled into their tankards.

I scowled at the one who'd spoken. One of these men could very well be the father. "She'll take as long as she's able. Good evening, gentlemen." I turned on my booted heel and made my way out of Madame Yolande's establishment and onto the dark cobblestoned street.

I was always followed by either my father's guards or my stepmother's. They never knew exactly *when* I left the palace, but I was easy to find. If you asked anyone in the local vicinity, they always knew who was giving birth, so naturally, that's where I would be. And by the glint of copper under the light of the moon, I knew it was my stepmother's guards— the *Queen's* guards, who were on the prowl tonight.

Ignoring them, I made my way down the main street, brightly lit with orange quartz, and into the retail district. Bluebell and her young husband lived with her parents above their bakery on Canty Street, so it was only a short walk for me through the vacant city.

Quartz City was as safe as any other. It had its share of pickpockets and criminals who only came out after dark, its gamblers, and its mobsters. With this in mind, my mother had insisted that my younger sister and I be trained in weapons from a young age. And even after her death, although my

7

stepmother hated it, we still drilled swords with the arms-master five times a week, and I made sure I took a lesson in knives since I couldn't be very well lugging a sword with me everywhere. So, I had two personal knives with simple leather hilts—one sheathed to my thigh and the other at my wrist.

Despite the minor risk, I crossed the empty town square and revelled in the nighttime stroll. In the moments of being out in the city alone, just me and the commonfolk, I had freedom. It was a tiny, delicate glass orb, this freedom, but it was all mine. It was not my father's nor my stepmother's nor the eagle-eyed advisor's. And in that orb glowed a peaceful power that I had all to myself. And once I returned to the palace, that orb popped like a bubble, and my magic, my skills, practically meant nothing anymore.

As I had guessed, when I reached the line of shopfronts that marked the beginning of the food district, a faint light shone from the bakery window. The Bakers, naturally, got up well before dawn to start off their loaves for the day. I rapped my knuckles on their glass front door.

A sandy-haired young man rushed across the shop towards me and unlatched the door.

"Your Highness!" Charlie was Bluebell's nineteen-year-old husband and a sweet boy who knew how to look after her. "Bluey is just here."

I entered the store, the smell of yeast and sugar making my stomach growl. "How's she going?" I asked him in a low voice.

He shifted nervously. "Okay, I think. The tightnings have been keepin' her up at night. So we just started the bakery up and let her parents sleep."

The tightnings were the pre-labour pains women often got

well before actual labour. And having twins, Bluebell's uterus was likely to want to 'practise' more than anyone else's. Contractions were a marvel to watch, using my own powers. Like a tide washing against a beach, the muscles bunched in brilliant waves across the abdomen. A woman's body was truly a marvellous wonder.

Bluebell, petite with a belly that seemed to dwarf her, was ferociously kneading a wad of dough on the bench. I raised my brows at Charlie, and he shrugged. Though she looked tiny and carried a mountain of grief on her shoulders, she was a strong, determined girl. Perhaps it was a lifetime of kneading dough that made her like that, I didn't know. She looked up and saw me standing there, gawking at her.

"Saraya!" she gasped, hastily wiping her hands on a towel before rushing towards me.

"Hello, Bluebell."

She grabbed me in an embrace, and when she pulled back, her anxious hazel eyes searched my green. "Were you at a birth tonight?"

"I was." I gave her my best smile. "Mum and baby are both bouncing and delighted."

Exaggerated, but I needed Bluebell to be positive. If there was one thing that hindered a birth, it was fear. She beamed at me as if I was a heroic warrior from an ancient tale returning from battle.

"Wonderful news! Charlie? Isn't that wonderful?"

Charlie rubbed the back of his neck nervously. "It is."

He was terrified of a repeat of last time. We all were. Second births were so different from first, as we'd been telling them over and over again, but that fear of the dark unknown was enough to cripple anyone.

Bluebell's hands were still clutching mine. "Can you check me?" she whispered. "Can you check if everything's okay?"

"Are they moving normally?" I asked, squinting at her tummy.

"Yes, too much sometimes." She smiled and placed her hands lovingly on her stomach. "They keep me up. Getting me ready for—" her throat caught on her words.

She couldn't say it. She couldn't say that her babies were keeping her up in preparing for nighttime feeds, and my heart squeezed in sympathy for her. She wouldn't let herself believe that she would come out of this with one or even two healthy babies. The hope was too much.

Bluebell had named her stillborn baby Rose, and it was the first funeral I had gone to since my own mother's. I knew grief, how it could weigh on a person like a dense cloud, suffocating and blinding you. I had gone through it with them.

If there was one thing that I knew, I would make sure, by the goddess, that everything went well for her birth. That all three of them came out of it with sighs of relief. All four, including poor Charlie, who could only watch and wait helplessly, whispering words of encouragement into his wife's ear.

I looked inside Bluebell's abdomen the way my mother had taught me as a thirteen-year-old girl. *Always get permission first*, she had said. *Invading someone's body is neither ethical nor polite. A person's body is their own. Never forget that.*

And I hadn't forgotten it. I never looked inside anyone unless they asked me to. This ability was fraught with ethical dilemmas, and my mother had done her best to warn me of them when my Power appeared at my first bleeding.

In my mind's eye, Bluebell's two babies, one boy and one girl, kicked each other in their sleep. I looked past them and into their thankfully fat tumble of umbilical cords, checking to see that the flow of blood and nutrients was sound. I followed one cord down to the placenta, checking its integrity. I felt the tension in my own shoulders abate when I saw that all was well. Her tiny frame was supporting her infants beautifully. When labour came, they looked like they'd be able to withstand the stress of the contractions.

I closed my inner eye and opened my physical ones, grinning at Bluebell and Charlie, who were studying my face with absolute focus.

They smiled back.

"All perfect!" I said happily. "Now, if you'll excuse me, I'll be off to my bed."

"Well deserved," said Charlie, reaching out to shake my hand.

I hesitated because it was highly unusual of a Lobrathian man to offer his hand to a woman like that. But I think Charlie was so thankful that he considered me akin to a man, so I shook it with a grin as Bluebell hurried off to the kitchen.

She returned to place a warm paper bag into my hands. I peered inside, and a hot sweet bun awaited within, slathered with white icing. I looked back at her with so much gratitude I could have burst. "Goddess, you're the best, Bluey! I'll see you any day now."

She smiled at me, but I could see it was strained at the edges. "Promise me you'll be here."

I took her hand, and my voice quavered with a seriousness I felt in my marrow. "I'll be here, Bluey. The goddess herself couldn't stop me."

I left the bakery through the back door, so I could lose the queen's useless guards as I made my way up to the palace. I tore into the warm, sticky bun just as the pre-dawn light cast

11

its eerie blue glow around me. Exhaustion clung to me like a heavy, invisible veil. I almost missed the dense grove of trees at the edge of farmer Thompson's land that marked my secret entrance—an entrance only visible to someone with a power like mine.

The palace had been built hundreds of years ago, in the days of the old kings, when, I guessed, magic had been commonplace. No one knew how I got in and out of the castle without being seen. I only managed it because of this tunnel —which I had stumbled upon by accident one day playing tag through the servants' corridors with my sister, Altara. Even if one of the guards was looking right at me as I went through my entrance, by some trick of the eye the ancient architects had come up with, it would just look like I had disappeared into thin air.

With my mental eye, I reached behind the layers of rock, soil, and tree roots. With my power, I flicked the latch that would open it. Rock grated against rock, and the ancient door swung open smoothly. I hurried into the passageway and let the door swing shut behind me.

In complete darkness, I reached into my satchel and fished out my tinder box and candle. Quickly lighting it with the ease of many years of practise, I used its circle of light to hurry my way through the dark tunnel of rock. There had to be some old magic in these tunnels because they were always in top shape. I'd never had any trouble with collapsed sections or blockages. And that was lucky because it was a long tunnel—about a thousand paces, at a guess. And when I emerged, it was always with a happy gasp of fresh air.

When I reached the exit, a mirror to the entry, I clicked open the latch and slinked outside, right into a vacant servant's corridor on the lower floors of the palace.

I hurried through the back passages, up a series of servants' stairs, and into my room through a narrow door hidden behind a tapestry.

As I entered my dark room, a voice like freezing ice stopped me in my tracks.

"Sneaking back in, are we, Saraya?"

2

SARAYA

It's commonly said that prostitution is the oldest profession in the world. That is very incorrect. The truth is that prostitution is the second oldest profession because the first is midwifery. Older women have been helping younger women give birth since the first humans walked upon the earth. And there was always one of them designated as an expert at the job.

In my humble opinion, there is no higher nor more noble a profession than midwifery. So, when my stepmother rudely inserted herself into my room and snidely accused me of sneaking around like some wanton thief, irritation spun through me like a spiked wind, grating and wild.

I could never openly admit what it was that I snuck into the city for because that would be admitting that I had magic —which wasn't supposed to exist in humans, for all intents and purposes, so my mother had forbidden me to reveal it to anyone unnecessarily.

My stepmother was in *my* room, in my personal space, like a foreign invader—which was accurate, really. My father had married her rather quickly, at the behest of his advisors, to secure relations with Kusha, the most isolated, northern-most kingdom of the human realm. We had not been on good terms since a trade scandal some decades back, and it was seen as a logical alliance. They were secretive people, and tall stone walls lined their entire southern border.

There was a soft whirr as the dark panel of a quartz lamp was opened. Yellow light filled the room, revealing my step-mother's cold, alabaster face, blue eyes trained, snake-like on me. It always struck me how different we were, like night and day. Me, dark and soft, her light and sharp-edged. Maybe that's why she hated me so much.

"I'm going to bed, Stepmother," I said stiffly. "I will see you at lunch."

"I think not." Her voice was like a serrated blade into my core, and it made the skin on my back twinge with an old memory.

Because I knew that voice. That feminine hissing, spiteful sneer that I had not heard in quite some months. That voice was only reserved for when the queen was feeling particu-larly malicious.

Her red quartz necklace glinted as she arose from my chaise, becoming an elongated shadow, the source of my fear and misery, the very reason I felt more at home in the city than in the palace.

"You are nineteen next week, and you still won't obey your father. I think you need another lesson."

It took all my self-discipline not to fall to my knees and beg. I had thought she had stopped. The last *lesson* had been months ago. I thought I had gotten too old for this. Not again. She couldn't possibly—

"Things are going to change around here, Saraya," she

said. "And for the better."

I only realised her guards were behind me when heavy hands grabbed me by my arms.

I refused to let the scream escape from my throat. "No," I said, hearing my own disbelief like the quiet before a thunderclap. "You can't do this."

But we both knew she could. Havlem and Yarnat wearing copper and black colours, standing behind me were not my father's guards. They bore no allegiance to me. She had brought them and two ladies in waiting with her from the Kusha Kingdom, and they were strictly loyal to her.

I hadn't known my stepmother hated me until a month after the wedding. It had been the first time since her arrival that I had left the palace for midwife purposes. The next morning, she had her guards escort me to her rooms, as they were doing now.

When she had taken out her whip, the shock of it had been so complete that when her ladies in waiting undid my dress and held me down across her red velvet ottoman, I did nothing. My own mother had been so gentle and kind to everyone she met that when faced with the complete antithesis of her, this monster in silk and chiffon, I completely froze.

As if the lashings weren't bad enough, after the queen was done, she bent down and whispered in my ear, "If you tell your father, I'll punish your sister too."

I had been fourteen at the time, my sister thirteen, and over the next five years, my beloved stepmother took out her seemingly endless anger upon me for any and every transgression. Telling my father was unthinkable, for half the time was too caught up in state affairs and the other half too caught up in a black grief that clung to his mind like tar. So each time my own guards would move to stop Havlem and Yarnat from taking me, I would shake my head with a firm 'no.' Confused, they stepped back every time.

Over the next four years, I wondered what I could do to stop it. But she was the queen and outranked me in all things, and I needed to protect my sister. Although she was only a year younger than me, I would do anything to protect Altara from this monster of a woman. I would die for my sister, and this torture was a small sacrifice for her safety.

Every time I looked into my stepmother's dead blue eyes, I saw something that made a shiver cut through me. A cold-blooded, life-altering rage lay sleeping within her. I wondered what she'd been through that made her feel the need to hurt someone as if her life depended on it. I'd seen a version of that look in the eyes of some of the veterans from the old war. Memories and trauma made them mean, and for some of them, it curdled their mind and made them insane.

I hated the fact that even at my age, a woman grown, her guards dragged me down the marble corridors of my own home like some child. These beautiful marble corridors and halls Altara and I had once happily played in. I wasn't a child anymore, and yet she still made me feel so small. I would have much preferred to walk to her rooms on my own terms, but I knew that would make it less satisfying for her twisted mind.

When we got to her suite, lit with a luminous red quartz hardly anyone else used, her ladies in waiting, Marissa and Tenna, took over, sweeping towards me as if this was some dark ritual. I knew she beat them too when she had nothing to punish me for because I had seen them cringe in their dresses on some days. But neither would ever seek to help me beyond first aid, and that was because they hated me.

Marissa had come to my rooms one night, crying and panicking. She was two months pregnant by the very much married palace stablemaster and asked me to terminate the pregnancy. I knew the consequences she was facing. She'd be sent back to Kusha in shame, losing her position here, and probably be shipped off to a nunnery to live the rest of her life in religious poverty. But if there was one rule my mother had, it was to never stop a beating heart without careful thought.

"You must always ask goddess Umali for wisdom," she whispered to me one night as we lay snuggled in my bed, all three of us. "She represents the space between life and death. If you are asked to stop a heart, it should be with caution, carefully considered, and *never* before you are an adult by law. Promise me that."

And so I had promised my mother.

I had only been fifteen at the time Marissa had come to me, and I heeding my mother's warning, I declined her.

I ended up sending Marissa to see Agatha, who gave her a special concoction. Marissa had returned a few weeks later, gaunt and pale from blood loss. I had felt sorry for her, but there had been nothing I could do. So, although she didn't need to do it at all, it was with great vehemence that she grabbed me by the arm and swung me down across the ottoman. I frowned up at her, and she scowled back, reaching for my dress buttons. I slapped her hand away and undid them myself.

Perhaps it was the exhaustion of assisting Chirra's birth, the emotion of seeing Bluebell so frightened, or the fact that my nineteenth birthday was just around the corner that made me snap back for once.

"How long?" I suddenly whipped around and faced my stepmother.

"Excuse me?" The whip was in her hands, and she held it like a lover, but when I had spoken, she'd gone as still as a snake looking at its prey.

Since the day she had told me that any resistance would land Altara under the whip, I had never spoken back to her for fear of the consequences. But my sister and I were almost grown women.

"How long will this go on?" I asked breathlessly. "I'm not a child anymore. Until I get married and leave here? And then what? Who will bear the brunt of this vile anger you have? My sister? She's old enough to fight back. You can't threaten her the way you've done with me."

I thought my words would make her angry, might make her remind me of who exactly was Queen here and under whose thumb I lived. But she didn't do any of those things. Instead, she smirked.

"Speaking of marriage…" her voice trailed casually as she stroked her whip. "There might be some news on that front."

"What?" My entire body went limp with disbelief. My father had always avoided talk of our marriages. In fact, avoided was putting it lightly. He outright refused to talk about it. Altara and I weren't so happy about that because we would rather know which brutish idiot we'd be expected to bed well in advance. But despite his advisors' persistence… nothing. So it was with a violent amount of surprise that I heard *this* news.

"What do you know?" I asked lamely, full well knowing she'd give me nothing.

"Turn around, Saraya."

I *hated* the way she said my name. In her mouth, the beautiful name given to me by my mother became something dirty. And at that moment, it was almost like the thought of a wedding being planned for me—of leaving the home I had grown up in with all the memories of my mother shattered some old contract I'd made with myself. If I was going, Altara would have to face our stepmother on her own. I had to end this once and for all.

"No."

The queen raised her eyebrows, her grip going tight against the leather.

"You are speaking to the queen," hissed Marissa.

"And you are speaking to the *princess*," I shot back at her.

My stepmother's lips went white, and I was suddenly very aware of the fact that it was three against one and that I had two knives on my person. Bearing steel against the queen was treason, and I wasn't even sure if my father's disease-ridden brain would be able to stop the consequences of that.

Physically? Marissa and Tenna were older than me by about five years, but I had been training in fighting since I was a toddler. I could easily take them and my stepmother down without even using my knives. But hurting women was something that went against everything my magic and I stood for. My magic was made to serve women, and something ancient and deep-rooted in me forbade me from hurting them.

So I ran. I darted towards the servant's stairs at the edge of the room because I knew the guards were waiting outside her official door. I ripped the door open and ran down the narrow stairs, Marissa shrieking after me.

But I'd never come down this way before. The servants'

stairs were an impossible labyrinth if you didn't know where you were going. So I just ran in the general direction of Altara's rooms, which were right next to mine. I would collect my guards and—

Abruptly, I wondered if I'd made a mistake. I halted in my tracks, panting and weary from my long night. The castle guards, even *my guards*, would take the queen's orders over mine. If she instructed them to drag me into her room, they would have no choice. It would be treason for them to disobey.

I couldn't go to my father. He would take her side. I was the disobedient princess. By now, everyone knew I snuck out night after night. He would think that I needed to be disciplined too.

Resignation hit me like a blacksmith's hammer. So I turned and went back the way I had come.

When I entered my stepmother's rooms, the suite was a jungle of raised voices as my stepmother, the guards, and the ladies in waiting spoke frantically over one another. I think the queen, still standing with her whip in hand, might have been in a sort of shocked disbelief at the fact I had finally fought back. But they all froze as I entered her room. Silently, I knelt down by the ottoman, undid my dress, pulled it down, and bare-breasted, lay across the red velvet in a way I had done a hundred times before.

In front of the queen, I would lose every time. This was an impossible knot. Something I couldn't fix with my mind the way I could fix an obstructed labour. I heard them shifting around me as I stared at the cream fibres of the carpeted floor. A floor I knew like an old friend. I had promised my mother I would never use my powers without a person's permission. And that also meant I could never use it for harm. I could have used my powers on the queen, or on the guards, or on Marissa and Tenna. But I wouldn't. My mother had been the better queen, but that thought was little comfort now.

The first strike came harder than it ever had. And I did not make a sound. Because silence was the sound of defeat.

3
SARAYA

As a girl, I saw my father as a strapping warrior, fearless, quick of mind, and of wit. A worthy leader my mother had grown to love quickly after their arranged marriage. A man who had valiantly led his army to meet the Dark Fae king and his monstrous horde on the battlefield.

But only a few months after my mother's death, he began to change. I don't know if it was the grief of losing her or some natural disease process, but his mental state began to decline. It started with forgetfulness, and often, he would look into the far distance, as if his mind was far away from his physical body. These trance-like states increased over the last five years until it seemed that lucidity was only something that happened twice a day. His advisors hid this from as many people as they could, restricting his public appearances more and more. I don't think anyone in the city suspected about his brain. The only rumours flying around were that his various injuries were causing him pains as he grew older.

It was important for our kingdom to maintain the appearance of strength. Not only because of our valuable luminous quartz quarry, but we were the major border kingdom. Our domain terminated at the foot of the Silent Mountains, which was also the divide between us and the fae realms. No human really knew what lay beyond the mountains in the fae realm except that there were five Dark Fae Courts, and of those, the Black Court was the major bordering court. We only knew this because the dreaded fae king Wyxian Darkcleaver had flown his sigil, a black dragon, during the war.

And it was this war my father fought at the base of the mountain on the human side thirty years ago. The fae usually stayed on their side, and we on ours. The only issue had come when they'd discovered the huge amount of luminous quartz we had. At that point, the fae king Wyxian had decided that he now wanted our land.

But what match are humans against an invasion of trained fae warriors? No match at all, and this was why my father was such a celebrated warrior-king. Somehow, using some genius tactical strategies, he had managed to lead his armies and meet the fae blow for blow, forcing them to retreat back into the mountains. We got our land back, but the mountains were no longer neutral territory. The fae gained a valuable asset that day, but my father saved our kingdom.

So it was a great shame for my sister and me to see my father deteriorate in such an awful way. In Lobrathia, females were not permitted to hold the crown, and as such, what would become of the kingdom when he died or if he was too ill to rule was not discussed with us. According to custom, both of us princesses were to be married off to neighbouring kingdoms. The next in line to the throne was my father's younger brother, Prince Ansel, who never really wanted the throne and was just happy to be away at sea, exploring the lands beyond the horizon. Until then, my father's office just ran on an army of advisors while he absently gave his signature and stamped the wax seal of the Voltanius House, a lightning bolt wreathed in storm clouds.

After my whipping, I slept all day, shirking my lesson with the history master. But we always had dinner together as a family, so that evening, we gathered together as usual in our small family dining room.

Marissa and Tenna always covered my wounds after a lashing, mostly so I didn't get any blood on my clothes showing through for all and sundry to see. But after a few rounds, I quickly learned to use my magic to tweak the skin tissue on my back to turn off the pain receptors. I could manipulate my body at will.

It just took a hell of a lot of effort to maintain.

It was like keeping your grip around a soft ball. You could do it for a little while pretty easily, but any longer, and it got more and more difficult and eventually painful. I could keep it up for a few hours, but more than that and I'd be on cue for a faint.

So I only cringed a little as I sat at the table next to Altara, whose beautiful, bronzed face was troubled as she watched me. I never openly mentioned the lashings to her, but she'd found me out one day when I'd forgotten and exposed my naked back to her. I shut the conversation down pretty quickly, but she knew what went on between my stepmother and me.

Altara and I looked alike, with long onyx black hair and brown skin courtesy of the mix of our milk-pale father and our dark as night mother. We were both curvy, with generous-sized breasts and hips and the high cheekbones of our mother's people. And our bright green eyes we shared with our mother's family—Lotus House. Altara's long silky black hair, which she hardly ever cut, was worn loose tonight. Mine was thick and wavy, more like my mother's, and each day, I had my maids braid and pin it to keep it out of my way.

Tonight, we were served a three-course meal of spinach soup, quail, and beets with a creamy gravy and a peach tart for dessert. The peaches courtesy of Kalaan Kingdom, whose capital, Peach Tree City, was even named after their famous and nutritious peaches.

"We have business to discuss tomorrow, Sara," my father said abruptly, sitting straight in his chair, his brown eyes as clear as I had seen them in a long while.

We all froze. My eyes met my stepmother's, and her lips pressed into a slow, malicious smile. Altara glanced at me in surprise, and I took a deep breath. "Yes, Father, of course."

This was it. This was the marriage arrangement. I could hardly wait to finish dinner to talk with Altara. After my father was led away by his manservant and carer, Derrick, we hurried to my room, and I quickly checked on my coloured candles, all seven of them, standing in their holders inside one of the cupboards in my room. Everyone simply assumed the multicoloured wax was for decoration, but my two maids and Altara knew better.

Altara plopped herself on my bed. "Do you know what it's about?" she asked earnestly.

"Stepmother let it slip," I said, moving a stack of heavy anatomy textbooks and sitting opposite her. "It's about marriage."

Her hand flew to her chest. "No," she said in disbelief, her beautiful face a mask of shock.

"It's about time, isn't it?" I said glumly, fiddling with my purple dress.

"But your nineteenth isn't for a week! It's a bit early, isn't it? Mother said we were to wait until at least twenty-one."

"Mother isn't here, so her rules don't apply anymore," I said quietly, looking at her. "But Tara—" My wounds stung against their dressings, and I hissed in pain. If I was being shipped off to a wedding, Tara would be here all alone. We needed to make plans. I couldn't just leave her here with that she-devil who prowled the palace.

"What?" she pressed. "If yours is being arranged, mine will be close too."

"We don't know about that," I pressed, "you have a whole ten months before your birthday. I'm worried about leaving you here alone." I couldn't meet her eye. I had let the pain receptors loose on my back and now felt every wound like a stinging hurricane. I couldn't let her go through that. It was unthinkable. "The queen—" I really didn't want to say it. But she should be prepared, she should know—

"I know, Sara," whispered Altara. "I know what she does to you. I…" She bit her lip.

I frowned at the odd note in her voice. "What?"

"I spiked her soup tonight."

"You *what?*" I leapt up from the bed and gawked at her, suppressing a grimace at the pain of the movement.

"It was just a laxative!" she said defensively.

I couldn't help it. The laugh came out of me in an unexpected flurry from my throat. "Are you joking?"

She giggled, covering her mouth as if she could hardly believe it herself. "No, I really did. Sometimes I give her the constipating one. Another time it was a herb that makes you itch."

"And all this time, you were supposed to be the nice one."

"She'll be on the chamber pot for hours."

A small act of defiance. But what would the consequences be? It wasn't enough. We needed to be smarter.

Altara's face suddenly became serious. "Is your back okay? Does it need medicine? I can send for some illegal herbs from Geravie."

Any remaining laughter died within me, and I sat back down, looking at my hands. Altara was as learned as I was about anatomy, physiology, and herbs, as our mother had made our education a priority. My sister was clever and had always had some guts. I knew that as much I felt a sense of responsibility for her, she also felt similarly about me. She had her own special type of magic, and she wielded it in the only way she could think of.

"I should have done something more, Sara," Altara whispered. "I should have sent the guards, told Father, sent someone—"

"We couldn't have done anything, Tar. Do you really want to know if your guards would obey her over you? Because I don't think it's a difficult choice for them to make. Uncomfortable at most, but we know what they'll choose."

"Father—"

"He would've done nothing, even if he was sane at the time."

She sighed loudly. "How can we be this powerless? We're princesses for the goddess' sake!" Then more quietly, "I miss Mother so much." Her voice caught, and I felt the backs of my own eyes burn.

I looked up at her, the fine panes of her face limned with yellow quartz light. "Me too. I'm glad we had the time with her that we did. I wish she could have done your bleeding ceremony with us."

She sniffed, nodding in agreement.

I was fourteen when I had my first menstruation. It was just a few months before Mother's death, and sometimes I think the goddess had waited for me to bleed before taking her from us.

It had been a full moon, and my mother, along with her three trusted ladies in waiting, took Altara and me into the grounds behind the palace, where there was a small forest. We all took off our dresses and stepped into the lukewarm lake.

My mother had taken my hand in her calloused one and pointed up at the moon with her other. "Bow, my daughter," she whispered. "For we are in the presence of the goddess."

The night sky was filled with stars, the moon sitting brilliantly with the barest pink tinge. They sang a song from their homeland, The Isle of Ellythia, where they all came from, and told us old stories of the mythical Ellythian jungles and the strange but handsome men who could turn into beasts.

That night had been perfect, and it is one memory I think about often. When Altara's bleeding had come the following year, although those ladies had been sent back to Ellythia by Father's advisors, I took my sister to the lake in just the same way. It had been a crescent moon then, but we followed the same ritual.

"I think we need to send you to that school Mother was talking about, the one in Ellythia."

Altara stilled. "You'd send me away from here?"

"You can't stay here alone with Stepmother. After I'm gone, I'm worried she'll—"

"I won't let her!" Altara said, her eyes glistening. "We're not children anymore. She can't do that."

"Don't underestimate her," I warned. "Besides, I think it'd

be good. And I'm pretty sure we have a cousin in attendance there."

"It's a finishing school," she scoffed, waving her hand in dismissal.

"I think we really should give it a good thought."

She pursed her lips. "Let's just see what father has to say tomorrow. Who do you think it'll be anyway?"

"I haven't even had time to think on it." It was the truth. Men didn't interest me in the slightest. I had more important things to worry about.

"You've been so busy with the city folk lately, Sara," Altara chided. "You need to think about palace matters."

"My magic isn't like yours," I said defensively. "I *have* to use it *on* other people. And we're just coming to the end of the birthing season. September to October was a mad rush of births."

And that was the other thing. Me being married off meant I would no longer be here to help the women of Quartz. If I was married to some other man in another city, how could I use my gifts? Would the women of another city even trust me? Would they be suspicious of me and call me a witch, or would I even be able to sneak out at night? But I knew the answer already. As a married woman, there was no way I'd be *allowed* to sneak out into a foreign city. There were nasty names given to women who snuck out at night. I rubbed my eyes tiredly as I thought about Altara's question. Who *were* my possible suitors?

"I do hope it's not Duke Maraven," Altara chuckled darkly.

"Urgh, please don't even say it!" The duke held a large fife to the south, was wealthy but very old, and been through six wives in his time. "Besides, surely it'd be a prince, no? Not that I'd care too much."

"No, as long as you have women to help, you wouldn't care who it was."

I smiled faintly. I couldn't argue with that because she was right. Midwifery was the only thing that truly mattered to me, after my family.

"Hmm…" Altara tapped her chin against her lip in a way that reminded me of Mother, and I couldn't help but grin. "Do you remember when Prince Isome came to visit?" she said suddenly. "He was quite handsome at the time. But we were only, what, thirteen and fourteen?"

We both went silent. On the occasion of his visit, sixteen-year-old Prince Isome had come with his parents from Waelan for our mother's funeral. A few princes and princesses of neighbouring Kingdoms, Kaalon, Serus, and Waelan, had come for it. Our mother had been easy to love and made friends quickly.

"Could be," I said. "And I suppose Serus Kingdom isn't so far. I could come back and visit…" I trailed off again as everything started to hit me. My coming of age next week, a marriage, a new family, moving away, leaving my sister—this was all happening too fast. I wasn't even half ready, half prepared for such a thing. And neither was Altara, for that matter, by the shining eyes that were trained on me now. I'd gotten too caught up in my 'work' to even think about my royal duties. My sister was right. I needed to make some preparations.

4

SARAYA

The next day, my father's runner, Lennard, a sweet boy in his early teens, knocked at my suite door. Tembry, one my maids, opened the door and let him straight in. I took the note from his sweaty fingers as he did his best to ogle me without being noticed. I pulled my thin robe around me a little tighter while Blythe, my other best maid, glowered at him with her arms crossed.

The letter turned out to be an appointment card to meet my father at midday. I nodded at Lennard, signing the note with a quill and handing it back to him. He left, glancing back at me twice.

Men had been staring at me from a young age, as it wasn't common to come across a biracial Ellythian-Lobrathian girl. Let alone a royal. But the stares hadn't gotten really bad until around my sixteenth year, when my breasts and hips had grown, and I'd really started to look like a woman.

My parents' marriage had been a little scandalous, but it was undeniable that a union between the two great houses, the Ellythian lotus princess and Lobrathian lightning king, as they called them, was the best thing that had happened to the Lobrathian economy since the discovery of the luminous quartz quarry three hundred years ago.

Ellythia now freely traded with us. Silks, rice, and cotton now ran here aplenty, making our kingdom of Lobrathia even more powerful. The commonfolk had come to love my mother quickly, as she spent a lot of time working the Sticks, where the poorest lived and worked alongside the orphanages and minor crime gangs. Through her work in creating schools and giving out free birth control potions, our city enjoyed the lowest poverty rates in the entire human realm.

My father had been incredibly proud of her, and in those days, Altara and I were freely allowed to snuggle in bed with both of them, and we would giggle and laugh while they told us stories.

But all of that had turned to ashes, just as my mother had with her Ellythian fire burial. And here I was reduced to receiving appointment cards from Oxley, my father's hawkish, lanky head advisor.

Instead of pacing around my room like an angry tiger and letting dark thoughts ravage me, I decided to see if one of my favourite people, the palace armsmaster, Jerali Jones was free for the morning.

Luckily, Tembry came back with an affirming 'yes' note, and I pulled Altara out of her history lesson with her professor of the month. My stepmother wouldn't be happy with that, of course, but I felt as if I was justified in doing so because who knew how much time I'd have to spend with her?

Once marriage agreements were made, weddings took place as fast as possible to avoid any incidents, so I could very well be off within the month. The thought crawled across my skin like something gross, so I knew the wise thing to do was to take my mind off it as much as possible. None of my special candles had been lit through the night, but I knew there were a few babies pending, Bluebell included. Clearly, the midwives had everything under control.

We changed from our day dresses into our practise uniform, which Mother had designed for us, modelled from the ones the women wore on her island home. There was a long-sleeved tunic and trousers with a skirt we could attach as we liked. She had always insisted that we knew how to fight both with a long dress on as well as in pants. When I asked her about it, she just said that it was best to always be prepared.

Our maids, Altara, and I headed straight to the practise arena in the back grounds of the palace, where Jerali would have been cleared of soldiers or squires to make way for us. We didn't keep it 'secret' these days that we practised fighting and weapons arts, but we did keep a low profile when we could. There were some in the kingdom who looked down upon women practising weapons.

No one knew whether Jerali Jones was a man or a woman. Not that my mother had cared what Jerali's gender was when she had brought Jerali here from the Waelan Kingdom— because the armsmaster sure didn't. To us, it was 'Armsmaster' when we were training or 'Jerali' when we weren't. Anyone who had an issue with it got the sharp edge of a sword or a tongue if it was improper to draw a weapon at the time. To date, no one had defeated Jerali in combat, no soldier, no Captain, no General, and it had been like that for years.

Jerali was always deeply tanned, mid-thirties, I guessed, and always wore the same loose, sleeveless white shirt and pants, long boots, and hair always shaved close to the skull.

The armsmaster stood inside the training arena under the blue banner of Voltanius house with our father's family motto written in silver. "Lightning does not yield."

"Good morning, Princesses." the armsmaster stood, hands behind a muscled back with the best posture I'd ever seen on a person. I immediately straightened my own spine.

"Morning, Armsmaster," we chorused back.

We were led into a jog around the arena, followed by a series of stretches. Then Jerali had us pick up our practise swords, made with a weighted steel intended to grow our muscle. Jerali graded up the weight every few months since we were three. It had worked to make us strong. Although neither of us had ever actually duelled with a man, Jerali said that because we'd increased our weight training and conditioning so much over the years that we'd be a real match for any man in actual battle.

Altara's maid, Lucy, along with Tembry and Blythe, set about grappling with each other while Altara and I duelled. I was ever so slightly stronger than her and heavier, but she kept a fine form, meeting me strike for strike each and every time.

Once we finished, Altara practised with her weapon of choice, a bow and arrow, and used the funny little men that served as moving targets. They were hoisted on a zip line at the edge of the arena. And once the lever was pulled, they flew, zigzagging down their line. She was an excellent shot, I'll admit, getting each one in the eye, sometimes *both* eyes if she was feeling up to a rapid-firing round.

Meanwhile, Jerali and I practised knives and then grappling. The armsmaster was ruthless with me, Princess or not, which I appreciated because it meant that if I got into a real fight, I wouldn't be caught unawares. It was the reason I was confident walking around the city all those late nights. Jerali knew I did that, and used that as motivation during our grappling.

"What are you gonna do if a mobster grabs you on the arse, hey?" Jerali would say in jest.

And I would whip around, grab Jerali's hand, and twist it painfully, leaving the armsmaster no choice but to swing around to avoid snapping a wrist.

"But then I would do this!" Jerali went for a right hook, which I usually successfully dodged.

Stepmother had walked in on me and Jerali wrestling once, and it was no doubt why she'd had such a distaste for it. I would have thought it inappropriate, too, if not for the fact that my mother had practised with us as children. Jerali terrified the soldiers of our military, training them with an iron fist, yelling and swearing at them until they were the best versions of themselves. I think that was why both Altara and I were as good as we were.

When it came time to finish, close to midday, I gave Jerali a meaningful look.

I took a deep breath, wiping my face on the edge of my shirt. "I'm going to miss this."

Jerali frowned deeply. "What do you mean?"

"Word is that I'm to be married."

Jerali stilled, grey eyes pin-point focused on me. "Who is it? I know the fighting style of every Kingdom in the realm. I'll teach you."

That was Jerali, always practical.

"I don't know yet."

We stared at each other for a miserable moment, and my eyes filled with tears. I closed them, pinching my nose. I rarely showed emotion in the training arena. This is where we put it all away. Where we spoke with our muscles and worked out our issues with steel.

Jerali sighed and sat me down on a bench, and we watched Altara go for another round of shooting practise.

"I know you, Sara," Jerali said in a gruff voice. "You'll face whatever it is that comes your way. *And* whoever it is. Your mother made sure you'd have the skills to do that."

I nodded, my throat tight. "It's not me I'm worried about," I murmured. "I'm going to send Altara to the ladies' school in Ellythia. It…won't be safe for her here after I'm gone."

Jerali growled in disapproval. Naturally, the armsmaster had known the moment Stepmother began the lashings as I had turned up to practise hissing in pain and unable to move properly. But that day, Jerali took my chin in cool fingers, forcing me to look into those steel-like eyes, and said, "Through pain, we are made strong. Lightning does not…?"

"Yield," I had finished in a whisper. I fought that day, eyes blurry with tears. And over time, I learned to fight through any injury, through any pain. Jerali had been right. It *had* made me stronger.

At the same time, having that much rage channeled into you for such a long time left its mark, and I knew something in me was a little broken because of it. Through my fighting training, I held the edges of that internal break together just enough so that the darkness from it never consumed me.

"Teach her a little grappling in the coming weeks," I said to Jerali. "I don't know what those girls at the jungle school are like."

Jerali made a sound of assent. "I'll make sure she's ready."

Freshly bathed and ready to meet my fate, I met my father in his office. His five advisors straightened immediately upon my entry. Oxley, the head advisor, looked down his nose and gave me a strange look I couldn't interpret. I had never really liked him, and neither had my mother. He had been put into this position just before her death and had disapproved of a lot of her initiatives with the poor. He was not a compassionate man and preferred practicality with all things, including the treasury. "Wasting" money on the poor was not something that Oxley approved of, and I bet my bottom dollar that he was the one who had ceased my mother's programs and sent the city's poor backwards after her death.

But today, I noticed that they were all eying me strangely. With varying degrees of…*sympathy?* I really couldn't tell, but I knew it made my stomach churn violently.

My heart plummeted straight into my nether regions. Why were they looking at me like that? The match couldn't possibly be that bad.

Discreetly wiping my sweaty palms on my dress, I came before my father.

He looked at me with a clear gaze that was all at once serious and resigned. "There is a matter of great importance for us to discuss, Saraya. Come with me onto the balcony."

His advisors bowed to both of us before rushing out the door. I braced myself, trying to control my breathing.

My father led me onto his office balcony and looked out at our city. The midday sun gleamed on the rooftops, quartz crystals glinting where people had left them out on rooves and window sills to charge up for the night. That was why they were so valuable. They were an endless source of light so long as you recharged them in the sun once in a while.

The familiar sound of people and horses reached my ears.

How long did I have before I couldn't call this home anymore? My stomach twisted again.

"I have never told you," my father said, in that stunted, slow way that was all he could manage these days, "what happened on the last day of the war with the fae."

Confused as to why we were talking about his battle against the fae thirty years ago, I shook my head.

"Not many know what happened that day," his voice was breathy as if he could see it playing out in his mind's eye. "But there I stood, on a battlefield soaked with the blood of my people, my army decimated, and myself, permanently injured." He rubbed his thigh, where his old injury still pained him. "I was ready to meet my death. All was lost."

I held my breath. This was not the story that had been told to us all this time—it was the exact opposite.

"He came to me, and we met on the battlefield amongst the dead and dying. All I could smell was blood, and I wondered whether he would just kill me right there and take my palace, take my wife and land. But I was ready to die fighting him—the fae King Wyxian Darkcleaver of the Black Court."

A chill swept across me, and my entire body erupted with goosebumps. I had not known that we had come that close to losing. So how exactly did we win the battle my father was praised for?

"He approached me like some god of death and sheathed his sword." My father's voice held a note of surprise as if the moment still confused him. "And he stood over me and said, 'We've both lost good men today, Eldon Voltanius. You've surprised me. I did not think the human race had such a fight in them. And yet I could take your lands, I could take your wife and enslave your people and proceed to take the rest of the human realm. But that is not the way I want to proceed.'"

I stared at my father, my mouth agape in the most un-princess-like way, hanging on to every word as if it were a life rope.

"Even on my knees, I was ready to swing my sword and kill him for his words," my father continued. "But what he said next gave me pause. 'I grant you peace, Eldon, but for one thing. Swear your firstborn daughter to me. Swear her to marry my firstborn son. And I will leave the kingdom of Lobrathia safe and intact.'"

I shut my mouth, and my stomach churned as if I were at sea. This couldn't be happening.

My father sighed and turned to look at me with a face gaunt with the knowledge of what he had done. "All was lost, Saraya. He would've taken everything from us and laid the human realm to waste."

The backs of my eyes burnt. I clutched my stomach. *It couldn't be.*

"I had no choice, Saraya. I swore my firstborn daughter to the fae king that day. And because of it, our people were saved."

I recoiled away from him. There had never been some genius tactical strategy. It had never been the might of my warrior father, the lightning king of Lobrathia and his brilliant human army. This is how he did it. This is how he saved us all. By signing me over. By selling me like property.

"No." The disbelief was thick in my voice as I tried to contain the emotional hurricane that was roiling within my bones, my skin, my gut.

"I'm sorry, Saraya," he whispered. "I've been trying to find a way out of this for the past nineteen years. But I signed my name on the contract with my own blood. And there is no way around a blood contract with the fae. You are nineteen next week. The debt is due."

This blow was worse than anything I could have imagined. I had been betrayed by my father before I was even born.

"You have no idea how much I despaired when you were born a girl. Your mother knew your fate from the day you were conceived."

"And…" I swallowed the lump in my throat. "And there's nothing to be done about it?"

In answer, he took out a letter from his pocket and handed it to me. I knew what it was the moment I saw the black foreign paper, the white foreign ink, the spiky foreign hand, the black wax seal stamped with a dragon.

Dear King Eldon Voltanius of Lobrathia,

We will arrive on the first morning of December to claim Princess Saraya.

King Wyxian Darkcleaver
Black Court of the Realm of the Dark Fae

THE LETTER FLUTTERED TO THE GROUND FROM MY HAND.

Claim. They even spoke like monsters. Devastation crawled around my heart like a black snake. I had been sold to the enemy. The creatures who fuelled the nightmares of

41

human children. The beings we were taught to hate, to fear. The monsters beyond the mountains.

It was the price of peace for my kingdom.

I'd been sold like a broodmare. And I would take it because that was my duty. But I couldn't help but feel betrayed by *both* my parents. My stepmother's cunning smile last night now made sense. She had also known before me and probably revelled in the idea of my eternal pain. Not only would I be gone, but I was going to spend my life in misery, living amongst monsters.

And those monsters were arriving in one week's time. The day after my nineteenth birthday.

One of the first lessons you learn as an apprentice midwife is that nothing truly prepares you for labour. That mysterious force that brings souls into this world is a rite that cannot be explained in words. The only thing you can do is prepare your mind to embrace the unknown.

And my mother had been preparing me for my marriage to the monsters since the day I was born. I had no idea then, of course, but looking back, it all fell into place.

The secret lessons in my magic. The constant weapons practise from the time I could walk. The lectures on ethics and languages, including what we knew of the runic language of the fae. I was going to spend my life with monsters, and my mother had done her best to give me the skills to deal with them.

But what I hadn't been ready for was the portal of grief that had opened at the thought of leaving my family home. It was a jarring, all encompassing thing. And if I mulled on it too much, I would've never gotten out of bed ever again.

And now, I had only a week to come to terms with the fate

that had been decided for me. That I would be leaving Quartz. The place where all my memories of Mother were, of my childhood with Altara, of everything that mattered to me. Now, my sister was my number one priority.

She was waiting for me in my room, bouncing excitedly. Altara, the romantic. When I told her, she didn't speak for a full minute, her mouth opening and closing like a blowfish.

"I can't—are you—is Father—what?"

"I know," I sighed. "It's hard to believe, but I saw the monster king's handwritten letter myself."

"By the triple goddess! But *one week*?"

I nodded. "Mother knew all along. That's why she made sure we had all those lessons."

Altara screwed her eyes shut. "This can't be happening! Goddess, I think I *would* prefer Duke Manaven instead of this."

Well, yes, I would have preferred it too. But, thinking about what could have been was useless. So instead, I decided to take the focus off me, and said. "We've already discussed where I think you should go."

"You really think I should leave?" Her beautiful eyes searched mine as if the answers to the universe lay there.

My back still stung. I levelled her an even look, and I saw in her eyes that she knew that I was serious.

"Fine, I agree, I suppose. But what if Stepmother tries to stop it?"

"We won't tell anyone. Geravie has contacts at the school. I'll get her to send a carrier pigeon. Then we'll smuggle you out, but you'll need a female escort."

"I want Geravie," said Altara firmly. "She hates it here anyway. All her friends are dead or poorly."

I considered it and decided other than our elderly nursemaid, we didn't have too many other options. After Mother died, anyone who was passionately loyal to her, and by extension us, were Ellythians. And they had all been ordered back to their island home. Except Geravie. She was too old by then and insisted on staying behind. Before being our nursemaid, she had been our mother's, and that bond held strong in the face of Oxley, who had bullied her until he realised Geravie was more stubborn than him. "The lotus is patient," Geravie said to me that night Oxley left her suite, storming about useless Ellythians.

That night, we collected Geravie from where she'd retired in a corner of the palace. Veiled in white, hunchbacked, and with eyes cloudy with cataracts that had returned since I'd previously removed them, she held my hand as I told her about my coming fate.

"Those devils," she muttered. "Typical fae! Coming to steal away a maiden."

"Next week, yes," I confirmed, darkly. "Both me and Altara will be leaving. We knew something like this would happen eventually. It was foolish of us to think otherwise. But I wanted to take some of Mother's things with me. Goddess knows what will happen to them here."

Geravie nodded, clutching the burnished gold goddess talisman around her throat. "Remember to go to the temple before you leave, Sara. Place an offering before the mother. You'll be a full-blooded, wedded woman soon. Even if it is to the darned dark fae."

I cringed at her words and thought of what rituals my mother might have planned for me on my entrance to adulthood and marriage. Whatever customs she might have shared with us would be lost forever if not for Geravie. I told the old woman so, and she smiled and crooked her finger at me. "I was never married myself, but I do remember a thing or two from my homeland."

Eagerly, we asked the head housekeeper to open the room where our mother's old things had been kept when they packed it all away in preparation for Stepmother's arrival. I'd really hated her then, invading my mother's rooms and replacing everything with foreign decorations. And five years later, wiping the dust off the wooden chest Mother had brought from her homeland still made my chest feel tight.

Altara sneezed, and Geravie held a handkerchief to her nose as I dusted the largest chest with my hand. It was a beautiful red-hued wood, carved with images of a moonlit beach, palm trees swaying, and her family symbol, a lotus with a crescent moon angled so it was a smile was carved into the top. I ran my hand along the strong panels of Ellythian fablewood. It was almost as if I could feel her there, her presence, her heart.

I swallowed the lump in my throat and opened it. Inside were her clothes and a number of books from the Isle of Ellythia.

I carefully laid them out, fully intending for one of us to take them. I didn't want anything of Mother left behind. I couldn't bear the thought of her things being here with Stepmother's nasty fingers nearby while we were far away, perhaps never to return.

I piled her clothes out next. Beneath her day-to-day clothes, which still smelled of her jasmine and hibiscus scent, I took out a set of rich purple silk.

"Is that purple I see?" asked Geravie, squinting through her cloudy eyes.

"I've never seen these before," I said, reverently stroking the finely embroidered material.

46

"Well, your mother didn't tell you everything, did she? We talked about this a few times, you see." She lowered her voice to a whisper, "Those are her wedding silks, Saraya. Oh, Yasani was a vision on that day, the *way* the men had no idea where to look first!"

"When *will* your wedding be?" asked Altara, frowning as we beheld the garments with new eyes. "The fae prince is coming here for a betrothal, right? So it'll be an engagement?"

I sat back on my heel. "I don't actually know. I don't know anything about fae customs."

Geravie let a long, loud sigh. "Oh, there are stories." She rubbed her lips together in thought. "But a human princess has not been wed to the fae for a hundred years at least. In fact, your father is bound to call the neighbouring kingdoms as witness. We have not treated with the fae since the last war."

I hadn't even thought about the actual *claiming* part. "I sort of just thought they'd take me away. They did say 'claim' after all, in the letter."

"Hm," Geravie said. "In which case you should be richly dressed, but your wedding will likely take place in the fae realm. This will be a *binding*."

"Is that like an engagement?"

"Oh no," huffed Geravie. "Fae bind with blood."

I screwed my face up, and Altara shot me a pained look. "Barbaric."

"Just the old ways. Your mother knew a thing or two about blood magic and…" She cast me a knowing look.

I, of course, knew a thing or two about blood myself. But I never did any scary sort of magic with it.

"They won't hurt her?" asked Altara timidly. "Will they, Geravie, do you think?"

Geravie grumbled into her paisley handkerchief. "She is *marrying* the crown prince, heir to their throne."

A cruel sort of realisation dawned upon me. I had never really considered *ruling* my dream. I just hoped I'd marry a second son and carry about my care of the local women. I hadn't thought about ruling a kingdom at all. So I listened fervently as Geravie continued.

"You'll be groomed to be Queen. But the hardest thing, no doubt, will be to win the favour of the fae people. They are as distrustful of us, as we are of them. They might not like you, Sara, as much as we do." She cast me a grim smile, and I didn't return it. "They might not be so happy to have a human woman ruling over them. What that Wyxian fellow was thinking...probably wants more quartz..."

Indeed. Of what use was I to them? Did they fae even need help giving birth? I wondered about their customs. If I was rendered obsolete...I couldn't even bear the thought of it. Helping women was my life's work, the goddess' gift to me. It was almost like a pulling, a tugging, a drawing. Midwifery pulled me towards it like a fishing hook. My work was who I was. I couldn't *not* do it. My heart hammered in my chest, a thousand questions in my mind. What did they expect me to do? Who did they expect me to be? I would have to bear his children—*could* I even bear a half-fae child?

"I don't think I can do this," I whispered. "I don't—how can I possibly—"

"You will!" said Geravie firmly, pointing a finger at me. "You are duty-bound. As your mother was duty-bound before you, to leave *her* home and come *here*."

"That's true," Altara said, eyes shining. "You're doing the exact same thing Mama did, Sara!"

I clenched my hands into fists. Mother hadn't married a

whole new species. But they were right, of course. I was duty-bound as a princess. But I was also duty-bound to my work.

Suddenly I found that I couldn't breathe. Bluebell's face flashed in my mind's eye, and so did Chirra and all the many other women I had assisted that month. What would Agatha say when she found that she wouldn't be able to call upon me anymore? I wanted to vomit. I wanted to—

"Look, Sara," whispered Altara. I clutched my stomach and turned. Altara held Mother's jewellery box.

"You should take that box with you," I said, trying to smile. But Altara was holding up a dainty gold piece of jewellery.

"Mother's anklet!" I exclaimed. I reached for it and felt the tiny links against my sword calloused fingers. She had loved wearing jewellery from her homeland. Anklets most of all.

"There's a couple in here," said Altara, holding up a matching second with a tiny gold lotus.

"You should wear one each," rasped Geravie from her chair. "To remember her by. On the ankle, so no one will see it. You can keep it private."

Altara beamed at Geravie. She knew us well. We had never publicly mourned Mother. It had only seemed right to keep it private like she had been when she was alive. So I took the second anklet and immediately set it about my ankle. Maybe I hoped it would give me some courage. Mother had the same magical gift as I had, and she used it as much as she was able. It was with her that I had first met Agatha and began my apprenticeship at thirteen.

I turned back to the wedding silks. "I'll take this with me," I sighed. "You'll have to tell me what type of rituals I'll need to do for the wedding. I'll be by myself, but..." I swallowed. I *would* be by myself. The only human amongst the fae. Father had told me that I was supposed to go alone as humans were not typically allowed in the foreign realm. "But I'll do whatever I can, on my own."

"So I won't be able to come to your wedding?" Altara's eyes filled with tears. "I always thought that we would—"

"I know," I whispered. "We just have to do the best we can...given the situation. Right?"

"Good girl," said Geravie. "I will have the bridal rituals written down for you. But you must take the texts and read from them."

"Texts!" said Altara suddenly. "We need to look up the fae in the palace library. You need to learn about our enemy before walking right into their den! There must be books there."

"Not much is known about them," said Geravie. "There is certainly only conjecture in those books. No...the best person to ask would be your stepmother."

"What?" Altara and I both asked in disbelief.

Geravie's mouth twisted in wry humour. "I know, I know. But her spies have been following the quartz carts to the Silent Mountains for years. They've been spying on the fae however they can. She knows some things, our queen."

Inwardly I cringed at the thought of asking the queen for any sort of help. We'd never really had a proper, two-way conversation in the last five years—I'd gone out of my way to avoid her. Perhaps she would get her claws into me one last time before I left her behind forever. It might very well be worth it. Because Geravie was right. I knew nothing about the fae or their customs except some of their language and the fact we called them monsters.

We had the maids help us collect everything of Mother's. Altara was keen to take as much as she could, as I wasn't much interested in clothes, except the wedding silks and a second crimson set that I wanted to wear for the engagement. I needed a part of her with me on that day, which was crucial for me. So we divided the other belongings evenly.

"Whatever I take…" I said slowly, looking at the neat piles of items laid out on Altara's bed. "Just choose wisely, I guess, because I'm not entirely sure I'll be able to…you know…"

Altara spun towards me, her face a picture of shock. "You don't think…you don't think they'll never let you *leave* the fae realm?"

I pressed my lips together to hold back a sob. The thought of never seeing Altara again was as shocking to me as my mother's death. She was everything I had. "They don't…" I swallowed. "They don't travel freely between, do they? I mean, this is the first time in thirty—"

Altara hurled herself towards me with all her might, wrapping her arms around my neck. Her hot tears fell onto my skin. "Promise me," she whispered. "Promise me that you'll do everything you can to try and come visit me." She pulled back, her face wet, her eyes red. "For all I know, Father will get me married off within the year too."

We *were* less than a year apart, as my mother had gotten pregnant right after birthing me. It would make sense for the advisors to get rid of Altara too. It was with this in mind that we made the arrangements with Geravie before we had escorted her back to her rooms. She was keen to leave the palace as Altara had suspected, telling us that she never planned on dying on foreign land. She wanted to see the ancient green forests of Ellythia again, and I couldn't blame her. Not with father the way he was and with Stepmother— well, the way *she* was.

"I promise, Tar," I said softly, tugging on a silken black

strand of her hair. "I don't know what awaits us out there, but we're going to do our best, you and I, aren't we?"

She nodded and wiped both cheeks with her sleeve. "Lightning does not yield."

I grinned back. "And the lotus is patient."

6

SARAYA

In the week leading up to the arrival of the fae, there was a palpable tension, both within the palace and the city. My father's advisors put out word that a royal announcement was to be made on Monday morning. I was tempted to head down to the town square and watch the royal crier and the people's subsequent reactions for myself, but in the end, Altara convinced me against it. So I sent Blythe and Tembry, who were more my friends than maids by this point, to attend and report back to me.

They returned flustered, with grave faces.

"What exactly did the announcer say?" I asked as they returned to my suite that afternoon, Altara sitting close beside me.

Blythe spoke in a low voice. "He said, 'In line with an old contract, the Princess Saraya Yasani Voltanius is to be wed to the crown fae Prince of the Black Court from across the mountains. The bond will maintain the current peaceful relations we have held since the last war. And on the day of their arrival, for the safety of the city, every man, woman, and child is to be locked down in their house.' That's what he said, didn't he, Tem?"

Tembry nodded. "There was a hush upon the crowd after that, Your Highness." She shivered and hugged her arms. "They didn't like that at all."

I didn't think they would. People knew me in the city and knew me in a way they had never known another royal. I walked among the commonfolk weekly, and most of the women called me by first name. Not only would they be losing me as their princess, but me as their midwife. I was their safety net, an assurance that their women wouldn't die in childbirth as they used to in the days before my mother arrived in Lobrathia.

"They don't want to see you go, Your Highness," whispered Blythe. She looked at me meaningfully because two years ago, I had saved her cousin from eclampsia—a severe blood pressure condition of pregnancy causing seizures. She knew that meant her cousin's sisters were at risk of the same illness. But I wouldn't be here to help them.

But no one said that out loud.

"What if—" Tembry stopped herself, glancing at Blythe, who vigorously shook her head.

"Don't say it, Tem!" the raven-haired maid hissed. "Don't you dare."

"But I have to say it!" Tembry exclaimed, her freckled cheeks now as crimson as her hair. "Or I won't be able to live with myself!" She took a deep breath and turned to me. I stared at her, my brows raised. "Your Highness, what if you ran away?"

I stilled, and I felt Altara stiffen beside me. Every molecule in my body sat poised, as if waiting for my response. I hadn't even given that option a thought. It had honestly not even occurred to me to shirk my duty and *run*. Where would I even go? We had extended family in other parts of our kingdom, sure. But who would take me, shelter me while I put the kingdom—the entire human empire—in danger? Because if I didn't marry the fae prince, that's exactly what would happen.

"If I ran, Tembry," I said slowly, sounding out my own thoughts for the benefit of Altara as well, "I would be breaking a binding contract with the fae. They would take that as a threat, a breach of the peaceful terms my father laid out with them. It would...it would mean that the fae had every right to wage war against us and take our land."

Tembry began crying into her hands. Blythe groaned and put her arms around the sobbing young woman. "I told you, Tem, I told you, Sara has no option."

I sighed and crossed the room to put my arms around Tembry, whose shoulders were shuddering under her sobs. Altara looked on as I tried to contain my own tears.

"It's not fair!" sobbed Tembry.

"No," I said softly. "It's not."

"Do you know what I just realised?" said Altara suddenly. We all looked at her.

"All this talk of 'the fae are coming,' 'do this for the fae,' 'prepare the city for the fae,' we've totally missed the fact that we don't know *anything* about the fae prince! The person you're supposed to marry! How old is he? What's his name? Is he a muscled warrior or a fat scholar, or what?"

"I don't even want to think on it, Tara," I grumbled, stepping away from Tembry, who was now blinking up at me. "He's a *dark fae*, and that means he probably just some brutish, bloodthirsty rake. I just...want to get past this next week."

"No!" she exclaimed, shooting to her feet. "This is important. There must be someone who knows *something* about this family. The Darkcleavers of Black Court."

"We must find out, Your Highness!" said Tembry, wiping her eyes. "Princess Altara, you should ask your father. He has met the King Wyxian."

"And *you*," Altara gestured at me. "Need to talk to Stepmother. It's only four days till they arrive."

THE NEXT DAY, I WAS STARTING TO GET ANTSY. NONE OF MY candles had gone off in the last few days, and I was getting worried that Bluebell wasn't going to go into labour until after I left. She would have heard the news. She would have known that I was leaving for good. And I can't imagine what that was doing for her nerves. So I did the only thing I could in such a situation. I did as my mother taught me and went to the temple of the triple goddess.

Altara and I headed down into the city where our two major temples stood. Since I was on official business, it was good for me to use the regular protocol for an outing, so I took a guard and a carriage. I had organised for Altara to leave straight after I left with the fae. In the hustle and bustle of my leaving, and with her own magic, her exit out of the palace should go unnoticed.

The sun warmed our carriage as we looked out the windows, the scent of roses wafting into our noses as two white marble temples loomed tall before us. While male pilgrims took the path to the right, to the father's temple, female pilgrims took the path to the left, to the temple of the mother. My guards dropped us off at the fork, where we would begin the long walk down the red paved path.

I treasured that walk, especially on beautiful days like this one on the cusp of summer, and I vividly remembered walking alongside my mother every month on the first day of my bleeding. I got four such months with her before she died, and doing it with my sister now, for the perhaps the last time, felt like another sort of ritual.

"Remember how Mother disapproved of our temple?" Altara said quietly. She looked radiant in the summer sun, and with the cool breeze coming off the coast to the east, it was a good day to walk among the tall pines.

I smiled at the memory as the marble monolith that was our city temple grew bigger as we walked towards it. "She said it was unnatural just to have three goddesses. She was far too used to the seven goddesses of Ellythia."

"She called it 'restrictive and demeaning' that women are only allowed to be three things," Altara chuckled softly, then looped her arm around mine. "I'm going to miss this."

Everything we did in the next two days would be our last together. Every walk, every moment was going to be just a memory for us. My heart clenched as if the fae crown prince already had sunk his claws into me. I wondered if my new husband would be kind enough to let me return to visit, but deep in my heart, I knew those monsters would never let me.

We reached the temple, took off our sandals, and washed our hands in the fountain. Then we donned the silk veils our mother had gifted us. They were matching with embroidered lotuses, but mine was purple, and Altara's was pink.

"In Ellythia, we cover the crowns of our heads before the gods in respect," Mother had whispered to us on our first trip as children here. "It's even more important for girls with magic because the powers within a temple might interfere with or exaggerate your own power. Consider it like a lid on a shaken champagne bottle."

We'd giggled at that.

The temple was a beauty of marble and stone. And the goddesses themselves, standing united at the end, were monoliths of marble and gilded edges, their faces carved to be benevolent and kind. The Maiden, the Mother, and the Crone. The three aspects of a woman. I blinked up at them, wondering if the men's temple was the same, only their three gods were the Father, the King, and the Magician. The goddess seemed to be bound in time, their forms chronological, whereas the three aspects of man were not.

It was my mother who scoffed at our temple. "Women can be so much more," she would whisper to us.

"You'll get to see the temple of the seven," I whispered to Altara, glancing around in case any of the priestesses were eavesdropping. "When you go to Ellythia."

When we got to the front of the short line, I passed my basket to Altara, and she took out one of the two red roses we'd cut from the palace gardens and one of the rosemary herbed loaves we'd made ourselves that morning.

The head priestess, a stoic, middle-aged woman in white robes, inclined her head as we approached and laid our offerings in the pile at the statue's feet. At the end of each day, the priestesses went around the city and distributed offered food to the poor.

"The queen awaits Princess Saraya in the garden of the blessed," came the priestess' breathy voice after we'd lain our offerings.

I glanced at Altara in surprise. "Just me?"

The priestess inclined her head demurely.

"I'll wait for you in the temple library," said Altara. "If I may, High Priestess?"

"Of course."

Altara strode off, and two waiting acolytes, priestesses in training, bowed and led me to the back of the temple, where there was a series of beautiful contemplative gardens.

I wondered why my stepmother had decided to ambush me here instead of at the palace. In the end, I decided this was better because any possible interaction with her in the palace would have me on tenterhooks, wondering if she was going to bring out her whip again. At least here in the temple garden, there was no risk of that.

To my knowledge, the queen was not religious and had only ever visited the temple on holy days when it was expected for her to be there. And indeed, when the acolytes led me to her, standing by a lovely temple-made pond surrounded by blooming purple hydrangeas, she appeared tense. There was a strain in her eyes, a rigidness in her shoulders. She seemed out of place and eager to leave. On some level, that made me feel satisfied—she didn't belong here, and she knew it.

"Walk with me, Saraya," her tone was stiff, and she turned, swishing her yellow chiffon gown, indicating we should walk down the garden path. Silently, I obliged, walking beside her, trying not to look suspicious. The garden was devoid of other people, and I knew then that she had probably had the priestesses close the entirety of the gardens just for us. The thought irked me. The gardens were a safe place for all the women of the city to use at any time. But then she spoke in her deep, serious, business-like voice, and any other thought was driven from my mind.

"In three days, you will be bonded to the prince of Black

Court. And in two days, you will become a woman, in the eyes of the law. Since your own mother has left, I take the responsibility of preparing you to be a woman and for marriage."

I stifled the urge to sigh. *Left*. Twisting her death into something nasty—as she'd made a choice to abandon us. I knew better, my mother had been preparing me for this years before it was time, and I had finished my midwifery apprenticeship under Agatha last year. Whatever she thought she was going to tell me about 'being a woman,' I probably already knew. I listened glumly as we followed the winding pave stones.

"And due to our trade of quartz with the fae, I am also one of the few people who have some knowledge of them, luckily for you." Her voice turned haughty—more haughty than usual. "King Wyxian has four sons and one daughter."

I almost tripped over my own feet. "Four sons?"

She smirked at me. "Four. Prince Daxian is the crown prince and heir to the throne. I believe he would be twenty by now."

So not geriatric. That was a bonus.

"The fae are protective of their royalty, so I have not been privy to the rest of their names, but the youngest is still a child at six, and his daughter around sixteen. But I want to draw your attention to fae customs surrounding marriage. These are old traditions, mind you, but I believe Wyxian to be a traditional creature who still believes in the old ways. So, naturally, he will follow them. Unfortunately, that is not a good thing for you."

A shiver ran down my spine. What barbaric rituals would they force me to take part in?

"It has only happened once before, with a human, but

when a princess is chosen for marriage she must be tested." My stepmother paused for effect, and I was hanging on to every damn word. "The fae believe a wife should be able to submit to her husband. So it is traditional for each son to test her psychic defences. The weakest son starts. When he cannot break her, the next eldest attempts, and so on until one of them breaks through. Only the one that is successful may wed the princess."

"Psychic defences," I repeated dumbly.

She stopped and turned to me, regarding me down her nose. "Unlike *most* humans, the fae never lost their magic. They teach their children the art of mental warfare from a young age."

I felt sick to my stomach. I didn't even know what 'psychic defence' meant. I only ever had to infiltrate women's bodies to help or heal them, and, in those situations, there was never any resistance, only gratitude for me.

It was likely then that I had no defence, and the six-year-old child would be the one to defeat me. I took a staggered breath, trying not to panic. Because in three days' time, I was likely to be humiliated in front of my new fae family.

7

SARAYA

I didn't sleep at all for the next two nights. I kept getting up to check my candles. But all of them, including Bluebell's purple one, remained dark and silent. They made a sort of *whoosh* when they lit up, so I never missed the lighting of one, but I couldn't help getting a bad feeling. Perhaps the midwives stopped lighting the candles after they heard the announcement? Maybe they had given me up for gone already? It was fair enough, I supposed, as I pushed myself out of bed on the morning of my nineteenth birthday.

What might have been a happy occasion was now overshadowed by the fact I was being taken away by monsters tomorrow.

At breakfast, our family chef of ten years, Minisri, brought a spectacular purple four-tiered cake with gold lotus and leaf decorations. There were tears in her eyes as she held it before me, the entire palace staff crowding inside the dining room. It was lit with nineteen candles, and I smiled sadly at Minisri before I blew them out.

We might have had a ball, inviting neighbouring royals

and their children to attend. Both Altara and I would have had extravagant ballgowns made. Instead, my maids and I prepared my engagement clothes. Instead, tonight would be my last dinner, the last time Minisri cooked for me. She had cooked my first meal as an infant, and now she would cook my last in the human realm. I looked out at the staff of our palace, most of whom I'd known since I had been a child.

"Thank you," I said, my voice catching and hating that I could see my stepmother passing off a smirk for a regal smile from the side of my eye. "You've all seen me grow up. And now I go to a new house, with a new family. But we all must do our duty. I am no exception. I will never forget any of you. Not Minisri's chicken dumplings, not Jerali's swordsmanship, not Tembry's flower arrangements, and not Blythe's beautiful paintings. Lightning never yields."

"Lightning never yields," they all murmured back.

I cast a glance at my father's disassociated face. But he had. He *had* yielded. To the fae king and to this disease. And now both of those things would damn me.

I spent the rest of the day packing, with Altara, Tembry, and Blythe sticking like honey to my side. I made sure Mother's wedding silks were packed safely, along with Geravie's instructional pamphlet on Ellythian bridal rituals. In the afternoon, both Altara and I met with our elderly nursemaid.

The old lady was also packed and ready for the trip. There was a gleam in her eye I hadn't seen in a long time.

"One more adventure for me!" she said excitedly. "A secret mission for an old woman is the best type of trip." Although her body had caught up with her age, her mind was as sharp as a knife.

"I'm going to miss you both," I said, my voice catching. I was upset on a number of fronts. I wouldn't see my sister again, or Geravie, but I had organised them to be safe. At least I had done my best there.

The only thing left outstanding was Bluebell and a promise I had made. I think that upset me more than actually leaving my family. I had kept every promise I'd ever made, and here was one whose weight bore down on me like a mountain.

"Well, one last present for you," croaked Geravie. "This one is from us both." She nodded to Altara. "And I think it's the best one yet."

Altara handed me a bundle of cotton tied in a thick red ribbon. I took it with both hands and laid it down on Geravie's lounge, kneeling to open it.

Inside it was a swathe of deep purple velvet. I stood and shook it out, quite shocked at its beauty. It was a royal purple cloak, and on the inside lining was a border of the finest embroidery I'd ever seen.

"Did you do this?" I breathed to Altara.

"I did the outer border," she eyed me meaningfully. "And Geravie did the rest. She's quicker."

"The pattern is one I learnt in the Isle as a girl," Geravie said gruffly, her chestnut skin wrinkling in a smile.

And I could tell because I'd only ever seen these patterns on Mother's clothes from Ellythia. A moonlight beach, palm trees, tigers, and colourful birds. And better still, having Altara's hand on the outer border meant that it would conceal me from onlookers. It wouldn't make me completely invisible like her magic enabled her to do, but it would be camouflage at the very least. It had many pockets sewn into it, and a few were concealed so that only I would be able to find them.

"I'll treasure it forever!"

We made our plans for Altara's quiet departure tomorrow, and then Altara sat me down.

"I didn't mention it earlier," she said seriously. "Because I didn't want to cast a pall over your birthday, but it can't wait any longer. In the temple library, I found some old books on the fae."

I scooted to the edge of my seat. "Tell me everything."

Altara took a deep breath. "Don't panic...but I found out that the fae realm is divided into two. Centuries ago, a figure called the Green Reaper, a fae turned evil, divided the two realms. So now, furthest south lies the courts of the Solar Fae, or Light Fae, but up north, beyond the border of the Silent Mountains, the fae that live there are called *Dark Fae*."

"So the Dark Fae are the ones we fought the war against," I said, vaguely remembering this from a history lesson.

"Right," Altara paused. "Those beings are darker, more violent than their solar cousins."

"Great!" I fell back into my chair. "So I get to marry the darkest sort."

"Well, there are five courts in the Realm of the Dark Fae. There's Black, Obsidian, Eclipse, Midnight, and Twilight Courts. Uh...apparently, Black Court is the worst sort. Obsidian is a step up."

"Lovely," I murmured. "So I get the worst of the lot."

"Could be worse," cooed Geravie.

I gave Geravie a dark look because how could it be any worse? But I suddenly realised she couldn't see. "Enough doom and gloom. Let me take your cataracts out, Geravie. You'll both need clear vision tomorrow."

After I cleared the lenses of Geravie's eyes, I bade them both goodbye, and I left to spend my last night in my childhood room.

I SHOULD HAVE KNOWN THAT THE PURPLE CANDLE WOULD GO OFF on my last night. The goddess works in funny ways. But in the dark of night, when I heard the whoosh of magic and the snap of the wick lighting up, my entire being relaxed in relief before leaping out of bed in a mad rush.

"Thank the goddess!" I said out loud. It was honestly a blessing, and I couldn't have thanked her more. I quickly changed my clothes and slung my satchel over my shoulder, getting into midwife mode. Agatha and I had spoken about what potential difficulties Bluebell might come across, and it was imperative I get there for the start of her labour. Bluebell had already given birth before, so this one would be faster, and the second twin faster still. I needed to make sure they all made it safely.

It was close to midnight when I left out my servant's door and practically sprinted down the stairs and through the long corridors. But when I turned into the corridor that led to my secret exit, a broad chest of copper plate metal barred my way.

Fear shot through my core as I looked up into the eyes of Havlem and Yarnat, my stepmother's guards.

I *felt* the blood drain from my face.

"What are you doing?" I asked quietly.

"You can't leave the palace tonight, Princess," boomed Havlem in his deep voice. "The queen's orders."

"I'm not running away, you dolt!" I snapped. "I have an urgent birth to attend."

"No."

Anger tore through me. Not tonight, any other night, but this one! "What do you mean 'no?'"

"We can't let you," said Yarnat, his voice slightly softer. "I'm sorry, Princess. The queen—"

I was fully prepared to barge around them and made to do so. "You can't stop me."

But they could. And they did.

They both lunged at me, and I flailed, kicking with as much force I could muster. They struggled for a moment, mildly unprepared as I had never fought them off before. But this was no whipping session. They were stopping me from seeing Bluebell. I saw red and bucked like a wild animal, and when that didn't work, their grip strong around my upper arms—

"Stop!" I screamed. "You can't!"

I'm not the lightest girl. I had weight on my side and muscle and the training of Jerali Jones, but it didn't matter. These were six-foot-tall soldiers in full plate armour, and they grunted and roughly pinned me down between them, practically carrying me back up to the palace. They brought me by the main stair since we wouldn't all fit up the narrow servant's passage.

Through the palace halls, they dragged me, but I wasn't giving up. I had to get to Bluebell. I *had* to. I thrashed my body, but they held me with such a strong grip I knew that if they didn't stop, they might injure me. I ceased my movement as I thought rapidly. They thought I was going to run away, and they couldn't risk letting me out. If I could just explain—

"Listen to me!" I cried. "There's a woman in labour. I *must* go."

"That's not your concern." The voice came from beyond

me like a whip. "And be quiet, you stupid girl, or you'll wake the entire palace."

The queen.

"Stepmother, please—" I said, as her guard's fingers dug painfully into my upper arms, hauling me before her, white face contorted in fury, a grey silk dressing gown wrapped tightly around her tall frame. "I'll just be a few hours, then I'll be back. I *have* to see Bluebell. Her baby died last time. She's high risk—"

"I do not care about the issues of the commonfolk," she said viciously. "I will not risk you betraying us or making us look like fools. Do you understand me?"

"I know, but I—"

"You will stay in your room until the ceremony. *That is an order*." She pointed a red-nailed finger in the direction of my room.

"No!" I screamed as Havlem and Yarnat hauled me down the corridor. "No, you don't understand! I promised!"

"Sara?" Altara's suite door opened, and she stood there in her pink nightgown, bleary-eyed.

"Tara!" I screamed. "Tell them! Tell them to let me go!"

My sister's eyes widened as she realised what was happening. "Sara! Havlem, let her go!"

"Go to bed, Altara," the queen snarled. "Tell your sister to behave."

Altara's head whipped from me to the queen and back to me. My maids' door opened, and Blythe and Tembry fell out of their room in a panic.

"Your Highness!" cried Blythe, bounding forwards. "What is going on?"

But the guards ignored them and merely pulled me past them all towards my suite door. I had to get out. I'd go back down the servants' stair, blast past them, and I'd have Altara create a distraction.

But as they shoved me into my room, my dress tore as I tried to twist out of their grip, and Havlem gripped me so hard I knew it would leave bruises.

"No!" I screamed.

They pushed me into my room, and I tumbled onto the floor. I shot back up immediately and ran at the door, only to have them shut it in my face, the sound of metal chains clanking.

I turned and ran for the servants' stair, but when I twisted the handle, it wouldn't budge. I groaned in frustration and looked around my room. A small crystal vase sat on my desk, with fresh cut flowers no doubt Tembry had placed there. I yanked it off my table and pulled the flowers out—aimed the heavy crystal at the handle, and rammed it down as hard as I could. It took three rabid downswings before the handle clattered to the floor. I sighed in relief, but when I pushed the door, it didn't budge. I threw my whole weight at it, ramming my shoulder into the wood. But it felt like someone had placed something heavy to barricade it from the other side.

I cursed so badly it would have made my sister gasp— I had learned more than midwifery from Agatha.

Agatha—she would be wondering where I was. It felt like a fist had gripped my heart, and I paced my room, thinking about how I could get into the city.

"Sara?" came a faint voice. "Let me talk to her, you fool!"

It was Altara. I ran to my main door. "Tara?" I called. "Can you let me out?"

"No, these two barbarians are standing here, *and* they've chained the door."

Metal clanked as if Altara had swatted at the chain. I

swore loudly, dragging my hands through my hair. My exits were barred on a level I couldn't fight against. There was no way out.

The sick realisation that I couldn't get to Bluebell hit me with the force of a horse kicking me in the sternum. I had never been the sort of person to wish harm upon others. Never sought to hurt or maim. But I felt that need in my being now.

"You'll pay for this!" I screamed at them with all the rage in my heart. "A woman and her babies could die tonight because of you!"

Bluebell's face swam in my mind's eye. She was probably in the throes of labour, wondering where I was, why I hadn't kept my promise. I imagined her in tears, holding a silent baby, all because I wasn't there. I imagined her with two tiny caskets, another funeral, all because I. Wasn't. There. Rage sliced through me, and the pain of it tore my throat open and made me scream.

"Did you hear me?" I screamed at my door. "You'll pay for this with your heads!"

My furore surprised even me. I fell quiet, my breath coming in heavy pants, my blood seething in my veins, thinking about who would pay for this.

"With all due respect, Your Highness," came Havlem's voice. "You're leaving tomorrow."

I slammed my fist into the wall in raw anger, hot tears sliding down my face. And I didn't say my next treasonous thoughts out loud. But I *hated* my stepmother. With all the hot-blooded rage in me, she would pay for keeping me in here, I would *kill her*. If Bluebell or her babies died tonight, it would be because of *her*. And my father. He let her do this to me. I hated him too.

"I swear," I whispered the words out loud in an oath that I felt in my bones. "You'll pay for this. And it'll be by my hand."

I had promised my mother that I would never harm anyone with my gift. But I had also promised Bluebell.

And I could break a promise to my mother for Bluebell because my mother was dead and Bluebell was not. But as I reached through the door with my mind's eye, I felt for Havlem's carotid artery, the big one that leads to your brain. But I came up against a black steel wall. Frowning, I pushed against it. I should have felt his skin, his muscle, his blood vessels, but the only thing I could see was a wall of black.

Punching the door again, pain shot down my wrist. But the pain felt good. It felt right. I knew in my core, the queen had something to do with this black wall around Havlem's mind. She had been the one to tell me about the fae psychic ritual, after all. She had knowledge of magic. That realisation silenced me for a moment.

They might be keeping me here now, but dawn would come. I cast my eye at the purple candle, its yellow flame now small and meek on its wick. I growled at the sight of it like some animal had emerged from the depths of me.

When dawn came, the fae would come, and then they'd *have* to let me out.

8

SARAYA

I swear that rage was the goddess' gift to women.

My mother had gone through every tissue of my body to teach me anatomy and physiology. And I felt my rage now, hot and icy at the same time, flooding every artery and vein and capillary in my body. I felt it from the coronary arteries in my pounding heart to the tiny vessels in my fingers. I seethed with it.

You would think that when I eventually fell asleep, slumped against my bedroom door, my anger would abate a little, or at the very least, I would be exhausted from it.

But it didn't.

I was a high-pressure system, like one of the dormant volcanoes that made up Ellythia's outer islands. I had been awakened and was ready to explode. Maybe I had absorbed five years of my stepmother's rage each time she had taken it out on me with cured leather.

Most of the night, I sat there watching Bluebell's purple candle, the flame sputtering in irritation, like me. But when I awoke with a sick start, I saw that the candle had melted down to its base, the flame out cold. It immediately spurred my rage back on.

I was convinced Bluebell was dead, or the babies were dead. Someone was dead, and it was all because I was barred from leaving to do my duty. It felt like a black poison coiling around my heart, choking the life out of it. Out of me. The fae were already playing a part in my demise, and they weren't even here yet.

My breathing was hard and heavy as I barely contained the desire to destroy everything in my room. I would have been quite happy to see the entire world burn right then and there—as long as I would be the one to kill my stepmother.

But the memory of the guards and the mental black walls I had met last night made me a little wary. She knew more about magic than she let on in the five years that I had known her. But she had no magic powers that I had ever identified or caught. I only knew her as a cold, angry woman who used the physical pain of others as an outlet.

And so this was the state I was in when finally, well past dawn, Blythe and Tembry were allowed in to get me ready, Altara hot on their heels.

"Oh, Your Highness," whispered Tembry, her face pale. I was still on the floor, not caring how I looked, which was probably horrendous. I had ripped the tie out of my hair at some stage, and my dress was still torn from last night's effort to escape from the guards—whom I realised were now standing hesitantly at the door, eyeing me warily.

I met them eye for eye, knowing that I looked a banshee out for murder. Both avoided my gaze, and I saw that Yarnat visibly grimaced at the sight of me.

They deserved death.

For that was what they had dealt to Bluebell. It was the only fitting justice.

"Do you know what you've done?" I rasped, not taking my eyes off them. They shifted awkwardly, exchanging an uncertain look.

"Goddess give me strength," Altara murmured. "Sara, are you alright?"

The anxiety in my sister's voice made my heart twang. Bluebell would have been just as afraid.

"I *said*," I snarled, getting to my feet, ready to run at them, to tear at them with my bare goddess forsaken hands. "Do you know what you've done?"

"We had to do it, Princess—" began Yarnet, shaking his head.

I took a menacing step forward. "Because of you, three lives might have been lost last night." I held up three fingers and whispered, trying to contain this raw anger. "Three. A mother and two babes."

"Sara…"

But I ignored my sister.

"I will *kill* her," I'm not entirely sure if I had meant to say it out loud.

"Sara!"

"Your Highness!"

I watched the guards' eyes widen, but I could only see Bluebell's face at that moment. "If they are dead. I. Will. Kill. Her."

The guards looked at each other. "That is treason, Princess."

"You restrained me. You ripped my dress. You stopped me from my duty. You stopped me from saving a life. *She* was the hand behind that."

I could see they were uncomfortable, and I revelled in every second of it.

I felt my sister behind me. "Let's get cleaned up, Sara," she whispered. "Come. Please."

Only the note of begging in her voice made me turn, and I let the girls do to me whatever they wanted.

They washed me, dressed me, combed the knots out of my hair, and the entire time, I remained silent, my stepmother's smirk in the forefront of my mind. I wondered if there was a way of getting to Bluebell or to Agatha to see what had happened. To explain—

I caught Blythe's wrist in a snake-tight grip. She was the cleverest of the maids in the palace. "You will go to see midwife Agatha," I croaked. My voice was raspy from the screams that came out of me last night. "And see if the girl, Bluebell—her parents own the bakery on Canty street—is okay. Go. Now."

She didn't argue and, white-faced, raced out of the room at full pelt.

I heard Altara swallow. "You can't say those things from before, Sara," she said. "You can't say you're going to *kill* the queen. Let alone in front of her guards."

"They should know," I said through gritted teeth. "*She* should know what she's done. And besides, I'm leaving, aren't I? She can't do anything."

"Let's just focus on what's going to happen in just a few hours, okay?" she pressed.

I let them dress me in the clothes we'd chosen from my mother's chest together. A red chiffon affair, tight at my waist, baring a modest amount of cleavage and flaring out at my hips. It was regal, and in the back of my enraged mind, I knew I had cut a striking image that would make heads turn.

75

Next, we affixed the finest diamond necklace inlaid with gold and matching drops. Tembry expertly curled my hair and set my official tiara in place—It was the shape of a lotus with gold, amethyst, and diamond gems.

They wanted me to look like a woman, strong and proud, but I think red was the worst colour given my current state. It only served to agitate me. All I could think about what how this dress was going to hinder me from getting my now mani-cured nails around my stepmother's neck.

We all looked at me in my vanity mirror, and Altara gave a choked sob.

"Don't," I managed in a soft voice. "Please don't. Keep Stepmother away from me, do you understand?" She looked at me wide-eyed. "It's not going to end well for her." And I meant it with all my heart.

"Saraya, the *fae* are coming. You need to be on your best—"

"Oh, I will," I snarled. "When I hear back from Blythe. *Only* then will I go to meet the fae."

"It should be quick for her," said Tembry nervously, rubbing her stomach as if she were queasy. "The city will be on lockdown. She'll just go right to this Bluebell's house and come right back."

I nodded firmly. I couldn't leave without knowing. I refused.

It was not half an hour later that there was a knock at my suite.

My father's runner, Lennard, practically fell into the room when Tembry opened the door.

"It's the fae! The fae are here!"

"In the castle?" I said sharply.

He flinched at my tone. "No, Your Highness. You can see their procession through the main street. Come and see!"

Havlem and Yarnet were still guarding my door, but I ignored them, not wanting to inflate my already gargantuan anger.

But they followed me close behind as we all followed Lennard through the palace and to the widest balcony that lined the front of the building. The entire senior household was standing there, and those who were not had their faces pressed against the glass of the windows looking out at the city.

My stepmother wasn't present, no doubt watching from her rooms on the level above us.

They made way for me, and I came to stand beside my father. He glanced at me and nodded once. I just hoped he would keep his mind for the duration of the interaction with the fae. It would be so awkward if he had one of the trances at the wrong moment. But I think the adrenaline of the whole thing kept him focused. I glowered on the spot, but then Altara took my hand in hers, and I swear it was the only thing keeping me from causing a scene. My father was as much to blame as my stepmother in all of this.

"There!" one of the advisors pointed, and we all almost snapped our necks to look. As they had planned, the entire city was quiet, the usual hustle and bustle completely absent. Everyone, out of both obedience and probably fear, was shut up in their homes. I imagined the shopkeepers and brothel workers peeking out of their homes to look out at the main street and get their first look at the mysterious fae.

The first look humans had of the fae for thirty years.

We only had images in books and the words of those who fought in the war. As the stories went, the monsters had pointed ears, snarling mouths, and blood-red eyes. They were supposed to be tall and beautiful in a fearsome, gruesome sort of way. And here I was, to be wed to one. To spend the rest of my life amongst them. I shuddered.

And then I saw it. A line of black winding down the main city road—the one that led right from the outskirts of the city and up to the tall palace gates, which currently stood wide open and ready.

In the lead were four black stallions bearing the plain white flags of peace. Behind them was another row of stallions bearing a grey flag with a rearing, black dragon. The sigil of the Darkcleaver Family.

Behind them was a series of horse-drawn carriages—I counted six.

"Looks like they've brought the whole family," murmured my father.

I glanced at him in mild surprise and wondered if Bluebell's family were watching the procession from the top of their bakery. I wondered who was alive to watch it.

The rage I felt scared me a bit. It was raw and terrifying to see that I had so much darkness in me. The need to hurt someone else, to take revenge.

But a part of me liked that. It was a new sort of power, and I felt it growing. And it wanted to be used to get justice. But at this moment, I didn't know exactly how to wield it best.

"We will invite them to stay the night," my father said to me. "They won't want to stay long, of course, but I will ask them to take you tomorrow."

I stilled in thought. Perhaps that would give me time to figure out a way to see Bluebell. I glanced at Altara, and I could see her mind working. I would still prefer her to leave tonight, if possible. Otherwise, we could delay it one day. After all, there was a chance they would decline to stay here.

Then in a show of rare emotion, my father put his arm around my shoulders in a move he hadn't done since before Mother died. I looked up at him, but his eyes were fixed on the procession. I swallowed through a throat that had suddenly turned tight.

"Use what your mother taught you, Sara," he said so that only I could hear. "I mean that. Use all of it."

He meant my power. I knew that any time during the years I had run into the city at all hours, he could have sent guards to stop me. But he never had. Instead, his guards would often watch over me, letting me attend my work without interfering. He had never sought to bar my way at all. At first, I had thought he simply didn't care anymore—after Mother died, he had withdrawn into himself. But now I realise that he had purposefully encouraged my work from afar.

"Thank you, Father," was all I could murmur. Because despite all that, his new wife still spent five years beating me. He should have protected me from her.

When the fae procession rode through the gates, our household all hurried downstairs to the entrance hall, where the king and queen would greet the fae royalty. Excited and nervous chatter flitted through the staff, and their energy fed my own, making my stomach flop on itself.

I was leaving. I couldn't believe they had come to take me away.

They made me wait with Tembry, in the wings above the entrance hall with the instructions to wait for them to call me. It meant that I would get a good view of the events preceding my own entry. Altara gave me a nervous smile as she headed to the hall behind my father. I wished she could stay with me, these were our last moments together, after all, but I knew I had to do this alone.

Oxley, with deep bags under his eyes today, came up to me and the hairs on the back of my neck prickled.

"Courage, Your Highness," he said formally, bowing. "The advisors thank you for your part in maintaining the peace. Lightning never yields."

I stiffly inclined my head, murmuring my house saying back. "What do you know of the ceremony?" I couldn't forget Geravie's words about the blood magic, nor my stepmother's warning about the magical testing.

"Just follow their lead, Your Highness. I think that's all we can do." And with that, he bowed and strode off, just as I heard the deep boom of a series of drums.

9

SARAYA

I cast a wide-eyed look at Tembry, and we both rushed to the red velvet curtain, peeking through it to get our first look at the Dark Fae.

My heart pounded in my chest as the drummers, who were a part of the fae group, stood in a black and gold uniform by the ten-foot-tall entrance doors. Outside and down the steps, I could see the tops of the first fae carriage.

"Here they come, Your Highness!" whispered Tembry, clutching the goddess necklace around her throat.

And indeed, what looked like the entire Black Court royal family walked up the stairs as one. Tembry and I watched on, transfixed.

There was a party of seven. The king and queen and their five children.

I noticed the king first since he was the most obvious. Although he must've been nearing sixty, like my own father, he was tall and still broad of shoulder and looked like he could take on any man in my father's army. His face was like cut marble, with high cheekbones and full lips. He wore his hair short, revealing finely pointed ears.

Next to him, the fae queen was a smiling beauty, slender with golden skin, rose pink lips, and an elegant silver gown that shone in the light of the sun streaming through the entrance. Long brown tresses coiled their way to her waist, and her pointed ears were decorated with shining gems that danced in the light.

They paused at the entrance, and one of their heralds came to stand just ahead of them.

"Presenting, His Royal Highness King Wyxian Dark-cleaver, ruler of the Black Court, deliverer of justice, defeater of the Nightwing! And Her Royal Highness Queen Xenita of the Corpse Flower."

Our own herald, an elderly man chosen for his deep voice, announced, "We welcome you to Lobrathia, our fae friends! Presenting His Royal Highness King Eldon Voltanius and Her Royal Highness Queen Glacine Voltanius!"

I held my breath as the fae king and queen stepped forward to my father and stepmother, trying to process what their names meant. Both kings shook hands, rather stiffly, I thought, although I couldn't quite see their expressions. The queens had generous courtier smiles plastered on their faces as they clasped each other's hands.

I peered at my mother-in-law to be and wondered about her personality. But I decided that she couldn't be any worse than my stepmother.

I didn't know if I was relieved or frustrated that they didn't look anything like what had been described to me in the past. I could almost imagine Agatha cackling at me. I wished I had gotten time to speak with her before I left. A chance to apologise.

It seemed a little unfair. The fae had all come as one family, and yet I had to make a grand entrance by myself. All I could hope was that I didn't launch myself at my step-mother when I got down there.

The announcer then called forth the rest of the fae, and I got my first proper look at my husband-to-be.

"Crown Prince Daxian Darkcleaver, heir to the Black Court throne, wielder of the onyx blade!"

Daxian sauntered forward with the ease and confidence of a trained warrior and swept a bow. He was tall, well over six feet, and his tanned face was devastatingly handsome. He wore a fine tunic of forest green with his family crest on the breast—a black dragon wreathed in gold. Somehow, his eyes, blue as a twilight sky, found me, peeking at him up in the wings. I flinched and hid back behind the curtain, but not before seeing his handsome face smirk.

"He saw me," I whispered to Tembry, suddenly finding my limbs trembling.

Tembry gave a nervous giggle. "He's the most handsome man—I mean person— I've ever seen. Oh, goddess, I need to sit down."

I made sure Tembry made it to the velvet chair, her face a little flushed, before I peeked back out the curtain where my siblings-in-law were being introduced.

Prince Ivy and Prince Dattan were in their mid to late teens, dashing boys with dark hair and square jaws, their expressions serious.

Princess Sage gave a wondrous curtsey in her gown of baby pink, brown curls a twin of the mother's, in a thick braid down to her waist.

And finally, tiny Prince Wren was called forth, his round face crinkled in concentration as he stepped forward, bowed, and swung back up a little too fast. He stumbled a step backwards before glowing red and stepping back in line.

I couldn't help but smile, so they had some human-like qualities in them after all. So much for being monsters.

Then the announcer called my sister forward, and I clutched the curtain, watching intently.

But my sister had always been the more graceful of the two of us. She breezed forward with a carefully crafted grace and swept into a curtsey that made me grin in triumph. She had matched the grace of the fae perfectly. And in her gown of russet and gold, her skin gleaming bronze under the quartz light, I thought that she was the most beautiful being in the room. I looked to the fae males and saw the appreciation in their assessing faces. They were going to be extremely observant of us, I knew. Watching us like hawks searching for any sign of weakness.

My father exchanged what seemed like stiff pleasantries with King Wyxian, but twice, the fae king shook his head. I wondered if father had asked them to stay the night and a spike of fear lanced through me. If we left straight away, I wouldn't be able to see Bluebell. I glanced behind me at the exit. Blythe still hadn't returned. I suddenly felt very hot.

I sat down on the couch next to Tembry and only had five minutes of her holding my hand before the herald hurried into the room.

"It's time, Your Highness."

My heart beat irregularly in my chest, and I stood on shaky legs. This was it. I was going to be bonded to a fae prince. Goddess, help me. I clasped my shaking hands in front of me. I suddenly thought of my mother, and with a sharp intake of breath, I scolded myself.

I was no quivering common girl going to face a king. I was Princess of this kingdom, and they were simply attractive people with oddly shaped ears.

And I bet my mother hadn't shown fear when she had come to marry the Lightning King. I bet she would have held her chin high in the air and carried herself with the grace of her people. So that was what I would do too.

I let out a cool breath and turned to take Tembry's hands in my own. She started a prayer. "Maiden, give us heart. Mother, give us strength. Crone, give us wisdom."

After I also murmured the words, I pulled her towards me, giving her a hug that made her sob, and then turned to follow the herald.

I came to stand at the front of the grand staircase, my mother's chiffon settling around me like water over pebbles.

The herald, now at the bottom of the stairs, thumped his wooden staff.

"The Princess Saraya Yasani Voltanius, first of her name. Daughter of the King of Lightning and the late Queen Yasani Lotus of Ellythia."

My breath caught as he spoke my mother's name and I urged back my tears. I hoped she would be proud of me.

I began my descent, feeling all eyes like a thousand tiny weights pressing on me. But I kept my back straight and my chin high, holding my hands demurely at my waist as I carefully descended.

They're not monsters. They're just like us. They're just like us.

But I felt it as I stepped off the final stair and came to stand before them, next to my father. Their gazes upon me felt like a cold kiss, and I tried not to let it get to me. Their presence sat heavy in the air, like the atmosphere before a storm.

A pregnant sort of power, just *waiting* to be unleashed. Perhaps it was my own magic warning me because I knew then that I should never underestimate the fae.

I gave my best curtsey, the one we spent hours practising from girlhood, and the movement came to me like an old friend.

I looked up into King Wyxian's inhumanely turquoise eyes, and he inclined his head, gesturing behind him.

The crown prince stepped forward and directly in front of me. I took in his impressive form. Broad, muscular shoulders tapering down to a narrow waist. He held himself like he was ready to strike at any moment. I knew him for what he was. A warrior through and through and arrogant to a tee.

"It is a pleasure to meet you, Princess Saraya," his voice was like the deep earth, and his eyes dragged down my form in a way that was, unfortunately, familiar to me.

"And you, Prince Daxian," I said lightly.

"How beautiful you are, Princess Saraya," purred Queen Xenita in a perfectly pleasant voice. "Was your outfit your own choice?"

Her blue eyes flashed with amusement. The only means by which I gave my offence away was to blink, slowly, only once at her perfectly sculpted golden face. I knew then that they looked down upon me. I cracked a broad smile to the fae queen. *Who does she think she is?*

"It was," I said evenly.

"Naturally!" She beamed at me, and that told me she was as fake as my stepmother. So I beamed back, inclining my head in most gracious thanks. But I didn't miss the fact that Daxian was watching me like a predator keen on prey.

"And so here we are," said King Wyxian. "A union thirty years in the making." His expression was unreadable, and I couldn't tell if he was happy with this or not. It had been his idea, after all. His terms of peace. *Why did you ask for this*? I silently asked. There had to be some reason, some ulterior motive, some grand plan for this union. That was something I would have to figure out.

"How do you wish to proceed, Wyxian?" asked my father, thankfully sharp for the moment at least.

The fae king waved a broad, golden ringed hand, and a servant was at his elbow in an instant, bowing deeply over the silver tray he bore.

"The magical contract."

The servant presented the tray to my father, and from next to him, I could see a parchment written with opalescent ink, the penmanship so perfect that it could only have been done by magic. I saw two faded thumb prints in what was clearly old blood—Wyxian's and my father's blood, from that day they had signed my fate on the battlefield.

"To seal the agreement, it requires one thumb print," Wyxian said, "each from the bride and groom, in their own blood."

My body relaxed a little, so that's all the ritual would require, a simple thumbprint of blood. It could have been much, much worse.

"Shall we—"

But the fae king cut himself off, frowning, and then Princess Sage muttered a dull, "Oh no."

A cold wind stirred wisps of my hair, and all at once, day turned to night. The entire hall became shrouded in darkness as if a storm had suddenly blocked out the sun.

I studied the fae king and queen. Both had stiffened, the queen pressing her lips together into a thin, hard line. The king and Prince Daxian turned and stared at the open front doors to the palace, and I saw with a little unease that the immediate sky around the palace had turned a stormy deep grey.

The voice came first.

"Apologies, Your Majesty," a low, deep drawl.

1 0

SARAYA

The hairs on the back of my neck stood straight at that deep, slicing voice.

And then came the chill. It swept over all of us like a wild wind from a blizzard. My stepmother flinched, and I felt my father grab her arm. I looked for Altara, but she stood still, frowning at the open entrance of the palace.

I followed her line of vision and saw three figures in the shape of tall fae warriors striding towards us. As they approached, their features became clear. I had been traipsing around the city at night for long enough to know the look of men I needed to avoid at all costs. Assassins, sell-words, mobsters.

I took one look at them and knew they were more dangerous than any man I had ever seen down in the Sticks. All three wore strange thick black armour that clung to their bodies like a second skin, the patterning akin to dragon scales. There were two warriors at the back, one dark-haired hulking mass of muscle, the other blond, leaner with a slinking dancers' walk.

In the lead was a male, Daxian's age, handsome, with a confident swagger that screamed for other men to avoid him —which meant that it drew the eye of every woman in the room—including mine. His skin was a deep tan, almost as brown as mine, and his face was ruggedly angelic with eyes of bright hazel.

And those eyes were set on me, the pupils dilated so much I could barely see the iris. It drew me in like a fishing hook, and I blinked twice, reminding myself to breathe. Something poked me at the corner of my mind, something familiar yet grating, but I pushed it aside.

I knew instantly that he was the one who had spoken first. It was like he was a tightly coiled power that lay silent and waiting.

"Your Majesty," he drawled as he stalked up to us, his hazel eyes taking in the entire scene and flicking to the king. He swept a bow. "Apologies for the delay."

I didn't fail to notice the malicious, black hilted sword he wore at his belt, nor the fact that each finger was tipped in pointed silver that looked sharp enough to tear a man's throat out. Elaborate runic tattoos wound their way around both his fingers and wrists, disappearing into his shirtsleeves.

"No need, Commander," said the fae king in a voice that I thought was slightly strained. He turned back towards us, the humans, as we all stared at the newcomers.

"Eldon," the fae king gestured to the newcomer and spoke in a dry voice. "Drakus Silverhand commands my elite forces. He is celebrated amongst our kind."

"A pleasure," purred my stepmother before my father could speak, her eyes trained on the fae commander.

I suppressed the urge to roll my eyes.

But despite a less than welcome greeting from the fae,

Drakus spoke with the grace of a prince, his silver-tipped hands casually resting at his belt. "The pleasure is mine." No doubt fae females swooned over him all the time.

Then his sharp gaze shifted back to me, and I felt an uncharacteristic flush creep through my body.

But Wyxian drew my attention back to himself. "Shall we proceed?"

It was at that moment that Blythe decided to make an entrance. A darting movement from the side of the hall made me turn, and I saw her standing there, uncertainly looking from between the fae party and me.

I beckoned to her, and, red-faced, she rushed towards me, her eyes so wide I could see the whites all the way around. She dabbed her brow with her dress sleeve as she reached me and slowed to a walk. My heart thudding, I leaned down as she whispered in my ear.

"Bluebell is alive. But barely. She lost a lot of blood. Both babies survived."

I closed my eyes as I felt first a cool wash of relief, followed by the heat of concern. I didn't care the fae were staring at me with heavy, suspicious gazes. A woman could die from blood loss quickly. Another funeral. Another casket. Bluebell's two babes could be motherless within hours. This news was a blessing but still a curse for me. That Bluebell was unwell. It was my fault. I needed to see her. I needed to apologise before I left and see what I could do for her.

"What else did they say?"

"I told them...why you couldn't come."

"What are you doing?" the queen hissed at me from behind my father.

My entire body stilled. And I tried. I really, really tried to contain my anger. But the rage returned anew, too powerful, like a heated sword thrust into my gut. I clenched my teeth as hard as I could. I fisted my hands for all I was worth, but I knew the slight tremble that it caused would be noticed by the keen-eyed fae. Their magical ears might have even heard what Blythe said.

I straightened from where I had bent to listen to Blythe and turned slowly to look at the queen with a face that promised murder. All she could do was frown deeply at me in return. I had not ever shown her open, public hostility, and I think that surprised her. Even through the whippings, I had learned to stay quiet and keep to myself, avoiding her whenever I could, being the good little princess the crown wanted me to be. She had too much power over me then. But not anymore. She had gone too far, and I was leaving now.

"Is all well, Princess?" There was the barest hint of resignation in Daxian's deep voice, but I didn't really care.

All I could manage was a whisper, but even to me, it sounded dead and dull. "My apologies for the interruption Prince Daxian." I glanced at the *other* interruption, the fae commander, whose hazel eyes were focused on me with an intense interest. I tore my eyes away from him and looked back at Daxian. "Please proceed with the ceremony."

The fae king announced to the entire hall. "The tradition is called *Salasangar*, which means 'to test the mind'. One by one, my children, starting from the youngest, will attempt to pierce the bride's mental defences. The ceremony will cease when one of them wins. In times gone past, that was the male you would wed. Although, of course," he gestured to Daxian, "we know it will be Daxian regardless."

The crown prince inclined his handsome head.

"It is an old tradition," piped the fae queen regally, a

cutting smile on her face. "Please do bear with us. It'll be quick."

Barbaric, she meant, and the sexual innuendo was not lost on me. They were eyeing me to gauge my response, I guess expecting me to blush or look uncomfortable. But they didn't know that I had started my midwifery training at thirteen and had long ago stopped blushing at such things.

So I gave my best amused smile and nodded regally. If I was to be embarrassed by the fae, at the very least I could do it with my head held high.

"Step forward, my dear," the fae king said, moving his family back a little. My father took his lead and also moved back, leaving a wide gap in the middle, into which I now stepped.

"Play nicely, Wren," said the fae queen loftily, gesturing her littlest child forward.

I swallowed, hiding my nerves as the six-year-old prince shyly stepped before me. He gave a bow and then set his shoulders and closed his eyes, scrunching his cherub-like face up in concentration. I would have smiled at his endearing face had I not felt a tiny presence at the front of my mind.

I slammed down a mental wall of brick, and my eyebrows flew up. Reflexively, I glanced back at Altara.

We had played this game before.

In fact, I had been playing it with my mother every night since I was three. Except we called it "palace siege."

Somehow she had known the fae ways and trained us both using a simple, fun game. Each player built a castle in their mind, complete with fortifications. The other person then sat across from them, and you both tried to 'enter' their mental castle. Whoever went in first won. I had thought it was an innocent game meant to help me in my training for magical midwifery and healing. It was a lot of mental work, and the game had really made me good at the magical side of my midwifery. I had never associated it with "magical defence," as Stepmother had warned me about.

So it came as a great surprise when the familiar feeling of someone trying to enter my mental castle came into the forefront of my mind. I hadn't played the game in years.

If this was the ritual, then I stood some sort of chance. I quickly built a castle in my mind. Upgrading my old castle with new fortifications, trick entrances, and traps. I built the walls impossibly high and right across into a cube, covering the castle completely.

Prince Wren winced as he came up against my wall.

I felt the fae shift in surprise. So I felt for his own castle gates and charged right through.

"Ouch!" he whined.

"Sorry," I murmured hastily.

The queen swept forward and pulled Wren back towards her, a smile plastered on her face, her eyes sharp on me now. None of them had expected this. "Next!" she called.

Prince Dattan stomped forward, looking a little uncertain. But I checked my castle walls as he stood in front of me, handsome, the beginnings of a moustache atop his lip. But I was ready this time.

I shot up to his walls and circled them, aggressively checking for any weak points. I felt him doing the same with mine, a deep frown on his face now. But I'd built my castle over the years. I knew there weren't any external weaknesses.

He wasn't expecting me to go *under*. In a trick I'd learned off Altara, I dove beneath his steel wall. It chipped away slightly, and I pounced, immediately breaching his mental shield.

He made a soft sound of dismay, considered me with cyan eyes, then gave me a brief smile and graciously bowed. I inclined my head.

Prince Ivy was steely-eyed as he came to stand in front of me. I took one look at his growing muscular frame and those cunning eyes and knew he'd probably be more than a match. So I brought out an extra layer of protection. It used to make me sweat when I'd go against my mother, but she'd laugh and clap at the beauty of my diamond wall. I had built it fractal by fractal with the same meticulous concentration it took me to repair vessels, cell by cell.

But it had always been there in the back of my mind, and five years later, I had gotten extremely fast at building and reinforcing. It was then, when faced with human tissue that I had been able to work at quickly healing any injury of childbirth.

Ivy made a surprised sound at the back of his throat as I felt his presence, heavy and strong, like a rhinoceros, in my mind. He prowled around, thinking.

Suddenly, he pounced upon my shield, soaring for the top, but my shield was ready before I was, and the fake weakness I'd anchored there swallowed him whole and plunged him into a cobweb of darkness. Ivy cried out and flinched like something had hit him, and I let him go.

"That was a trap," he announced. "Where did a human learn to do that?" he asked suspiciously.

I opened my mouth to answer, but Daxian swaggered forwards. "You've had your turn, brother."

I flushed a little as he stood, tall and proud, opposite me, a fae warrior full grown. But—arrogance. Pure, unadulterated arrogance shone in his eyes. He wanted his turn. He wanted to break me. I was suddenly reminded of my stepmother's ice chip eyes.

A sudden fear filled me, and I flung up three layers of diamond for all I was worth. A sharp intake of breath through his nose told me he had not expected that.

Surging forward, I inspected his palace shield.

It was a wall of obsidian, smooth and sleek. There would be no obvious weaknesses here. I circled, and so did he, stalking the edges of me with a panther-like growl.

I dipped under and over, but the obsidian went all the way around. And then something thorny lunged for me, and I danced backwards in fright. He penetrated my outer shield.

He let out a low, satisfied laugh.

Traps then. Two could play at that game. I had them all along the inner perimeter. None of the others had even gotten close enough to test them. But I knew he would. It would take me a little time to find a way through his obsidian. I needed a fragment, a splinter, a fractal of insecurity to wheedle my way in. *Everyone* had some weakness in their defence. I just had to be wiley enough to find it.

I darted around the obsidian, and he poked at my next layer of defence quite hard. I flinched as one of my traps went off unexpectedly, pinching at him.

He hissed, and I smiled.

We danced around each other's shields warily for a minute, but I couldn't find a thing. I was considering a brute force attack when he murmured, "Do you look as good under all those clothes?"

Shock spun through me, and I stared at him, but he'd taken a moment to poke a hole and then shatter the second wall of diamond.

"Daxian," scolded his mother. But her gaze shone in approval.

Monsters indeed. They had no idea their human princess frequented brothels. Dirty talk was not something I was afraid of. But irritated at his audacity, I punched his shield.

He grunted, and I drilled into the obsidian with a pin of diamond. Daxian flinched, taking a step back.

Someone gave a snort from the fae group.

"I think that's enough," said the fae king, the barest crease between his brows as he studied me. Daxian and I both ceased our attacks immediately. I straightened, not realising I'd hunched a little in my concentration. Behind the prince, Drakus Silverhand, a name I was not likely to forget any time soon, had a smirk of amusement on his lips.

But Daxian was eyeing me now, and I think he was a little shocked. Or as shocked a fae could show on their face. I doubted anyone had dared to drill into the fae crown prince's defences in a while. He had fully expected me to submit to him. But I had not. I knew my mother would be infinitely proud, and that would carry me all the way to the fae realm.

The entrance hall was eerily quiet, and I'm not sure whether the humans had understood what happened except by reading body language. I was sure the fae had been able to see each battle using their own magic. I couldn't believe I had been able to stand up to the *fae*. I wondered what they were thinking, what they made of it. But the fae king was gesturing to one of his servants, and I had more urgent matters to think about.

Because as the servant brought the silver tray forward, my mind was a whirlwind of thought as I counted all the different possible ways that I could sneak out and see Bluebell and help her with her blood loss.

Daxian came to stand by my side so that we were facing our families, and I felt his presence next to me like a mountain of heat. It might have been a fae thing, but his smell was something I couldn't quite pinpoint, but it came to my nose as the darkest places under the sea, cold and narrow.

"The proper wedding will be in *our* palace in Black Court," piped the queen, her voice a little bit stiffer than before. "Where we can adhere to the proper fae traditions that are *thousands* of years old."

"Lovely," I said lightly. "I will also be adhering to my mother's *ancient* Ellythian bridal traditions."

Queen Xenita's eyes widened so fleetingly I could have sworn I imagined it, but her smile remained fixed in place as she observed me. They had expected a meek, weakened human girl, and my strength and magic surprised them, and I revelled in that.

King Wyxian strode forwards with a gilded pocket knife and handed it to Daxian. The fae prince took it and pricked his thumb. He squeezed the blood out of it, then pressed it onto the parchment under his own father's print.

Then he handed the knife to me.

I'm sure that, judging by the impossibly acute way the fae were all watching me, they were wondering what type of Princess I was. Would I balk at the sign of blood or refuse to stab myself?

Luckily for me, I was quite willing to stab anyone at that point. So I slashed my finger a little too vehemently, the blood poured out, and I quickly pressed it onto the parchment, leaving more of a bloody smear than the neat fingerprint Daxian had left.

I stared at my bleeding thumb, the sting of the pain abating a bit of my anger. I was about to seal the wound together with my healing magic when Daxian took out a handkerchief from somewhere, took my hand in his own, and pressed the wad of cloth onto the wound.

I stared up at him in shock and was a little more alarmed to see him in such close proximity. We were close enough to kiss, really. I had been kissed before, incidentally, though I'd only ever told Altara. After assisting the sister of one of the city's Blacksmiths in birth, he, a strapping young man with arms like logs, had swept me up and planted his mouth on mine. He'd be thoroughly scolded by Agatha afterwards, but it had made me giddy and craving more, though I'd never acted upon the desire.

But as Daxian's hand was hot against mine, and as I looked into his fae blue eyes, I felt no kindness in his gaze, only possession and...*ownership*.

"Thank you," I murmured, tugging on the handkerchief, and took my hand hastily back from him. I had not liked the feeling of his skin on mine, of his clear intent to overwhelm and dominate me. He was a warrior, and he was treating me as an enemy to conquer or property to obtain. A chill swept through me, and I suppressed an angry shiver. *I was not property*. And the fae would learn that.

"Well!" said one of the warriors behind the Drakus Silverhand, the blond, with the dancer's tread. "So it's done, then! Is there going to be food afterwards?" He looked around with raised golden brows as if expecting someone to lead him to a dining table.

"No Seargent," said the fae king disapprovingly. "I'm afraid we cannot eat the human food."

I glanced at my sister in surprise, and her eyes narrowed a fraction. I had never heard of this rule. Perhaps they simply didn't want to eat lowly human food because that was certainly the impression that they were giving, with the fae adults looking down their noses at us.

"Are we leaving immediately then?" I burst out, my heart rate rising in panic.

"Yes," said Daxian, his voice making goosebumps erupt all over me once again, "we are."

"It's a week's journey to the border," said Wyxian. "I will allow you half an hour to pass your luggage to our servants and say your goodbyes."

I will allow you.

The words struck me like a hammer. Was this going to be my life now? Control over what I did, where I went, who I went with?

But my mind rapidly focused itself upon one thing— because I had *half an hour*. I gave a swift curtsey and hurried out of the hall as fast as I could without actually running.

11

DRAKE

I walked out of the human palace with Slade and Lysander stalking behind me, my entire body twitching and hissing with adrenaline and desire. I needed a drink, an extremely strong one that would burn my insides. But I wasn't going to get one vile enough for my fae body in the human realm.

The Princess Saraya was nothing like we'd imagined.

"Daxian is an ass, as ever," drawled Lysander. "But more importantly, what do you think human brothels are like?"

"They'll take one look at you and run for it," Slade gruffed, stomping down the palace steps. "They shut down the whole city for us."

"I swear I saw one of them smiling at me from a window, though." Lysander gestured at the brick buildings beyond the palace walls.

"Are you sure that wasn't a look of horror?" I glanced back at my best sergeant, whose blue eyes were contemplative in deep thought. Fae females fell at his feet wherever we went. I doubted human women would be any different.

The fae attendants the king had brought with him

retreated behind their carriages as we passed on our way to the front lawn. If our reputation proceeded us, it wasn't our fault. Well, actually, I guess it was.

In Obsidian Court, they called my unit of elite guards the Shadow Bastards, but they're poetic people. Everywhere south of Twilight Court in the solar kingdoms, they call us what we are: the Black Drakus Devils.

We collected our horses, obediently waiting for us. The human handlers who had crept up to marvel at our steeds ran away at full pelt when they saw us approach. I didn't blame them for gawking. Our beasts were massive fae *zekar* stallions that we'd hand raised ourselves —more monster than horse. There wouldn't be any beasts like them in the human kingdom.

I patted my faithful Razor and swung onto him. He'd never balked or failed me, even when I'd pressed him into charging at a hazilem one time. And those things would take a horse and swallow it, given half the chance.

"Did you see her, though?" asked Slade as we trotted out of the gates and into the empty city, allowing the light back into the palace. I couldn't control the storm that followed me around, a consequence of an old bargain. But this time, it matched my mood perfectly.

Did I see her.

"Daxian's bride?" asked Lysander. "Hmm, she's some-thing, that's for sure. The Ellythian complexion, those emerald eyes. All that fiery rage. She mustn't like her step-mother that much."

No, the look she'd given her stepmother would have wilted steel. My hackles had raised at the sight of it. Queen Glacine was someone who needed to be watched.

"And she's got magic somehow," said Slade in a low voice. "So strong I could practically taste her anger."

I bristled a little at that. Magic only got that insanely strong if you were using a lot of it and often. I wondered what the hell she was using it for. I wondered what the hell had made her so angry. We had all heard what the raven-headed servant had told her, but without any context, it didn't make sense.

"She's wasted on Dax," said Lysander. "Did you see how she drilled into his shield? I've never seen a woman ballsy enough to do that at a Salasangaar."

"You haven't seen a woman do many things, Lysander," I snorted.

"That's because they're always on their back when I'm with them," he retorted. "Oh, look—" he jerked his chin up the second-storey window of a bakery. A haggard old woman stood there, bold as brass, watching us with an assessing look. Then she raised one finger in a universal sign I hadn't seen directed at me in…well, ever.

Slade chortled, and Lysander waved his fingers at her. I gave her a nod. If the old lady was telling us to fuck off, then good for her. To my surprise, she nodded back.

Humans were odd creatures, and Quartz City was more beautiful than I had imagined. More civil even. I had envisioned humans crawling in the streets, eating filth. Luminous quartz deliveries were made without much contact so most fae knew virtually nothing about them because we'd never needed to. Nothing truthful anyway. I would have to rectify that.

I led the horses into a trot then, not bothering to hide my amusement as I surveyed the main city road. In the fae realms, people fled at the sight of us. They'd heard the stories, and they were smart enough not to risk hanging around. But here, no one knew a thing about who we were, and that gave me a sort of levity.

But as the beautiful, furious, bronze face of Princess Saraya swam in my mind's eye, I kept coming back to one thing.

"I still haven't figured out why the king made that contract," I murmured irritably. "It just doesn't make sense." The thought itched under my skin like Eclipsian fire ants were crawling inside of me. It made the monster lurking in the shadows of my mind want to kill something.

The three of us quietened as we circled the city once more before heading back south.

Because now I knew the city's various weaknesses in and out, and as Commander of the Black Court's elite warriors, if the time came for us to ever take over Quartz City, I knew exactly how I'd do it.

12

SARAYA

Altara and the girls followed close behind me as I stripped off my gown before I even got into my dressing room, passing the red gown chiffon to Blythe while Tembry passed me a travelling dress and leggings.

"I'll be right back," I said, huffing. I knew my servant's door would still be blocked, but I knew a dozen different ways to get to my entrance.

So I sprinted.

Through the palace, through the servant's labyrinth, through the underground tunnel, and out into the empty city.

I ran to Bluebell's bakery and rapped my knuckles on the door, and sagged there, bent over double, gasping for air.

The door opened, and it was Charlie.

When I saw his pale face, I burst into a body-wracking sob right on their doorstep. "I'm so sorry!"

His arm came around me, urging me into the bakery. "Shhh, Princess, it's alright."

"Where is she?" I gasped.

"Upstairs, come on."

I followed him up their rickety stairs, wiping snot and tears off my face with my sleeve. Down a corridor and in a darkened room, Agatha sat in a rocking chair in a corner, and Bluebell lay tiny and pale on clean sheets. A babe nestled on either side of her, both pink and snuffling at a breast. The sight of them all alive healed the ragged edges of my rage. I barely stopped my knees from buckling right then and there.

"Princess!" Bluebell whispered.

"Oh, Bluebell!" I carefully stepped around the bed onto her side and knelt on the floorboards, relief pouring through me like a king tide, every intention of begging for her forgiveness.

"I'm so sorry." I couldn't stop the tears.

But she shook her head with a smile. "I'm okay, Princess. There's nothing to apologise for. That lovely Blythe told us what happened."

"They locked my door," I whispered. "They—"

"We saw the fae come," Agatha croaked from the corner. "Is it done?"

I held up my still oozing thumb. "I'm bonded to the fae prince. We're leaving right away. I don't know if I'll ever be back—"

Agatha sighed long and loud. "Destiny. Can't thwart it. Those scumbags thought they'd try for the quarry again!"

I gaped at Agatha, but Bluebell, with her arms around both her babies, smiled tiredly at me. "But I did it, Princess. I thought I couldn't do it, but I surprised myself. I'm more capable than I thought."

I smiled at her. "You are. You definitely are."

"And guess what," Bluebell whispered, eyes earnest. "I'm calling her Destiny." She nodded down to the baby suckling at her right breast. And then the baby on the left. "And he is Luxon. Lucky for short. Because the goddess meant it to happen this way. And I *know* you would have been here if you could have."

My heart clenched so hard that I felt like I was going to choke. She had done this all on her own, and she was right. Perhaps it *was* destiny. She'd come out of this with a renewed faith in herself.

"Check her uterus, will you?" Agatha groaned as she got off her chair. "I'll make you do one last bit of work before you leave us forever."

"Of course." I sniffed and closed my eyes, checking Bluebell's abdomen for any abnormalities. A twin birth made the uterus tired, and sometimes the placenta didn't come away properly. In amongst the inner lining of her womb, I spied a small discrepancy. A fragment of the placenta was still stuck to the wall. That was why she was still bleeding so heavily. I coaxed it out, ensuring the blood vessels of her uterus were all safely pressed shut.

Unfortunately, it wasn't in my power to give her more blood, but I could see that she was severely dehydrated. So I encouraged her bone marrow to work a little faster in their production of red blood cells. The ones that looked, to my eye, like Bluebell's cinnamon donuts without the holes all the way through.

"Should be fine now," I said. "One lobe was leftover. But she'll need a lot of food and water."

Charlie nodded, rushing out of the room to comply.

"Thought so," said Agatha stretching her back, old bones cracking. Then she fixed me with a beady blue eye. "The fae are no joke, girl. Be wise. Be smart. Be cunning if you can, although I know you don't have that in you."

I swelled at the advice and sideways compliment. "Thanks, Agatha. I'll miss you. I'll miss you all."

Bluebell gave me a tired smile. "We'll miss you too, Princess."

"I just wish I could stay and—"

"Oh, we'll continue on as we did before we had you, girl," Agatha said evenly. "You were a great help, but I think you made some of the young midwives lazy. It'll be good for them."

Naturally, I was late returning to the castle. I was able to give Altara a quick hug in my rooms as Blythe and Tembry took out my luggage.

"Be watchful," my sister said, looking up at me, her leaf green eyes brimming with tears. "Remember what Mother told us. And…think of me."

"You know I will," I murmured, pulling her towards me. We only had a beat before Lennard, the runner came puffing to the door looking panicked.

"I'm coming," I said, disentangling from Altara. I took her sweet, round face in my hands. "Use your gift wisely. I love you. Never forget that."

I saw her off to Geravie's rooms, sending a prayer to the goddess that her passage to the docks and then over the sea would be undisturbed. Altara was a clever girl, cleverer than me even, but she was going into the unknown now, and neither of us had been to Ellythia before. But our mother had fed us bedtime stories of beasts who could shift into men, magicians so powerful they needed to be bound under the earth, wandering ghosts and ghouls…Mother had always hinted they were more than just stories. Altara would need all her smarts.

I took my last walk through the familiar gilded halls of my home, taking a short detour into the deserted corridor where my mother's portrait had been moved. In her prime, when the portrait had been painted, she looked just like Altara, with bronzed skin, heavenly features, and a voluptuous body dressed in the finest Ellythian red silk. She was a sight that deserved to be painted, and indeed, I remember when the painter had come to do our childhood portraits, he had begged my mother to paint her just one more time. She had smiled and waved him away, saying something about vanity not a becoming trait of Ellythian royalty.

I kissed my fingers and touched them to the gilded frame. I had her anklet on and her silks packed in my bags. I had a part of her to take with me, and that gave me heart.

When I got to the entrance hall, I turned to give it one last look, nodded to myself, and went to see my father.

The entire household was standing at the entrance of the palace. One by one, they curtseyed or bowed as I passed, and I smiled fondly at them all. Tembry and Blythe rushed forward to hug me, and I whispered my thanks and goodbyes in their ears, promising to write if I could. The tears fell when Blythe presented me with a miniature painting she had done of my mother dancing in the back garden. Blythe was deft with a paintbrush so it was an exact likeliness. I clutched it to my heart and kissed Blythe on both cheeks. I was more friendly with my maids than a princess had a right to be, but I didn't care.

Jerali Jones waited patiently beside them and bowed deeply to me, eyes shining with rare emotion, throat bobbing. I immediately moved forward to take Jerali's hands in mine.

The armsmaster nodded firmly to me, eyes silently conveying a message.

Lightning does not yield.

Then came the king and queen. I glanced down the palace stairs. The fae were already in their carriages. One door was open for me. I wondered who I'd have the misfortune of spending a week's ride with.

I ignored my stepmother and focused on my father. But his gaze was distant, and I knew at once that whatever lucidity we had for the engagement was now gone. Perhaps he was dissociating from the pain of seeing me leave.

I sunk into a deep curtsey and, just for a moment, for the very first time, looked into my father's mind. It was almost as if the crevices of his brain were warped in the most obscene way. I abruptly sprung out of his body, suppressing the urge to shiver. Rising out of my curtsey, I turned on my heel and left. My stepmother never uttered a word, and perhaps that was for the best.

A fae footman offered me his hand as I stepped into the carriage. I took it with thanks and entered to find the courtier-faced Princess Sage and a bouncing Prince Wren with a demure fae I took to be the young prince's nursemaid.

They had put me with the children, and I knew their game well enough now to know they were telling me where in their household they thought I belonged.

The youngest members of the fae royal family stared at me as I took my seat opposite them.

"So," said Princess Sage in a deadpan voice. Then she grinned. "I've never seen my eldest brother *matched* like that. It really unsettled him. Thank you for humbling him."

One of the things I learned early on as a midwife was to be forever expecting the unexpected. I was definitely a better royal for it. So I was quick to grin back at the fae princess. "I honestly didn't know what would happen."

"He fought dirty," said Wren with his nose in the air. "Father says that's a commoner's method."

"Indeed," said Sage, prissily adjusting her pink skirts. "But you must tell us, how you got such enormous power? I was under the impression humans didn't have any."

"I guess these things pop up from time to time. That's nature for you."

"Hmm." Sage didn't look convinced. "You'll be a target now, in the fae courts."

"I imagine I would've been a target, anyway."

She smiled. "True."

"What's it like? The fae lands?"

"We live in the Dark Fae Realm," said Wren importantly. "So there's monsters. You don't have monsters here, do you?"

Oh, how badly I wanted to say I already knew about the monsters and that I thought I was supposed to be marrying one. But I bit my royal tongue. "Our wild animals are like bears, and deer, elk. On the Ellythian Isle, they have crocodiles and tigers."

"A hazilem would eat a tiger whole," said Wren. "And you must never let a kraasputin ask you for a secret."

"It talks?" I asked, shocked.

Wren nodded, wide-eyed. "Father bought me an encyclopaedia of fae monsters, and it says that over half of the fae beasts know some common tongue. The magic makes them smart."

We only spoke for a little while before both the prince and princess began dozing in their seats. It was then that I turned to Wren's nurse, who told me her name was Nettlie.

"What can you tell me about my husband to be, Nettlie? I'm afraid I know nothing about him."

Nettlie twisted her hands in her lap. "He's a fine fae, Your Highness, very fine. But I doubt you'll see him much."

"Oh?"

"All the fae males attend the Mountain Academy for most of the year. It's about to start back up again."

"Even at his age?"

"Fae males are particularly dangerous and troublesome in their youth, Your Highness. So hundreds of years ago, it was decided they should go to an Academy until the age of twenty-five when they become less volatile and better rulers of their kingdoms. When we...acquired the Silent Mountains, the Academy moved there."

I sunk back into my seat. So what was I supposed to do in the fae kingdom? Sit on my ass in the palace until my fiancé came back from school?

Eventually, I, too, began to doze and only woke when the carriages halted late in the afternoon.

I emerged behind the fae to find the Lobrathian country-side and a sea of white tents.

"We had most of our convoy camp here and wait for us," the Princess said, seeing my confusion. Their convoy looked like a whole heap of fae soldiers to me. Resting horses all lined up on one side, and maybe thirty plain white tents in organised rows. It would be a week of this, I despaired, before we got to the Silent Mountains and over to the other side into Dark Fae territory.

I watched the king and queen sweep out of their carriage and head into the camp without even so much of a glance at me.

"We'll take you to your tent." Princess Sage said tiredly as Wren was led ahead of us by his nurse.

"Where are your brothers?" I asked, following her. I'd not seen them emerge from any carriage.

"They've already gone," she said lightly, "to the Academy. It was faster for them to take the horses. They wouldn't make it on time, otherwise."

I hid my annoyance that they hadn't even told me beforehand. And I was slightly disappointed I wouldn't get the chance to observe the prince. I mean, he was nice to look at, but I had planned on watching him closely to find out about his character. But now, I wouldn't even be in contact with him at all. Sage led me past a group of guards sitting at a table. They were armoured with fine steel and stared at me curiously as we went past. I nodded at them. One of them raised his brows.

"Do the girls not go to an academy of their own?" I asked.

"We do, but only until sixteen."

She led me to a line of slightly larger tents.

"Mine and Wren's is the one next door," Princess Sage pointed to a line of tents. Wren and his nurse were entering a huge white tent. Next to it—mine was the smallest by far. I wondered how long I would be treated as lesser than by the fae.

"Thank you, Sage."

"I'll show you the latrine, and then we'll eat dinner in my tent together."

As Sage showed me the tent they used as the women's toilet, I silently thanked the goddess that Sage was here and pleasant with me because the queen seemed keen on ignoring my presence entirely. It didn't bode well that my mother-in-law didn't like me. I could only hope to change her mind over time.

Back in Sage's tent, which was divided into three, one compartment for her, the other for Wren, and the middle as a common and eating area, she abruptly turned to me.

"The fae think that humans are disgusting and uncouth," she tilted her chin, and I stilled. "I disagree. Even before I saw your people, I knew there was more to my nursemaid's stories." She shot a look at Nettlie, where she was unpacking food for Wren. The young nursemaid flushed.

"I had a different nursemaid back then." Sage looked back at me. "I want you to know that the fae are not going to like you."

"I guessed that would be the case."

"Let me clarify, there will be an assassination attempt, or at the very least a kidnap attempt."

My stomach flopped nervously as she continued. "But our forces are the best in all the fae lands. I just want you to be ready for something like that."

The servants brought us dinner, and we ate in quiet tiredness. It was roast vegetables and chicken, crusty bread, and a fresh salad. I was naturally impressed at their 'camp' food and decided I might take a wander to their kitchen tent tomorrow.

I bade Sage and Wren goodnight and headed into my own tent, which turned out to be quite comfortable. They'd given me water to wash with, and the cotton sheets on the soft down mattress smelled like lavender. I lay there for some time, just listening to the foreign sounds outside my tent. The faraway voices of guards, the chirp of crickets, the rustling of the tent. I knew this wasn't going to be easy. But that someone would want to kidnap me, and that there would be open hostility directed at me— it didn't make any sense. If they just wanted access to the luminous quartz quarry, surely marriage wasn't the best way to do that? With all their fae magic, why did Daxian need to marry me?

I barely got any sleep.

The next morning, the fae packed up their camp, and we continued our way down south. The next three days passed roughly the same, and we didn't talk too much in the carriage, as the prince and princess mostly dozed in their seats. The king and queen continued to ignore me, and I continued to twitch and jerk at any unexpected noise, half expecting some dark fae to kidnap me at any moment.

I'd never been this far south before—I'd never needed to. But word was, the closer you got to the dividing mountain range, the more fae the air was and the more strange the beasts. On the third night, I was walking past a group of guards from the latrine when I heard a sort of jeering.

I paused to watch as they gathered around a table, poking at something and laughing. One of them shifted a little, and I caught a glimpse of a plump creature no bigger than a kitten, its coat a beautiful rainbow of colour, its face contorted into fear as it looked up at the five fae soldiers looming over it.

"Her mum was dead," gruffed one of them. "Took her right from the pouch. She'll fetch me a fortune at Eclipse Market."

"I'll say," said another. "Lumzen are worth a couple hundred kruzos at least."

The creature gave the softest mewl of protest, and I scowled. One of the soldiers glanced behind him at where I was standing staring at them, but he paid me no heed and turned back to the creature they called a lumzen.

If I could have taken that baby animal off him, I would

have. But as it had stood, I'd been considered human trash by the guards and basically ignored the whole trip so far. I didn't think I'd get away with taking something worth that much money from a grown soldier. It wasn't bound to end well.

So, thoroughly irritated, I walked back to my tent for the night.

I should have known this trip wouldn't go smoothly for me.

Deep in the night, just as I'd fallen into a troubled sleep, I felt something tapping at the side of my mental defences. Frowning in my sleep, I peeked at it. The hazy image with a ghostly blue, translucent sheen became apparent, hovering at the edge of my mental walls. Was this the kidnap attempt Sage warned me of?

Thoroughly alarmed, I said, "Who are you?" My heart was hammering, but though I'd never met one before, my mother had always told me to wary, but respectful of spirits.

The ghost spoke in a stern, business-like voice, "My name is Arishnie, warrior midwife of the most sacred Order of Temari."

The name sounded vaguely familiar, but I couldn't put a finger on where I'd heard it. This woman also looked very human. "Why are you here?" I asked breathlessly.

Her face was grave, but her voice was urgent. "I need you to follow me now. You cannot leave with the fae."

I woke up with a start, sitting bolt upright in my bed. Before me, the spectre glowed blue-grey in the night, a middle-aged woman in heavy plate armour, a broadsword at her belt.

"It is time, Princess."

13

SARAYA

"Goddess, help me!" I exclaimed, jumping out of bed and squinting at her. "Time for what?"

I'd never seen a ghost before, but now I was actually before one. I somehow didn't feel as frightened as I thought I would be.

"You need to follow me." She said impatiently. "The Temple of Temari is not far from here."

"What do you mean 'I can't leave with the fae?'" I hissed. "And I can't just go out in the middle of the night with a ghost!"

"Your mother was Princess Yasani Lotus of the isle of Ellythia, and her mother was Queen Cheshni. Your gift has been passed down from mother to daughter for generations. Your duty calls you."

"Duty?" I whispered, conscious of the fae in the tents around me. "My duty is here, fulfilling a blood contract with the fae."

"There is something more important at play here,

Princess. I urge you to listen to me." She gripped her sword as if she were irritated.

"I'm listening," I hissed. "But what could be more important than the safety of my kingdom?"

She spread her hands out. "The safety of the entire human realm."

I sighed. I was arguing with a ghost, in the middle of the night, from my tent in a fae camp. I didn't know which part was more ridiculous to me. But what the warrior said to me next made my racing mind stop in its tracks.

"Your mother was never preparing you for your fae husband, Saraya. She was preparing you for something else. Something much greater."

"And what is that?" I whispered angrily. "And how can I trust you? There are assassins and kidnappers out to get me, apparently!"

"I'm long dead and very human." She twisted to show me her rounded human ears. "And it wasn't until this week, on your nineteenth birthday, that we were called back to the temple."

"Who's we?"

"The Order of Temari. The last of us that were murdered."

The memory came back to me. My mother had mentioned the Temari to me once in an old story. An order of female warriors tasked with protecting women. There was something in this warrior's eyes that reminded me of someone from an ancient story. I count myself as a good assessor of people, and in her ghostly form I saw only a stubborn determination. In her eyes, I saw no lie. My mother would have told me to take this offer seriously.

"I can't just go out into the dark of night alone."

The spectre raised an eyebrow. "Did you not do that regularly in your home city?"

How on earth did she know that? "I guess, but I'm not familiar with this area. How will I get past their guards anyway?"

"We won't be seen." She sounded so sure.

I cast a look around my tent helplessly. I was curious about this temple, and this woman in plate armour. But the likelihood of me getting into trouble was high. On the other hand, I'd basically been sold to the fae, for some reason that was beyond me. I owed these fae nothing and what did I really have to lose? I'd already lost everything that mattered to me. My family and my work.

"Fine." I pulled on leggings and boots. "But let's be quick about this. The fae already don't like me. Goddess, help me if they think I'm doing something suspicious."

"We will be fine. Stay close to me."

As a midwife, I appreciated her no nonsense matter. She had an efficient way about her that said she wanted to get things done. Maybe it was this fact that made me want to trust her.

I followed her into the night, a full moon lighting up the entire camp in the most beautiful way. Waves crashed nearby, and a cool breeze made the sea of tents thrum against their moorings.

I crept as quietly over the grass as I could, following the floating spectre as it wove through the tents towards the southern edge of the camp.

But then I paused. Because I was in front of a familiar soldier's tent, and right outside was a canvas-covered metal cage, its corner pulled up, so I could see the colourful lumzen kitten curled up in a corner, sleeping.

Arishnie, the spectre paused ahead of me, turning to see where I was.

I barely gave it a thought as I mentally unlatched the cage and slowly opened the door. I reached inside and curled my fingers around the creature's buttery soft warmth. It opened its rainbow-coloured eyes, staring at me with its mouth slightly agape. I wondered how intelligent it was because it was observing me in an unnerving way.

"Good idea," the spectre suddenly appeared by my side. "I have not seen a lumzen for some time. She will be useful. They are master illusion makers. Let's take her with us."

My sister was not an illusionist, but the creature's ability reminded me of her. I knew I was making the right choice in saving her. But how I would hide her the rest of our journey was beyond me. She was small enough to put in a pocket, though. I might be just able to get away with it.

"Stick by me, little one," I whispered. "And I'll look after you. I won't be selling you like those nasty fae."

To my surprise, the baby lumzen nodded slowly, and I grinned in surprise. "They are marsupials," said Arishnie, "their babies sleep in pouches."

I glanced at Arishnie. The fact that she was telling me about this creature made me trust her even more.

"You sleep in a pouch?" I asked the creature, "Here, sleep in my pocket. Its got extra padding."

I held her in front of my breast pocket, and she nuzzled my thumb before climbing in. Warmth spread through me, and suddenly I felt not so alone anymore.

Arishnie continued forward, and with less suspicion in my heart, I followed closely.

I knew there'd be at least two fae guards this side of the

camp. But I also knew they'd be lax because what possible human enemy would be stupid enough to creep up on a group of armoured fae? I saw the glint of metal in the distance, at the edge of the camp. I crept around the corner, peering out.

"Do not pause," the warrior whispered. "Keep behind me and do not stop." She proceeded right out in front of the guard, and I tiptoed after her, heart pounding, one hand cupping the baby lumzen from outside the pocket.

But whatever magic the spectre possessed, it worked, because neither fae guard noticed us pass. My brows raised in interest, I followed Arishnie into the forest at a brisk pace, almost tripping over a fallen branch in the process.

After minutes of me cursing and stumbling, there was somewhat of a path, crumbling and overgrown with leaf litter and vines. Ten minutes after that, I started to get a little nervous. I didn't know if I'd be able to find my way easily back to the camp at this point, even with the light of the full moon to guide me.

And then Arishnie spoke again, "We're here."

My head snapped up from where my eyes had been trained on the forest floor, and when I saw what we had come to, my breath caught in my throat.

The ancient temple had been huge in its prime. High domed roofs and tall stone walls now stood crumbling and half-collapsed.

And the travelling fae had woven closer to the shoreline than I had thought, such that I could see the ocean through the distant trees, the moon glinting on the water's surface like shards of diamonds. The overall effect was so ethereal. I honestly felt like we had walked into a different world. My feet felt light on the ground, the very air smooth against my skin.

The warrior-spectre proceeded straight into the magnificent shadowy maw that was the entrance of the temple. The lumzen rolled around in my pocket and crawled onto my shoulder, holding tight with tiny claws.

I stroked her head with a finger, and she made a soft purring noise. "Here we go, kitten." Steeling myself, I followed Arishnie into the darkness.

I flinched as fire lit itself in the sconce on the wall next to me, and I ended up gaping as, with a whoosh, flames sprung to life in sconces periodically set around the spherical hall. When I saw what was before me, I almost fell to my knees.

It was as Mother had described the temples in Ellythia. Seven goddesses carved out of marble stood in a circle, each incredibly different. From the shadows between them, another two armoured spectres floated towards me. One was reedy with a top knot, the other tall, with a mass of bulky muscle.

"Is this her?" asked the one with a top knot.

"I'm Princess Saraya," I said hesitantly, stepping forward. "Is someone going to tell me why I'm here?"

Top Knot looked me up and down. "I am Epelthi, and this is Silent Tara. Her tongue was cut before she died. We were senior members of the Order. The last to die."

Silent Tara opened her mouth, and indeed I saw the jagged severed stump of a tongue, looking as if it had been roughly hewn away. I suppressed a grimace.

"The Order of Temari has been activated," said Epelthi. "That's why you're here." I gave her a disbelieving look, but she continued. "Our order died out more than a hundred years ago. We were hunted and burned at the stake until there were none of us left. After that, there was no one to protect the humans from their magic being dissected at birth, and no magical adults were left to become members of the order. Until now. Until you had your nineteenth birthday two days ago."

I started, "What do you mean, 'magic being dissected at birth?'"

"No one has told you about this?" asked Arishnie.

I shook my head. "I don't know what you're talking about, sorry."

"I think you'd better sit down, Princess."

Vaguely concerned, I obeyed, sitting on the flat surface of a broken stone pillar.

"You know that at one time, all humans had magic?" Arishnie asked.

I nodded. "But that was in ancient times."

"We don't know when exactly it happened, but someone decided to start harvesting human magic. We think it was to stop us from getting too powerful. They quickly found that the only way to take someone's magic *completely* away forever was at birth before a baby had completely crossed over into the physical, human realm. Their demons would come from the astral realm, where no one could see them, and snip the magic right from their crown, their anterior fontanelle."

Shock coursed through me. The anterior fontanelle was a diamond-shaped gap in a newborn's head. They fused over time but allowed the bones of the baby's head to shift so it could pass through the pelvis more easily during birth. My own mother had told me to cover my crown when entering the temple of the mother. That was where our magic sat.

How was this possible? How did anyone not know this? Agatha, in her midwifery training, had taught me long ago not to accept the words of others as facts. I needed more information.

"What do you mean, the astral realm where no one could see them?"

"We have the physical realm, where you are now. And the astral realm exists as another layer on top. That is where we are, as spectres. Only you can see us since you turned of age. You'll be able to see the demons as well now."

A chill crept up my spine. "Do you mean to tell me that every birth I've attended, one of these demons has come in there without my knowing and taken the baby's power?

"They are drawn to birth as mosquitoes are to blood. They rarely miss one."

"Then how do *I* have magic?" I crossed my arms.

"Your mother killed every demon that came after you. The window is twenty-four hours. She could see them."

"That's mad."

"That's the truth," snapped Epelthi.

"Why didn't she tell me about it, then?"

"It's hard to believe something you can't see," said Arishnie gently. "She didn't want to frighten you from your training. I believe she was waiting until your nineteenth birthday."

I quietened. If everything they were saying was true, then it needed to be stopped. Why would these ancient warrior ghosts lie to me? What good would it do to lie to me under the eyes of the seven goddesses? I looked up at three ghosts, trying to make sense of this new information.

"So demons are coming from their subterranean realm to steal our magic..." I repeated slowly. "And they use it to make themselves powerful?"

The warrior-ghosts glanced at each other.

"We believe it's to make someone else more powerful," said Arishnie, "But that doesn't matter right now—"

"Wait a minute!" I jumped to my feet, bracing the baby lumzen with my hand where she still sat, wobbling on my shoulder. "You think they're giving the magic to someone else? The fae were looking for more power, weren't they? That's why they tried to take the quartz quarry! They've always wanted to be more powerful, especially the Dark Fae. *They're* sending the demons, aren't they?"

Epelthi sighed as if she hadn't wanted to tell me this part. "The Dark Fae Courts do have relationships with the demon clans. It's always been something we considered a possibility. It could very well be the fae doing it."

I seethed on the spot, clenching my fists. Those fae bastards from the Dark Court had the gall to come into the human realm, seek to marry me, all the while stealing the magic from our people? Perhaps it was to make us all weak so that they could swoop in and steal our land. If we humans all had magic, we could match them in battle. It was a brilliant plan, I had to admit. But it couldn't go on. I had to stop it.

I guess Arishnie wanted to distract me from my sudden outburst because she asked me softly. "Guess which one of the seven is the goddess of childbirth?"

Brightening, I strode up to the first statue to examine her exquisitely carved form. A cherub-faced girl shyly regarded me. In the stone inscribing her name under her was crumbled beyond reading.

"This is Cherimani, the sweet maiden." Arishnie went around the goddess and told me about each one.

"Lasanthi, wealth, the all mother. Luana, the seductress.

Agnolthi, the witch. Cholnayak, the widow. Xalya, the warrioress. And Umali, the dark goddess."

I stilled as I took in the final one. More fearsome than the armoured warrior goddess, Umali's depiction was ferocious. Her hair was flying around a face contorted with rage, a sword in one hand, the severed head of a demon in the other. She wore nothing except a garland of skulls. She was large breasted but also well-muscled. It was an imposing sight, but something in her drew me in. On my shoulder, the baby lumzen cooed in wonder. "It's her," I breathed. "She's the one."

Arishnie made a sound of agreement. "She is the force that creates the hurricane. She is the tempest, the tsunami. She is the darkness of the womb, the strength that brings forth a child. She is feminine rage made manifest."

Rage. That was something I knew.

"She is the patron of the Order of Temari. You knew it without being told. Do you need more convincing?"

I took a deep breath. I didn't. "If I leave the fae, it could very well cause a civil war. None of this—" I waved my hand to indicate the temple "—will matter then."

"I will construct a golem," said Epelthi. "It was a technique we used to fend off the demon hunters in our last days. It's an impersonation of you made out of the earth and a strand of your hair. If your lumzen helps me, it will be more convincing. By the time they figure it out, you'll be well and truly hidden."

The lumzen gave an affirmative squeak by my ear, and I knew then she'd understood the whole thing. What a wonder fae creatures were.

"So, what am I supposed to do now?"

"You're already a midwife, having studied under one for

several years," said Arishnie. " You need to master the warrior aspect. You are a good fighter, but these are no human adversaries. These are grown demon males and females."

I didn't like to admit that a nervous tingle had seeped into me. I was good with a sword, but I had never fought a demon.

"So you will need to learn from the best," Arishnie said carefully. "You'll train undercover at the fae Academy."

I raised my brows at that. "They train them to fight at the fae women's school?"

Silent Tara laughed, her shoulders shaking.

"No," said Arishnie. "You need to go to the male academy. To learn to fight supernatural males, you need to learn alongside them."

Every molecule in my body froze. "Is that…a good idea? I mean, you want me to fight and train with *fae male warriors?*"

"Yes. You can change your appearance?"

I could make it so I looked like a man, I supposed. But…I glanced at my baby lumzen.

"You cannot use the lumzen for a major illusion," said Epelthi. "The fae warriors will figure it out within days. It must be your own magic. Only that will be undetectable."

It was something that I'd never done before. But I would do what needed to be done to defeat this enemy. If it was the fae stealing from our newborns, I would learn what I needed to do the job.

"This is how we trained in days of old, Saraya," said Arishnie. "With men."

The image of King Wyxian and his family being welcomed into our palace swam in my mind. The fae of the Black Court were scheming behind our backs. They were the enemy. They had *always* been the enemy. They had tricked us. A bubbling anger tore through me, followed by sheer determination.

Well, I knew their dark secret now. I nodded at the three dead warrior midwives before me. "Tell me what has to be done."

14

SARAYA

Epelthi had me collect mud from where the sea flowed into the little channel on the temple grounds. I dumped a heap of it in front of her, and she was able to morph it into my height and shape. After a moment of the ghosts' concentration, I was surprised to see that between one blink and the next, it had taken the shape of a walking, breathing version of me. Epelthi spoke quietly to my baby lumzen, and under the ghost's direction, she cast her magic and produced a shimmer of colour over the golem, and suddenly the golem looked so real I had to turn my back on the thing before it got too weird. Arishnie led the creature that looked exactly like me, by her hand, walking back into the forest, where she was to deposit her back into my tent.

"They'll just think you're a little grumpy and giving them the silent treatment," said Epelthi, sitting down on a fallen part of the temple wall. "The fae don't know much about humans, really. They'll think it's normal."

Arishnie returned half an hour later, followed by an

obedient chestnut mare, saddled and bridled, carrying bulging saddlebags. She also had a map.

"I've put all your important possessions into these bags," said Arishnie. "Including the Ellythian wedding silks I found. They were your mother's, I'm guessing?"

I hurried to the bags, immediately checking their contents. "Yes," I said, relieved. "They're of no use to me for a wedding now, but at least I have them with me."

The ghosts nodded. And I suddenly realised that I was taking Tembry's advice back from the start. She was the one who told me to run away. And now, that's exactly what I was doing. I hoped the golem would buy me some time because I really couldn't stomach a war on my hands.

Arishnie cast a wary eye up to the sky.

"How can you touch everything if you're a ghost?" I asked, following her line of vision and looking at the moon.

"Only on the full moon to assist you," she replied. "In between, we go back to the ether." After a moment, she indicated that I look at the map she'd obviously stolen from the fae camp. "We are not far from the mountain pass. If you follow this map through the forest, you'll reach there a day ahead of the fae convoy because they have to take the longer route on the roads for the carriages."

I nodded nervously, studying the map. It was a direct track south, and the mountains would be impossible to miss.

"One last thing," Arishnie said. "On the night of a full moon, every month, I will come to you and will educate you on the ways of the Order. There is much you need to know."

Relief flooded through me. I wouldn't be alone in this. "Got it."

"It will be dawn in a few hours. You had better go."

I swung up on the chestnut mare as Arishnie gave me my final instructions, and it wasn't until then that the whole thing suddenly got real. I was heading into the Temari forest on my own, making a beeline straight for the fae warrior Academy. If this wasn't completely insane, I didn't know what was. Anxiety pulsed through me, sharp and acidic. "You can't… come with me?"

I hated how small my voice sounded, but all this was too new, too strange.

"I'm afraid not."

I had never been this far from home, let alone by myself. Something wet touched my cheek, and I turned to see the baby lumzen with her tongue sticking out. I let out a tiny chuckle and scratched her head. Not completely alone then. And with a useful friend. I took a deep breath and looked back at the three ghosts. "Alright then, I'll see you at the next full moon?"

Arishnie nodded. "I'll be there."

I nodded back, checked the baby lumzen was settled back in my pocket before I swung the mare around and headed into the forest.

My heart hammered in my chest. I was running away, sneaking out of the fae camp and leaving them in my wake. I wondered how long it would take Sage to figure out that I was a golem and how the fae king and queen would react. Would they be angry? Or had they expected something of the sort from me? They'd never taken great pains to guard me, but I did get the feeling they thought humans were rather simple. Perhaps they just didn't expect that I'd be smart enough to successfully run off under their noses.

In the absence of the three ghosts, the forest became eerie, and the irony of that was not lost on me. It was also lucky this mare was sure-footed because I sure as hell couldn't see through the dark. If any beast or creature came at me, I wouldn't know until the last minute. I kept us at a trot through the dark until the baby lumzen sighed in her sleep and I had a thought.

"Hey, little one?" I whispered to it. She popped her head out of my pocket and rubbed her eyes with a paw. "Do you think you could put an illusion around us to stop anyone from seeing us pass through the forest?"

Anyone or *anything*, but I didn't want to scare her. I also needed to give her name. She and the mare both.

She yawned and nodded, sliding back down into my pocket. A heartbeat later, a shimmering opal light encased the horse in an opalescent orb. I grinned up at it in wonder and decided on her name right away.

"Opal," I whispered to her. "I'm going to call you Opal. Is that okay?"

She crooned sleepily from her pocket.

I suddenly thought of Altara and Geravie, hopefully by now safely docked in Ellythia and heading towards the jungle school. I suppressed a mad laugh as I thought of her reaction to me telling her that I'd run away. There had to be some way I could get a letter to her, but if I was undercover at the fae academy, I doubted I could risk it.

The thought of this 'school' sent me into a buzz of nerves. My place was with women because that's what midwifery was. That's where I spent most of my time, my speciality. And now I was going to spend all my time with fae warriors? I took a deep breath and a long exhale to try and calm myself. I'd have to make sure my disguise was top-notch.

How would I look as a male? If I kept my hair long, I could probably hide my ears. But a moustache would be necessary, I think. A beard might even be better. But what about my breasts? I panicked a little. They were a decent size. I couldn't shrink those! But I looked at the shimmering illusory magic around me. Perhaps Opal could help with that part. I'd have to keep her hidden on me at all times. It was lucky she was so small.

Cloaked in the illusion, I felt safe as the blue light of predawn swept across the spiky branches of the Stickly trees that made this part of the forest. Thankfully, we hadn't come across anything yet, but that could change as morning came around. This close to the mountains, there wouldn't be much traffic, but you never knew.

But the three of us, mare, girl, and lumzen, travelled during the day without incident, even when I made sure I rested and watered the horse. I decided to call the chestnut steed Silentfoot because her tread was so sure, so silent despite the leaf litter and debris that she deserved the name.

As night fell, I scouted a potential spot behind a series of large bushes where a brook bubbled nearby. I didn't quite like the idea of sleeping so out in the open and so close to the road, and I had no idea how to make a fire, but I didn't have a choice. So I brushed down Silentfoot, gave her some oats I found in one of the saddlebags, refilled my canteen in the brook, and settled down against a tree.

Opal and I had a dinner of hard bread and cheese that Arishnie, in her great wisdom, had put in my bags. But it still took a considerable amount of water to get down. And even with Opal's protection around our little camp, I didn't feel safe at all. Crickets sounded, leaves rustled, small animals darted in the distance. This close to the fae-human border, the forests were untamed, wild, and unkempt, and I was just waiting for the moment some strange fae creature thundered out of the bushes and came at us. But that night, none did.

The stars were beautiful in the inky black sky, and I couldn't help it when the tears fell. I missed Altara and Geravie. I even missed Jerali Jones. While I'd travelled to other kingdoms with my parents as a child, I had never slept on the ground before, and the prickly blanket I had felt awful against my exposed skin. I only slept when sheer exhaustion took me.

At dawn the next day, we took off again, and by midday, the trees grew sparse, and the land started to make an incline. I knew then we would be approaching the mountain pass.

I consulted my map multiple times, and luckily, the old track, perhaps by some magic, was obvious to me, and before I knew it, I was out of the cover of the forest and into a rocky landscape littered with saffron-coloured boulders.

I was quite worried that since this was the way to a fae Academy, we might meet some fae within the mountains, but as I travelled eastwards, following the map into a path between boulders, we didn't come across anyone. It was late afternoon by the time I consulted the map again and saw that I was supposed to be close.

Arishnie said the entrance was hidden, and I'd have to use my magic to find where to go. So I pulled Silentfoot into a corner and closed my eyes, searching through the rock in segments. I had never actually cast my mind out further than just in front of me before—I'd never really had to—but I found it was easy. I swept down the mountain path, looking side to side, and suddenly came across a long cavern passage leading into the mountain itself. I blew out air. That had to be something. I kicked Silentfoot into a trot and headed right for it.

Hidden behind a boulder was a huge gaping tunnel, completely black. I closed my eyes again and mentally went through it, looking for any bears or fae cave monsters who might be sitting waiting for prey. But in that hollow darkness, there was no beating heart, only cold rock. About two hundred metres in, however, my mind hit on steel, and I recognised the shape of a gate. I'd found it.

I pushed the Silentfoot inside the tunnel. When we emerged back into the sunlight, we stopped dead. In front of me was a sprawling complex of huge stone buildings behind a tall wall.

Opal let out a faint "oooh."

My heart leapt into my mouth. We had reached the Mountain Academy.

I pulled Silentfoot back into the darkness of the cave, panic bubbling through me. I had to focus on my physical appearance. Otherwise, I'd be caught out immediately. *A man, a man, what would I look like if I were a man?*

I decided a beard would be best. I had fine peach fuzz on my face already, so encouraging them to grow thicker and longer seemed natural. I was sweating within minutes of the effort, but when I reached up to feel my face, I burst out laughing. A prickly, full thick, black beard now surrounded my upper lip and all around my mouth and cheeks, my face now warm. I touched my eyebrows and focused on growing those a little thicker too. I needed to be completely disguised in case I came across Daxian at some stage.

"How do I look?" I asked Opal.

She looked up at me, and a wide smile spread across her silver lips, and she nodded eagerly. I laughed. "I hope I can revert it all back afterwards. Imagine if I was stuck like this forever!"

I got off Silentfoot and rummaged through the saddlebags and found a bandage meant for wounds. I took off my shirt and bound my breasts down. It hurt a little, and I still couldn't make my chest completely flat.

"Do you think you can hide my chest a bit more?" I asked Opal. "I can add things, but taking these both away might be a big job. I'd have to destroy all the cells and grow them back later. And make my eyes brown, the green is too obvious."

Opal nodded and squinted at my breasts. Sure enough, when I looked down, it looked like I had nothing there at all. It was completely flat. I reached up to touch my chest and found my breasts still there. As long as no one went touching my chest too much, I should be okay.

"Phew. Okay, what else?" I quickly changed my clothes, I was already wearing pants, but the riding dress would have to come off. I put on a plain cotton shirt instead. "I'm going to have to change the way I walk a bit." For some reason, my mind went straight to the swaggering walk of the fae commander Drakus Silverhand when he had entered the palace on the day of my engagement. It was the type of walk that spoke volumes, and if I could emulate it just a bit, that'd be enough.

I felt around my face and decided that I had better make my ears pointed just in case. It took me a good minute to encourage the cells on the tips of my ears to grow. It turned out a little wonky, but I was sure no one would look at me too closely. Then I made my nose a little bigger for good measure. I got back onto Silentfoot, adrenaline coursing through me.

"Here we go, Opal, into enemy territory. We'll learn their tricks and use them against them, hey?"

Opal crooned in reply.

"Alright, you can take off the hiding illusion now."

The shimmering magic dissolved around me, and I urged Silentfoot back into the light and through the curling metal gates of the Mountain Academy.

I scanned the warrior academy, and my eyes found a barn-like building that could only be the stables. I headed towards it. It was the largest stables I'd ever seen, rivalling ours back at the palace. I supposed it had to house all the horses the fae rode to get here.

When I reached it, I made sure Opal was hidden in my pocket and swung off Silentfoot. An ostler came out leading a beastly stallion. He was a deeply tanned, gangly fae with long red hair tied back, speaking softly to the horse.

"Oh, you're a sourbottom today, aren't you, Willow?"

Then he saw me.

"Good afternoon," I said, trying to hide the nerves that was like a knife twisting in my gut.

He beckoned to another ostler and expertly reached for my reins, the stallion eyeing Silentfoot appraisingly. "Afternoon, I can take her, but you're a bit late?"

Oh no. "I...had far to travel."

"What's your name?"

"Sa—" I swore under my breath. I needed a male name. "Sam."

Awkwardly, I unhitched my saddlebags, all too aware of the ostler staring at me. Would I pass for a fae male? I wasn't entirely sure about how successful my morph was. I didn't have a mirror to check myself out after all. I'd just have to hope they bought it.

I cleared my throat. "Where do I…enrol?"

He looked me up and down and frowned. "The parchment pushers sit in there," he pointed to a double-storey building.

"Thanks," I said, awkwardly hoisting my saddlebags onto my shoulders.

He led my horse away, glancing back at me once. I sighed. I'd have to get better at pretending to be fae. The ostler had taken one look at me and known something wasn't right. I strode across the grass to the building the ostler had pointed to, practicing my man-walk.

I entered the building, clumsily banging my saddlebags against the glass doors as I went. Inside, there was a long desk, behind which three old fae men sat, dressed in flowing long white robes. I walked up to the one in the middle and set my bags down.

"Hello."

The fae clerk looked up at me in surprise, and I suddenly realised how high-pitched my voice had gone, especially tight with my nerves. Hastily, I gave a small cough, simultaneously elongating my vocal cords. When I spoke next, I sounded like a croaky teenage boy whose voice was still in the process of breaking. Cringing inwardly, I said, "I'm here for the Academy."

"Are you?" he said slowly, brown eyes taking me in. "Is this…your first time at the Warrior Academy?"

I knew right away this was going to be difficult. But I tried to keep my spine straight as I said, "It is."

He frowned bushy grey brows at me. "How old are you? Why have you not presented yourself before this late age?"

I blurted out the first thing that came to my mind. "I'm nineteen. I…I was unwell."

His brows shot up. "Where are you from?"

I quickly made up a fae-sounding name. "T-Talathia, a small village really far south. Very rural. Small population."

He sighed and brought out a sheet of parchment and began writing on it with a quill. "Name?"

"Sam."

"Surname?"

I blurted the first thing that came to mind. "Sourbottom." Oh shit. Why was that the first name I thought of? Damn that ostler.

But the clerk said nothing as he wrote it all down in fae script. Anxiety bubbled up in me again. My mother had made sure we learned both human and rudimentary fae runes. It was something all royal children had to do. But it had been a while since I'd read it because we didn't have many fae books in the palace library. I'd have to brush up on it.

"Well, in your age group, we only have one dormitory left this late. I'm afraid we're going to have to put you in there." And then he began muttering to himself. "Nothing can be done about it. If he ends up dead, it's not our fault. I'll have to write a letter apologising to the prince."

My heart leapt into my mouth. Who on earth were my roommates going to be? *In my age group,* he'd said. That meant

I'd be with fae male adults. Why had I assumed I'd be in a room alone? *Because,* said a nasty voice in my ear that sounded awfully like my stepmother's, *your royal backside never had to share a room before.* But I wasn't going to be a royal here. I was going to be treated as a commoner. I had better get used to that.

The old fae held up a key on a cord. "Don't lose your room key."

"Got it." I placed it around my neck and felt Opal rolling in her pocket. She wanted to get out and look, but I couldn't risk it. I patted her from the outside of the pocket while the fae clerk was looking down.

"Map." He handed me a piece of paper with an illustration of the complex. "The noble's adult dormitory is the building left of here. You are on the seventh floor, room seven oh one. That second slip is a note for your...roommates. You are common, know your place, and do not speak unless spoken to by a prince. Let them skip any line. Always give them way. Understood?"

They'd put me in the noble's dormitory? I resisted the urge to gape at him and nodded stiffly. "Understood."

"See these mountain forests on either side of the Academy?" The clerk pointed out areas on the map marked with black skulls. "Under no circumstances do you wander in these areas without an escort. Understand?"

"Yes, sir."

"Good luck, Sam. You'll need it."

I pursed my lips and nodded, my heart sinking. How hard was this going to be exactly? I walked out, but not before catching the old fae talking about me with the clerk next to him.

"He's an odd-looking fellow, isn't he?"

"Hm, inbred perhaps, you know how those back-water fae can be."

I swallowed my laugh. So I hadn't done that great of a job with my physical changes. But as long as they weren't suspicious of me, I could work with that backstory.

I lugged my saddlebags into the building on the left. A huge, seven-storey red brick structure that was supposed to house the older students.

The moment I entered, the ruckus of fae teenagers assaulted me from the floors above. Nervously, I walked up the steps and suddenly realised I'd have to walk seven flights of stairs. Sighing, I did so, Opal rolling and fidgeting in her pocket. Adult fae students—noble students—loitered about their corridors as I passed their floors, shouting, throwing things at each other, laughing in many cases. My nerves doubled. I'd have to emulate their behaviour to be accepted here. I mentally took note. I'd have to practise laughing like a man. Giggling wouldn't do at all.

When I got to the topmost floor, huffing and puffing, something small and red came hurtling towards me. I ducked just in time, collapsing into the wall in front of me.

"Sorry!" came a call. A spiky black ball bounced down the stairs.

I straightened and looked up at my attacker. He was a tall fae, skinny as a stick with a mop of blond hair. "Are you new?" he asked, looking me up and down. Sizing me up, I noticed fae males seemed to do that a lot.

I nodded as another noble came to flank him.

"Look, it's a new one," he said to the other—a wide-set young man with a moustache and long black hair tied in a bun at his crown.

"I'm Sam," I said, hoisting myself up the final step.

The ball owner stuck his hand out. "Emery, my father is Duke Nightsong of Black Court."

I shook his offered hand. "Nice to meet you."

"This is Briar," he indicated the one with the bun. "His father is King Wyxian's advisor, the Viscount Nightclaw."

As I shook Briar's hand, I mentally noted all the names to look up later.

"Where are you staying?" asked Emery.

"Uh, seven o' one."

"Thought so," he replied darkly, looking me up and down again. "We're the only ones with the spare bed. Come on through then."

I followed the two fae into the first room off the corridor. It was wide and spacious, the beds surprisingly luxurious, fluffy with wide mattresses. And lounging on one of them with a naked sword in his hand was a tall, muscular fae male with a healthy amount of onyx hair. My fiancé, Daxian, himself.

I dropped my bags in shock. Daxian looked up from the sword he was polishing, frowning.

"Sam's our new roommate," Briar said cautiously, eyes darting between the prince and me.

I hastily bent down to pick my saddlebags back up, taking a beat to recover. *I was going to be sharing a room with Daxian.* I couldn't have thought of a worse room assignment. No wonder that clerk had been worked up about it. Daxian slid off his bed with a menacing grace only a fae prince could muster. He stalked up to me like a tiger pursuing its prey, and I gulped, fumbling with the papers in my hand, doing every-thing I could to avoid eye contact. Would he recognise me under the beard?

"Uh, the clerk gave me a letter for you, Your Highness."

Daxian all but snatched the note out of my hand, and I looked up at him, towering above me, as his blue eyes scanned the script.

He took a deep breath through his nose and dragged his eyes down my frame. "Sourbottom, is it?" his voice was already thoroughly unimpressed with me. I almost sagged in relief. I'd fooled him then.

"Yes, Your Highness." My voice cracked like a thirteen-year-old, and I blinked rapidly at the floor.

"You are aware this is a dormitory for nobility?"

I nodded, opting to stare at his tanned, muscular chest.

But Daxian was a relentless prick because he said in a low voice, "And you are aware that you are *common*?"

I blanched, but surprisingly, I did not feel fear but anger. How could he treat people like that? I clenched my saddle-bags and nodded stiffly. Briar and Emery shifted in the corner.

Daxian crossed his arms over an expansive chest. "How is it that you've avoided service until this age?"

"I was unwell, Your Highness. I couldn't come. I live in the country." It was the only storyline that seemed the most likely, the least suspicious.

Daxian made a disbelieving sound at the back of his throat and stepped threateningly towards me. "Do not lie to me, *Sourbottom*. You can be sure I will have my officers *check in* with your family when I return to Black Court."

I clenched my bags tighter, fearing for my imaginary family, my knuckles going white. I couldn't believe he could be so cruel. But then he abruptly stepped backwards, and the air between us became light. I felt as if something heavy had been lifted off me. I glowered at the floor.

"So," he said lightly. "Keep out of my way, and we will

be fine. Listen to Briar. He's the clever one around here." Daxian stalked back to his bed and sat back down on his mattress.

I glanced at the others who were finding their books very interesting at that moment. Then Briar saw that Daxian had finished with me and hurried to my side. "Bathrooms are on the first level." He said, smiling at me earnestly. "Our time slot is five a.m. Room checks are done at seven p.m. and seven a.m. by an angry bastard from Obsidian Court called Seargent Sharpfang. He's our housemaster. Don't give him any lip, or he'll split your face in half. Half the time, he doesn't show up for checks, but we always have to be ready in case he does."

I nodded. "Understood."

"That's your bed." He pointed to the empty one by the door.

It looked comfortable enough, with a single pillow, crisp white sheets, and a blue coverlet. "Make sure it's pristine at seven and seven," said Emery. "Otherwise, we'll all be put on bathroom cleaning duty. They turn the magic off and make us do it instead."

"*If*—" came Daxian's nasty growl. We all turned to look at him, but he only had eyes for his weapon, "—you land us on bathroom duty. I'll shove you down a toilet myself."

Briar laughed awkwardly, pulling my attention back to him. "You missed the first three days," he said hastily, "but you should be able to catch up." He lugged some books over to me. "You can look at my notes if you like."

"Thank you," I cringed at the stack of books the large fae was setting on my bedside table. No doubt all of it was in the fae language. I'd have to catch up on fae quickly. Otherwise, I'd be super suspicious.

"We should head to dinner, though," Briar said upon straightening.

"Urgh, agreed!" Emery bounded to the door but didn't head out, only hovered beside the door. "I hope it's not rabbit again. There's only so much rabbit I can eat."

I *was* hungry. I'd eaten only crusts and hard cheese for two days. So I dumped my saddlebags next to my bed and made to head out the door, but Briar held me back with an arm, narrowly missing my breasts. I jerked backwards and stared at him, his pointed ears twitching. I arched my eyebrows but shook his head slightly. I looked at Emery, who was staring at the ceiling. It was then that I realised who we were waiting for.

Daxian dragged himself back off his bed and casually sauntered out the door. Only then did Briar let me go, and we followed Emery and the prince to the stairs. *Royal prick!* I thought savagely. He was the type of man Agatha would say was 'in need of a good thrashing.' And to think I was engaged to him. I scowled at his back all the way down the stairs.

Other fae nobles began joining us, heading down the stairs, the scent of men's cologne enveloping me, making me dizzy. They cast me curious and, in some cases, hostile looks. Having never been on the receiving end of hostile looks from any sort of male my own age and older, it had me flushing at the attention.

What if I got into a fight? Young human men did that, so the fae would be the same. Would I be able to handle myself? I didn't know for sure because although I could change a lot about my physical appearance, I hadn't been able to change my height. I was a good 5'7", but a majority of these fae warrior nobility were over six feet tall.

I trailed along to the dining hall, a building west of ours. From the map I'd seen, the school was split in half. The under eighteens had their own section on the eastern side of the school, including their own dining hall, while the adult fae were on this western side altogether. That meant every fae male here was older, taller, and stronger than me, and it really hadn't hit me until I experienced them all—athletic male bodies walking around me, towering and glowering, joking and laughing in deep voices. They were also a little rough, jostling each other until we all funnelled into the hall, that is.

Then, the students began talking in hushed voices as if something serious was happening. Lines of long tables waited empty as we filed in. And sticking close to Briar, the most welcoming of my roommates, I saw a line of five tall fae warriors at the front of the hall, standing with their hands behind their backs. They were observing the students with the eye of teachers, ready to punish for any wrongdoing. I'd known tutors like that in my time, but none of them had the hardened look that these fae did. They wore leather and cotton over tanned, well-muscled bodies. I avoided eye contact at all costs. My disguise had fooled Daxian, but I didn't want to draw unnecessary attention to myself. I didn't know how well my new face would hold up under close scrutiny.

The line shuffled on at a steady pace, and when we got to the food, my stomach grumbled loudly. I glanced at the fae behind me, a tall, black-eyed handsome one, and he gave me an unimpressed look. I quickly hurried after Briar. We each took ceramic plates and quietly loaded them up with bread, three different types of meat, seven different types of vegetables—fae types I didn't recognise—colourful fruits, and a tankard of watered wine. Most of the students filled their plates to bursting, and I tried to copy the foods Briar put in his plate.

A single long table had been set against the wall, facing the other tables. A line of fae students was sitting there already, and I saw Daxian head over to them.

Briar caught me looking as we went past to another table, just adjacent to the prince's. "The five princes all have their own dormitory floor with fae from their own court. It's to avoid any fights. But they're still princes, so they dine together up there. We dine with the other nobles. And then the lower born take the tables furthest away."

As I sat at the table and the fae young males began systematically shovelling food into their mouths, I was suddenly reminded of the golem that was travelling with King Wyxian in my place. I wondered how long it would take for them to notice and what the consequences of that would be. Would they start hunting for me? Would they write to my parents or send soldiers to the castle?

I almost dropped my plate as we sat down at a table, suddenly feeling too nauseous to eat. Sitting here in the dining hall with all the fae, I had the sudden and intense feeling that I did not belong. I was a female human imposter, and if I was discovered under the ever-watchful eye of these teachers, the punishment could very well be severe. I started to wonder if I should leave and head back to safety.

Back to where I belonged.

Opal rolled around in my pants pocket, and I discreetly slipped a piece of meat to her, glancing up at the others. But they were too focused on their food to notice me. I almost snorted. Fae males were the same as human males then.

Arishnie would be here the next full moon. I had promised to be here to meet her. I had to remember that these fae I was sitting with were the enemy, and I needed to learn their secrets and their fighting techniques. It was the only way I could stop them from stealing human magic. I had to remember them for the monsters they were. I was here to learn, to beat them at their treachery. And over in Ellythia, Altara was possibly doing the same by now, a stranger in a new school of her own.

I began eating.

Next to me, Emery glanced over his shoulder and swore under his breath.

"What is it?" I asked.

"The psychopaths are here."

I swung my head around, almost cracking my neck. But any pain I had was long forgotten because swaggering in was a form and face I wouldn't ever forget.

Hazel eyes, a lethal stride and silver tipped fingers. It was Drakus Silverhand, the commander of the elite forces of the Black Court, followed by his two warrior companions. The hulking mass of muscle and the slender, dancer-like one. I wondered how old they were and decided they couldn't be much older than Daxian—early twenties at the latest. They were the last to get their plates. I turned back around, my heart pounding, glancing at Daxian at the high table, but he was concentrating on his plate. I couldn't believe we were all going to the same academy.

"Why are they psychopaths?" I asked Emery.

"You've never heard of the Black Drakus Bastards?" Emery asked. "You must really come from far away."

I gave a one-shoulder shrug I'd seen Charlie do a few times. "Why is everyone scared of them?"

"Drake might be the commander of the elite forces," murmured Emery. "But before that, the three of them were cutthroats, hired to kill. Monsters, fae, or anything. Wyxian saw what they were capable of and offered them a job with pay and incentives they couldn't refuse."

"We've grown up watching them," said Briar. "All three refused to come to the academy, but Wyxian gave them some sort of threat. Their first year here was when they were sixteen. They brought them in a locked cart with ten armoured guards! I saw the whole thing."

"I heard he had to have a knife to the throat the entire trip. Otherwise, they were never able to get him here," said Emery. "But when he came to classes, he thrashed everyone."

"Well, Wyxian's word would've carried some weight," said Briar reasonably.

"So he comes voluntarily now?" I asked.

"The *only* reason they come," said Emery, stabbing his chicken. "Is to beat the shit out of the seniors in fighting class. The Dean hires them to fight the seniors. They're the final exam."

Briar snorted. "And yet no one can beat any of them. You pass if you survive getting beaten up."

"No one's bested him?" I asked, Jerali Jones coming to mind.

"Nope."

"I heard Sharpfang say," said Briar, "he comes here for fun and the free food."

"Of course Sharpfang loves him," muttered Emery. "Just stay away from him, Sam. At all costs. Those guys live for a kill."

16

SARAYA

We returned to our dormitory after dark, where Emery and Briar started on some homework. Daxian left, and I spent the next few hours pouring over Briar's textbooks by the light of a quartzlamp Briar lent me, trying to remember how to read the fae language. It came back to me quickly enough that I felt satisfied I'd be okay in the theory part of the schooling.

Just before lights out, Daxian returned and promptly began taking his clothes off. Heat spread through me as Briar and Emery continued their conversation about spear types. I didn't know where to look because wherever I did look, I could still see Daxian's naked back from the side of my eye. He was built with muscle, and it wasn't until he bent down to take his pants off that I turned around completely, fussing with my own bed.

"Never seen a naked male before, Sam?" joked Emery.

I swore inwardly, realising my discomfort was obvious. At the sound of Daxian throwing himself into bed, I turned around, thankful my beard was hiding most of my surely red face. Daxian glowered at me before turning and shuttering the quartzlamp on his bedside table. So he liked to sleep naked. I guessed that was something males did commonly, then.

"I, uh, only have sisters," I muttered as Emery took his own shirt off and climbed into his bed. Meanwhile, Briar bundled himself up inside another jumper, and Emery threw a sock at him.

"What?" Briar said, affronted. "I always get cold at night, you know that."

"It's to hide the tattoo on his chest," said Emery, turning on his side to look at me. "Of his long-lost love, Seraline, the blonde from Twilight Court."

"It is *not!*" cried Briar, throwing the sock back at Emery and missing by a mile. "I get cold, Sam, that's all."

I smiled at Briar, climbing into my own bed, careful not to squash Opal in the process. We all shuttered our quartzlamps and very happy I got to sleep in an actual bed tonight, I fell asleep quickly.

THE NEXT MORNING, EMERY WOKE US ALL UP WITH A LOUD, prolonged yawn. So much for having the manners of a Duke's son. I couldn't really speak, though. Half the time, I had the verbiage of the commoners I spent so much time with.

"It's five a.m., Sam," whispered Briar, stumbling out of his bed. "Hurry, or we'll miss our bathroom slot."

I suppressed a groan as I got up and rolled, almost squashing Opal, who'd curled up under my neck. I quickly scooped her up and pulled on some pants under my night-shirt, putting her into my pocket. Following the boys out of the room, a shirtless Daxian naturally in the lead, a cold sweat suddenly swept over me. I realised they meant to shower or bathe or do whatever males did in the bathroom. I hesitated at the top of the stairs before hurrying after Briar. I might as well see what I was up against.

When we got to the first-floor bathroom, summer dawn light making an appearance through the windows, I entered a vast white-tiled room. In front of me was a series of five sinks, and on either side of them were dividing walls in which shower heads were positioned. With relief, I noted that each shower had its own stall, but on the downside, there were no doors on the stall. They were open. Beyond the showers were latrines, to which the boys immediately fled—except Daxian, who lazily sauntered after them, flexing his shirtless muscles in the mirror as he went.

"What do I do?" I whispered to Opal, letting her stick her head out to see the bathroom.

I couldn't risk having a shower. Not with the boys, the prince, right next to me, and anyone able to look into my stall. My heart hammered against my chest like a war drum. I went to a sink and hastily washed my face and underarms with a cake of soap sitting on a stack by the wall. I'd come back tonight, I decided, after everyone was asleep. I wet my hair so that when Briar came out from the latrines and washed his hands, I told him I was done and hurried towards the latrine to avoid further questions.

"Hold on, Sam," Briar said, a strange note in his voice.

I froze and turned around. "Yes?"

"These," he said, walking slowly forward and pointing to a shower stall. "Are called *showers*." He paused and spoke with exaggerated slowness as if explaining something to a child. "You turn on the tap, water comes out, and you wash yourself." He mimed washing his body. "Using this soap." He picked up a cake and mimed again.

"Right," I said, nodding as if I'd learned something new.

"It's alright," Briar said gently as Daxian and Emery came out to wash their hands. "We don't judge here. I'm pretty sure back home Emery had a special friend he saw every night whose name was 'pig.'"

"Hey!" Emery cried, affronted.

"*And,*" continued Briar, smirking. "I know for a fact that when Emery first came here, he thought the soap was for eating."

"I did not!" choked the lanky fae.

"Then explain why you smelled so bad all the time in the first year?"

Emery chucked a soap at Briar, and it caught him right on the forehead before falling to the floor. Briar bent down to pick it up, but it slipped out of his fingers.

Emery guffawed as Briar chased the soap around the bathroom. When he finally got a hold of it, he flung it at Emery and missed completely. Daxian caught the soap before it fell and gave Briar an unimpressed look. He took the soap, and stalked into a shower cubicle, immediately stripping down. A tanned backside came into view, and I immediately turned on my heel and hurried to the latrines, which were, thankfully, closed in their own stalls. I had never seen or imagined a setup like this. I supposed, in theory, it was meant to humble the princes and noble-born sons. But it didn't look like it had worked on Daxian.

When we finished in the bathroom, we casually went back to our dormitory and cleaned up the room before inspection by the House Master, Sharpfang. Briar and Emery corrected my bed after I made it, tucking in folds here and there so tightly that by the end, you could bounce a coin off the spread. We opened our dorm door and stood at the feet of our beds with our hands behind our backs. I made sure Opal was tucked, unseen in my pants pocket, where her magic sparkled outwards to hide the ridge of my bandaged breasts and the colour of my eyes.

Sharpfang arrived at exactly seven a.m., and we knew it by the thumping of heavy boots up the stairs. Daxian's posture was straight, but he looked bored while Briar and Emery stiffened, thrusting their chests out. I emulated them. This would be my first real test with one of the frightening warrior fae.

He appeared at the door, standing as if ready to reprimand. I took one glance at him and immediately turned my gaze back in front of me towards Briar, whose eyes were tight with nervousness. Sharpfang's significant height was not the only thing that made him intimidating. He was in his fifties, I guessed, muscular under his fighting leathers with short, greying hair. But it was his lined face that terrified me. There was a keen intelligence there, as well as a sense that he could give a thrashing without warning or reason. I was familiar with all the various commanders and generals of my father's army, but they all paled in comparison to this Seargent Sharpfang.

"Good morning, Seargent!" shouted my roommates.

I caught on a little too late and finished a beat after them. Sharpfang took the opportunity to step menacingly into the room, and from my periphery, I could feel him assessing me. He came to stand in front of me, and I ended up simply staring at his chest. Opal trembled in my pants pocket.

"Name yourself, student," he commanded.

"Sam Sourbottom, Sergeant sir." I had been around the

palace guard enough to know roughly how they spoke to one another.

Silence. I looked up, craning my neck to look into his stone-grey eyes, and then quietly, "Explain to me why I've never seen you before."

I broke eye contact and swallowed the sudden lump in my throat. "I have been unwell, Sergeant. I live in the rural village of Talathia. I only…heard about this place recently." That part wasn't a lie, at least. But I don't think Sharpfang took kindly to any of it because he stepped closer to me.

"That's not in Black Court," he said sharply.

"No, sir," I shook my head, my mind racing, trying to remember the names of the courts in the Dark Fae Realm. "Um…er…it's in Twilight Court." Altara had said that court was closest to the Solar border, meaning furthest from here, which I hoped meant these fae would know the least about it.

"Hmm," Sharpfang said slowly. "If you are hiding something, Sourbottom, I will find out."

I looked up into his face with alarm. "I'm not, sir! I'm just here to do my duty." And it was the truth, just not in the way they thought of it.

Sharpfang's nostrils flared and made a sound at the back of his throat. "I actually might just believe you."

I could have collapsed with relief, but I maintained my posture. "Thank you, Sergeant."

He stepped away from me and spoke in a booming voice better suited to a training field, "I'm sure your roommates have told you the rules. Head down to the field."

He stood aside, and one by one, we all filed out after Daxian, Emery casting me a placating look. So I'd survived the House Master, but that was surely going to be the easiest part of the day.

"We start each day with physical training," said Briar. "They make us exercise, then we do fighting training. First is hand-to-hand combat and then weapons. Then we have breakfast and go to our written classes."

"We don't get to eat first?" My stomach and no doubt Opal's would be growling soon.

Briar shook his head sadly. "These monsters like to train us fasted. Apparently, it prepares us for adult difficulties and discipline or some shit like that."

We joined the stream of other students heading down the stairs as we made our way to the field behind the Academy. It was set to be a bright day, and even being this far south, I could feel a warm summer breeze on my face. Looking around at the strapping fae around me, it looked like all the adult fae males, from eighteen to twenty-five, trained together, and I wondered how on earth I was going to keep up. There were about a hundred of us total, and many were already jogging around the grassy oval when we got there, so my roommates and I simply joined in the procession. With a pang, I noted Daxian joining some other princes ahead of us, sprinting confidently at the head of the group.

After two laps, we were all huffing and sweating, but I had managed to keep up with the centre of the group, thanking my lucky stars that Jerali Jones' made us do the same thing every time we trained. We came to stand in a big group in front of the five scary warriors from last night. The students began sorting themselves into five groups. Briar grabbed my elbow and steered me to the group on the far left.

"We self-sort into weakest to strongest," he panted, face ruddy from the run. "After the first week, they assign us a ranking, and we train in rank groups. It's the only fair way to make sure us less physically able folk—" he gave me a pointed look, "—don't get beaten up too badly."

I frowned, looking around at the ten boys in our group. Some, like Briar, looked like they never did physical work, either very skinny or very chubby. And they were all stumbling over their feet and cringed away from the other students. I was pretty sure I would beat them bloody. I noted Emery had put himself in the group next to ours.

"Group five!" came a cry, and we all jumped. A short, stocky warrior with brown hair beckoned our group aside. "Babies of the group, let's head over to the shade, shall we?" I was a little shocked at his kindly voice and the way he addressed us like children. Trying to hide my surprise, I followed the group to the far end of the grounds, where shade sails covered a sandpit. "You know the drill."

"Officer Sunny!" Briar called, pulling me in front of the older fae while the other boys positioned themselves around the sandpit in pairs.

"Yes, Briar?" Officer Sunny looked to be about thirty and looked me up and down. Heat filled my cheeks. "Who's this young lad?"

"This is Sam," said Briar. "He's a country boy, first day here."

I decided that the country backstory probably ended up serving me well because Officer Sunny smiled at me as if I were a simpleton. I returned a toothy smile.

"Nice to meet you, Sam. Any combat training?"

"A little," I shrugged, side-eyeing the way two students were wrestling like toddlers in the sand. They looked like they hadn't been at warrior school since they were children, but I knew that they had. Looking around, I was starting to get the idea that the fae liked their hierarchy more than humans did. They seemed to want to keep groups of their people within their own lines.

"Alright," said Sunny gently. " How about I work with you a while? I think we have an odd number anyway."

I gave him a curt nod, eying his athletic form. A burst of anxiety shot up my spine like an arrow.

I had never touched a male intimately before—bar the Quartz blacksmith that had kissed me— let alone fought one. We hadn't actually been allowed, my sister and I being princesses, no man was to touch us in the way hand-to-hand combat required. It had only been Jerali Jones or my sister. My father had once told me that Jerali had the strength of a strong man, though, so I had some idea of what to expect. So when officer Sunny came to stand in front of me, I couldn't help but get extremely hot under my cotton shirt collar. I hoped he wouldn't feel my breasts this close. I discreetly prodded Opal out of my pocket and watched as she darted out under her own illusion and buried herself in the sand in the furthest corner of the pit.

"Alright, Sam," Sunny said brightly. "I'm going to come at you, then you can try and defend yourself, is that okay?"

I nodded, shifting into the fighting stance Jerali had been drilling into me since I was three. Sunny actually paused and considered me before setting his shoulders and running at me. But I was ready. I came in low, crouching down, and grabbed him around his lean abdomen, tackling him to the ground, trying to avoid chest contact and shoving him with my shoulder instead.

He landed with an 'oof,' but I rolled off him, and he jumped to his feet, a surprised grin on his face. "Very good, Sam! Again!"

We grappled for a bit, and when he saw I could defend

myself, he upped his game, getting rougher, trying to get me on my back. But Jerali had emphasised the importance of never letting anyone get me on my back, so I knew all too well how to avoid it. Jerali had roughed me up on a number of occasions, and Sunny wasn't any worse.

He called quits when I, trying to avoid his forearm from pushing against my breasts, accidentally elbowed him in the crotch.

"Sorry!"

He only grimaced for a second before grabbing my hand and vigorously shaking it. I felt his callouses right up against mine. "Well done, Sam, but let me see your sword skills before I move you up a group." I looked up to see Briar and the other boys had scrambled out of the sandpit to watch us, mouths agape.

Panting and very sweaty, I took the wooden practise sword he was offering me. I stared at the feather-light thing in dismay as I heard the sound of steel on steel in the distance. I hadn't trained with wood since I was a child, but I supposed the better students were allowed to practise with real steel.

But Sunny was lunging towards me again, with his own wooden sword, and I met him with mine. Jerali had me lifting heavily weighted swords for years, and with how light the sword was, I was able to move incredibly fast. Sunny started slow, but I got bored quickly and pushed him into reacting faster until we were a flurry of reflexes.

My muscles happily relished in the familiar movements, and I saw Sunny's eyes widen as I pushed him back, engaging him in heavy blows. Perhaps it was because I was still resentful of being treated second class by Daxian's family, but a sudden anger took over me, and I aggressively attacked the fae teacher until I had backed him to the end of the pit.

But then he twisted his sword in a way that made me lose my grip and sent my sword flying. He pointed his sword at my neck, and I raised my hands in surrender.

He was no longer smiling at me, instead regarding me seriously. "Well done, Sam. Tomorrow, you'll go to group three."

"Three?" I repeated lamely.

"Don't bother with four." He grinned at me.

17

SARAYA

After a huge luncheon, which had me feeling like I needed to go back to bed, my roommates collected their books from their dormitory and headed to a double-storey building where our written classes would be. There was a huge lecture amphitheatre, where all one hundred of us sat for two hours listening to a rasping fae academic talk about strategic warfare and doing a play-by-play of some historic battle between the Green Reaper and the fae courts from a hundred years ago. I listened for about half an hour before falling asleep. Briar shook me awake at the end of it.

After that, we split into small classes of about twenty and attended one class on the structure of fae swords and another on tactical strategy.

By dinner time, I was exhausted and ready for bed, but when the boys took their five p.m. time slot for the bathroom, I made an excuse about going to see my horse. Instead, I snuck back up to bed for a half an hour nap. I desperately needed a shower after a morning sweating and tumbling in the sand with Officer Sunny.

The boys settled down into what seemed like their regular evening routine. Briar read what looked like a thick romance novel while Daxian and Emery left to find their friends in the recreation building out the back of the complex. They returned just before ten p.m. when we were expected to shutter our quartz lanterns.

It was then that I made a mad dash for the bathroom.

If I wanted to avoid being seen in the shower, either I went extremely early in the morning or very late at night. Since there was no point showering before training, I decided night was my best option. Opal crooned sleepily at me as I darted down the seven flights of stairs, yellow quartz lamp half-shuttered in my hand.

"Sorry to wake you, Opal," I whispered. "But I need to make sure no one will see me. Imagine if one of the fae saw me naked!"

It would be a disaster. I'd probably be put in fae prison and tortured for information. That was probably what my own father's advisors, especially Oxley, would do.

I got down to the first-floor bathroom and snuck inside. Bright lights stung my eyes, and I held my breath to listen in. But it was empty, thank the goddess. I took the last stall, furthest from the entrance.

Setting my fresh clothes on the stool inside the stall, I placed Opal on top. Then I rapidly stripped down.

"Okay, Ope, make it look like no one is in here."

Opal sleepily nodded and squinted her multi-coloured eyes at me. Her shimmering magic encased our entire stall in a glittering, multi-coloured cube.

I relished in the hot shower, going to great efforts to use the soap in case I'd have to skip a day's washing once again. The fae had a keen sense of smell, I'd realised pretty quickly. There was no way that they'd miss that I wasn't bathing.

I had just turned off the water when I heard the distinct click of the bathroom door opening. A cold spike of fear shot through me. Had someone seen me and followed? No, they wouldn't have waited this long to come in. It had to be a coincidence.

Deep male voices echoed towards me, and I goggled my eyes at Opal, placing a finger on my lips. She placed a paw over her mouth, her eyes wide. Quietly, I slipped my clothes on. But I didn't know whether to risk moving out now or staying until the others left.

When a distant shower turned on, I blew out a breath of relief. I wrung my wet hair out and tucked Opal back into my pocket, bundling up my dirty clothes. I slipped out of my stall and made a dash for the exit. I would have to wait to use the clever hole in the wall that cleaned the fae's clothes. I passed the other stall in use, not even daring to look inside. I lurched for the entry door handle.

I would have made it out if it weren't for a deep grumble that stopped me.

"I haven't seen you around here before."

Freezing dead in my tracks, like prey caught in a snare, my heart leapt into my throat. Then I slowly turned.

Clearly having just finished washing his hands by the sink was the Commander of the Black Court forces, Drakus Silverhand—Drake, Emery had called him for short, in all his six-foot-tall, black leathered glory. I swallowed and gripped my clothes as if my life depended on it. His eyes were fixed on my face, and to my horror, they were black all the way around. I couldn't see any of the whites.

"Uh, yeah," was all I managed to get out.

As he wiped his hands on a small towel, he studied me, and I felt his gaze like a hot iron on my skin. "What's your name?" he asked, stepping up towards me.

I mentally said every swear word Agatha had ever taught me. "Sam Sourbottom."

To his credit, he didn't laugh. His face remained serious as he leaned down, his face only a handspan away from mine. "Unfortunate name, Sam."

His breath was warm on my face, his masculine scent enveloping me. As I stared into those all black eyes, my magic stirred lazily in me and my head began to swim.

"Fuck!" came a deep voice from the still-running shower stall. "Pass the soap, will you?"

Drake abruptly stepped away from me and I pressed a hand to my forehead. I glanced at the stall and saw the backside of a tall, muscled male, his back caked in what looked like dried blood. I tried to keep my expression blank at all that crimson liquid, but I knew it was the more slender of the commander's companions from the day of my engagement. Without taking his eyes off me, Drake took a cake of soap from the bench next to him and tossed it over the stall. His friend caught it without effort and began violently soaping himself.

Drake spoke again, casually leaning against the stall wall. "Be careful, Sam. You never know what you'll meet in a place like this."

I nodded vigorously to show him I was heeding his words and then spun around, yanked open the door, and ran outside, Opal bouncing in my pocket. I jogged all the way back up the stairs to the seventh floor without stopping and then sagged down against the wall of our landing.

"That was close, Ope," I said breathlessly.

She crawled up to my shoulder and licked my face, cuddling against my neck, both of us trembling just a little. We sat there for a moment to calm ourselves down before heading back to bed. I was suddenly very glad to have Opal with me.

THE NEXT DAY, WHEN IT CAME TIME TO SORT OURSELVES INTO fighting groups, I nervously strode towards group three, which was nothing like Briar's group. These students all towered over me and looked like they knew how to handle themselves. I knew I'd probably be alright with a sword against these fae, but hand to hand would be a different matter. They all stared down at me, either confusion or irritation on their faces. They hadn't seen me fight yesterday; I'd have to prove myself all over again.

Officer Wingback looked after this group. He was a middle-aged fae with black hair and a smart mouth. He paired me with a very attractive student by the name of Dreven, who looked to be on the lower end of the skill group.

He was good, but he'd underestimated me due to the size difference so that when I fought aggressively, he didn't expect it. In the end, I pinned him down with my legs, trying to ignore the fact that his very muscular body was pressed close against me for a very long time. I prayed to the goddess that he didn't feel my breasts. Opal was tucked away behind a bush, doing her job unseen.

"Yield," he grumbled in annoyance.

And then they gave us real swords. They were fae-wrought steel, patterned with beautiful geometric designs along the blade and flowers over the hilt. I knew I'd have to be careful then, as Dreven was already annoyed at me. He fought well, I'll give him that, and he was stronger than me by quite a bit. But it didn't matter so much because I was more skilled. I disarmed him within minutes.

Officer Wingback came up to me afterwards. "You don't belong here, Sourbottom," he grinned around my family name. "You don't look like much, but somehow you can handle a sword. I want to see you fight the group ones tomorrow. See what you can learn from the princes, eh?"

My brows shot up as I thanked him.

Being in group three, I was close enough to the group one students to observe them in between bouts. All five princes were in group one, and the rest of them were the best of the fae nobility. I'm sure Wingback was just being nasty when he told me to go there, some effort to bring me a peg down. I would be the only 'commoner' as far as I could see, and these were the physical best of the fae, trained from boyhood by the best warriors. Every single one was also older than me.

But I had to admit to myself, that Dreven hadn't actually been much of a challenge. I was here to be a better fighter, to fight those demons. I needed to train with the best if I wanted to be the best, even if I was sure I would get hurt a little. Daxian was in that group, and goddess help me if I was asked to fight him.

The next day, with a massive storm cloud hovering over the field, I tried to look confident as I strode towards Daxian's group. Two of them laughed in disbelief at the sight of me, small and probably inbred looking—entering their domain under an expansive tree. They all loomed above me like warrior giants, and I felt like a child playing at being an adult. Opal dashed out of my pocket and up into the tree.

I glanced at officer Wingback with his group across the

field, and he was openly smirking at me. I swore under my breath. I was going to get beaten up. I knew it. It got worse when I realised who the officer in charge of this group was.

"Who's this?" Sergeant Sharpfang said, frowning at me. "Sourbottom, what are you doing in this group?"

"Officer Wingback—"

"What? Speak up!" he shouted at me.

Every eye in group one turned to look at me, including Daxian, who looked incredibly handsome in a black cotton shirt that showed his substantive chest muscles. I felt all my blood rush to my face.

"Officer Wingback told me to come here," I said.

Sharpfang turned to watch Wingback's retreating figure walking away with his group and made a disapproving noise at the back of his throat.

But then Daxian spoke, and every cell in my body froze. "I'll take the newbie, Sergeant."

"If you're sure, Your Highness," said Sharpfang dully. "Rough him up a little. It'll be good for him."

"Yes, Sergeant." Daxian sauntered up to me, looking me up and down as if to tell me I was no opponent for him.

"We have a guest supervisor here today," continued Sharpfang. His mouth suddenly twisted, and I realised that was his version of a smile. "Commander Drake will be joining us."

The fae in my group stiffened as, from across the field, I eyed the storm cloud above. Weirdly, a storm seemed to follow the commander. I grumbled under my breath as he walked over to us. It was just my luck to have both Wyxian's boys here to watch me make a fool of myself. Yet again.

But I hadn't made a fool of myself at my engagement.

I had made my mother proud.

And yet *still,* the fae had looked down upon me.

I heard Daxian swear under his breath as Sharpfang gestured us to make pairs in the practise area. Drake met us there, and I swear I saw his lips twitch in pleasure when he saw me. Psychotic indeed.

Daxian led me to a corner while the others began grappling. I swore in as many ways as I knew as he looked me up and down.

"You know," he said. "You look familiar to me."

As ice trickled down my spine, I shrugged, trying to look nonchalant.

"Where have I seen you?"

I stroked my beard, more to check it was still there than anything. But I couldn't miss the thing. It was as coarse and itchy as all hell. "Don't know, Your Highness."

"What's your father's name?"

I thought quickly. "Same as mine, Your Highness."

He nodded absently, never taking his eyes off me. "Let's see what you can do. You'd better come at me. I'd probably hurt you if I started."

I hesitated, looking at his height and considerable mass.

"Come on, *Sourbottom,*" came a deep drawl. "Show us why Wingback put you in this group." I turned to see Drake standing there with his arms crossed, looking at me with a frown, his eyes a normal hazel today. Sharpfang was next to him.

"I suspect he did it for laughs," I muttered.

"What was that?" asked Sharpfang.

"Nothing."

He raised a brow.

"I mean, nothing, Sergeant."

Drake smirked at me. "This one's trouble already, Sharpfang."

Daxian crouched down in a fighting stance, lowering himself to better match my height, and beckoned to me with two fingers. "Come on, Sourbottom, come to Daddy."

Oh shit.

I took a step a tentative step forward. I really didn't feel like touching Prince Daxian. Not like this, anyway. I remembered his hand warm around mine when I'd cut my hand too much at our engagement. *At our engagement.* This man was my fiancé. And he'd left without saying goodbye. Left as if I'd been nothing to him.

But I could feel three pairs of fae warrior eyes on me.

I ran at Daxian, jumping up to launch my weight on him. I wasn't light, but he was so much heavier. He caught me, roughly turned me around, and slammed me into the dirt.

"Oof!" I choked, gasping for air.

"Get up, Sourbottom," jeered Sharpfang. Drake was no longer smiling.

I jumped to my feet and wiped the dirt off my cheeks. "Give me a sword, and I'll show you what I can do."

Sharpfang raised his brows. "Thinks he's good, does he?" But Drake was already handing me a steel sword, heavy, made for a fae male. But as I hefted the weight, I felt my muscles flex happily. My lightest sword at home was heavier than this. Jerali, in great wisdom, had trained me like that on purpose. Drake tossed a sword at Daxian, and he snatched it out of the air with a wicked smile.

"I'll go easy on you," Daxian said, sounding exactly like he intended to do the opposite.

"Don't." I snarled as I flew at him, hard and fast. He got his sword up just in time as mine came down on him. I could tell he was shocked by my speed because he only just met me blow for blow, his blue eyes wide. When I'd pressed him enough, I fell back, stepping back towards Drake and Sharpfang. Briefly, I became aware that the other noble fae in the arena had fallen silent, watching us from afar.

"That was unexpected, Sourbottom," the prince said, stepping towards me. "You have surprising strength for someone so puny."

Only small when compared to a fae warrior, I thought. Both Altara and I had the same build as our mother. It was lucky this shirt was so loose that he couldn't see my curves.

But I remained silent, watching the way he moved, assessing his weaknesses, where he needed improvement. The fae were physically stronger and quicker than humans, I knew that, but I did have some suspicion that the magic I inherited from my mother made me somewhat faster than a regular human woman. I wondered if I could match fae speed, though. I had more to give yet.

The prince's demeanour suddenly changed, and now he stalked me, his eyes intent, expression focused. He looked more fae than I'd seen him previously, his corded muscles rippling as he moved. I realised I may very well be outmatched. I blew out an even breath in the way Jerali had taught me, watching his gait. I knew he fought dirty from the way he'd tried to penetrate my defences the day of our engagement, but I didn't know how that translated to swordplay.

He lunged, but I was ready. Steel clashed, and pain seared up my forearm. He was strong, far stronger than me, but I knew how to fight through the pain. So I met each of his heavy blows keenly and then parried, stepping away to give my forearm a rest. It was going to be close. My whole right arm stung up to my shoulder.

He prowled, eyeing my form as closely as I was eyeing his. I tried to ignore the way the entire group were now watching us. I needed to focus.

He lunged for me again, and I got my sword up just in time before tripping and stumbling backwards, landing on an awkward angle, and dislocating my shoulder with a sick sort of pop.

But I reflexively turned off the pain receptors in my shoulder and dragged my arm upwards, popping it back into place as I rolled to my feet, flicking his sword away with mine with a grimace. Someone in the crowd hissed. I scowled as I realised I had done real damage to the major tendon and surrounding ligaments of my shoulder. I'd have to heal it tonight, but for now, I kept the pain sensors off. I'd be damned if I let Daxian get the better of me.

Daxian smirked at me, and, as he prowled again, I felt him feeling out my mental protection. Alarmed, I covered my diamond shield in black. If he saw the diamond, he would immediately recognise me. Either this is the way fae nobility fought, or he was playing dirty again. He mentally punched into my shield, and I flinched, glaring at him.

He smirked.

Arrogant prick!

This man was going to be King of Black Court one day. One of the leaders of the fae was responsible for stealing our magic. The magic from infants. And he was old enough that his father had probably discussed this treachery with him. Anger tore through me. They thought *we* were scumbags, but in reality, it was they who were the vile species.

I engaged him in a flurry of blows and distracted, he

stopped punching my mental shield. Simultaneously, I slammed into *his* mental shield.

Daxian seemed not to be able to both mentally and physically attack at the same time. I, on the other hand, had been practicing both for a very long time.

His handsome face contorted in shock.

I thrust my sword and twisted it the same way Officer Sunny had done to me just two days ago, simultaneously mentally breaking through his shield and pinching his Achilles tendon, hard. He cried out as his sword was thrown from his grip, and he stumbled backwards, grimacing and reaching for his heel.

He landed on his back, and I stood over him, levelling my sword at his neck.

He frowned at me. "I yield," he muttered.

I stepped backwards and looked around to see the fae princes, Drake, and Sharpfang staring at me in a mixture of confusion and horror.

I had just bested the crown fae prince of the Black Court. And he had no idea I was the human fiancée he'd looked down upon just days ago.

It was then that I knew that I was worthy of being in the Order of Temari. They needed someone to lead the campaign against the fae. And I wanted to be the one to do it. The fae scumbags needed someone to go up against them who was determined and ruthless. Only then could they be brought down. And I would revel in doing just that.

fter I'd bested him, Daxian stalked off with his prince friends, glancing at me and muttering with them. I saw him talking with the prince of Twilight Court, and I hid my concern, wondering if he was asking about my fake rural village of Talathia.

At the back of the group, Briar and Emery suddenly became my best friends. Emery swung his arm around my shoulder and declared me the king of the school while Briar chortled.

"I bet Dax was livid!" whispered Briar. "He's never been embarrassed like that before."

"*And* both Drake and Sharpfang saw it. Everyone will be frightened of you now," said Emery shaking me. I was thankful I'd kept my injured shoulder numb.

Three fae students I didn't know came over to shake my hand. Others warily observed me from a distance.

"Double dessert for you, Sam Sourbottom!" one of them said.

"King Sourbottom!" cried Briar. "King of the village Talathia!"

It seemed that Daxian wasn't as popular as I thought he was. It made sense. He was as arrogant as anything.

"Shhh!" I hissed at them. "What if they hear?"

"Well done, Sam," came a deep voice from behind us.

Briar shrieked, and Emery jerked off me as we spun around to see the Black Court Commander walking silently behind us.

I took a solid second to collect myself. "Thank you," I said.

Drake gave me a nod and walked off, leaving Emery, Briar, and I gaping in his wake.

Emery blew out a breath. "Dear gods. That's the nicest thing I've heard come out of his mouth."

Briar shook my hand. "Congratulations, Sam. You've got a fan."

ON FRIDAY AFTERNOONS, BRIAR EXPLAINED TO ME THAT CLASSES were off, and they all went out to the waterfall south of the school for a swim. Nervously, I followed them all out, towels over their shoulders, happily chatting away. The storm cloud that came with Drake seemed to have blown off into the north, leaving blue skies above us.

The waterfall was a bouncing mass of pouring water, and I had to stand and marvel at it for a moment because I'd never seen one before. I didn't realise I was gaping until Emery came, placed a finger under my chin, and pushed my mouth closed.

He chuckled and jumped into the lake, splashing me with water.

I spluttered and shook the water out of my hair before realising that all of a sudden, all the fae nobles were stripping down and jumping into the impossibly blue lake.

By the goddess. Opal stuck her head out, and I pushed her back into the pocket. Daxian was standing next to Briar, both of them naked. Briar turned to me.

"Come on in, Sam!"

I smiled and shook my head, trying my best, and failing, to keep eye contact. I glanced down between Daxian's legs and immediately regretted it. Heat surged through me, and I shook my head, plonking myself down on the grass.

"Hey!" I suddenly called to Briar. "So Emery wasn't lying about that tattoo!"

Briar turned crimson and stumbled into the lake, so I couldn't see the naked blond woman tattooed on his barrel-like chest anymore.

Chuckling, I watched the boys splashing about in the water, using the chance to heal the torn ligaments in my shoulder. Every so often, some daring fae would climb up onto the tall rock next to the waterfall, announce for everyone to get out of the way, and they would jump, plummeting hard into the lake. I cringed every time they did, less because of the drop and more because of all the penises now blatantly visible to me. I wondered if human males were any different because I hadn't really had any chance to see something like this before before.

I felt a little odd sitting there by myself and it made me stand out, but I hoped they wouldn't be suspicious of it. They seemed to accept it was just a strange part of me being a country-raised inbred weirdo. Which worked fine with me if it made them leave me alone.

Eventually, I let Opal stick her head out of my pocket, and

she watched, wide-eyed, with her little head cocked to the side. She ended up taking a little dip as well, and it made her coat shine like a real opal gem in the sunlight. I hid her behind the rock, drying her vigorously with the towel, but she ended up sunning herself, stretching out on her back and wriggling around happily.

About half an hour in, a dull ache began in my lower stomach, and I immediately recognised what it was. I shot to my feet, grimacing. Shit. Shit. Shit. I looked within my own uterus and saw it was ready to start its monthly shed. I would start bleeding soon. How could I be so stupid? I was able to stop my own ovulation at will. I'd been doing it for ages if there was a big event or for travelling. I did it for Altara as well, if she asked. But the Warrior Academy had been such a distraction, and being around, so many males had me almost forgetting that I was, still, a woman.

And then I felt it. A pooling between my legs.

"What's wrong, Sam?" Briar floated up to me, concern all over his face. Then his face changed, and he tilted his head upwards to the wind, sniffing. "Are you bleeding?"

Oh, dear Goddess. His nose was extremely sensitive.

I clutched my shoulder, which was, in fairness, injured. "Yeah, just a scrape, though."

"Oh, sorry. Maybe head over to the infirmary? I can take you—" He made to climb out of the lake.

"No!" I said, my voice sharp with panic.

Briar looked up at me in surprise. "It's no trouble, Sam. Really."

I snatched up my towel and backed away from him, "No, no, really, I know where it is, I'll go myself."

Briar almost looked disappointed that I'd declined his help, but I couldn't think about it. Opal scrambled onto my shoulder and I ran, hobbled rather, back to our dormitory. I had to get into the shower and wash my clothes. Wash everything.

But when I got to the showers, they were full of fae males, loud, boisterous, jovial fae males. The noise echoed all around me, and heart hammering, I ran to the latrines.

"Is that blood?" someone asked. "Who's bleeding?"

I shut the latrine door and willed my uterus into a stasis. I stopped it from contracting and commanded it to cease its bleeding. Panting, Opal scurried up to my shoulder, and I told her to close her eyes. She obliged, covering her multi-coloured eyes with a paw, and I took off my underwear and wiped myself down as best I could. I put my pants back on and went outside, dodging Dreven as he passed me and headed straight for the magical laundry hatch. But there was already someone there.

The student turned as I approached, and to my dismay, I saw it was the Prince of Twilight Court.

"Hello, Sam," he said, leaning against the wall as the laundry hatched whirred as it worked.

I crossed my arms and hid my bundled-up underwear under my armpit. "Hello, Your Highness."

"No need for that here. I'm just Skelton, or Skel for short," he said, waving his arm in a friendly manner. He had the handsome face of a fae royal but had kind brown eyes. The antithesis of Daxian. "But I was wondering if you could tell me—where was it in Twilight Court that you're from?"

I cleared my throat and kept my voice light. "It's called Talathia."

"See, I've never heard of it." Skelton smiled, and I could see he was trying hard not to scare me. That made me soften to him a little.

"It's very rural...I don't get out much, you see." I smiled back, looking at my feet as if I were ashamed of myself.

Skelton placed a large hand on my shoulder. "It's alright, Sam, you don't need to be worried about me. But if you need *anything*, Sam, *anything* at all, you just let me know, alright? You fall under my jurisdiction, so you come to me, not Daxian."

I looked up at him in surprise. "Okay, thank you."

The laundry hatch shut itself off with a magical hiss, and Skelton turned to take his clothes out. He left, glancing back at me to smile. I stood there in a sort of shock for a moment before a snide voice said behind me. "You keep your dirty inbred hands off Skel."

I whirled around and saw a handsome waif of a boy, blond and hazel-eyed, glowering at me. "He's looking at you funny, and you need to know, don't get any ideas. He's *mine*."

A passing fae jostled him. "Yeah, but does *he* know that, Gerard?"

Two others chuckled, and Gerard scowled at them all and pointed a menacing finger at me. "Watch your back." He stalked off, sashaying his hips.

I gaped at his departing back for a moment. Prince Skelton was making a move for *me*? I couldn't fathom it. I thought about it before shaking myself out of it and putting my underwear into the laundry hatch. I sincerely hoped it would take blood out. Opal stuck her head out of my pocket, her magic sparkling around her, and I patted her comfortingly on the head with a finger, but I think it served to comfort me more. I hadn't known how weird pretending to be a male would be.

As the weeks went by, my routine was fairly simple, it was the same every day, but we got the weekends off. I met the other fae nobility, the princes of the other fae courts, and the various heirs to this or that land. Each had a different way of fighting, though none of them ever tried to psychically pierce my mind like Daxian, and it seemed an impolite thing to do.

Daxian, for his part, kept his distance from me, and I never fought with him again. I knew that he watched me, probably because it irked him that I'd humiliated him in front of his friends, but the other princes, especially Skelton, were nice enough to take turns training swords with me and teaching me how to grapple better.

Because of it, I got a lot better quite quickly. I imagined what Jerali Jones would think, knowing that I was training with fae princes, possibly the best warriors in both the human and fae realms. I also learned a lot about my fae roommates. Briar hid romance novels inside thick textbooks. Emery was frightened of nothing except Sergent Sharpfang and Drake

Silverhand and regularly lectured me on his exploits with his various lovers in Black Court. But Briar told me later that his stories were either outright lies or heavily exaggerated.

I also learned that the fae knew or cared nothing about humans. They thought of us akin to animals and imagined that we could do nothing of importance except hog the luminous quartz. Even in our lessons, humans never came up.

The only time humans were brought up was when *I* was mentioned in relation to Daxian. Me as Saraya, that is. The news that Daxian had been engaged to a human was treated as an unnecessary political manoeuvre by Black Court, but no one was stupid enough to mention it while Daxian was around. It was almost brushed under the carpet, treated as if it were nothing. Emery even made out that Daxian would have a fae wife anyway.

That blistered me more than I cared to admit. My only consolation was the smugness I got from knowing that I was capable of defeating the majority of them in sword combat.

And Daxian? Well, Daxian preferred to spend time with the other princes more than with us. He was either lounging with them in the recreation room or sparring with them in our spare time. Other than that, he remained strangely and eerily quiet.

LESS THAN A MONTH LATER, I LOOKED UP AT THE NIGHT SKY AND knew it would be a full moon the next night. I had been sneaking to the bathroom for weeks now, but sneaking *outside* would be a different matter. We weren't allowed out of our buildings after lights out, but there were no locked doors or anything barring me from doing so.

So the next night, I crept out of my dorm with Opal sitting on my shoulder. She had been a faithful companion and extremely good at hiding around so many fae eyes. I thought at one stage Briar had spotted her, but I think he put the rainbow-coloured blip down to eye strain from the phenomenal number of romance novels he read.

The grounds were wreathed in the blue glow of moonlight, and I knew that anyone looking out at the lawn from one of the dormitories would no doubt see me, so I stuck to the shadows. I decided that since the forest was out of bounds, the best place to go was by the lake, which was a solid fifteen-minute walk from the school complex itself.

I jogged over the grass, and cicadas chirping so loudly in the night that I had to really concentrate to make sure no one was following me or that I didn't come upon some teacher's night-time walk by mistake.

When I came upon the lake, which glowed like something mystical in the moonlight, I was reminded of my mother and my full moon ceremony on the night of my first blood. My heart ached a little as I realised how much I missed my family. I sent a prayer for Altara, hoping she had found some friends amongst the other girls in the Ellythian jungle school. I had never been without her for this long, and it was really starting to grate on me.

"Saraya."

I hadn't been called that name in a month, and it honestly took me a moment to register. I turned to see Arishnie, smiling softly at me, blue-grey under the moon. Opal chirped in greeting.

"Hello, Arishnie. Long time no see."

"Indeed. You did well with the disguise." An amused smile played on her lips.

I grinned, stroking my beard, a practise I'd perfected by watching Sharpfang do the same. "It has them fooled so far, at least."

"Good, you've already gained more muscle."

"And am a better fighter. What are we going to do tonight?"

"We're going to the capital. I need to show you what you're up against."

I stilled. "Now?"

Arishnie smiled and pointed at the grass in front of the pool. "Sit and, in a moment, have the lumzen hide you completely."

Once I was seated, my warrior mentor said, "We are going to astral travel."

My eyes widened. "I've never done that before."

"You've done enough mental work that it should be easy. It's only a different version of what you do with your midwifery. Close your eyes and imagine the world around you as you saw it just now."

I did as she asked and found my mental vision surprisingly sharp.

"Now feel yourself rising up into the air next to me."

I did so and gasped as I physically felt myself leave my body.

"Now, look down at yourself."

I opened my mental eyes and tuned to see myself sitting on the earth with Opal on my shoulder, looking confused. It was such a jarring experience that I opened my physical eyes, feeling a *whoosh* as my astral self came back into my body.

"Goddess!"

"I don't mean to sound rude, Saraya," said Arishnie

hastily, "but we really don't have too much time. Can you try again? Opal, make her invisible"

I closed my eyes, shaking myself a little as Opal's magic settled around me in a shimmering dome. But I knew what to do now. It felt almost natural to me after years of looking into other people's bodies.

This time, when I emerged to float alongside Arishnie, I looked down at my hands and found them to be the same transparent blue-grey as hers. I couldn't feel the wind anymore, nor the temperature. But my hearing was intact.

Without warning, Arishnie grabbed my arm and flew us upwards into the sky. I let out a cry as the world under me fell away, and I gained the most resplendent bird's eye view of the whole Mountain Academy. And I did feel like a bird. It was the most exhilarating feeling to be airborne, but also odd that I couldn't feel the wind on my face.

"Travel is much faster this way," explained Arishnie, as we zoomed up further and further until the entirety of the mountain range became visible to us, the school like a series of caterpillars lying sleeping. It was a beautiful and terrifying sight.

My warrior mentor then flew us northward at such a rapid pace I was thankful that I didn't have a physical stomach. The land zipped past beneath us: forest, land, rivers, shimmering lakes, minor villages, all sprawled as if I were looking at a map. Within minutes we reached the bright multi-coloured blanket of Quartz City, the rainbow of quartz lights glinting beneath us in a tapestry of colour.

My throat did feel tight back in my physical body as I looked upon my birth home. Arishnie led us down into the city, and it was honestly the most fun I'd had in months, zooming around like that. I was keen to try and do it again—until that is, I saw what Arishnie had brought me to see.

"Quiet," she whispered as we rounded a corner between two houses. "The humans cannot hear us, but the demons will."

"There are demons here?" I asked, whipping my head around so fast I almost pulled muscle.

She gave me a pointed look, "They frequent the cities because this is where the most births are."

I felt sick to my stomach.

"Come on."

We floated up to the second story of a townhouse, where I heard the unmistakable sounds of a woman at the end of labour.

I found myself holding my breath as we came into the room. Before me was Agatha and a younger midwife called Christie. A woman was rapidly birthing a babe into Christie's hands.

"Goddess!" the mother cried as the babe was born, and Christie brought him to the mother's chest. The child was silent for a moment before Agatha roughly dried him off with a towel, and he gave a lively wail. Immediately, something skulked through the ajar door behind them.

Arishnie grabbed my arm and hid us outside the room, hovering just so we could peer in. It was a frightening creature. Black and red-skinned, in the shape of a hunched man. It walked on four legs right up to the bedside and reached right through Christie, who gave an unconscious shiver.

"We have to do something!" I hissed.

"We can do nothing," Arishnie whispered back dully.

Rage tore through me, hot and fiery, as we watched the demon, fangs bared, reach with black fingers, and pinch something at the baby's crown. The child gave a whimper as a silvery stream of light came forth with the demon's fingers, linked to the baby's head. He drew it forth to his nose and inhaled it in, drawing upon it until the silvery stream thinned and disconnected from the child and was no more.

Disbelief tore me like an oily black shadow. I wanted to tear open that black demon, rip its head off, cut open its bony body. How could this have gone on for decades, and no one had known? How were the warrior midwives from the Order of Temari systematically killed off until their Order was completely destroyed? We watched the demon scuttle out.

"Could you not kill it?" I asked. The backs of my eyes were burning fiercely, and so was the pit in my stomach.

Arishnie sighed. "I wish I could, but I am dead. I have no reach to kill it. They have a twenty-four-hour window to claim the magic," Arishnie rubbed her eyes in frustration, drawing me away from the window. "But they get there every time. They smell a labouring woman as a wolf sniffs out its prey."

"How do we stop it?" I asked through clenched teeth.

"To reach them in this dimension, you'll have to learn how to summon an astral sword in your physical form. A normal one won't touch them at all. "

"Teach me," I growled. "Teach me how to kill them, and I will kill every single fucking one."

Arishnie smiled a savage smile. "Then let's begin."

20

SARAYA

Another two months went by, including two full moons. In these sessions, Arishnie taught me everything she knew about killing demons. Summoning the astral sword took me three sessions to do. You had to picture a sword, creating it in your mind, and somehow merge the physical with astral and call it forth.

That first full moon, even with the anger of what I'd just seen urging me on, I couldn't manage it.

On the second full moon, I managed a flicker of *something*, and I swear I felt something in my hand, but it was gone in a flash.

At the third full moon that we met by the mountain lake, I finally got it. It was like trying to capture the ghost of a thought. Or a long-gone memory. I've always had good focus because of my midwifery work but trying to pull something out of nothing felt impossible.

Arishnie guided me in constructing the sword in my mind, and I used what I had learned about fae weapons from three months of studying blacksmithing in theory classes. So I had it there so clearly in my mind. I stood there, thinking and feeling deeply. And between one heartbeat and the next, a burst of light came through my eyelids and my fingers closed around something heavy. I was so surprised I almost dropped the weapon.

Arishnie cheered, and I simply stared. In my right hand, the sword gleamed blue in the moonlight, diamond-plated steel, a hilt of lapis lazuli in the shape of a lotus, and a lightning bolt. The sigils of my mother and father combined. The weight was just heavy enough, the diameter of the hilt perfect for my grip. I gave it a swing in a figure-eight through the night air.

"I can't believe I did it!" I breathed.

Opal chirped in delighted congratulations.

Arishnie made me practise letting it slide back into the ether and manifesting it again. We practised all night, and a few hours before dawn, she let me go back to bed.

THE NEXT DAY WAS A SATURDAY, AND ON WEEKENDS I DECIDED to take my showers during the day when everyone was likely out or busy and not using the bathrooms. That way it was safe to spend the extra time washing my hair. With Opal getting brilliant with her illusions, I was confident that we wouldn't get caught even if someone walked up directly behind me. Even so, I took the last shower before the latrines.

But that day, as I turned off the water, I heard Briar's curious voice behind me. "What's this?"

I whipped around to see Briar crouching down to look at Opal, who seemed to have fallen asleep and rolled out of the shower cubicle. Naked, with hair dripping all around me, I watched on in horror as Opal sleepily blinked her eyes open and saw who was staring at her.

She gave a frightened squeak and bolted towards me for safety. It was then I realised none of her illusory magic was around the cubicle. She must have been tired from being up all night with Arishnie and me.

Briar's eyes followed Opal as she frantically scrambled up to my shoulder. I watched his eyes widen as he took in my naked body.

"Urgh!" I cried, covering myself with my hands.

"Argh!" shrieked Briar. He ran out of the bathroom.

Opal began squeaking in panic and apology. But I had to act fast. I didn't even dry myself off before pulling on my pants and shirt and bolting out after Briar and up the stairs, the running making me realise that I'd not bound my breasts.

But Briar had seen me naked.

He knew.

He would tell Daxian.

I would be outed. He would tell everyone, surely. And I wouldn't just be kicked out. I'd probably be interrogated, held captive. He'd probably gone to tell our roommates. I was going to be in huge trouble.

My heart thundered in my head, and I skidded into our dorm room to find Briar sitting on his bed, hunched over with his hands over his eyes. Opal, who'd dashed up the stairs behind me, scampered up to my shoulder. I hurried up to my fae friend.

All my thoughts came out as a blur of words. "Oh goddess, Briar! I'm so sorry, I'm sorry! Please don't tell anyone. Don't tell Daxian. I can explain, I can—"

"Don't apologise, Sam," he looked up at me, the distress showing in his dark eyes.

"I know it's probably a shock—" I said, then I realised what he'd actually said to me. "Wait, what? Why?"

Briar took a slow exhale and nodded as if he had come to terms with something. "I understand everything now. At first, I was confused why you hadn't been to the Academy. And then you said you were sick. And I was like, what? Fae don't get sick. And now it all makes sense."

No wonder they'd all looked at me strangely at the time. But how was I supposed to know fae didn't get sick? "I know. I don't even know what to say."

"That's why you say goddess all the time!" he slapped his forehead. "That's why you've taken showers alone and never come into the lake with us! I should have known! I'm sorry. Being a eunuch must be so difficult."

I opened my mouth and then abruptly closed it. Carefully I said, "*Pardon*?"

Briar looked like he was about to cry, his chubby face beet red. "How did it happen? Wait, that's insensitive. Forget I asked. It's awful. I'm sorry it happened to you, Sam. We'll all support you, don't worry. Don't feel any shame about it."

He thought I was a eunuch. He mustn't have looked at my privates properly, or my breasts for that matter. I threw myself back on my bed and covered my unbound chest with a blanket, not caring that my hair was thoroughly saturating my pillow with water. I was trying to decide if this was a good or bad thing. I guess my cover really wasn't blown, was it? Opal crooned apologetically next to me, and I patted her head to tell her it was okay.

"And you have a lumzen!" Briar came over to my bed. "Fascinating creature, has it been helping you somehow?"

I sat up on my elbows, my mind racing. "I guess I thought

she could—she could make it look like—" I gestured to the area between my legs.

Briar pressed his hand against his face and swore. "You don't need to do that. You don't need to feel any sort of inferiority with us. You don't need balls or a penis to be a good fighter. And you're the best of us! Look at that!"

I could've laughed. Right there, I could have laughed in his face. But I figured this would actually help me. No one would have a reason to be suspicious of me anymore or call me weird.

Opal stared at me with googly eyes. I supposed she could've made me a fake penis. By now, she'd seen enough of them at the lake to model one. But it didn't matter now. There would be no need. Looking back at the incident, it was just luck that my tumble of thick, wet hair must have covered my breasts at the time Briar had come along. *And* I was lucky that Briar was a bit of an idiot. In his mind, it was more likely that I'd be a eunuch than a girl.

Relief washed through me like an ocean tide. I imagined how my sister would react if she knew about the strange things that were happening to me. I'm sure she was up to something interesting too.

Briar ended up telling our roommates about me being a eunuch, and to their credit, Daxian and Emery didn't treat me differently at all. If anything, Emery seemed more impressed, and it gave Daxian even more permission to ignore me. But as long as they didn't start calling me the eunuch king, I was happy. Plus, we had the added bonus that now, Opal was allowed to roam freely on my shoulder. Briar made it out as if she were some sort of trained assistance animal for me. Apparently, they used such animals in the fae realm to assist with the odd fae who needed it. There was even one mage in Obsidian Court who used a creature to keep him calm.

But I was stupid to think that Daxian wouldn't want a little revenge for me humiliating him in front of the other princes. But he was smart, and a good enemy knows how to wait until the right time. And, of course, quite quickly, word spread about my lack of male parts.

21

SARAYA

I was fast asleep when he came for me.

My covers were ripped off, and I was yanked out of bed, a black cloth sack thrown over my head. The smell of garlic consumed me, and I retched.

"Gods, don't you *dare* vomit, Sourbottom," growled a voice that I recognised immediately.

Daxian.

"Your Highnesses!" Briar's voice. "What—"

"Not a word Briar," snarled Daxian. "Or you know what I'll have done to your father. You too, Emery."

There were others in the room. Briar had said 'highnesses,' so that meant Daxian had hauled another prince into this too. I should have known the arrogant ass would want payback. He'd just waited long enough that I'd be caught off guard. He'd been so quiet I'd assumed he was over it. I had been so very wrong.

Resisting the urge to vomit or cry, I allowed myself to be shoved over a shoulder and carried down the stairs. Realising that I had no idea where Opal was, I thrashed, gaining me a punch to the head that had me seeing stars.

"Where's Opal!" I croaked.

"Your lumzen, do you mean?" snarled Daxian. "We've got him, don't you worry."

His dark tone had me terrified. "Don't hurt her!" I cried.

"Shut your mouth, or I will!" he hissed.

"It's alright, Sam," came a deep, even voice I recognised as Prince Skelton of Twilight Court. "I'll keep the lumzen safe."

Opal gave a frightened warble by my ear, and relief washed through me. Skelton wasn't a brute like Daxian. He wouldn't needlessly hurt a tiny creature.

Daxian hauled me out into the night, the cold air biting at my bare legs. I had a shirt on but no pants. My fiancé, my monster of a fae fiancé, wanted revenge on me...and he didn't even know who I was. The irony of it made me want to giggle hysterically. But the idea that these fae males were out to punish me, had me quivering to the bone. What awful thing did Daxian have in store for me? How much damage would I get tonight? I struggled to control my panicked breathing.

We trudged into the night, their boots crunching on grass then dry leaves. Eventually, Daxian plonked me down and roughly grabbed my hands. I felt the rough bark of a tree against my back, and I cringed as it scratched at my old scars. Daxian wound prickly rope around my wrists and tied them to the back of the tree. Only then did he remove the garlic sack from my head.

I gasped the fresh forest air as, in the darkness, I tried to make out the small group gathered in front of me. They had brought me deep into the forests on the western aspect of the school. I was met with the satisfied smirk of Daxian, a grave-faced Skelton, and Gerard, the fae who had threatened me about his crush, the Twilight prince.

"We know you're lying about where you come from." Daxian scowled at me. "Skel looked it up with his staff. There's no village called Talathia in Twilight Court."

Behind him, Skelton stepped forward. "Just tell us the truth, Sam," he said evenly. "We won't hurt you. We just want to know the truth."

"I'm not lying!" I cried, twisting within my bonds. I'd been caught out, and my mind raced trying to find purchase for some reason, some answer that would placate them. "Why would I lie?" I asked.

"There's something weird about you," sneered Gerard, pointing a skinny finger at me. "You're suspicious as all hell. Even if you are a eunuch!"

I groaned. "You guys are insane. I'm not hiding anything!" But I'd never been that good at lying, and these were sharp-eyed fae who were now staring at my face very closely. I should have known that I couldn't get away with my ruse for this long.

"If you won't tell us," said Daxian viciously,"you'll have to be punished for it." I see that hate in his eyes. I cringed under it, terrified of what was coming.

"You guys are making a mistake!"

"Shut up!" snarled Daxian. "You need to be taught a lesson." He suddenly stepped away from me, and it was only then that I realised how terribly dark the forest around us was. "On the night of no moon, something dark moves through this part of the mountains," said Daxian in a low voice. "He is called *Kraasputin*. Also known as the gonad stealer."

My face contorted with disgust as I cringed. What the hell was he planning?

"Are you sure this is a good idea, Dax?" asked Prince Skelton. I could see Opal's squirming, rough outline in his hands. "I don't want him to wind up dead. Imagine the—"

"Oh, he'll be fine. Do you know what a gonad is, country rat?" Daxian gave me the ugliest smirk I'd ever seen on a person's face.

I gulped. "Ovaries."

The prince of Black Court narrowed his eyes. "And testicles." He turned back to the others. "Which he doesn't have. So he'll be safe from permanent injury. He'll just be scared out of his mind. Kraasputin will teach him who his betters are. He'll teach him not to lie to us."

He turned his back on me, and they all followed him back to the Academy.

But I did have gonads. I had goddess forsaken ovaries! "No, you don't understand! Daxian—"

The prince stiffened and turned around. "What did you call me?" His voice was dangerous

I gulped. I was his damned fiancée! I had every right to call him by his name. But instead, I bit my tongue and said, "I'm sorry, Your Highness."

Skelton cast me a slightly disturbed look before turning around and heading away with Gerard.

It was dark, so incredibly dark out here that I couldn't see a thing. I also had no idea how to get back to the Academy— I'd never been this far from the main buildings. The forest around me rustled and swayed in the night, and I was sure they had brought me deep inside of it. I looked up, seeing barely a speckle of stars through the dense canopy of trees. I twisted my hands. If I could get free of my bonds, I could just run back. But the bonds were tight. I closed my eyes and focused on the bonds, trying to loosen them the way someone else would if they were releasing me. Daxian had bound me tight, but thankfully, I had excellent mental prowess. I had just managed to undo the first knot when a sudden wind bit at my skin.

My eyes flew open just as the smell of burning flesh hit the insides of my nose.

Something moved in the trees beyond.

I took a shuddering breath, telling myself to calm down, to concentrate. But that awful smell was so strong that I wanted to gag and hurl and cry at the same time. Whatever this Kraasputin was, it wouldn't be a friendly spectre like Arishnie.

I managed to undo the second knot, but that bastard Daxian had done a third. I set onto it just as the snapping of a twig echoed around me.

I opened my eyes to see a figure standing there, and my heart stopped dead in my chest.

Holy mother goddess.

It was cloaked in a black cloak that seemed to suck in any of the remaining light around him.

And from within the cowl were glowing eyes. Eyes that burned like fiery coals. It stepped towards me and lifted its head as if sniffing the wind. All I could smell…was *it*.

"Why hello, little…*person*," the Krassputin's slithering voice crawled all the way up my spine and back down again. I shivered in the sudden chill.

"W-What a-are y-you?" I asked, despite the chattering that had taken over my teeth. I didn't want to look weak in the face of an evil creature, but if it could be engaged in conversation, there was a chance I could talk myself out of this.

"A being of the night," it hissed. "Darkness incarnate, grief and worry incarnate."

"Y-You speak so highly of yourself, sir." I kept my voice light, just to give myself courage while I loosened the third knot. The ropes fell away, and I brought my wrists to my front, rubbing the soreness out of them. "I was told you steal certain bodily organs."

"Oh yes, those are *most* useful…"

I summoned my astral sword in a flash of blue-purple. To my satisfaction, the creature flinched. "I'm afraid you're not going to steal mine tonight."

"Is that a threat?"

"It's reality." I snarled. "I have work to do. The goddess Umali herself granted me this work. I cannot let her down."

"Umali?" There was a lilt of surprise…and pleasure. "It seems we are both servants of the night sky."

I shrugged. "I guess we are."

"But you understand…if I let you go, I have been denied a meal. This is my source of life, what I require to survive. Predator, I am. Prey, I must have."

I stiffened. "What are you saying?"

"I deal in the precious, little midwife. Precious things like secrets."

I froze again. He knew what I was. How on earth did he know?

"Give me one precious thing," he insisted, "and I will grant you one in return—your ovaries. Thus we have struck a balance."

Logic was something I could work with. "If I spare your life and you spare mine, we are also equal then, no?"

The creature cackled, a bone-rattling, spiking sound that sent my knees quivering. "I do not deal in lives, midwife. I deal in *precious* things. *Secret* things. And ovaries are quite precious to a young princess, no?"

My stomach churned as I understood what he meant. "You know everything about me. How could I possibly have secrets?"

"Oh, there are things that even I do not know...give me something secret, my midwife princess, and I will give you the precious gift of your ovaries, deal?"

Deals with fae creatures were the stuff of nightmares, fodder for stories of warning. It looked like I could talk my way out of this after all.

"Deal." I sent my blade back into the ether.

Greedy eyes glowed in their own fire. I looked at those eyes and took a deep inhale and a long exhale.

"A precious secret, hey?" I said, crossing my arms. Agatha's old face swam before my mind's eye and her words before I left Quartz City. *"The fae are no joke, girl. Be wise. Be smart. Be cunning if you can, although I knew you don't have that in you."*

She was right. She knew me too well. I wasn't a cunning person. I kept no lies, had no cunning plans...except one. A secret only three ghosts knew.

I swallowed. "I was to marry the prince of the Black Court," I said slowly. I wondered if this was a good idea, but I had just the one secret to give, and maybe this being of the dark knew that, seeing as he knew everything else about me. "Did you know about that?"

"Perhaps," a voice full of cunning.

I sighed. "I escaped to come here under disguise. In my place is a golem."

The creature sighed. It would have been a mirror to my own sigh if it wasn't filled with such gluttonous pleasure.

"Oh, Princess, this is a precious gift indeed."

I shook my head sadly. "I'm not a cruel person, nor out to hurt others. But know this." I pointed a finger at him. "There is a special place in hell for those who take advantage of the kindness of others."

The creature regarded me. Its glowing eyes seemed to pulse in their sockets. I regarded him evenly back, thoroughly displeased with myself.

"You are a precious thing," the creature said slowly. "Precious to those of us who have walked the earth for millennia. I will gift you one thing for free."

Uh oh. "What is it?" I asked sullenly.

"Knowledge." It floated closer to me, the smell of decay filling my nose, my pharynx. "Your stepmother," it said slowly. "Is not human."

I froze.

"What?"

"Do with that gift what you will."

I scowled. "What—"

"Farewell, warrior midwife. I hope we do not meet again."

And with that, the Kraasputin slithered back into the darkness between the trees.

I was barefoot, but I ran anyway, into the direction the two princes and Gerard had left. I twitched and scowled as twigs stabbed me underfoot, but I jogged in a straight line until I could see the distant quartz lights of the Academy. I sighed in relief as I reached the soft grass of the compound, and then a wailing croon blasted for me.

Opal pitched herself right at my face, chattering and warbling, shrieking and stuttering.

"Shh!" I said, holding her against my cheek and stroking her. She was trembling so much that she was vibrating. "Oh my poor, poor baby Opal, you're okay, I'm okay. You got out, you clever thing."

She crooned, her wide eyes wet, and I realised she had been crying. "You are far too precious—" I caught myself just in time, the word precious taking on a whole new meaning. "Oh goddess," I said tiredly as a wind stirred on my bare legs. I tugged my sleeping shirt down. "Let's get out of here before something else gets to me."

I set into a quick jog, Opal bouncing on my shoulder as if I could run off the Kraasputin's words that now clung to my skin like a spiderweb. We jogged around the junior's wing and into the senior's, right into my dorm. I took a moment to take a quick shower, in attempt to wash the icky feeling covering me, and headed up to bed.

Back in my room, everyone was sound asleep, including the big lump that was Daxian. Opal and I slipped into bed, but it was a long time before either of us closed our eyes. *Your stepmother isn't human.* In the stories, these trickster demons were known to twist words around. Perhaps he meant it in a metaphorical way? I had often called her a monster in the full sense of the word, after all.

The next morning I acted like nothing had happened, and when Daxian woke up and saw me, safe and yawning in bed as per normal, I thoroughly enjoyed the look of profound disbelief on his face.

AT LEAST ONCE A WEEK, I THOUGHT ABOUT THE CONSEQUENCES of my running away from my fae marriage. It was what drove me to work so hard at my training with both the fae warriors and Arishnie every full moon. Surely, they had discovered the golem by now. And surely, they were furious about being deceived.

But it turned out that Epelthi and Opal's golem had been a good one because it was only three days after my meeting with the Krassputin that I learned Wyxian had figured out that I'd duped them. And I knew instantly that it must have come by revealing the information to the Krassputin. Perhaps the old devil had sold the information, but coincidence or not, all hell broke loose.

While the news of Daxian's human engagement had caused barely a buzz within the Academy, that was nothing compared to the reaction to what happened next.

One morning, Daxian had disappeared. His bed unmade and his possessions gone. He had clearly left in the night.

Classes had also been cancelled for the day. We all loitered about our dorms, nervously wondering what could have gone wrong. And then we heard the news that the fae nobility had left this morning. They'd called their sons home.

"What does that mean?" I asked nervously. "Is something going on in the fae realms?"

It was then that Emery rushed through the door, having come back to see his gambling friends on Eclipse's floor.

"I've got the news!"

We all jumped off our beds.

"The Black Drake has taken the human city."

Every muscle, tendon, and bone in my being froze. "What?" My own voice sounded far away.

"Yeah, remember how Daxian got engaged to that human princess? Well, apparently, she's just run away. So Drake and his elite guard have taken Quartz Palace. They're calling for war!"

"Honestly, I was waiting for this to happen," said Briar,

shaking his large fae head. "There's been rumours about it for ages. Drake probably jumped at the chance. He wanted more land to terrorise. The fae lands were getting too small for him."

I was going to hurl my dinner right there and then. Opal licked my face, trying to see if I was okay.

But only one thought was in my mind. This was my fault. I had to go back.

LATE THAT NIGHT, I TOOK MY SADDLEBAGS AND FOOD I'D TAKEN from the kitchen, perched Opal on my shoulder, and together, we snuck out the door. But just as I was about to hurry down the stairs, I stopped and turned around, looking at the shadowed sleeping shapes that were my friends. I did feel a small pang of sadness then. These boys had become my friends over the last three months, and I knew I would probably never see them again.

Opal pressed her cheek against my face, and I patted her soft head.

"Goodbye boys," I whispered into the dark.

Then I turned and swept down the stairs and across the lawn to the stables. I thought I would have to sneak Silentfoot out, but to my surprise, the ostlers were running around, a small queue of fae students standing waiting.

"You going home too, Sourbottom?" came a voice. I turned to see Avery, a fae from Briar's fighting group, lugging a backpack.

"Yes," I said, after hesitating.

Avery nodded. "Lots of us are, don't want to get caught up in some noble's war. They've already taken *their* sons home to safety. I don't care how dangerous it is. I'm not waiting for morning. It's going to get even more dangerous if a war starts. We all know that."

I swallowed. *Some noble's war.* It was my war. I wondered what Daxian was thinking. I watched as Avery and the others were slowly given their horses and rode out into the night. When it was my turn, the red-headed ostler nodded at me. "I remember you," he said. "The chestnut mare."

When they brought Silentfoot out, I gave her an apple, and she whickered, nuzzling me. "Good to see you, girl. Let's go home."

I led her out of the stables into the night. It was a half moon, which gave me some light to see the great arched gates that was our exit. I led us through and into the dark earthen tunnel.

I hadn't actually used my magic in a while, and it felt good to use it now, like stretching out a muscle after a long day. I checked the tunnel and the remaining path through the mountains for any signs of life. Travelling by night wasn't ideal, but that was how I'd started this trip. I supposed it was poetic that I'd leave by it too.

Opal's magic shimmered around me in a comforting way, and we rode silently through the mountains. We travelled through the night, and by the time dawn reached us, we were well into the Temari forest.

We were going home.

W e rested off the track beside a familiar stream, and I was able to sleep under Opal's illusory shield, huddled into the purple cloak Geravie and Altara had gifted me. It was approaching Autumn now, and at night, there was now a bite to the forest air.

By midday, we were back to it, travelling through the Temari. It took me another day to get out of the cover of trees and to the first village.

A tiny wooden sign read "Albani Village: home of the sweet Lavender." I recognised its name and knew it to be the southernmost village in Lobrathia. When I had travelled with the fae, we had camped a few kilometres from this village in a wide grassy field. But I was alone this time and needed a warm meal to eat and somewhere to stay. Silentfoot needed a proper meal too. It was lucky I had a small amount of gold tucked away in my saddlebags. It was only a small town, but there was an inn called *The Lazy Duchess*. I wondered if the good Duke Garner knew they made fun of his wife this far south of his lands.

I made for the inn's stable, and a boy no older than eight ran out in a dirt-stained shirt and muck on his pants. I smiled at him as I got off Silentfoot and prodded Opal back into my pocket. I'd kept my male appearance for good measure but returned my ears to their regular rounded human form.

"Name?" he squeaked, expertly taking the reins from me.

I'd have to use a different one here. My mind cast around and found purchase on the town signboard I'd just seen. "Uh, Lavvy Smith."

He nodded and led Silentfoot away as I headed into the inn. Opal squeaked excitedly from inside my cloak.

"Shh," I warned, but I knew she was just excited about the food. A happy innkeeper in a purple apron took one look at me and showed me her upstairs rooms, and offered me a bath. I thanked her for both, and Opal and I bathed then ate a hearty meal in our room.

The bed was a little lumpy, but it did the job because I went to sleep immediately.

I woke up in the middle of the night to the sound of a woman wailing in the distance. I sat bolt upright in bed, my head cocked and listening.

The wail came again, followed by a deep-throated grunt. I knew that sound.

A woman was giving birth.

I changed my clothes in a flash. Opal woke with a croon and leaped onto my shoulder.

"There'll be a demon nearby," I hissed to her. "We have to hurry."

"Mmm-hmm!" she warbled in assent.

I was already out of the dark tavern when I realised I still looked like a man. No one was going to be letting an unknown man into their birthing room.

Swearing in a way that would have made Agatha proud, I strode down the road, muttering to Opal.

"We'll look awfully suspicious hanging outside the birthing room, Ope. Make it so no one will see us."

Opal obliged, her shimmering magic falling around us in a manner that was practically ritual by now.

I followed the sounds, and sure enough, I found the odd one out, the only house brightly lit with luminous quartz-zlights..

The birthing woman grunted deeply, followed by a shriek. I scouted around the perimeter of the house, on the lookout for any skulking demons. There were none. Arishnie said that no one else would be able to see the demons, just me and anyone else with magic. I couldn't very well barge in there with a sword, illusion or not. They would all think something foul was afoot, that foul thing being me. I couldn't afford to let any demon inside the house at all.

"Carefully. Carefully," a woman said softly. "Just breathe, my love. The head is just there."

The confident coo of a midwife who could see that a baby's head was about to be born.

The birthing mother groaned. "I can't, I can't!"

"All is well! Don't push now. Just breathe!"

I narrowed my eyes and summoned my sword. With a small burst of light, she appeared in my hand, her heavy feel comforting my pounding heart.

"Keep an eye out, Opal," I whispered. "I don't want to miss it."

"There we go!" laughed the midwife.

A newborn baby gave a wet, gargling cry. I smiled at Opal. It was always the best sound.

And then I saw it

It was hunched and gangling, pale skinned and snarling. As if it had done this a hundred times before, it was headed straight towards the cottage at a rapid pace. I stilled, suddenly wishing Arishnie was here. This would be my first ever kill and I didn't know what killing a creature would have me feeling like. I was midwife, life was my domain. But at the same time, it was life that I was protecting. Opal leapt into the shadows of the house. Now, it was just me and my astral blade.

I strode towards it, gripping my sword. Its gleaming eyes met mine through the dark of the night and a slight confusion crossed its face. It had never been *seen* before. I scowled, ready for blood. "Come and meet your death, demon."

Its surprise gone, it snarled and lunged at me, clawed hands outstretched. It was fast, but I was faster. I struck it in the chest, and it shrieked, reaching for my face with sharp black claws. I retreated, pulling my sword out, and, in one swing, beheaded it. Its head and body thudded onto the dirt ground and dissolved. I stared at the charred patch of earth. I had just killed my first demon.

"Did you hear that?" a nervous voice asked from inside the house. "Franklin, go and take a look."

Filled with rippling adrenaline, I signalled to Opal, huddled under the eaves of the birthing house. Her magic shimmer around me just as the door to the house opened.

Panting, I gazed at Opal, holding out my hand. She jumped right into it. I evaporated my sword and held her up to my cheek to give her a kiss. Yellow quartz light spilled out onto the stoop. A man in his late twenties peered outside. He turned his head left, then right, and then shut the door.

"It was nothing," he called. "Must be Jon's tomcat."

"That was my first kill, Ope," I whispered. But I remembered everything Arishnie had told me. There'd be more. A baby had twenty-four hours to have its magical essence taken away. There might be more tonight and then again tomorrow night.

I began my guard.

ONLY WHEN THE SUN CLEARED THE HORIZON DID I HEAD BACK TO bed, bone-weary. I'd taken down another demon, and that had been the end of them. But this was the countryside. There wouldn't be as many pregnant women here to give the demons reason to prowl about in larger numbers. I was sure there would be more of them as we got closer to the city.

Rosali, the innkeeper, was bustling about as I went in, but under Opal's protection, I trudged up the stairs unseen and we threw ourselves back into bed.

That evening, Opal and I had a dinner of bread and meat and resumed our guard of the new mother's cottage. At just after midnight, at the twenty-four-hour mark, I got a peek inside the house when someone opened a window. A sweet-faced, pink newborn rested in the crook of his mother's arms, both sleeping in a peaceful bubble of their own exhaustion. I mentally looked within the baby and spotted a tiny core of magic seated at his crown and grinned to myself.

"We did it, Ope," I whispered. "That's one more human soul with magic."

Opal crooned, and I went back to the stables, woke the stableboy sleeping on a bale of hay to tell him I was leaving.

Silentfoot, Opal, and I headed out of town and rode into

the night. The cart-worn roads were quiet, and it took me a another whole day to get to the next village.

It became routine for me then. By day I slept in village inns, and by night I prowled their streets with my sword in hand and Opal's magic around me. Each village had at least one demon lurking after dark, whether they had birthing mothers or not. I made it my aim to get rid of each one, and I was successful every time. Demons varied in shape and form and how good they were at fighting, but they were all unprepared for me, having gone so long without having a predator in the human realm. They were easy to destroy and one by one, as each fell by my hand, my confidence grew.

We travelled across the countryside, and as we got closer to Quartz City, the townsfolk got more and more agitated with news of the capital being taken over by the fae. The night before I knew I was going to arrive in the city, it was the full moon. I stepped outside and waited for Arishnie to find me.

Her transparent face was grim, her eyes tight around a hardened mouth.

"I flew over the capital," she said. "It seems a bit of a mess."

"Great," I said darkly. "For good news, I've killed a good number of demons on my way here."

She cast me a proud smile, and emotion rose up my gut, scalding and intense. Arishnie might have been my mother's age when she passed away, and the look on her face was all I'd ever hoped to see on my mother's.

"But my absence has come at a cost." I said dully. "My home city has been taken over by the Black Court. My father is probably dead. Who knows what they're doing to the humans?" I took a deep breath as hot-blooded anger and fear tried to overwhelm me. I didn't know any of that for sure, of course. They could very well have held my father hostage until I was found. I told Arishnie so, and she clucked her tongue.

"It's all a part of a great war. They have to be stopped."

"The fae haven't tried to invade the capital in thirty years!" I whispered in frustration. We were standing by a fountain in the town square, but all was quiet this late into the night. "The last time, they just wanted the quarry. This is all my fault."

Arishnie bristled. "You did your duty, Saraya, even if others won't see that at first."

"But what about my duty as a princess? It's always clashed with my midwifery. I...I don't know what's going to come of this."

"You'll do what you do best, Saraya."

"And what's that?" I fought to keep the anger from my voice.

"You'll watch, you'll learn, then you'll fight."

I looked at her until my eyes swam with tears. I pinched the end of my nose in frustration, willing my tears not to fall.

"You have work to do, Saraya," said my mentor gently. "You are the sword that guards the vulnerable. The shield that protects in the night. The guardian of human potential."

I took a shaky breath as Arishnie's words fell over me like a veil. She was right, this was far more important than anything I'd ever come across. In my heart, I knew I was doing the right thing, even if it was the most difficult path. My mother would have said the same. It was the Ellythian way.

"I am. I know. I'll do what needs to be done. I'll do what's right."

"And that," said Arishnie, smiling at me, "is how a warrior midwife speaks."

The next day, I arrived in the capital.

23

SARAYA

Under Opal's protection, the three of us arrived in Quartz City at sunset. Heavy storm clouds circled the palace, black and grey on the cusp of a storm.

I bristled because they reminded me of one person. Drake Silverhand.

But he didn't know my father's family motto used a storm as inspiration. *Lightning does not yield.*

Up on the battlements of the city wall, I spied a familiar form lounging across a ledge, looking out at the surrounding lands. It was Drake's huge, muscular companion. In place of my father's city guard stood tall, muscled fae warriors dressed in all black, a dragon with its wings spread painted over their chest armour. My heart stuttered in my own chest. Hearing about the city being taken over was one thing, but to see fae standing on the walls as if they owned the place? It made me livid. I gripped Silentfoot's reins tightly, and she whickered with nerves.

Stranger still was the fact that there was barely any traffic going through the gates. In front of us was one cart, which looked like it held a farmer's wares, but otherwise, the streets beyond were empty. It was like the day I had left when everyone had been told to go into lockdown. It looked like the fae preferred it to control the humans this way.

A pair of fae guards stood at the entrance, and I thanked my lucky stars that my man-disguise was solid enough to trick fae eyes. As I came up to the gate, Drake's huge companion climbed down off the battlements and gestured to me while another warrior sat at a desk with parchment and quill poised at the ready.

"Name and business?" he asked, looking me up and down.

I looked down at him from my saddle, stroking my beard out of habit. "Lavvy Smith, come to see my grandmother, Agatha Penrose. She's the head midwife in the city."

"We know her," said the fae warrior darkly, a pulling at his collar as if it were too tight. I noticed fine brown scars at the base of his muscled throat and wondered where he'd gotten them. "New city rules are in place. Humans are to remain in their houses unless obtaining food."

I frowned. The city's economy would be destroyed if they kept this up. "For how long?"

"As long as it takes to rectify the situation. Go on in." He turned away.

Suppressing a scowl, I trotted through the gates.

I needed to understand what had happened here before I went to the palace to see what had become of my father, and there was only one person I trusted with my entire being.

Agatha would no doubt be in her ramshackle townhouse in the Sticks, so I headed straight there. I left Opal outside, invisible, but perched on Silentfoot's head to keep watch. Standing on her doorstep, I decided it was time to let go of my disguise. Aggressively, I commanded the follicles of hair on my face to drop out of my skin. With a hurricane of fire on my cheeks, I felt every single hair comply. I staggered on the street, hissing in pain as I watched my beard fall onto the road in black clumps. Then I reversed every other slight alteration I had made, shrinking my nose back to its usual size and getting rid of the excess eyebrow hair.

I patted a cool hand against my face, trying to reduce the inflammation I could feel popping up like a thousand angry bee stings. It felt odd to feel the cool dusk breeze on my cheeks after so many many months. I'd miss the beard just a little bit. I'd have nothing to contemplatively stroke now.

I didn't bother knocking as I opened Agatha's lock with my mind and walked right in.

She was sitting at her fireplace, drinking a cup of herbal tea. She didn't look up when I walked in.

"Decided to come back, did you?" she croaked.

I couldn't help but smile as I realised how much I'd missed her bone-dry humour. "How did you know it was me?"

"Your smell. Magic always has a smell."

"I hope it's a nice smell." I came to sit on the red patterned couch opposite her.

Her blue eyes pierced right through my core. "Urgh, you look awful."

"I know. I've been…far…and back."

"You look different."

I rubbed my sore cheek.

"More muscled," Agatha clarified.

Observing my old midwife mentor, her long silvery hair, perfectly combed, her patchwork cardigan warm around her —some things hadn't changed. Agatha was always the same, no matter what difficulty befell her or her patients. That's what made her the best midwife in the city. It was something I don't think I could ever muster. "There's something I have to tell you, Agatha."

She put her flower patterned cup and saucer down on the doily covered table next to her, a yellow quartz light giving her eye an eerie sort of glow.

"Have you heard of the Order of Temari?"

She froze in her seat, recognition, marking her face. Of course, she had. She remained silent while I told her my story from the start when Arishnie had come to me in my dream and then led me to the seaside temple. When I finished, I stood and summoned my sword. She leaned back in her armchair, blinking at it.

"When I was a young girl," Agatha rasped as I sat back down, "I apprenticed under an elderly midwife called Ruth-ann. She was a cranky old thing. At the end of her days, I sat with her on her deathbed. She'd had no children of her own, of course. Lived to serve the people, like me. She told me about the old days, the Order of Temari, and the atrocities the warrior midwives suffered. I didn't know whether it was deathbed talk or real. But I never forgot it."

"It's very real. And I've made a war happen because of it. The fae are here because of me. I have to fix this." I clenched my jaw. "I'm going to go to the palace tonight."

She nodded. "I thought you might."

"I don't know what's going to happen. But I know one thing. The fae are the enemy. And somehow, I need to get rid of them. How did the invasion happen?"

Agatha took a sip of her tea and spoke matter-of-factly, seemingly unperturbed by the chaos going on around her. "They came at night, took the palace like sweets from a baby.

216

The town crier made the notice in the morning, the big, brauny fae in armour standing there waving the bell. They said that you'd run away and had forsaken your blood contract. They said they were going to hunt you down, and until then, we're not allowed to leave our houses except to go to market."

"It's a strange thing, though," she said. "The fae king isn't here. It's just that dark-looking fae, the one that looks like he's gonna kill you where you stand."

Drake, she meant the Black Drake. "I guess he does the king's dirty work."

"Be ready, girl. It might not be what you expect in there."

I stood. "I learned to fight them, Agatha. I know what they're like."

"He's different," she said, searching in her cardigan and bringing out a hand rolled cigarette. "Put the kettle on before you leave, will you? If I'm going to be sitting here a while, thinking about your exploits, I might as well keep drinking."

As I left, I saw her spike her tea with the Grey Dove whiskey she kept on the floor beside her armchair.

I SWUNG MYSELF BACK UP ON SILENTFOOT AND SETTLED OPAL ON my shoulder. This was going to be difficult. I didn't know what awaited me inside the castle. And what was my plan anyway? Storm in and do what? Say that I'd returned to marry Daxian?

No, I wasn't going to marry him. He was my enemy. *They* were the enemy of all humans. But to bring about war to the entire human kingdom? How could our military forces possibly fight the fae? I didn't think it could be done. It would have to be subversive. I would have to destroy them from the inside. I knew what I had to do.

I trotted Silentfoot through the main road, thanking my lucky stars that I knew this city inside and out. I took her to Madame Yolande's brothel and stabled her there, filling her a bag of oats. I kissed her on the nose, and Opal and I took off at a jog under a blanket of her magic.

"Let me show you my home, Ope," I whispered, jogging towards my secret entrance. "This is how I used to get in and out without being seen by the queen."

The queen. Both my stepmother and father were now prisoners of the fae. I wondered how they were treating them. It was lucky I'd thought to get Altara out of the city. At least she would be safe in Ellythia, away from the conflict.

I clicked open the entrance and jogged through the tunnel. When I reached the entrance to the servant's tunnel, I took a deep breath and checked the space beyond with my mind. It was clear. I clambered through, a sudden prickling feeling enveloping me. My home was no longer mine. It had been taken over, and I now had to sneak into it like a thief.

My stepmother's voice echoed in my ears. *Sneaking back in, are we Saraya?*

Well, yes, I was, and those years practising would now serve me well. I bet she was doing nothing at all to save us.

Your stepmother is not human.

I shivered as the Kraasputin's voice sung in my ear like a fell tune. But my father was my priority, and I needed to see that he was alright. So I headed first to his suite. Even though I was basically invisible under Opal's illusion, Arishnie had warned me that there was a chance a fae could figure out an illusion was present, especially if I was moving directly past them. I moved swiftly through the servants' passageways, where there was no sign of any human or fae.

I chose a servant's entrance that came out directly into my father's bed-chamber. I felt for movement in the room and, sure enough, felt shielded minds right through the door. I abruptly recoiled, coming back into the tunnel. A well-trained fae mind would be able to feel a foreign presence probing around the room. I couldn't risk having a look around, even mentally. No, I'd have to go in the old-fashioned way.

I moved back to a corridor that might not be guarded. How many fae could they have brought with them after all? Not enough to man every aspect of the palace, that was for sure. I checked a potential corridor entrance and found it to be clear. This one came out from behind a tapestry, so I sent Opal out first, in case anyone was watching from afar. She returned and gave me a nod, and I swiftly stepped through, closing the door behind me.

Opal jumped back onto my shoulder, and we resumed our slow jog to Father's suite. I looked around a corner, jogged through, then peered around the next, which was the hallway that led directly to the king's suite. A spike of fear lanced through my spine. A line of fae warriors stood guard down this corridor.

I let out a silent breath and glanced at Opal, pressing a finger to my lips. Then down the corridor, I crept. I moved slowly, knowing that Opal's illusion left a rippling demarcation where her illusion met the natural air. If I moved too fast, they'd see that ripple very clearly. I stepped slowly, pressing my heel onto the glossy marble tile, then my toe, and continued on.

The fae warriors did nothing but stoically look forward. The only problem was, at the end of the corridor was a door.

Cursing at my lack of forethought, my mind raced to come up with a solution. But I didn't even get there.

"That's a lumzen construction if I've ever seen one," drawled a voice.

I whirled around, only to find the Black Drake himself was leaning against a column, his eyes narrowed and trained directly upon me. "Your mistake was thinking that no one was watching the servant's entrances and that Slade wouldn't recognise you. Reveal yourself before I make you."

The fae guard all drew their weapons and turned towards me. I was an idiot to think I could enter unnoticed.

Letting out a resigned breath, I carefully picked up Opal from my shoulder and whispered in her ear, "Hide, Opal, but keep nearby."

She nodded, a worried expression on her face before she jumped onto the marble tile and zipped off into the distance. As her magic dissolved around me and I became seen by the fae warriors, I watched as Drake Silverhand's lips twitched into a smirk.

"Look who it is," he sounded extremely amused. "It's Sam Sourbottom."

2 4
SARAYA

It took me a full second to realise what he'd called me. Then my hand flew to my face, and I remembered I was back to my female self. Icy surprise shot through me. I stared at him.

Drake's handsome face surveyed me and missed nothing. "Or should I say, Princess Saraya?"

I blinked at him, trying to look unimpressed. "How did you know?"

"You could never hide from me, Saraya."

Heat rose up in me as his voice caressed my name in the most unexpected way. I couldn't gauge the strange note in his voice, but it left me feeling extremely unsettled.

Stony-faced, I crossed my arms. "So am I your prisoner now?"

His face was a mask of happiness, and I couldn't believe he looked like he was enjoying this. "Just because you bested the fae prince doesn't mean you call the shots around here, Princess."

"That's exactly right," I shot back. "I made him fall on his ass."

The fae guards shifted in surprise around me, and I didn't think the Black Drake's grin could get any more disgusting, but it did. "She's got a potty mouth."

Stay away from him, Emery had said. *He's a psycho.*

I was itching to draw my sword and swipe through these warriors. I had just spent a week cutting down demons in the dark, so I knew I could do it. "You have no idea who I am," I growled. "You don't know anything about me."

To my surprise, his smile faltered. "You're right. I don't." A beat passed between us, then he said, "I want to know why you ran."

I rolled my eyes. "A better question would be, how did you make that amazing beard, Saraya? It's much better than anything I could grow." His eyes danced, but I continued, "Or a better question would be, why is Daxian such a jerk? I got away from the Kraasputin he set on me too."

His face darkened for the briefest moment before he nodded. "They're good questions."

"And why is everyone scared of you anyway?" I asked, having no idea why I was baiting him, but it just felt right. "You don't look so scary to me."

He smirked again and was in front of me so fast my head spun. He stared down at me, his scent like earth and wine, his hazel gaze so sharp I swore it saw right through to my beating heart. I hated to admit it, but he *did* look scary—more than any other fae I'd come across. There was more to him than met the eye and I knew it by the way my magic shifted inside of me. The hairs on my arms raised, and I suppressed a shiver, raising my chin to maintain eye contact with those hazel eyes. "Nup, still don't see it."

"You're right on many counts, Saraya," his voice was so low I felt it rumble through me, but I didn't dare break eye contact. "You are my prisoner. Have you ever been to the dungeons under your blessed palace?"

I narrowed my eyes. "You wouldn't."

"Oh, I would." He stepped away from me. "Guards."

But I wouldn't have it. I summoned my sword, and it appeared in a flash of blue light. The warriors who were about to advance on me stopped in their tracks. Drake stilled.

"How do you have an astral sword?" his voice was dark as night and as cold as frost.

"None of your business." I hissed. "But if they come towards me, I'll kill them all. I know who you are. I know *what* you are. I know what you're doing to the humans. Your secret is out."

He cocked his head. "Stand down," he shot at his guards. They stepped back, retaking their positions against the wall.

He thought for a moment—calm, with his tattooed hands behind his back as I stood there, on guard with my gleaming sword.

"One of your maids is pregnant," he said softly. "Beautiful, waif-thin, red hair?"

I flinched. *Tembry.* "Excuse me?"

How was Tembry pregnant? She'd had a lover, a captain in the army, but I assumed she'd been more careful.

"I thought you might want to know that before..." he waved his hand to indicate his guard. "And you forgot one thing. *I'm* here."

Anger rose up in me like fresh lava. "Wouldn't stop me from trying."

To my chagrin, his rugged face twisted with delight. "I'm sure. But you wouldn't win. You know that." He flexed his tattooed, claw-tipped fingers, and I grimaced. He was right. Of course, he was right. *Goddess help me.*

"I'm not going to your dungeon."

"Not suited to Princess, is it? But you've been living with dirty fae noble's sons for the past three months, can't be that different."

"I want to see Tembry. You'll bring her to me, in my old rooms. And where is my father?"

"The human king is…fine in his rooms. Though no one told me he's brain-addled."

I levelled my sword at him as fury swept through me. No one spoke about my family without respect. "Watch your mouth, fae scum."

He nodded slowly, eyes wary on my face. "And no one can find your stepmother. I was properly thwarted on that count. I'll give her credit for that."

Surprise filled me like water bursting from a dam. How had she gotten away while Father had managed to stay here? That seemed…so much like her, actually. The words of the Kraasputin slithered into my mind. *Your stepmother is not human.*

I sighed. "Where's Tembry?"

"I'll take you to her."

He turned on his heel, and I had no choice but to return my sword to the ether and follow him.

We walked in silence to the servant's quarters, where five fae warriors were standing guard.

"Are they getting fed?" I asked. "Are they allowed out for fresh air?"

He glanced at me in mild surprise. "Yes to the first, no to the second."

"You'll allow them out."

He stopped and turned to face me. "You misunderstand. You're a prisoner here."

"I understand exactly what is going on, *Drake Silverhand*." I snapped, my anger making my entire body taut. The corner of his mouth lifted, and that only served to infuriate me. "What are you doing exactly? The whole point of this invasion was to find me, wasn't it? So why haven't you taken me straight to your King? To my fiancé for punishment?"

Indeed, what punishment was I in for?

"Wyxian is on his way here, as is Daxian. In the meantime, you are *my* prisoner, not theirs."

I briefly wondered why this commander spoke so familiarly of his own royal family. "And when they *do* get here? What then?"

A tic pulsed in the plane of his jaw. "Then you will be theirs to do as they wish."

"No," I said firmly. "I am not anyone's property, Drake. I am a princess, and you will treat me as such. *Your* princess, in fact."

"You're not married yet," he said smoothly, making for the servant's door. "You're not my…anything."

He turned the handle and held the door open for me with a raised eyebrow. I strode in, and I was met with a shriek. There was a blur of red hair, and someone lunged towards me with a cry. I was pulled into a fierce hug, the sound of Tembry's sobbing filling my ears.

"Oh, Saraya!" she sobbed. "I'm sorry, what happened? I'm so sorry."

"Oh, Tem, it's alright," I murmured into her hair. A rounded tummy sat between us, and I pulled away from her to have a look. Surely, she was almost term by now. But I'd only been away for four and a half months. I frowned. "Tem? You look *very* pregnant."

My maid and friend's pale face went crimson, her red-rimmed eyes blinking over and over. "I know, I'm sorry," she whispered. "I didn't even know for a while. I thought it was the stress that made my monthly bleeding stop."

My mind clicked into midwife mode. "You must've been at least four months when I left? Or just under?" Tembry had always preferred looser dresses, and to think on it, that day of my engagement, she *had* almost fainted.

She shook her head. "I don't even know."

The door shut behind me, and there was a definite click of a key. I whirled around and ran to the closed door trying the handle and finding it locked.

"Hey!" I thumped my fist against the wood.

A thump came back. "No noise!" a guard shouted.

I swore under my breath and felt for the lock in my mind. It was surrounded by the rippling sparkle of fae magic. I scoffed, and I pushed at it. It wouldn't budge, and I'd never seen this type of magic before. It would take me time to break it. I wondered where Opal had gotten to and hoped she had either followed me or was safely hidden somewhere.

So I sighed and turned around. Blythe and Altara's maid, Lucy, stood behind Tembry. Blythe rushed at me, and she hugged me so hard I'd thought she might crack a rib.

"Tell me everything," I commanded.

The maids had been sleeping in this room for over a week. They were allowed out three times a day to use the latrines and then escorted back by no less than two fae warriors. Their meagre meals were brought to them once a day by the kitchen staff, also under guard. They informed me that the rest of the palace staff had either been sent back to their homes in the city or shut off in rooms like this one.

I didn't really tell them my story. How could I? Even if they believed it, telling them about the demons wouldn't be a good idea. Not with Tembry pregnant and every single one of the maids already thinking they were going to die. They seemed content to think that I had just gotten scared and run off and then returned out of guilt. It was the easier explanation.

But none of this worried me as much as the fact that I felt Tembry's uterus giving preparatory contractions. Part of it was her nerves, I'm sure, and women in extreme distress often went into labour earlier than they would have otherwise. And if anything gave a person distress, it was being held captive by the people you were raised to believe were monsters. Who *were* monsters as far as I was concerned.

My fingers itched for my sword as night fell around the city. How many demons were prowling around, looking for prey? I wanted to go out there and kill them. I needed to be out there. Instead, my stomach churned as, stuck in a cramped room, waiting for that prick Daxian to come here and claim me as his unwilling bride and probably punish me for escaping. I had only just escaped from his Kraasputin by the skin of my teeth.

Around the time I would have expected dinner to arrive, there was a knock at the door, and it promptly opened. I had been ready to rush at the guard, but it wasn't an ordinary guard that came through the door. It was one of Drake's companions. The tall, dancer-looking fae, with long blond hair and black armour, stepped boldly in. He gave me a sensuous once over and smiled.

"Princes Saraya," his voice was as silky as a courtesan, and I wondered whether he had been one, at a certain stage in his life. I had been around enough sex-workers to know that particular look in their eye.

"Yes?"

"Drake requests your presence at dinner tonight. He asks that you wear appropriate clothing. I'm going to escort you to your rooms. You may bring a lady in waiting."

That silken voice, that gracious demeanour. He was no brutish fae warrior.

"No." I crossed my arms and immediately regretted my words. I desperately needed a bath. I smelled like horse and soil. "Actually...fine."

He raised an elegant blond eyebrow and smiled, showing straight, white teeth. "Good choice, Princess," he purred.

I met eyes with Tembry, and she nodded, hurrying forward. The fae warrior raised his brows at my choosing of the heavily pregnant maid but said nothing.

"What's your name?" I asked.

"How rude of me," he said, genuinely shocked. He gave me a gallant bow. "I am Lysander of the water lily. A pleasure to meet you, Your Highness. And—" he leaned towards me, and I was surprised to note he did actually smell like flowers, "I—particularly enjoyed your performance at your engagement ceremony."

"I don't know if I'd call it a performance," I mused. "But thank you. It was as unexpected as your presence was."

His eyes flashed in amusement. "He might not look like it, but the Black Drake does like to have a little fun. But come, that devil will be cross with us if we delay his dinner."

He led us out and into the palace proper, and I thought I'd better take the opportunity to ask him a few questions. "Lysander of the water lily," I mused, "is it normal for fae to be named after flowers?"

He gave me a wicked grin. "Only bastards. But the courtesans get the prettiest ones."

Tembry flushed next to me, and I suppressed my own smile. I had been right. But I only said, "Interesting."

"Oh, it is. Though I cannot say I have been with a human woman before." He gave me a curious look, and I pursed my lips.

"Nor have I."

He chuckled. "I imagine not."

"Have you known Drake long?" I asked casually.

He gave me an amused look to say he knew that I was poking for information. "Yes, since we were teenagers. He won me in a card game, actually."

I almost choked. *"Won you?"*

He smiled as if it were a fond memory. "It was a dramatic game, let me tell you. Oh—don't look at me like that. I'm sure your people have told you all about how the fae are cruel people. We can be, that much is fact. Anyway, I had been sold since I was quite young in the black markets that run through the demon kingdoms. At the time, Drake had been Princess Celetine's champion, and she had her eye on me. Drake was a brilliant gambler, of course, and won me." Lysander glanced at me. "He cheated naturally, but he was the best because he never got caught. Princess Celentine took me under her wing for years, a smart woman of Eclipse Court. Brilliant actually, if it weren't for her vicious brothers who got her married off to that old porcupine Guttlechest."

I kept my mouth shut as he prattled on, revealing potentially valuable information. So Drake was good at gambling and liked to cheat. Well, he was no better than Daxian, then. I ground my teeth as we got to my old room. Lysander opened the door with a flourish. With a pang, I noticed all the furniture had been covered in protective white sheets. It had never occurred to me that I'd ever be back here. I turned to the blond courtesan turned warrior.

"Who's the other fae warrior you and Drake travel with?"

"Oh, Slade?"

"Slade." I nodded slowly. He definitely looked like a Slade. "What's his story?"

Lysander gave me a coy look. "Oh, we have to be drunk to tell that one, Princess." He bowed. "I will stand guard and ensure no vagrants enter your sacred princess bathing room." He indicated my bathroom with his eyes and wriggled his brows, then turned to Tembry. "Make sure it's a nice gown." Then promptly left through the door and shut it behind him.

I gave a long sigh and glanced about my room—it was as if a ghost had lived here a whole lifetime ago. The last time I'd been in here, I had been livid with rage when Glacine had stopped me from going to see Bluebell. I had been captive then, and once again I was a captive. The backs of my eyes burned, but I shook it away and made to set about our baths. I made Tembry go first, as I knew her hips were bound to be aching her by this point. She put up a fight, but I wasn't having it. Secretly, I hoped it would relax her tightening uterus and calm her down. As she bathed, I sorted out some clothes for her and the other maids because it had looked and smelled to me like they'd been wearing the same dresses for a week.

I heard Tembry draining the tub and refilling it for me, and I opened the wardrobe where my more beautiful dresses were kept. I couldn't believe that bastard of a commander wanted me to dress up for dinner. Like he was some king that I needed to please. Well, seeing my beloved home being taken over had put me in a barbaric mood, and so I would sure show him.

Back at the Academy, he'd seen me as Sam Sourbottom and apparently, had known the entire time who I was. I needed a little revenge on my part. Especially considering that day, he'd met me in that goddess-forsaken bathroom. I'd been scared out of my mind that he was going to find me out, and all along, during that conversation, he *had* known and let me go. Had let me fight Daxian the next day. I didn't understand him at all.

After I took my turn to bathe, I pointed to Tembry what I wanted to wear, and her eyes nearly popped out of her head.

"Are you sure, my lady?"

"Oh yes." I grinned.

She helped me into my dress and then piled all my ebony hair into a beauty of curls on my head.

"Oh goddess," Tembry whispered as we both looked at my reflection in my full-length, gilded mirror.

"It'll do." My grin was sly.

I'd been dressing as a man for four months, and I had sorely missed being a woman. Altara had this dress made for me on my seventeenth birthday, and at the time, it had been a secret joke of ours. A costume for us to laugh at, and although we were too old for playing dress-ups, it was something that had still made us giggle.

It was a deep crimson satin and clung to me like a dream. Dangerously low cut, it showed the curve of my ample breasts in the most obnoxious way. I had been binding them down for so long that having them out made me feel like a completely new person. And better still, there was a glorious slit up the side that came up to the top of my thigh. I loved every silken inch of it.

I mentioned this type of dress to Altara after one trip to a brothel for a birth one night. I'd been stunned at how a scandalous dress could have looked so beautiful. Little had I known that Altara, in her brilliant sense of humour, thought to gift the same sort to me, with a little princess touch of the finest material money could buy.

"Let's not forget a tiara," I said with a start. I chose a gold and ruby set that included a diadem, necklace, and earrings. "He needs to remember that this is *my* home that he's in."

"Yes, Your Highness," Tembry said, frowning faintly behind me. "I think you look wonderful. Imagine if your step-mother saw."

I turned curiously when I saw her frown in the mirror, and she abruptly straightened into a smile, rubbing her tummy. I glanced down at her heavily pregnant form and back up to her anxious face.

"I'll be here with you, Tem," I said gently. "We'll make sure it goes right, together." She smiled up sadly at me, and I knew she was thinking about her captain lover and his whereabouts in this whole thing. I'd have to track him down in the midst of this invasion. They had to have restrained our armed forces in some way.

There was a rapid knock on the door, and Tembry hurried to open it. Lysander's grin faded when he saw me.

"Dear God," he whispered.

"How do I look?" I said seriously.

"Like a dream." He breathed. "Like a dream within a dream. Like a flower within a dream. Like a—"

"Oh, do stop it," I chided. "Take me to the Black Drake. Let's see what he has to say."

He looked back up at me then, from where he'd been staring at my chest. His lips spread into a grin. "You are a clever thing, aren't you?"

"Hm, sometimes. Let's go. I have a war to discuss."

Lysander bowed, and he led us to the royal private dining room that I had spent my entire life eating in with my family. The two fae guards standing by the open double doors shifted in surprise, and I saw both of them sweep their eyes up and then down my form. Satisfied, I said goodbye to Tembry as one of the guards made to escort her back to the other maids, fresh clothes in hand. Lysander behind me, I entered with my chin in the air, my spine straight, and my hips set to saunter.

When I entered, the massive Slade had his back to me, pouring wine, while Drake was standing by the window, drinking from a gold chalice. He paused mid-chalice-raise and stared at me before proceeding to drink deeply. *My father's* chalice, I reminded myself. He never took his eyes off me.

I sauntered over to him, the same way I'd seen *him* saunter so many times. And then Slade turned from the wall, taking a swig from his own chalice, but when he saw me, he choked, spluttering into his goblet.

I deigned to give him an unimpressed look, then turned my attention to Drake, who was still staring at me, not at my chest to his credit, but my face. His eyes flicked to my diadem.

"Pretty," he said.

He only said one word but for some goddess forsaken reason it made my heart flutter. I had to keep it together. So I made a non-committal sound at the back of my throat. "I'm hungry," I announced loudly. "I haven't eaten since this morning." I turned and appraised the dining table, and I saw it was laden with three roast chickens, loaves of fresh bread, and various sautéed vegetables. I thought about my poor kitchen staff working under duress. "I do hope you've been treating my staff well."

Drake's lip quirked up. "They're *my* staff now."

"Are they?" I said loftily, turning my back on him to sit on the other side of the table. I didn't realise everyone in the room had gotten quiet until I turned back around, my hand ready to pull out my own seat.

But I paused when I saw that the tension in the room had suddenly changed. All three fae eyes, Slade's black eyes, Lysander's blue eyes, and Drake's hazel, were all staring at me with an acute focus.

I searched their gazes, one by one, but couldn't place what was wrong. "What?"

Drake strode towards me and came to stand behind the seat to my left, at the head of the table. As he placed his goblet down, I swore I could feel his fae magic pulsing with a tempest of red hot anger.

He glowered at me, his eyes simmering, but the rest of his body was calm. His voice was barely restrained rage. "Who did that to you?"

Taken aback by his reaction, I blinked at him.

Then his eyes flicked towards my back, and my very soul froze. The back of my dress dipped low around the base of my spine. That was why I'd never worn it outside my room. I had forgotten every single one of my stepmother's lash marks that was seared into the skin on my back—my only weakness —was now on display to my enemies. *That* was why Tembry had been frowning behind me. I had come in here thinking I was Princess of this place, my nose up in the air, trying to seduce this warrior. Only to be humiliated. The backs of my eyes pricked as an embarrassed heat rose up in me. Stupid. Stupid little girl. I was so stupid. What was I even doing here? Trying to negotiate with my invaders? Embarrassment shot through me like a burning whip. I felt each and every scar on my back with a sudden and terrible clarity.

I did the only thing I could do. I ignored him.

I sniffed away the sudden sharpness in my throat and swallowed it down with brutal force. Ignoring the knife currently twisting in my gut, I pulled out the heavy wooden chair and sat in it.

"I'm hungry," I repeated, keeping my voice light. "I can't eat all these chickens all by myself."

Without a word, Slade and Lysander took a seat at the table. I watched them each pull a loaf of bread and a plate of roast chicken towards themselves. I served myself some vegetables, trying not to notice Drake glowering over us all. Finally, he silently took his seat and began eating, the wheel of runes and the lines of black tattoos on the backs of his hands coiling and bunching around his silverware. He'd taken his silver claws off at some stage.

We ate in silence for a solid ten minutes.

"They'll arrive tomorrow," Drake finally broke the silence, wiping his mouth on a napkin like a gentleman. "Wyxian and Daxian."

Again, I wondered why he didn't call them by their titles. He behaved as if he were equal to them, a part of their family. Perhaps it was a fae hierarchy thing.

"They'll be surprised to see me here, I'm sure," I said, sipping my wine.

Drake studied me with hazel eyes that seemed to glow under the quartz lights but said nothing.

"What will they do with me?"

"Ask you questions."

"Hm." I met his stare, eye for eye. Slade and Lysander looked between the two of us.

Suddenly, Drake stood and offered me a hand. "Shall we?"

"Where are we going?"

He smiled, slow and mischievous. "To take a turn about the palace."

I felt the blood drain from my face. I had never really ever been alone with a man. I had been discouraged from it at all costs, taught from a young age that I should never *ever* find myself alone with an older man for my own safety. And here I was now, a legal adult, having travelled to the mountains alone and back again, spent four months in a dormitory with fae males, a fighter of demons.

And now, here with my breasts out, it all felt different. The thought of being alone with him, *outside* at night…I didn't quite know what to do. I would almost rather face the Kraasputin again. My confidence dissipated like a bubble bursting in the sun.

I'd taken so long to think those thoughts that Drake dropped his hand.

"Well," he said, brushing it off, "I—"

I stood abruptly. "I want to show you something."

Drake's handsome face showed no trace of surprise though I knew he would be. I pushed back my chair and turned my back, gritting my teeth as I did so, as I knew they'd be looking at my scars again. "Come on, don't keep me waiting."

26

DRAKE

I had been all over both fae realms, seen all manner of fae high queens, sirens, creatures made by the gods to lure men with lust.

And yet.

This young human woman was by far the most beautiful being I'd ever seen in my entire sorry life. My cold black heart stuttered in my chest the moment I'd seen her appear out of the lumzen illusion. And seeing her fight Daxian back at the Academy? My blood had boiled and come to life at the same time. It was like having clear vision after a long time in the dark.

Gods, I'd had enough blasted concussions as a child to know what blurry vision was like. I'd let the princess play her Sam Sourbottom game, curious about her motives, watching her from afar. She played a good trick, but I'd known that as soon as she'd heard word of me taking her palace that she'd come running back. All that was left for me to do was sit down and wait.

And then she'd come here tonight, in that goddess blessed

dress, hoping to raise some lust in me, no doubt, and it had bloody worked. I couldn't take my god-forsaken eyes off her. Her body was a gift from the goddess, but her *face*, the way her green eyes danced and seethed with each emotion, contemplated and seduced. I'd never seen anything like it. Much to my displeasure, she drew me in with every breath I took.

Then, when she'd turned around and bared those scars on her back, I thought I was going to murder someone, *anyone* right there and then. I wanted to hunt down the *creature* who had done it and taste their blood in my mouth. Tear them into so many pieces, no semblance of a body would be left.

She didn't want to tell me who had done it to her, but I was sure as hell going to find out. She couldn't keep that from me. Not when I had this boiling, madness-provoking rage at the sight of each scar. How many times had she been whipped? How many times had the princess of Lobrathia endured this torturous pain? And for what? I couldn't even imagine. The fae were cruel and cunning creatures, but I had never, in all my travels, seen a princess getting *whipped*.

And now, she was leading me away from the dining hall. I didn't even cast a glance back at Lysander and Slade—I knew they'd find their own entertainment tonight. Slade would never take another woman, not after what happened to his last love years ago, so he'd probably play quiet cards with our warriors.

And Lysander, odd, eccentric Lysander, was quite happy conversing with his new toy, a kitchen wench with 'amber eyes like sweet honey,' he'd said. He wouldn't even sleep with her. I knew him by now. He'd get to understand her first, learn what made her tick, her deepest desires, her most lofty dreams, her darkest secrets. *Then* he would make love to her

—give her the time of her life. Only then would he would be satiated, knowing another woman's entire being. He was a strange fae.

Princess Saraya, or Sam, had secrets of her own I needed to know. But I wanted her to tell me of her own accord. I didn't want to play a game. The Master of Games, so they used to call me, didn't want to play one, I mused. Oh, what my old mentor would say. So when I followed her out of that room and into the vast hallways of the place I now owned for the Black Court, I counted each of her scars and seared them into my memory for later. Right now, I lengthened my stride so I could walk beside her. She smelled like jasmine with a bit of agitation.

"Are you planning on finding a dark corner in which to murder me?" I asked, shoving my hands into my pockets if only to try and stave away the itching of the magical runes that bound me.

Her beautiful pink lips curved into a smile, and for some bizarre reason, my breath felt like fire in my chest.

"I am, actually," She said, so seriously that it made me tingle. "There are a number of potential spots I think you would find rather poetic."

I tore my gaze off her face before it consumed all of me. "Death can be poetic on many fronts," I mused and then immediately bit my tongue. Morbid thoughts were no conversations for a princess.

And yet, she'd done what she'd done—gone undercover as a male at the Academy and fought like a seasoned fae warrior. I'd known from the start she wasn't any run-of-the-mill royal and seeing Daxian thrown down like that almost soothed the white-hot anger of knowing she shared a dorm room with him.

Almost.

"You look dashing with a beard." I threw her a smirk, hoping she'd give me a clue as to how she'd done it.

She let herself smile before it fell away, and I observed her fine, bronzed features. Something I said hadn't sat well.

"What?" I asked. "Do you miss it?"

"Pardon?" she asked, affronted.

"Do you miss the beard?"

She choked back a laugh, stroking her chin. "Maybe. But tell me, do your kind enjoy stealing from humans?"

I turned her words over carefully in my mind. I felt the need to be honest with her. "I enjoy what I do, yes." But I couldn't let her know how depraved I was. That I enjoyed the hunting, the invading, the taking and consuming. How much it filled my veins with satisfaction like a drug. How it soothed the writhing monster inside of me.

She bristled beside me, and I knew she was angry. Which was fair considering I'd taken her home from her. Anyone would be angry. Fae had been angry at me before, for doing such a thing. Warfare was, after all, one of the many things I was good at.

Before I knew it, she came to a stop in a deserted, dusty corridor tiled with a mosaic pattern. She stood by the wall, and it took me a moment to realise she was indicating something.

"This is my mother," she said wistfully.

I glanced up at the massive oil painting. Royals and their fascination with paintings. Except this one was a portrait of a beautiful Ellythian woman, bronzed of skin, ebony hair, glowing green eyes that promised secrets under the moonlight. I looked back at the princess.

"She looks like you."

"Indeed," she said. "She died just five years after the portrait was made."

"How?" I frowned. I couldn't even think about how incredibly old my own mother was. But as little as I knew about humans, even I knew that they lived far longer than Queen Yasani's age was depicted in the brushstrokes.

"Poor health," the princess said. "I don't even know why I'm showing you this," she said. "But—" abruptly, she stopped, her gaze fixed upon something out the window opposite the painting.

She rushed to the glass, all but pressing her nose against it. She swore, and I smiled in delight. I stood a respectful distance behind her, looked over her head out the window, and saw a chinga demon stalking across the grounds, illuminated silver by the moon floating in the gap of my heavy storm clouds.

"Huh," I said, mildly surprised. "You see that demon?"

She growled in her throat, her fingers twitching like she—light flashed, and to my great shock, an astral sword appeared, diamond-sharp and thrumming with a power I could *feel* in through the air. And then she was off, sprinting down the corridor.

A primal drum beat through my core, and I ran after her.

She led me the quickest way she knew, down a series of steps, through a corridor, and out a back door into the cool autumn night. She sprinted on the gravel, down the length of the back aspect of the palace, her legs practically bare with each stride. It was lucky that the gown had a split that high.

We reached the side of the palace, turning the corner, and I got a bit of a kick running after her, like I was pursuing her. Doing what I do best, *hunting*. My nostrils flared as the familiar rush hit me, the wind on my face, the scent of my prey in my nose. I shook it out of my head. This was her hunt, I realised. I was just a spectator.

And then we reached the chinga demon, and I saw there were actually three prowling in the night, but I wasn't watching them. I was watching *her.*

She sprinted towards them, glowing sword in hand, a ferocious scowl on her face. They realised her intention with all the surprise of monsters that were not used to being prey. Their glowing red eyes widened as she struck, like silver lightning, fast and brutal. She beheaded one, stabbed another, and slashed the third. In seconds they had dissolved onto the ground.

It was the most beautiful thing I'd ever seen. She stood there panting under a glowing moon, her face not triumphant, but raging, like a wild, feral thing. Her shoulders moved with each breath, and she gripped her sword, scanning the grounds, ready for more. Then she saw me as if for the first time, standing there watching her, and her expression changed. She stalked towards me, frightening in the most wondrous way, a siren of the dark. Heat spread through me, fiery and blazing. My heart felt like it was the size of the moon.

"I want you to know something," she whispered, making gooseflesh erupt all over me. I leaned into her. "Those monsters that were sent by your people. I will kill *every single fucking one.*"

The primal rush I felt coarse through my body with all the force of a king tide caught me by surprise.

At that moment, I knew nothing else but the beauty of her form, the strength in her arms, and the fire burning in her eyes. And I believed every word she said.

27

SARAYA

The next day, Drake let me see my father. Something in him changed when he saw me kill those demons. I didn't understand it when he clearly knew what I could do with a sword. It wasn't like he was seeing me use one for the very first time. But I couldn't spare it any more thought because I was keen to see my father and his advisors to discuss what our plan was.

Opal had not reappeared, to my dismay, and I was missing her comforting warm weight on my shoulder. I sincerely hoped she was just keeping hidden and watching from afar. She was a clever little thing. Surely she'd be alright.

Drake had kept them in their rooms under guard so that they couldn't communicate with each other. Lysander took me to my father's suite, humming a strange and whimsical fae tune as we went.

"Did you sleep well, Princess?" he purred.

"Of course not," I replied smoothly.

"Oh."

I hadn't slept at all. The adrenaline from killing those

demons had me tossing and turning all night, thinking and wondering and raging. I'd barely spoken to the maids, who'd given me as much for a wide berth as they could in that tiny room.

"If anyone touches my father, I'll kill them," I said to Lysander.

He cast me a wary look. "He's...been very compliant."

I made a dissatisfied sound at the back of my throat. Of course he had. He'd probably mentally withdrawn at the sign of the fae army. Dissociated from the world so he didn't have to deal with it. It wasn't totally his fault, I knew that it was just a part of that disease that warped his mind.

When we reached my father's suite, Lysander knocked on the door and escorted me in. My father sat in his receiving room, on his favourite red leather couch. His manservant, Derrick, was kneeling before him, tying the laces on his boots.

My father's face was pale and blank, his eyes heavy-lidded and staring into space. My throat went tight as long-held emotion bubbled up in me. I hadn't seen him in almost five months, and when I had left here, I had assumed I would never see him again. He looked older, the hairs around his temples now snow white.

I strode right over to them.

"Hello, Derrick," I said softly, sitting on the couch beside my father. "How is he?"

Derrick drew a deep breath when he saw it was me who spoke to him. "Your Highness." He stood and bowed. "He is not well, I think. There have been no lucid moments for some days."

"*Days?*"

Derrick nodded sombrely.

I looked into my father's face, the backs of my eyes stinging. If there was one time I missed him having his sane mind, it was now. I needed my father, but I could see that he was lost to me. Perhaps forever. Perhaps this would be the thing that finally killed him. I swallowed the tightness in my throat away.

It was then I noticed the Lysander had remained in the room. I raised my brows at him. "Can I have some privacy with my father, Lysander?"

He shook his head, his face drawn. "I'm afraid not, Princess."

I narrowed my eyes at him, but it wasn't worth the fight at this point. I looked back at my father's lined face and wondered if I could do anything to help him. But I remembered the way his mind had appeared when I broached it last, and it hadn't been pleasant at all. I didn't think even I could heal such a thing. My powers worked best on women, after all.

"And the queen?" I asked Derrick in a low voice. "When did she disappear?"

Derrick's eyes flicked to Lysander, then back to me. "The day of the invasion, Your Highness. She, her people, and the head advisor Oxley were gone as soon as the city gates were breached. I did not see them leave."

Stunned at the revelation that Oxley had run off too, I searched Derrick's face to see if there was anything he might not have wanted to say in front of Lysander. But his features were only a picture of stress and anxiety.

"How on earth did they get out?" I murmured to myself.

Cowards. That's all they were. That's all my stepmother would ever be. If I ever saw her again, I would make her regret ever marrying my father. A real queen would have stayed to negotiate for her people and protect them. I'm sure she would have headed to one of the closest kings to seek protection. Perhaps she'd even gone back to her walled home in the Kingdom of Kusha. I wondered if I could get a message out.

"I need to talk business with Drake," I said, standing. "Since my father is not able to, nor my stepmother or any of the advisors, I will negotiate on my kingdom's behalf."

Lysander gave me an amused look that made me want to punch him. "There is no negotiation, Princess. We own this land now."

The memory of the demons prowling in the castle grounds last night, filling me with a burning, and, unbidden, my astral sword beamed into my hand. Lysander's jaw went slack as I strode towards him.

"Over my dead body will fae rule this kingdom, *Lysander.*"

The fae warrior's mouth became a grim line as his pretty blue eyes darted from my astral sword to me. "Let's hope it doesn't come to that, Princess," he said softly.

My voice was as cold as the breath of the Kraasputin. "Take me to him."

He slowly turned around and strode back out into the corridor. I glanced at my latent father over my shoulder. He hadn't reacted at all to me, my sword, or Lysander. His face sat fixed and blank. I nodded at Derrick, who was staring at me in shock.

"You don't know how much it means to me that you've stayed to look after my father," I said to him. "When this is over, I'll make sure you are appropriately rewarded."

All Derrick could do was bow before I went after Lysander and dissipated my sword.

Lysander led me to the entrance hall, where the Black

Drake was talking to one of his fae warriors, a scroll of parchment in one hand. He turned and seemed unsurprised to see us walking towards him.

"Princess," he said. "I have news."

"And what might that be?" I kept my voice as calm as I could.

"Wyxian and Daxian will be arriving this afternoon."

Before I could reply, Lysander clapped his armoured hands. "Brilliant! They'll be in time for the ball."

I choked. "*Excuse me*?"

Drake gave Lysander a bemused look. "It's not a ball," he said firmly. "It is a meeting between royals and nobles so that they may come to terms with the fact that the fae are extending their territory."

I simmered, fighting to suppress open hostility. Anger never made for good negotiations. "I didn't authorise this," I said through gritted teeth. "Who have you invited?"

Drake smirked at me. "When you learn to accept that this is no longer your kingdom, *Princess*, things will go much more smoothly."

I all but scowled at him in a very un-princess-like way. "If this is no longer my kingdom, then why do you keep calling me 'Princess?' And if I'm not a princess, then I'm no better than a commoner."

"You often speak like a commoner," said Lysander curiously. "Why is that?"

Drake spoke before I could reply, his face brightening. "You're right, Saraya. But you're too pretty not to keep around. I'll be calling you Sara from now on. Or do you still prefer Sam?"

My fingers twitched in anger. But I didn't want to give in to his baiting. "The fae cannot rule over a human kingdom. It doesn't make sense." I announced. "This land is still mine as far as I'm concerned, and you monsters will be driven out."

"With whose army?" Drake asked, gesturing around the hall. "Your human military are all locked up."

So he *had* locked them up.

And so he was right. I needed to get out of here and find my military. I needed to make a plan. But the Black Drake continued his verbal assault, his hazel eyes fixed on mine. "The dignitaries of Waelan and Kalaan are on the way to pay their respects to the new sovereign leaders of Lobrathia along with the others. They'll accept the humans into their own kingdoms as refugees, allowing us to make this an all fae city."

I crossed my arms and stared right back at him while shock pulsed through me. So they were serious about this and had a plan for how it would work out. But it was a dumb plan. Quartz City was huge. There was no way half a million refugees could just pick up and leave for a new city. These fae monsters knew nothing about humans.

"They told me to be frightened of you," I said in a low voice. "Emery and Briar. They said you were undefeated and so terrible that no one wanted to get on your bad side. But do you know what I just learned?" I paused to see if he'd say anything, but his face gave nothing away as he remained silent. "I learned that you're just your king's lackey. Your plan will never work, you stupid fae. You disgust me."

He shifted a little, meeting my cold gaze, and I stepped closer to him. "And all you fae have been doing is stealing human magic for generations. And guess what? I'm going to stop it. You look down on humans as if we're scum, but the way I see it? Only scum take from the vulnerable. And that's exactly what your kind is."

He opened his mouth, but I held my hand up. "I'm leaving, and you're not going to stop me."

"We can't let you, Princess," Lysander said quickly. "You need to be here when Daxian comes. It doesn't matter whatever it is you think we are. A blood contract is unbreakable. You can't walk away from it."

"And what if I do?" I asked evenly. "Break it, that is?"

Lysander spread his palms out as if I should already know this. "You'll die. The magic will kill you."

Well shit. I had nothing to say to that.

"Fine," I said. "But you'll move the maids to a bigger room. It's disgusting where they are now. And Tembry is pregnant."

Lysander gave me a short bow. Drake opened his mouth, then closed it, seemingly thinking better of whatever he was going to say.

"What will they do to me?" I asked him. "Daxian and his father? If I'm your prisoner, at the very least, you should tell me what I'm in for."

His eyes skimmed the open doorway as if he could see the king and prince of Black Court riding towards the city. "I don't know."

We stood in a sort of contemplative silence for a while, staring into the distance.

"Princess," said the commander, finally. "Your problems would be solved if you married Daxian and joined your kingdoms. I assume that was what Wyxian was planning all those years ago."

Marry that royal, dirty playing ass of a creature? It was unquestionable. I'd be whisked away to fae land and never be able to kill the demons here. They wouldn't even let me prowl the streets at night if I was married. The Order of Temari would be over before it could even be resurrected.

"I can't," I said through gritted teeth.

His voice was low, and I noticed that he was stiff, as if poised for a fight. "Why?"

I was a little thrown off by his posture and turned sideways in case he was going to come at me or something. "I—I just can't. I'd never be free in the fae realm. I'd be a prisoner for life."

I could see his mind considering my words. "But that's the life of a princess. Did you not know you'd be married off to some prince to serve the kingdom?"

"Of course," I said. "But that was before—" I abruptly stopped myself. I had been about to tell him about the Order of Temari. Had been about to tell him about my powers and my midwifery. Why was I revealing all this information to my enemy? There was something about this fae commander that made me run my mouth. That made me want to trust him. But I couldn't. He was my enemy. "That's not for you to know," I finished softly.

"But if you don't adhere to the contract, you'll die as an oath breaker. You signed in blood; we were all there."

As if a cold breath had slithered down my spine, I realised that there was no way out of this. No way out of marrying Daxian and being his prisoner. With a feral and dark twisting of my gut, my mind flashed to the first time my stepmother had laid me down and gotten out her whip. I struggled to draw in breath as I remembered that first lash stinging my skin and how that hadn't hurt as much as the realisation of what my life would now be.

I had been a prisoner from that day onwards...until I had

run off to the Mountain Academy. And now, after a precious and momentary freedom, it was happening again. I was trapped in an iron cage of duty, and I would never be able to get out of it.

There were some demons no astral sword was capable of defeating.

28

SARAYA

The king and the crown prince of Black Court arrived at dusk, and I watched, as the two warriors rode through the palace gates from a high window. For the second time, I was watching a fae prince come to steal away my fate. Bile rose up in my throat, and I itched to draw my sword. But what good would it serve? I couldn't very well kill Daxian.

The thought hovered at the centre of my mind. *Could I?* If I killed Daxian, that would be the end of everything. I remembered the contract I had signed with my own life's blood. It had stipulated "firstborn son." Did that mean the contract was null and void if Daxian died? It seemed like it would be. But the thought of killing him made me sick to my stomach. He was not evil. He was an ass, to be sure, but he'd never actually hurt me badly in any way. The incident with the Kraasputin had been a mistake on his part—for my pretending to be a fae eunuch. And besides, murder would be a sure-fire way of getting a bounty on my head and inciting a massive war. People could get hurt.

No, killing him wasn't an option. There *had* to be another

way around the blood contract. The fae were cunning people and were experts at swindling their way around these kinds of things. I would just have to beat them at their own game. As I ran through the words of the contract over and over again, the brilliant golden seed of a plan began to form in my mind.

"Are you ready?" asked Lysander. I realised he had been watching me from afar. I started and shook myself, giving him a small, fake smile and nodded.

He gave me a strange look and escorted me downstairs. To my surprise, he led me to the throne room.

I was no animal, but I literally felt my hackles rise. When Lysander led me to the open door, cold anger rose up my spine, and I paused upon the threshold, held in place by the image before me.

King Wyxian was sitting on my father's throne.

Daxian was standing on his right.

Lysander looked behind him to see why I wasn't following, and his eyes widened. "Princess," he muttered in warning, "don't do anything that might endanger your *people*."

I shot him a look of loathing. They were already hurting my people, our city's economy, and goddess knew what they had done to our soldiers. I closed my eyes and took a breath, and then put my chin in the air and strode forward, quickly overtaking Lysander.

Wyxian looked more terrifying on this throne than my father ever had. Than any human ever had, no doubt. He was all muscle even at his mature age, tall and powerful, his face handsome perfection and his expression currently livid. I had no doubt that I wouldn't be able to defeat him in battle.

The thought tangled in me, and I pushed down the urge to vomit. I avoided Daxian's gaze, but I could tell he was glaring down at me. He'd never been denied anything in his sorry, cushioned life, and I'd defied him on multiple levels. Some of those levels he didn't even know about. I wondered if Drake would tell them about me being Sam. But the memory of being 'Sam' served to make me more furious. The reason I had ran from the far convoy in the first place was to thwart these monsters.

"How dare you sit on my father's throne," I snarled, even before the powerful fae king could open his mouth.

The room felt perceptibly colder.

"How dare you break your blood oath," he shot back.

"I haven't broken it," I said, through gritted teeth, remembering my plan. Finally, I looked at Daxian, who was frowning at me with narrowed, blue eyes. His stare was intent. His eyes raked down my body, taking in every pore, every breath, every movement…and finding it eerily familiar. I knew he realised I was Sam Sourbottom when all colour drained from his face, and those brilliant eyes filled with rage.

I allowed a slow, spiteful smile to spread across my lips. Would he tell his father? No, that would just be embarrassing for him. Because then his father would find out that I'd bested him in one on one swordplay. I straightened my spine a little further, knowing I had a tiny upper hand at this moment.

"I fully intend to marry my *fiancé*," I said the words slowly, smiling at Daxian, whose face was now slowly turning crimson. "But we never stipulated a timeline. I had every right to leave when I did."

One tiny loophole in the wording of the contract. But I'd manipulate it for all its worth. I'd decided that I would marry Daxian. But only when we were both old, if I hadn't found a way out of the contract by then.

"How did you make the golem?" asked the king. "It fooled us for months."

I smirked on behalf of Epelthi and Opal, and shrugged. "I'm sure you hardly interacted with it much, though, did you? Easy to fool if you just kept her locked away in a room somewhere?"

Wyxian bristled in a way that told me I was right.

"Where were you?" he growled. "Tumbling with some commoner?"

"I can't say that I've ever *tumbled*," I shrugged as my four months at the Academy ran through my mind. My eyes met Daxian's when I said, "I was just...out."

"Why are you doing this?" the fae prince's teeth flashed like the predator he was.

"For reasons that are my own," I said snidely.

"You stupid girl," growled Wyxian in a voice that made my blood rush to my head. "You would risk your entire kingdom over nothing? I suppose your *mentally crippled father* couldn't teach you to do your duty."

I closed my eyes to try and abate the fiery anger that rose up in me again. I had been doing so well at controlling this rage of mine. I opened my eyes and hissed, "You will *not* speak my father's name with your filthy fae mouth."

I'm sure both royal fae were shocked, but the king remained still, the true warrior that he was. He blanched, and I could feel his anger projected at me like a blast of winter wind.

"I know what you're doing," I spat. "It hasn't gone unnoticed, and I *will* stop it."

"Shackle her," said the King with dangerous calm. "And put her in the dungeons. That might make her think twice about her disgusting commoner's tongue."

Ten fae warriors advanced towards me from behind the marble pillars lining the throne room. Behind them, I saw Drake standing in the shadows, his arms crossed over his fighting leathers, his face unreadable. But he never took his eyes off me, as a fae captain I did not recognise, roughly took my arms and put them behind my back.

With all the venom and rage I'd accumulated over weeks of killing demons, I said in a dark and quiet voice, "You'll pay for this." I stared at the fae royalty on my father's throne with hooded eyes. "I'll make sure of it."

In Daxian's eyes, I saw a tiny, itsy, bitsy spark of fear.

I WAS MARCHED BELOW THE CASTLE INTO THE DUNGEONS, WHERE the city's petty criminals were housed under palace guard.

The dungeons were expansive and spanned a large rectangle dug into the earth. There were one hundred and forty-eight cells, I knew from listening in to Father's various conversations as a child. But I had never actually been down there. The air got heavier and more humid as they marched me down the slippery stone steps, and when we finally reached the bottom, I suppressed a gag.

It was dark as hell, wet, and smelled like human waste and perspiration.

There was only one way in and out, making the dungeons practically impossible to escape from. I briefly wondered if I had made a mistake in antagonising the fae king. I doubted they would keep me here long, though, because of the meeting between nobility or 'ball' as Lysander had dubbed it. They led me a little way down one row and shoved me into an open cell. I stumbled in, surveying the stone bed and latrine with distaste, and turned around.

But this unfamiliar fae captain knew nothing about me. So when he locked the cell with the cast iron key, he used no magic to reinforce the door. I smiled softly to myself and sat down on the hard stone bed, drawing my legs up and closing my eyes. I would bide my time, and when I was ready, I would make my move.

THAT NIGHT, TO MY SURPRISE, BECAUSE IT WAS NOT A FULL MOON, Arishnie came to me in my dreams.

"Where are you?" My ghostly mentor frowned.

"Captured. Prisoner. Put in a dungeon," I said wryly. "Why?"

She made a disapproving sound. "It's a basket moon tonight. Can you meet me above the palace? We will have to do it tonight."

I raised my eyebrows because I had no idea what she was talking about but inclined my head regardless. My body woke up instantly, and I closed my eyes once again and ascended into astral form, wondering why I hadn't thought to use this new skill of mine earlier. I flew up through the layers of the place, slicing through them like they weren't solid floors, and broke through the roof into the dark of night.

"I could spy on the fae king in this form," I said to Arishnie, waiting by a golden capped spire.

"No, you couldn't," she warned. "The fae can see into the astral realm. They would see you, and you would be outed for the witch that you are." Her face twisted into a wry smile as I mentally kicked myself. "Witches is what they used to call us when we didn't have a sword in our hands," she mused.

"And what did they call you when you did have a sword in your hands?"

Her mouth twisted in memory. "They used to call us, 'Oh no, RUN!'"

I let out a humourless laugh. "What are we doing here, Arishnie?" I asked, looking out at the city, multi-coloured quartz lights glinting like tiny jewels.

"Tonight is a basket moon," the warrior pointed to the moon, and sure enough, a crescent moon sat like a smile in the sky. I smiled back, remembering that moon was carved into my mother's Ellythian wooden trunk. "That means," she continued, "it is Umali's night. Tonight is the night of your initiation."

My stomach did a flip. An initiation? Did I deserve to be in the Order of Temari when I couldn't even go out and fight the demons plaguing my people? How many were out there now while I was stuck inside a dungeon because of my big mouth? How did I deserve to be in the ancient order when I couldn't even fend off the fae holding me captive?

"Don't be nervous," Arishnie said. "This is the start of something important, and you are the only one who can do it. The only one who is ready."

I took a deep breath and nodded. As soon as I untangled myself from this situation, I would be back to fighting these demons. "Let's go."

We flew out of the city and over Lobrathia in that rapid way of astral travel, until I saw the ocean laid out under the moon like a thing of dreams. Ripples of water caught beams of moonlight and played with them, and eventually, my eyes set upon the remains of the old temple. We descended down into the trees and to the gaping entrance. There was a sacredness here, and neither of us would breach the temple from its roof.

Arishnie led me into the dark mouth of the temple, and once again, the fiery sconces lit themselves up one by one around the sacred space. But this time, an inhuman being stood at its heart, flanked by all seven marble goddesses.

I froze on the spot, every cell in my body fluttering in a static haze. Power, so much power in that one being that I felt it coming towards me in a hurricane or turbulent energy. And it wasn't just her presence that affected me. It was her form. I recognised her immediately.

Her skin was navy blue, the colour of the deepest parts of the ocean. Her obsidian hair was long down to her waist and unbound, wild around her head and stirring in an invisible wind. Her face had a pristine beauty that far surpassed any mortal creature, and her midnight eyes were currently trained upon me in the most intense way. Her teeth were bone-white fangs peeking out under her upper lip. She wore nothing, her breasts heavy under the long garland of bleached white skulls hanging around her neck. In one hand, she held a sword. In the other, a gleaming scythe.

The goddess Umali.

I couldn't move any part of my body. But then the goddess tilted her head to me as if beckoning me forward, and I realised that I had no use for fear here. The only appropriate state for me at this point in time was reverence. I swept forward on gentle toes, my gaze locked upon hers, and breathlessly, I did what felt right and knelt down on one knee, bowing my head.

Saraya.

A voice like midnight whispered all around the temple,

and goosebumps erupted all over me. As ancient as the universe, as dark as the void, more powerful than a shifting tide.

A thumb of infinite power pressed against my forehead and burned my skin. Something in me shifted.

I bless you.

I bind you.

The Order of Temari.

You are the sword in the night.

The protector of human potential.

The shield against all that is evil.

Do you accept this pledge?

I was enveloped in a powerful magic that I couldn't fathom. It felt like a tornado was whirling inside my body, and I grunted with the strain. The goddess Umali removed her thumb from my forehead, and the whirlwind of power receded, leaving me reeling and breathless. I realised that she had asked me a question.

I looked up at her magnificent form and found my voice caught in my throat. This was really happening. I swallowed and whispered, "I am the sword in the night. The protector of human potential. The shield against all that is evil. I accept this pledge."

She straightened, and I felt the weight of her gaze like the weight of the earth on my shoulders.

"Then rise."

29

DRAKE

I strode out of the palace gates and into the night. The city was quiet, which was, I'm sure, something that had not even happened during the last war. This morning, I had lifted the lockdown between sun-up and sun-down to prevent the local economy from being destroyed. Lysander had kindly reminded me that brothels needed to feed their staff, and without customers, a business couldn't make money. The human city, oddly enough, worked similarly to a fae city.

I obliged and reinstated the quarry miners under a strict fae guard, harshly enforcing the lockdown at night. Any stragglers were reminded to move on, but as the humans quickly learned, execution was something my warriors were not afraid of. I should know. I trained them to be as ruthless as I. The humans were unsettled and showed it, the males playing up and trying to be defiant every so often. They didn't know their fate, and in all honestly, neither did I.

I passed bakeries, farriers, seamstresses, and shops, all vacant and quiet, cloaked in a night-time hush that rarely frequented large cities. Perhaps that contributed to the jittery feeling that crept up my spine like a stream of angry fire ants. That feeling that made me want to kill someone. To hunt something. To be frank, it was lucky that a majority of my power had been magically bound at the age of thirteen. Darkness like that, couldn't be allowed free reign. Even though it prickled at me, those bonds on my mind, it was for everyone's safety.

But about half of my agitation was because of Saraya. The wild bronzed princess with an insane sort of defiance in her eyes. Yes, her appearance made me itch, but tonight, her words had fallen upon my ears like a mace.

I know what you're doing.

My wild princess fought the demons as if they were a personal affront to her. As if *I* was a personal affront to her.

So it was just as well I was good at hunting because a hunt was exactly what I was going to do. I stopped in the shadow of a street light, its yellow quartz glow vibrant in the night. I lifted my nose to the air and sniffed.

A hint of baked bread from that afternoon, cheap women's perfume, human perspiration, horse dung, cow, dog, cat. I turned my head and sniffed again. A fae warrior and a human woman were making love a distance away, roast meat, ale, whiskey, beer....*demon.*

I shot eastward, like a hazilem on the chase for its mark. I had become familiar with the humans of Quartz City this past week, and it seemed to me they were more like the fae than I had realised. They cried the same, they were jealous the same, they made love roughly the same, and they used the latrine the same.

But Saraya was a different story completely. She had an interesting sort of magic. I knew that for certain now, by that astral sword she had summoned as if she were born to do it.

I'd watched her kill three chinga demons with the air of someone with a personal vendetta against them, and I wasn't getting any closer to discovering how she, as a human, had this magic and of what type it was.

I had heard her name whispered reverently in the city on a number of occasions, but when I questioned the humans on it, they kept their lips tightly sealed. So she had loyalty or respect among the common people, which was a rare thing for a princess. I fit that to the jigsaw puzzle in my head that was the Princess Saraya Yasani Voltanius of Lobrathia, who seemed more Ellythian by the day. Those ancient and noble people I had only heard stories about, or read in books, were even more mysterious to me than these Lobrathian humans were.

Surging through the quiet streets, I registered that the demons were moving swiftly in the dark, and there were a number of them. I caught up to the pack quickly but made sure I wasn't seen. Prowling in the shadows under the eave of a house, I came upon four lacren demons, fat, fleshy types with rolling muscle that could swipe the head off a fae warrior. They were slow but strong, and I knew their smell from a mile off. I watched them confidently, *hungrily* pludge up to a cottage with whitewashed walls. Someone in the house gave a loud yelp.

It was the smell of childbirth. And I noted that human amniotic fluid smelled the same as the type the fae produced. Like something new mixed in with brine. Like the sea in its youth. Alkaline. Being around military men most of my life, it wasn't a smell I came across often, but it wasn't something I could ever forget—it was too distinct.

The four lacren strode right through the wall of the human dwelling.

Silent as only a fae could be, I crept up to the glass window of the house. A woman lay on a birthing bed, sweating but smiling at her new babe, still shiny from birth. Two women cooed and wept around her. Her mother maybe, and a midwife.

The lacren demons, all four, crowded around the birthing bed, two of them standing through the women. Simultaneously, they leered over the new mother and her babe. The biggest one, their leader, plucked something from the baby's crown and drew it out as one draws a needle through cloth. He then lifted it up, and the three others leaned in. All four demons inhaled, their broad shoulders heaving, and a golden thread of magic split into four and shot into the demons' noses.

I exited the house immediately, put myself back inside my body, and strode away from the cottage.

There were few things in my life that disturbed me—that made me feel as if I needed to scrub my skin with a wire brush. But I could put this on my list of things that did.

I strode back to the palace. I needed to send a letter.

30

SARAYA

I woke up the next morning from my astral projection with a headache the size of the Silent Mountains. My forehead burned like someone had pressed a white-hot brand there.

Not someone. A goddess. The patron goddess of the Order of Temari had officially initiated me into the Order. I was the first warrior midwife for over a hundred years. The first of what I hoped would be many.

I groaned, getting up from the concrete slab that served as my bed, my joints cracking as I stretched them out in a pattern of movement Jerali Jones had taught me. I stopped dead.

Jerali Jones.

Where was my armsmaster? Where *were* all the soldiers of my father's army? They had to be around here somewhere, perhaps locked up and hidden away. The Black Drake would not have killed them all. That wasn't his style. He was too clever, too cunning.

I massaged my temples and took a drink from the pitcher of lukewarm water that had been left for me. As I leaned

266

down to place the pitcher back on the stone floor, I froze. The darkness of the pitcher allowed me to see a hint of my reflection. And on my forehead, something glowed. A symbol. I squinted, trying to make it out. The goddess Umali had seared a symbol into my forehead. I touched the skin, heat bursting forth. I wondered if everybody else would be able to see it.

There was no mirror in this cell, but luckily for me, I had a useful skill.

I sat back down on the concrete slab and closed my eyes, ascending into astral form. As I came out of my body into my translucent, ghostly form, I turned around to face myself.

Oh, goddess.

There on my forehead was an intricate glowing symbol, a crescent moon, a 'basket moon' as Arishnie had called it, linked with delicate lines to a lotus.

Already it was starting to fade. I breathed a sigh of relief, thankful that it wouldn't be a visible thing. There would be too many questions about it otherwise. With me having magic, at least I had some small upper hand.

But I needed to get to work. I needed to find Jerali Jones and the others. I crept through the cells. While I might be invisible to humans, the fae, as magical beings, would be able to see me, as Arishnie had said last night. I'd have to avoid fae guards at all costs lest they find out about my magic.

I swept systematically through the dungeons, corridor by corridor, hiding around corners to allow the patrolling fae guards to pass me by. It wasn't until I got to the part of the dungeon furthest from the entrance, where it was darkest, that I found familiar faces. Jerali Jones sat meditating against a cell wall, looking slightly gaunt with a healing black eye. Commander Starkis, head of the palace guard, was in a cell a row away from Jerali, lying on his stone slab with an arm across his eyes.

If I was to escape out of here and make a plan to take back the city, I would need both of them. They knew more than me about tactical manoeuvres.

So now I knew where *they* were. I left the palace completely, flying through the layers of earth, and ascended through the levels of the palace. They had to be somewhere separate but close by.

I flew above the castle, eyeing the surrounding land. There was nowhere in the city that could house a whole army. I looked northwards, behind the palace, where the palace grounds and forest lay.

Out eastwards was some farmland where we grew wheat. Behind it, a series of large barns stood. Barns big enough to house a large group of people.

I flew towards it immediately, eyes fixed on the surrounding area. By day, a ghostly astral body would hardly be visible flying through the air, but I'd have to be careful. Sure enough, as I got closer, a whole squadron of fae guards patrolled three of the barns. Breathing hard, I angled myself, so the sun was above me. That way, none of the fae would spot me unless they were dumb enough to look straight into the sunlight. I flew a little lower, trying to make out any potential weaknesses in the fae defences. They patrolled around each barn in pairs, and there were four pairs in total. I needed to get inside and make sure the soldiers were okay.

I waited, watching their pattern as they walked, but it seemed they'd gotten a little bored with days of doing the same thing, so their stride around the barn was slow and meandering. As soon as the back aspect of the barn was clear, I shot straight down and through the wooden panels of the barn. I was met by a sea of packed bodies. Men sat or lay down on the straw of the barn floor. One man moaned. I sought him out and saw a soldier in a bloodied mess of cloth and wadded bandages. A soldier medic sat next to him, his face drawn and defeated.

All around me, men sat pale and glum. I wonder how often they were fed and where they went to the bathroom. Anger torpedoed through me. This is what the fae did to humans, and it was unacceptable. This couldn't go on. I had to get them out. I needed a plan.

When I woke up back inside my physical body, I found my eyes wet, my blood turbulent through my arteries. This was awful. The fae would pay.

I felt out my options and kept coming back to one choice. I had made a promise to my mother more than ten years ago. To never use my magic to harm a person.

And now I was about to break it. The vow had felt sacred at the time. But in the face of a heinous crime, the sacred became a luxury.

Shame crept through me like a poison. All these years, I'd kept this vow, but now I simply couldn't. It was a matter of life and death. It was a matter of losing a kingdom.

As much as it felt like a black poison snaking around my heart, I knew I would be more ashamed if I left my people to suffer like this.

I WAITED UNTIL NIGHTFALL. IT WAS ONLY A MATTER OF SECONDS to open my cell door. I strode confidently out, wishing I had Opal to disguise me at least a little bit, simultaneously hoping she was somewhere safe. But since I had no idea where she was, I crept along my row, keeping flush to one side.

My first pair of fae guards came more quickly than I would've liked. They spotted me immediately and rushed down the lane with a cry.

I took a deep breath.

"I'm sorry," I whispered before mentally charging straight into their mental shields. I had never tried this with anyone since the night before my engagement when my stepmother's guards barred me from leaving the palace. I knew it would be difficult and require brute force, as I had no idea how strong their mental shields would be, and my power had always worked better on females.

But they had not expected a magical, mental assault, so as they ran towards me, the battering ram that was my anger actually threw them backwards as it shattered both their shields like glass. I halted, frozen by the realisation that my own power had done *that*. Perhaps Umali's initiation was giving my power a bit of a kick? It seemed plausible, but I couldn't think on it now as the fae guards began to stir.

I swore, running towards them and taking the greater vessels of their neck in my mental grip. I squeezed just enough so they would lose consciousness, and with that part done, I sprinted past them and down to the next intersection.

Jerali Jones and Captain Starkis were some distance away from me, but luckily from my astral scouting of the dungeon, I knew the quickest way to get to them. I knocked out another pair of guards, not even breaking my sprint, jumping over their bodies and continuing past them.

When I got to Jerali Jones' door, the armsmaster was still sitting on the floor in a meditative pose.

"Jerali!" I hissed through the bars. Eyes flew open, and I

opened the cell, continuing past to Captain Starkis'. The older man was sitting on his bed, drinking from a ceramic cup. He dropped it when I appeared through the bars and scrambled to me.

"Princess!" he hissed in disbelief.

"I'm going to get you guys out," I said. "You and the other soldiers."

I magically unlocked his door and pushed it open. He stared at it dumbly for a second before his mind kicked in, and he lurched out. I ran back to Jerali's cell, but the arms-master was quicker than either of us and met us halfway.

"Keep close," I said. "And follow me."

Jerali's eyes shone as they regarded me, but we had no time for greetings. They both nodded, and I jogged ahead, scouting left and right at the intersections.

But within moments, the thundering of fae warrior boots sounded in the distance, followed by frantic, masculine shouts. They'd found the collapsed guards. I'd have to be fast.

I increased my speed, hoping the other two would be able to keep up despite living for however long on meagre scraps. But their steps were sound as we rushed towards the entrance.

We were close. We might just make it.

But just as the steps to the outside world should have come into view, six armoured fae stepped in front of us, their swords drawn.

I never stopped. Fuelled with the vision of my sick and injured army forces, I beheld their various shields of steel, ice, obsidian, amber, quartz, and earth and shattered through them with a diamond fist, smashing through every last shield, deep into their brains, effectively giving each a concussion. As one, they flinched and collapsed where they stood.

Captain Starkis let out a surprised shout, but when neither Jerali nor I ceased in our escape, so he continued behind us. Panting from the strain, I jumped over fae bodies and shot up the stairs, my lungs burning, my thighs feeling like acid was flowing through them instead of blood.

We needed to get out of the palace quietly. We would never be able to survive being chased to the barn the soldiers were being kept in. When we got up the long dungeon stairs, I paused at the top, looking left and right, wheezing where I stood.

"Which way?" I murmured more to myself.

"Left," said Jerali.

"I want to get to the soldiers in the eastern barn," I said quickly to them both. "We need to get everyone out of the city and get to the closest—"

Jerali sighed. "Kingdom? Saraya, both Kalaan and Waelan are at least a week's walk! We'd need horses, food, provisions."

"You should see them," I said, looking between them both. "The conditions are awful."

"That's war," said Captain Starkis, shaking his head. "We need to get out of here and into a hiding place in the city."

"Yes. Right, of course." My eyes were seeing spots, my mind was a little fuzzy from the strain of so many mental assaults at once, and I knew a worse headache was budding. But we couldn't afford to delay. "Around the back then," I said.

We shot down a servant's stair, hoping that it would be deserted because, after all, how could they man every exit to this place? And, of course, there were some exits that were hidden from everyone. I led them to my own secret entrance, but when I opened the hidden panel in the wall, both Jerali Jones and Starkis hesitated.

"I've been using this tunnel for years," I said. "This is how I've been getting out of the palace all the time. It's dark and long, but no one uses it. It comes out just outside the city. No one knows it's here."

Jerali Jones gave me a pained look. "We don't have a choice, the way I see it. Goddess help us all."

I nodded and led them inside.

Leading them down the dark tunnel, with no light and only suffocating darkness around us, we stumbled. With our hands skimming the earthen tunnel walls, I scoped ahead to make sure there were no hidden fae ahead of us. I was so intent on scouting ahead that by the time I knew the exit was close, I didn't realise we were being followed.

I felt him like a fish feels an ocean current, his power radiating into my core.

"Go!" I shouted, simultaneously opening the tunnel's exit door with my mind and pushing them both past me.

I gave a cry as something powerful stroked my mental shield, and I shook with the vibration of it.

"Saraya," a voice like deep earth held my brain in a steel grip. "Stop."

31

SARAYA

Blue light flared, and Drake appeared, ghoul-like before me, dwarfing the tunnel. His handsome face was grim, lips pressed into a thin line. Internally, I screamed with frustration.

I had been so close. So close to escaping. The golden rays of the setting sun glared behind me, and I turned to see Jerali and Starkis shoot out of the tunnel into the forest beyond. With the last ounce of magical energy left in me, I slammed the tunnel door shut in their faces, just managing to get a view of their eyes widening as they saw who stood in front of me. I needed them to get out. I needed them to be safe and make plans to get the soldiers free. They would know what to do, I hoped. There was no one else.

I looked back at Drake, seeking to distract him from pursuing the others. There were no soldiers I could see behind him. I wondered if he had come by himself. "How did you find me? How did you know that I'd escaped?"

His face was stormy in that blue light and it made my

heart hammer against my ribs. "You could never hide from me, Saraya."

I seethed. "That's all good and well, *Drake*. But what are you going to do now?"

"I'm going to take you back inside." He turned to the side in a silent instruction to have me move in past him. But the tunnel was far too narrow and not meant for two people to stand side by side. I'd have to skirt past him—touch him, to get by.

So I set my jaw, and I did. And did it in the most inconvenient way possible...for him.

I strode up to his powerful, towering form, never taking my eyes off his, turned so that I was facing him and slowly, very slowly, slid past, making sure I pressed every inch of my body against his.

It was more satisfying for me than I thought it would be. His body was all hard, lean muscle, his belt scraping against my abdomen, and I tilted my head up to keep my seething gaze on him, making sure he knew I meant to get him back for stopping my escape. But as I passed him, something unfamiliar flickered in his eyes, and his face leaned down the barest inch, his lips parted almost as if he wanted to kiss me. A primal heat shifted deep in my core and every cell in my body stood at attention.

I sucked in a breath before snapping myself out of it and hastily moving into the tunnel past him. That had been a mistake. This fae —possibly the most dangerous fae warrior his race had—was my enemy, and I had no idea why I had the urge to seduce him, to taunt him. It was only natural that I desired him. I was only a woman after all, and I'm sure he had women running after him on all fronts. But I couldn't let my self fall prey to his fae wiles.

I glanced at his hand suddenly, looking at the blue ball of light that sat in his calloused palm, giving the tunnel an eerie feeling. Now *that* was useful magic. I wondered if my magic could do that. I'd never tried. Perhaps without fuel, it wouldn't work...

"You have magic." He stated in a low voice that still seemed to take up the whole tunnel.

I started, realising I was standing right next to him, staring at his hand, completely consumed by my own thoughts.

"Hmm," I replied. It was neither yes nor no. "I can't do *that*." I nodded at his hand.

"Why did you bother trying to escape?" he asked. "You knew that I would find you."

Well, no, I hadn't thought that he would or could. "Do you have some type of magic that helps you find people?"

His grin was sudden and wicked, showing all of his white teeth. "You have your secrets, and I have mine."

"You're torturing my people," I spat. To my chagrin, my vision went blurry with tears. But Jerali and Captain Starkis were safe. I had to remind myself that all was *not* lost. "How can you do that?"

"I'm not torturing anyone," he said, his voice upturning at the end as if he really believed what he'd said.

I sniffed away my tears and looked up at him. I saw no lie in his hazel eyes. "You have my soldiers living in squalor. Injured, wounds festering, living in their own filth, how is that not torture?"

He frowned as if he were confused.

"Did you not know this?" I asked.

"I knew..." But his eyes were searching the air behind me, thinking.

Something struck me then. Briar, Emery, and the others...

they had known nothing of humans, spoke as if we were some alien creatures they were confused by. "You know that humans need hygiene and food and medicine just like fae do, right? Even animals need that." This, close, I saw his pupils dilate. He was surprised. I scoffed in disgust at him. "Oh, come on, Commander of the Black Court's *elite forces*. Surely you knew that humans don't heal themselves, that they have different requirements than the fae?"

He looked at me like some door had opened in his mind. "I'll sort it out," he growled.

I gave him an unimpressed look, trying to ignore the way his gaze seared my skin. "You'd better." I turned on my heel and walked back down the tunnel, right into the dark, Drake's blue light at my back, trying not to feel him behind me. But his presence was so sure, so absolute I couldn't *not* feel him.

I couldn't believe the fae didn't know anything about how humans functioned after a week of invading us. It was beyond me. How self-centered could they be? But on the other hand, before the fae came to our city on the day of my engagement, I thought they'd be red-eyed monsters out to kill us. We had known nothing about them. I supposed it was only fair that they didn't know anything about us either. Well, these interactions would fix that.

"Are you going to put me back into my cell?" I growled, trying to hide the exhaustion in my voice, in my frame.

"No." He said. "I need to keep a closer eye on you."

I let out a short laugh, then said snidely, "Are we going to bunk together? Share beds?"

"Would you prefer that?" he asked quietly.

I shot him another disgusted look over my shoulder. "That's rude. I am a lady."

He didn't reply, but I could *feel* him smirking.

We continued on for the rest of the kilometre in silence, and when we got out, it was then I was dismayed that my once-secret tunnel was no longer secret. If the fae commander knew about it, then all the fae basically did.

Drake turned towards me, and right there in the servant's tunnel, he procured something from behind his back, grabbed my arms with his tattooed hands so fast he was a blur and secured something around my wrists. When he moved back, I could only stare in shock at the magically glowing steel shackles.

"These will stay on," he said. "You won't be able to use your…magic. Or whatever it is you have."

I stared at him in disbelief. "Are you serious?"

"Do I look like I'm joking?"

I tried to mentally feel out my surroundings and found that I couldn't. It was like being underwater and knowing you couldn't breathe. I tried again. Nothing. I came up against an impenetrable, dull barrier in my mind. "No," I whispered. "No!"

He turned away. "Come on."

Trembling with anger, I followed, staring down at the shackles. I had no magic. I had no power. I wouldn't be able to astral project or summon an astral sword. I couldn't believe it. I was powerless now. *Weak.* I looked up and stared at the fae commander's back with hatred because that's all I could do.

We walked a long while down the servant's corridor, and in the distance, I heard a bone-rattling scream.

We both froze. I recognised that voice.

It was Tembry. And it sounded like she was in labour.

I pushed past Drake and ran towards her voice as she

wailed again. I came to a large door, guarded by two grimacing fae warriors. True to Drake's word, they had put them in a more spacious room. The guards hastily let me in when they saw Drake striding behind me.

I ran into the room to see Tembry rocking on her hands and knees on the floor, Blythe and Lucy kneeling by her side —and to my surprise, Opal was on Tembry's shoulder.

"Saraya!" Tembry gasped, "Oh—" she reached for the bowl and vomited right into it, but it was only water that came out of her. Opal slid off Tembry and shot right for me, chattering as if to explain herself. Something in me warmed as she jumped into my arms, licked me, and jumped back to Tembry's side. Opal had seen a pregnant woman and had chosen to stay with her, perhaps in some attempt to guard her in my absence.

"This little creature has been helping us," said Blythe from where Tembry was clinging onto her. "Getting us extra food by sneaking in and out!"

"She came with me," I said hurriedly, kneeling beside them. "But tell me, how long?" I indicated the swaying and sweaty Tembry.

"Hours, Highness. Hours. We begged them to call you, but they wouldn't. They wouldn't listen!"

"I'm here now," I said, biting back my annoyance. I would have a word with the guards later. "It's alright."

"I need to poo!" Tembry screamed, reaching for me. "Help!"

"That's good, Tem." I grasped her hand. "That means she's coming."

"She?" choked Tembry. "You didn't tell me—oh no!"

Another contraction blew through her, and she grunted deep and low in her throat— the unmistakable sound of a woman's body pushing a baby out. We were already in the second stage. She was close.

"How long has she been making that noise?" I asked.

Blythe thought for a moment. "About an hour."

"Alright." I looked around the room. Naturally, we had nothing for a birth.

I stood and went to bang on the now-closed room door, and it opened quickly. Drake stood there, wary-faced.

"I need things for a birth," I demanded. "Another bowl for the placenta, clean towels, two tiny pieces of clean cloth to tie off the cord…and more towels. Understood?"

He glanced at Tembry behind me and seemed to understand the urgency. "I'll arrange it."

I slammed the door back in his face and managed to snag the stupid handcuffs. I hissed in pain. I couldn't even use my magic to see if everything was alright with the labour. But as I heard Tembry go through another contraction, I knew I wouldn't need it. She would give birth soon.

"Sara!" she groaned.

Agatha would scold me for relying on my powers anyway, and Tembry looked like she was progressing normally. I rushed back to my friend.

"I'm here, Temb. It looks like it's time to take your underwear off."

The three of us helped her, and by the sounds she was making, I knew things were getting close. Between the two maids and myself, we kept Tembry in a squatting position, leaning on Blythe and Lucy. They kept her calm as the baby descended through her body with vigorous contractions. Sure enough, within the next half an hour, Temby began instinctively, actively pushing of her own accord. Eventually, she let out a tiny whimper, and I saw the back of the baby's head peeking between her labia. I beamed at her sweaty, red face.

"She's coming, Tem."

There was a knock at the door, and I leapt up and ran, opened the door, grabbed the bundle of material from the sheet-white fae guard, and slammed the door shut. I passed the towels to Lucy to set down. Then I paused. *The baby. The demons. The cuffs. I couldn't summon the sword without my magic.*

A demon was probably already in the room, and I had no means of even seeing it with these magic stealing shackles on.

Tembry groaned as she pushed.

"Don't push, Tem!" I called, watching the baby's head descend even lower out of her. "Just breathing now."

"Oh goddess," she shook, grasping Blythe around the neck for all she was worth while Lucy dabbed her forehead with a cloth.

I yanked open the door, stepped outside, and strode right up to Drake, who was waiting against the wall.

"I need these cuffs off right now."

"No."

I growled in frustration. "Now *is not* the time to argue. Take. Them. Off."

"Why?" he asked. There was a curious note in his voice.

I almost punched him as Tembry screamed. The demons would arrive at any second. "Drake. Take these handcuffs off me, or so help me, goddess, when they *do* eventually come off, I will hunt you down to the ends of the earth and destroy you."

3 2
SARAYA

He fixed me with an intense gaze, unperturbed but taking my threat seriously. "Swear on your goddess that you will tell me about your magic afterwards."

I groaned in frustration. "Fine!"

He flicked his fingers, and the shackles fell off with a hiss, clattering to the ground, their glow now absent. As my magic rushed back into my awareness, I strode back inside, just in time to see the baby's head being born. I rushed to Tembry, kneeling down beside her. Blythe gave me a frightened look, but I nodded to her encouragingly.

"You're doing so well, Temb!" I said, eyes darting around the room. Thankfully, there were no demons present in the room yet.

Tembry nodded, sweat dripping off her face, chest heaving with the effort.

"She's almost here!" whispered Blythe, supporting Tembry as we all knelt on the floor around her.

With the next contraction, the baby's head turned to the

side, and I knelt behind Tembry and caught the baby as she came out.

"Oh, goddess!" Tembry cried, leaning back into me as I passed the baby through her legs. She reached for her. "That's my baby!"

I passed the bawling babe into Tembry's waiting arms, and she instantly cuddled her to her chest. We assisted Tembry onto her back and into the supportive arms of Lucy.

I covered the baby with a towel, checked her perfect, screwed up little face to make sure she was breathing, made sure Tembry was covered, then I stood. I prowled around the room, searching.

"Try and put the babe to the breast," I said reflexively to Blythe, who was wiping tears from her eyes. "Dry the baby off. Keep her warm."

From the side of my eye, I saw Blythe and Tembry comply. I swept my eyes around the room. No demons yet. I didn't want to scare Tembry, so I pretended to fiddle with the bundle of equipment the fae had given us.

"Do we cut the cord?" asked Tembry.

"Not yet, love," I said, "We wait for the placenta to pump the rest of the baby's blood back into her. Might take a few minutes."

I looked through the tiny slit that was the window. It was all dark outside, the grounds quiet as far as I could see. It was only a matter of time before a demon strode right through the walls.

There was a male shout outside, and two of the biggest demons I had ever seen lumbered through the door, at least seven feet tall. One was a male and the other female, which I could easily identify by the lack of any coverings. Their skin was a mottled black lined with red glowing veins. The male was slightly taller and his muscles bulged as he moved, his breath slow as he fixed his all-black gaze on Tembry's babe. The female seemed to jitter with anticipation. I wondered how many newborns they had stolen magic from.

The door slammed open next to them, the fae guards swinging their swords. Of course, their blades swung right through the male demon's body. Tembry shrieked. Blythe jumped to her feet, cussing.

I summoned my astral sword just as Drake strode through the door.

"Move her back against the wall!" I commanded, pointing at Tembry's startled face. "Do it. Now."

I moved forward, stepping into the demons' path as the maids struggled to comply with my instructions. Drake looked between me and the demons.

"Drake!" I urged.

He obliged, walking past me and hauling both Lucy and Tembry, who was leaning against the maid, back into the far wall of the room.

"Watch for the placenta, Blythe," I called over my shoulder. "It could come any time now. Don't pull on the cord. Hold the bowl ready."

I heard her scampering for the bowl, and then I looked up at the demons, my forehead growing warm. The male cocked his head at me and stomped forward.

I angled my blade at him, glancing at the female. It was a small space, and there were two of them. I was the only one with a weapon that could touch them. I needed to act fast.

I launched myself at the male.

Still tired from the use of my powers in knocking out the fae guarding the dungeons, I came at him too slow. With incredible speed, he knocked my sword away, where it clattered to the ground and dissipated. He grabbed me right around my throat in one gigantic red-lined hand and crushed my airway. My hands flew to grip his thick muscled one.

I couldn't even scream as the air was choked out of me.

The female darted around me to Tembry, and fury tore through me. I let go of his hand and summoned my sword, thrusting it into his abdomen. He let me go immediately, and I dropped to the ground, taking my sword with me.

"Sara!" came a male shout. "Hurry!'

I wheezed, clutching my throat with one hand, trying to get up with the knuckles of my sword hand, turning to see the female demon pinching her fingers angled in mid-air. Opal must have made an illusion to hide Tembry and the baby. But it didn't seem to matter because the demoness seemed to know where the baby's crown was anyway. Drake rushed over to me, hauling me to my feet as I wheezed in air. I realised my windpipe was partially crushed, and I was still choking, but Drake used his strength where I could not and gripped me with strong arms and dragged me towards the female demon.

With my last ounce of strength, I jumped on the female demon's back, clawing my way up to her neck, and dragged my sword across her throat.

She choked on her own blood as we fell to the floor, but before I could fall off her, strong hands gripped my sides and pulled me backwards. I fell into Drake's muscled chest, barely able to get any air in as the female demon dissolved before me. I gripped my own throat, trying to stay calm while I analysed the damage.

I rapidly reconstructed my airway first, pushing the fibres of crushed muscle back out where the demon had crushed my trachea, closing the gaps between cells and allowing air to flow freely back into my lungs. The muscles around my neck would be sore and bruised, but I didn't have it in me to heal them just now. I realised Drake's arms were still around me, and I hastily dissipated my sword and scrambled over to Tembry, as Opal's illusion fell away.

"Saraya?" she asked, sitting up and clutching her baby tightly, all three maids staring at me as if I had two heads. "What just happened?"

"Two demons," came Drake's deep voice, "in astral form, just tried to take magic from your baby. Your princess killed both."

A gurgle across the room made my head snap towards the source. At the doorway, the hulking male demon was twitching, not having dissolved yet. I crawled to my feet and summoned my sword again, hobbling over to him, Drake close behind me.

The demon was gurgling, trying to talk, I realised. I angled my sword at his carotid. "What did you say?" I rasped through a burning throat.

"They're coming for you," he rasped, guttural and dark. "They're coming..." His body went taut and he died, dissolving into nothing.

I turned to look at Drake, who was looking at me with a strange darkness in his eyes. I shifted past him to Tembry.

"I'm sorry to scare you, Tembry," I said earnestly. "But it's the reason I fled from the fae to start with. Demons have been attacking humans for hundreds of years from the astral realm. They hunt every childbirth and take each baby's magical seed. They—" I pointed to Drake. "The fae kind have been stealing our children's magic to make themselves stronger. I'm the only one right now who can stop it."

Tembry looked between Drake and me, then shook her

head. "I trust you, Sara. We always have. Don't we girls?" She looked up at Blythe and Lucy, who were staring at my sword open-mouthed.

"We believe you," said Blythe. "You've been midwife to the women of the city since you were thirteen. How could we not trust you with everything we have?"

Relief flooded through me like a warm breeze, and I felt like I could finally take a good and proper breath. I had been worried about their reaction and had hoped that I had time to explain things to them before the birth rather than see it full and terrifying like this. But they trusted me, thank the goddess. Years of them seeing me helping the city's women had them trusting me on all accounts.

Perhaps in some midwife intuition, I had chosen tonight to hold our escape. Somehow, I knew I needed to be here on this night. If I hadn't been here—I couldn't bear the thought.

I glanced at the fae warriors who were standing in the corner, their swords still drawn, unsure of what to do. "You two—" I angled my sword at them. "If you ever stop me from attending a birth, your friends will be attending your funeral. Got it?" They nodded frantically, clutching their useless swords. "Right then. Get us some food. It's going to be a long night."

I turned around to look for Drake, but he had already gone.

33
DRAKE

As I strode out of the birthing room and into the palace proper, my mind was a fucking whirlpool of shock and disbelief.

Saraya had some of the most powerful magic I had ever seen. Every fae had magic of their own and the truly talented of us rose up the ranks into high ranking positions like I had. The strongest among us were kings and queens, who belonged to long lines of extraordinary magic wielders.

I had already known the princess was excellent with a sword. So excellent that she had no doubt been trained from infancy to wield one. Mixed with natural talent, she matched our own royalty when it came to swordplay.

But her magic.

I had watched her. Even while being choked by a seven-foot-tall charangula demon, the worst of demon-kind, she'd still summoned a sword and killed it and then its mate.

On top of that, I'd then watched her heal her own bloody windpipe, something no fae warrior would have been able to do after a battle. That kind of intricate, detailed healing took an insane amount of discipline and focus.

And *then*, I'd seen the carnage she'd left in her wake down in the dungeons. I had no less than twenty fae out of service with severe concussions. She'd done all of that with a wave of her mind, by the accounts of the groaning captain I'd briefly interrogated before tracking Saraya down.

Her maid had also called her a midwife. Had said that she had been serving the people of Quartz City for years.

If I hadn't heard or seen any of this, I would never have believed it.

Sure I was no expert on humans, Saraya herself informing me that I wasn't treating her military properly. I would change that now, of course. I had a reputation for being brutal, but even I had no intention of torturing the humans for no actual reason.

I mean, give me a reason, and then sure.

But for all my lack of knowledge about humans, I could tell that Saraya was something else. Something more.

She might even be like *me* in that way.

My heart was beating faster than it had any right to. I slowed my breathing down as I reached the dining room and poured myself a glass of wine. I was looking for the whiskey, turning over what I'd just seen, when realisation thudded through me like a blacksmith's hammer.

Saraya had just told her maids that the fae were sending demons to take human magic. She had hinted at it twice now. Once when I'd seen her kill those first demons, and the second time was when Wyxian summoned her to the throne room. But this was the first time she'd actually made the full accusation out loud.

But surely it wasn't true. Wyxian had spies all over the realm of the Dark Fae, and if either the Obsidian Court or Midnight Court were doing something as big as this…surely it would have been found out. But Saraya believed it so vehemently that she hated us, hated me with a burning passion. I was still waiting for a reply to the letter I had sent. Until then, I could do nothing.

So there was one sick, twisted question that remained. If it wasn't the fae that were sending demons after the humans, then who the hell was?

34
SARAYA

Tembry ended up delivering her placenta ten minutes after the attack, assisted a little by me. Shock can sometimes delay a placenta from birthing, as a strong contraction is needed to push it out. And these contractions come best when a mother is *not* scared out of her wits.

Opal took a great liking to Tembry and the baby. She always sat somewhere she could get a good view of them both, softly crooning a little lumzen song when she thought no one was listening. I thought it was impossible to love the little creature even more than I did, but I was proven wrong yet again.

Tembry named her daughter Delilah after her grandmother and I watched over the new mother and baby for the rest of the night. Twice more, we were attacked. The fae guards alerted me both times when they arrived from the front entrance, shouting out in warning.

The first was a sliming yellow thing that squelched across the floor. I could tell that in its physical form, it would smell awful. I plunged my sword through its squashed face, and it died with a squirting cry.

The second lot was a group of tiny demons, the top of their spiked heads coming to my waist. They didn't know I was waiting for them with a sword on the other side of the wall, so I was able to slice my way through all five of them pretty quickly before they got three steps into the room.

My throat was still sore from the attack, and I was desperately exhausted. So when dawn arrived, and Blythe woke up, I gave her instructions on how to help Tembry and then promptly tumbled into her bed and fell asleep. I woke up to find Opal smooshed against my cheek.

I'd sworn to tell Drake about my magic at the time of Tembry's birth, but I didn't see him all of the next day. I was thankful because it gave our smitten little mother time to rest and learn how to breastfeed her new baby. To our dismay, our request to see the baby's father, Captain Markus, had been denied. It left a bad feeling in my mouth because they had taken some time to deny us. Blythe told me that there had been some fighting during the initial stages of the invasion, and I was sure that meant human deaths as well. Markus would have fought. For all we knew, he could be dead.

The fae would pay for all the wrongs they had done in the name of a stupid marriage contract.

But if I thought that was as bad as it could get, I was wrong because the next day, I was escorted by Lysander to attend the throne room.

When I strode through the giant oak doors, the first thing I saw was Daxian. His spine was ramrod straight with his hands clasped behind his back. As I met his turquoise eyes I saw they held a dark shadow of anger.

A sense of dread wound its way around my heart as I

warily came to stand before him. I felt Lysander hovering protectively behind me and the movement would have confused me if I hadn't seen Daxian's face. He looked like he wanted to wrap his hands around my throat and throttle me.

"*Princess*," the fae prince said through gritted teeth. I got the feeling that he was still bitter about my being Sam, I thought. But what he said next punched any thought right out of me. "The other dark fae courts have pledged their support for my father. There will be no question. Tomorrow, we are getting married."

I simply stared at him as realisation came crashing down upon me like a falling tree. Daxian continued, his face snow white. "With your countrymen to bear witness, we will have our union, or you will be breaking your oath."

He abruptly turned and strode swiftly out of the room without looking at me again. I stood there lamely for a moment before movement at the edge of the room caught my eye.

Drake stood there, preternaturally still, his knuckles white as he gripped the pommel of his sword with those tattooed fingers. His brown eyes held mine, and there was some meaning in there that I could not read. Some message he was trying to send me.

I frowned, but just as I made to move towards him, Lysander stepped between us.

"Come on, Princess," he said quietly. "I think you have some things to do...some type of preparation for the wedding."

I blinked into the middle distance as my entire life came suddenly crashing down around me. My stepmother's pale as milk face loomed over my head, blue eyes hooking mine, telling me I had no power here. Each garish scar on my back reminded me of exactly how powerless I was. That to protect everyone around me, I had to do what I was told. Had to sacrifice myself.

My father was the one who had sealed my fate for me. And Drake was enforcing that now. Everyone else's actions to take over my life had always come to fruition. The moment I had moved to carve my own path, I had felt liberated. Free to do what I knew I was meant to do. But it had lasted all of four months. Here I stood again, in my birth home, a place that should have been my safe haven, but was instead, my worst nightmare.

And there was nothing I could do about it.

I shattered, at that moment, like a quartz crystal being crushed against the marble tile. I looked at the pieces of me, lying there, glittering and beautiful but useless.

There was a tug on my arm as a shadow fell over me. Warmth spread through my elbow, and I looked up to see Drake's eyes. His nostrils flared as if he were scenting me.

"Are you alright, Saraya?" he asked in a low, rumbling voice, like thunder rolling in the far distance.

I stared at the shards of me and decided in that moment that I would not let the fae—let Drake— see me shatter like something delicate and breakable. So, like knitting together a wound made of flesh and blood, I tied my pieces back together, their seams made of a pledge I'd made to a goddess. Of a pledge I had made to the women under my care.

"What does the lotus have in common with lightning?" I breathed and my voice sounded far away.

His dark brows knitted together. "I don't know."

"Both are born from struggle. Lightning is born from the charge between clouds, and the lotus is born struggling out of the mud."

His eyes searched mine, unsure of my meaning.

And I spoke in a voice that did not quiver. That sounded to my ears like a cold, southern wind. "I am the sword in the night. The protector of human potential. The shield against all that is evil. *This* is my pledge. And I will *never* be broken. *Lightning does not yield.*"

I turned on my heel and strode out of the hall, leaving Lysander, who was hovering by the door, to hurry after me.

3 5

SARAYA

I was getting married tonight.

And it clawed at my heart as if all ten of Daxian's fingers were inside my chest, digging my flesh out. I couldn't escape it. I had tried and failed to thwart this blood contract, but no amount of clever thinking could get me out of it.

But there was no way I'd let them break me. I would go into this in a way that befitted my station, both as a warrior midwife of the Order of Temari *and* as Princess of Lobrathia.

Lysander moved me back into my own suite, and the girls and I began preparations in the early afternoon.

Tembry insisted on getting me ready, and I insisted that if she did so, her babe's cot should be set up in my room. Blythe and Lucy also came, with Opal sitting protectively on the edge of the baby's cot, watching over us all.

I bathed myself, and just as I was getting out, I heard a knock at my suite door. Wrapping myself in a modest gown, I hurried to the door to find Lysander there, as I'd requested.

"Good afternoon, Princess," he said, bowing.

Tembry blushed, trying to cover me with her body, but I

was sure Lysander was more than familiar with women in dressing gowns.

"I need something from my bags," I told him bossily. I wanted no arguments from him tonight. "They are in the stables of Madame Yolande's establishment down in the city."

He gave me a look as if to ask if I was serious. "The wedding is just in—"

"Lysander."

"Yes, Princess?" he didn't look exasperated, only curious.

I swallowed the sudden lump in my throat. If I was to do this, I would do it properly. "In those bags are my mother's wedding silks and the instructions for Ellythian bridal rituals. The rituals of my mother's people. Do you understand?"

His face softened. "I understand."

"Are there fae rituals I should know about?"

Lysander grimaced. "Yes, um. No."

"Which is it?" I said impatiently.

"The Dark Fae are barbaric people..." he rubbed the back of his neck uncomfortably.

"I can handle it, Lysander. Just tell me."

"I don't know if they'll do it this time, but tradition is for someone to try and kidnap the bride on your way to the moon alter. The groom has to fight the intruders off."

Tembry gasped.

But I had heard only one part of that. "Did you say moon alter?"

"The Dark Fae worship the moon. The Light Fae, the sun."

I let out a slow breath. "Perhaps we're more similar than we thought. There are moon rituals for the Ellythians too."

He nodded as if he knew that already. "Ellythians have been sailing across the sea to Midnight Court for hundreds of years, I'm sure there's a lot that we share."

The thought surprised me, though I knew it shouldn't. Ellythia's southern-most island fell in line with the Dark Fae Realm. I had just never actually thought they would be communicating with each other.

"Will you get my things for me? Please?"

He gave me a small, handsome, courtesan smile and swept a bow. "Upon my honour, Princess, I accept this quest and will return your treasure to you."

I LEFT MY ROOM IN A WHITE SILK GOWN WITH A WHITE LACE CAPE hood that Blythe had managed to find in someone's closet. I think it was supposed to represent the leaving of my innocent single life behind. We left baby Delilah behind with Lucy watching over her as I would need Tembry for the ritual.

As instructed by Geravie's notes, kindly delivered by Lysander, I readied a silver tray with a matching sapphire encrusted goblet. But there was one thing missing. I went up to Drake, waiting for me outside my room.

"I need something from my husband to be. For the ritual." I shifted uncomfortably. The heat I felt in my cheeks was senseless. *Husband-to-be* sounded awful. Like something dirty and far removed. Something other people had, not me.

Drake stood preternaturally still in front of me while every muscle in my own body was seizing up. When he didn't say anything, I looked up at him, frowning. "What?"

His face was a little pink behind his golden tan. "You look beautiful."

Heat spread through me, and I blinked back down at my tray. "I'm not even dressed for the wedding." I scoffed. "Can you get something or not?"

"Will one of his eyes do?" he growled so only I could hear. "Or how about his tongue?"

I choked on a sudden laugh. I glared up at him, but there was a smile on my lips. "This is serious, Drake."

A mischievous smile played on the corner of his mouth. "One moment. I'll meet you at the doorway."

Our little troupe marched down to the end of the palace and down to the golden doors, a smaller version of the entrance hall at the front. The dusk air was cool on my skin, the smell of jasmine filling my nose. My mother had requested those be planted at the back of the palace because she had them at her palace in Ellythia. My vision blurred as tears overcame my eyes. I hoped my mother was watching over me from above because these rituals were the only way I felt like she was with me tonight.

Quicker than I thought was possible, Drake was at my elbow, a ring in his hand. It gleamed fat and gold on his palm as he offered it to me.

I took it, and he smirked.

"Looks like I beat Daxian to giving you a ring."

"Very funny." I palmed the gold ring, wondering why he was taking extra effort to flirt with me tonight. The ring had a black dragon carved into the top of it. It was just like Daxian, a brutish, arrogant thing. I placed it on my tray and led the girls away towards the queen's forest. I knew Drake would be tailing us and I could feel his gaze on my back, heavy, like obsidian, but I knew he'd keep a respectable distance—and well, if he didn't, he'd regret it.

The sky progressively darkened above us, and a slither of a moon appeared in its waxing phase. It was honestly a perfect night for the most tragic thing that could be happening to me. Marrying the fae prince of Black Court.

Why couldn't the war have been between a happier Court like Midnight or Twilight? Marrying Prince Skelton wouldn't have been so bad. But alas, I knew the answer already. It was only Black Court that had the gall to wage that war in the first place.

We reached the forest, and the ground became prickly underfoot, but I didn't pause in my step, knowing I was due for a splinter any second. Drake was silent behind us in that strange way of his.

The lake was like a gaping hole in the black of the night with the absence of much moonlight, and it wasn't until Tembry and Blythe opened their yellow quartz lanterns that I could see properly. I set the silver tray on the wet earth and lit the tiny candle with a match. I filled the goblet with lake water and set it so the tiny bit of moonlight fell on top of it as Tembry made her way to the other side, and Blythe shivered in her woollen shawl behind me.

Standing, I dropped my white lace cape. I glanced to my left in the distance, between the trees, the darkness shifted, and I knew Drake was watching.

I slipped the delicate strings of the silk dress off my shoulders and let it slink to the ground. The cold night air kissed my skin, and goosebumps erupted all over me, less from the wind and more from the fae warrior I knew was watching closely.

Tembry's birth had brought us girls all closer, and I blessedly felt rather indifferent about being naked in front of them.

Blythe picked up my silver tray, her eyes shining, and handed it to me with a tiny curtsey. "Maidenhood delivers you to the mother," she said softly, reciting the words Geravie had written. "Go with the love of the goddess at your side and fond memories of your old home."

I took the tray from her, bowing over it, the backs of my eyes burning. This was it. Turning towards the lake, I clenched my teeth as I padded over the wet earth, the cold of the world stinging my bare skin and the rabid scars on my back. I stepped into the lake without hesitation, and my jaw pulsed as I suppressed the urge to cry out against the chill. I persisted, wading deeper and deeper until the light of the moon shone upon me from overhead, and the water reached my nipples. I balanced my tray high above my head, careful not to let the goblet spill.

When I reached the other side, the air chilling me to the bone, I presented the tray to Tembry, who represented a mother figure. "Come, bride of the Crown Prince of the Black Court." She said the words carefully, not stumbling, and reached for the goblet. She tipped its contents over my head, and I gasped as cold lake water stung me. "Mother Moon, cleanse this bride on this sacred night, for she is about to be maiden no more." She set the chalice back on the tray and took up Daxian's fat ring. "May her husband see she is moon touched and goddess blessed. May he worship the goddess at the feet of his bride, at the lap of his bride, and at the lips of his bride. For tonight, she *is* the goddess."

I smiled a little at the words, as I *had* been blessed by the goddess in the form of the dark Umali. She had already blessed me to work in her name. But the smile fell from my face as I realised what those words to a bride really meant. Daxian and I would be required to consummate the marriage as soon as possible. I'd have to share a bed with him. Lose my virginity to him. I swallowed down the acid that now crawled up my throat. *Mother, give me strength.*

Tembry put the ring back down with a heavy clang, and I arose out of the water into her arms, where she wrapped me in a red velvet robe. The night's chill was abated, and now I was a bride in the eyes of the goddess.

"Is it done?" asked Tembry, rubbing my arms. "Is that it?"

My teeth chattered. "Y-Yes, let's go."

I huddled within the robe, took the silver tray, and led us out of the forest. Something shifted ahead of me, and with a sober knowledge that with his fae ears, Drake had probably been the first fae to witness an Ellythian bridal ritual. It didn't feel tainted, somehow, though it should have. Perhaps because it was more like he had been watching over us.

He is your enemy, I chastised myself as we hurried across the lawn, Drake darting behind our group again. *Don't let your guard down. Nothing good will come of it.* But my eyes always seemed to find Drake in the dark. I found myself wondering if this would be less awful if it were him waiting for me at the end of the aisle instead.

36

DRAKE

I walked back from Saraya's room, my insides hot and pulsing despite the cool of the night. I had stood transfixed at that forest pond as she'd taken off her robe. No force on earth could have torn my eyes away as she'd let her gown fall off her body. And, like some mythical fae creature, had taken on the grace and grit required to walk through what I'm sure was ice cold water without breaking a sweat. She'd looked ethereal under the crescent moon, and I had gaped at her like some sort of juvenile who'd never seen a naked woman before. I shook my head as I strode across the marble tile, trying to get the vision of her, the scent of her, the sound of her, out of my god-forsaken head.

But it was impossible. She would always be burned into the grooves of my brain. I knew that down to my marrow bones. I had always known from the moment I'd first seen her.

I swore under my breath as Callan, one of my captains, a meaty young fae with the sharpest eyes on the team, strode up to me.

"They'll be here in half an hour, my lord. Just coming up the eastern road."

I nodded at him absently. "Good. Very good."

Lysander appeared out of nowhere, probably from lurking in some shadow, scoping out the situation.

"Penny for your thoughts, Commander?" he sniggered at me. "How did the ritual go? I read those instructions on my way back. Something about strolling naked?"

I growled at him, and he smirked happily, knowing full well what was going on inside my head. He and Slade always knew how I was feeling. We'd been in each other's company for too long.

"Grumpy doesn't do for Daxian's wedding night," he said, now sobering up. "Shouldn't you be doing best man duties?"

I grunted irritably, because we both knew full well that me being Daxian's best man was a farce at best. We walked together to the suite we'd taken over to get changed as we were still wearing full fae armour, our uniform of choice on most days.

Slade was already there, coming out of his room into the suite living room. He grimaced, looking down at his new shirt. "Urgh, do I have to wear this?"

"Yes," piped Lysander. "It's only appropriate for a fae wedding."

Slade and I both chucked our friend a dirty look, to which he turned his back and held up a swathe of black silk. "This is yours, Drake," he tossed it at me, and I snatched it out of the air.

"Awful."

"It's lovely, handwoven by the looks of it." Lysander picked up his own sky blue shirt. "Ah, nothing beats silk.

What do you think the princess will be wearing? I don't know what Ellythian brides wear."

Slade grunted. "Fae brides always look like puffed-up pudding. I've never liked it."

"Well, lucky you don't have anyone that will wear one for you," shot Lysander. "*I* happen to like them. Though I'm sure they're hard to take off…"

Lysander and Slade argued about the merits of fae bridal garments, and I left them to it, fleeing into my room for a cold shower that I very much needed.

It was not often that I was caught out of control, and this irked me more than anything. I needed to be sharp and collected, completely in control as Commander of the Black Court elites. I needed to think about tonight. Any number of things could lead to disaster, political or otherwise. As much as this was a wedding, it was a political meeting of royals. Something that had not happened between the humans and the fae for a hundred-odd years. Half of the humans still thought we were black-eyed beasts, and the other half child-eating killers. Wyxian hoped to change that tonight and show that we meant well and that all we wanted was control over the luminous quartz quarry.

I ran through the strategy for tonight. The Lobrathian nobility had all been collected and brought to the palace days ago, so we had Saraya's liege lords under our control. Tonight was about the royals of the other human kingdoms.

Lysander had one set of warriors following each human monarch into the city, as well as scouting the area in general in case one of them decided to be stupid and bring an army with them. Because chances were, they would assume that if the fae had taken one human kingdom, we might be on the move for more.

But that wasn't the king's intention.

I had warriors hidden all around the castle on the outside perimeter, set to alert me in case anything out of the ordinary happened. Both Lysander and Slade would be doing their rounds, outside and inside, to make sure everything went as planned. That left me free to wander inside the ballroom and eye out the human royals and their retinues.

From what my spies had told me, the human royalty all met at the Kaalon Kingdom last week before they set out to get here. Everyone, that was, except the northernmost Kingdom, Kusha, the desert kingdom, which was too far for any of them to get here on time. Wyxian hadn't wanted to wait. But by all reports, their meeting was fairly inconclusive. What could they do in front of a fae army after all?

I donned the black silk shirt and pants I was supposed to wear and strapped my sword belt on as well. Wyxian wanted to put on an undefeatable front, so a little steel message wouldn't go amiss.

Lysander, Slade, and I left our suite to go and greet the royals. It was a little strange, thinking that this massive palace was now ours. That we owned it, the land, the humans, and of course, the princess Saraya with it. Her sister had been rumoured to have escaped to another Kingdom, and to my chagrin, had been impossible to trace. But tonight, Daxian would seal that ownership of Saraya and cement our hold over this land.

Irritation sliced through me like a hot, jagged knife.

"You can't murder anyone tonight, Drake," Lysander drawled. "Peaceful human relations, remember?"

I growled in assent. I *did* want to kill someone, and it was no human. I gripped the obsidian hilt of my sword until I thought my hand would stay fixed in that shape.

I had a job to do. A blasted job, and I would do it well. I always had.

We arrived at the entrance hall, my captains already lined up and waiting. I nodded at Callan, standing at the open doors. I lined up next to him and checked my pocket watch.

"It's almost time," I said. "Send word to the king."

I sent a line of warriors to stand either side of the palace steps and a few more leading up the driveway.

A little domineering, maybe. But it was control. Complete control. Retaliation was useless against my warriors.

The king arrived with Daxian, dressed in elegant finery, showing our wealth with heavy gold rings. Daxian had a ruby stud on one ear and the massive gold family ring on his finger. I smirked, just a little, patting the pocket where my own ring sat.

A carriage rattled in the distance, and the fae all stood to attention. After a few tense moments, a carriage with the peach tree insignia of Kaalon arrived. Kaalon was Lobrathia's eastern neighbour and the closest, as the crow flies, to this palace. I vaguely wondered if Wyxian would give this city a new, fae name once he claimed it properly.

King Osring was a balding waif of a human, as tall as a fae, and would have been graceful if not for the need for a walking stick.

How on earth these humans kept their thrones was beyond me. At Osring's age in the Dark Fae Realm, someone would have knocked him off his throne already, usually a son or other relative. He hadn't brought his queen along. Apparently, she was a poorly old thing, likely bedridden.

Osring ambled up the steps with his stick, and Wyxian greeted him formally. To his credit, Osring barely gave away any nervousness, simply nodding, exchanging formalities before being escorted by a human manservant to the refreshments.

It wasn't long before the rest arrived. Both the king and queen of Waelan came, which I thought rather bold. Waelan shared a border with the northern aspect of Lobrathia and were apparently friendly neighbours.

Indeed, when they arrived, neither looked happy about the new occupation. King Desmond was shorter than his wife, Queen Helena, who stood tall and proud with a stature that made me think she could take me to the ground without any difficulty.

Next to me, Lysander tittered in excitement before I shot him a look as they walked up the stairs. He quietened, but his face glowed under the quartz lights, taking in every aspect of Queen Helena. Slade covered a smirk with his hand next to us. We both knew Lysander's favourite type of woman.

The queen marched right up to Wyxian and shook hands with him, her brown eyes sparkling with suspicion and the urge to dominate. She sized up the fae king and prince Dark-cleaver, almost standing eye to eye with both.

"I hope you're not keeping the Voltanius family in the dungeons," she said superiorly.

"That would be inhumane," said Wyxian with a smile.

I cringed inwardly.

Helena sniffed and walked past, her husband hurrying after her. I almost felt sorry for King Desmond because, by the way Lysander was twitching, I knew Desmond would have competition tonight.

Then was Serus Kingdom, which was north of Kaalon. But it was only tiny King Junni, barely thirteen years old, with his regent, Duke Lee. To his credit, the young king, clearly having spent the trip practising, swept a bow.

"King Wyxian Darkcleaver," he said softly but regally. Then he politely gave his name.

And finally came the Traenaran, King Omni, a mahogany-skinned man, built tall and broad like the ox that was his house symbol. He wore his hair in neat twists that I'd never seen before. It was not often that Traenara visited Lobrathia, since it was so far, no doubt Omni had set out as soon as he got the letter a few weeks ago.

"Fae King," he boomed, his voice like a drum. "One hundred years since the fae graced our lands, and now here, you stand, usurper and conqueror."

The two kings sized each other up before stiffly shaking hands with what looked like a bone-shattering grip. I cringed for the Traenara king, fae strength was far superior to a human's, as I'd learned in the past two weeks, yet Omni didn't so much as a grimace.

I was impressed by the humans. I didn't know why I thought they would be stuttering kings like the one we took the throne from. Saraya's father appeared to be the anomaly here. But we all knew they came out of fear and curiosity. Everyone knew that theoretically, the fae could take over the entire human realm easily.

But we had no reason to do that. The fae realm was where the fae belonged, as Saraya had so politely told me. Too long in the human realm, and we pined for our own earth, we just couldn't let the humans know that.

But the quarry was here. The other realms had no such valuable resource.

One question remained. The Lobrathian queen, Saraya's stepmother, had not made an appearance. That would be something that had to be addressed tonight. One of them could be hiding her, and we had to figure out which. My guess was actually on Kusha, the secretive walled kingdom at the northernmost point of the human realm. That's where Glacine supposedly hailed from, although I had thought Kusha people bore the darkest skin. There was some mystery there—Wyxian would have to get it out of them.

We left for the meeting room. Servants bustled about around us, putting the finishing touches on the ballroom for the wedding.

I was about to enter the meeting room when Callan arrived at my elbow. "My Lord Commander," he said. "A raven has arrived for you."

I t took all three maids to help me get dressed in my
mother's purple wedding silks. We followed the instructions and diagrams Geravie had given us in the little
pamphlet she had made. And when it was done, they all
stood back and appraised me.

"Are you sure it's supposed to be like that?" Tembry
asked cocking her head.

Blythe held up Geravie's diagram, and they all squinted at
it, then back at me.

"It's exactly like the picture," said Lucy. "And I think it's
the most marvellous thing I've ever seen!"

"Can I look in the mirror now?"

They cheered me on, and I gave them a small smile to
bury the sinking feeling in my heart. This day that should
have been the happiest moment of my life was pinched by
sacrifice and laced with sorrow. I had been bound by a savage
duty at every corner. But I did freeze like an icicle looking at
myself in the mirror. The girls had outdone themselves.

I knew I was considered beautiful by most people; from

the moment the stableboys began staring at me goggle-eyed around the time I turned sixteen. But this? This was something else entirely. I looked like an Ellythian Princess from some old tale.

The silk blouse, finely embroidered in gold, bared a hint of my upper midriff in the traditional Ellythian style my mother had known and loved. The full skirt sat high and then flared out at my hips in a tumble of silk and intricate, glittering embroidery.

A sheer purple fabric covered my mouth and nose, and the matching purple veil made me look like a vision.

But the whole thing was completed with the best jewellery I had. We'd taken out my finest to match the thread of the embroidery. A gold necklace in a staggered chandelier design, dotted with amethysts, matching gold drops, and a matching tiara, my biggest one, that you could see from a mile away. It screamed "Princess" to anyone within fifty metres, and in the quartz light, it sparkled jauntily.

It was a lot. It was too much. And I told the girls so.

"It's your wedding!" chided Tembry. "It's supposed to be a lot."

"You're the eldest princess of Lobrathia!" said Blythe in a soft voice. "This is the *one* time you get married. And the only time a human has ever married a fae. The only time a fae has taken over a human kingdom. You represent all of us. And you'll make every person in the city proud!"

Tears threatened to spill from my lined eyes. I took a deep breath through my nose.

"I love you guys," I whispered, trying to keep it together. We had been here before, just months ago, when my engagement was supposed to lead to me being taken away.

312

Now, with my wedding, my kingdom was being taken away.

They each took one of my hands.

"How could everything have gone so wrong?" I whispered.

"It's no one's fault," said Tembry. "Your father is ill. Your stepmother ran away. You couldn't do anything."

You couldn't do anything

Those words haunted my very core.

I can't do anything.

I failed to save my people.

This whole thing had sat in my hands, and I hadn't been able to handle it. At every turn, I hadn't been able to change anything. If anything, *I* had caused this. Did the goddess not want me to join the Order of Temari? Because the sole thing that could stop me from fulfilling that role was happening.

But that couldn't be right. The goddess Umali had met me at the temple, had placed her blazing thumb on my forehead herself. She wanted me to lead the Order of Temari. She had made me the first Warrior Midwife in a century.

There was something that I was missing. Some crucial piece of this puzzle that I was overlooking.

But as the clock struck eight, I knew it was pointless. My time was up.

"Where will you sleep?" asked Tembry in a hushed voice. "Have they prepared the marriage bed?"

Lucy's eyebrows shot up. "I must go check!" she cried. "We have no idea! That prince has been sleeping by his father's suites." She rushed out of the room, and I imagined having to spend my wedding night in a room next to the king of the fae. Thank the goddess for Tembry's quick mind.

There was a knock at the door, and Tembry opened it to

find Lysander leaning on the doorframe with a crooked smile on his face.

His mouth fell open when he saw me.

"By the gods," he whispered.

"It's customary to bow before a princess," Blythe said snidely.

Lysander looked at my friend in shock for a moment before looking back at me and bowing. "Your Highness."

"She will be *your* princess soon. And one day, your queen," Tembry added.

Lysander pressed his lips together into a small smile. "Of course, of course."

"Shall we?" I said.

Opal crooned from Delilah's cot, warbling sadly like I'd forgotten her. I turned and smiled at her, and she leapt for me, and I caught her in my arms.

"Do you want to come and see me get married, Ope?" I said, my eyes burning. Opal nodded and wiped an eye. "Okay, well, you can be on my shoulder. Just hide yourself." She sniffed and leapt up. Suddenly, her familiar weight on my left shoulder made me feel so much better. We had been through so much. It was only fitting she be with me all the way.

THE BLOUSE FELT A LITTLE TIGHT AROUND MY RIBS, BUT I KNEW IT was just nerves. I told myself to breathe and nodded to the girls before I strode forward past Lysander, catching a whiff of lilies as I passed him.

The fae warrior-courtesan led me through the palace to the ballroom, where two fae warriors stood guard. Some kind person had placed hibiscus bouquets on either side of the entrance. The servants were thinking of my mother.

Oh, Mother, how I wish you were here to tell me what to do.

Derrick appeared from the corner, guiding my pale-faced, vacant-eyed father in a wheelchair. A lump formed in my throat, like a fat piece of coal.

"He cannot walk, Derrick?" I breathed.

"I'm sorry, Princess," Derrick said stiffly. "I tried this morning, but he wouldn't even stand for me. I'm not sure what's happening. He won't take his medicine either."

Things were getting worse and worse. "He won't eat or drink anything?"

"I all but tried to force it down his throat, Your Highness, but it's too dangerous. He only chokes on it."

"Can I see that?" came a sharp voice from behind me. We turned to see Slade striding forward and reaching for the dark vial in Derrick's hand.

Alarmed, the manservant handed it over, staring at the huge warrior. I watched on as Slade uncorked the vial and delicately sniffed it. The warrior's dark eyes shifted to me and then back to my father. "Who gave you this?" he asked the manservant

"The palace physicians," Derrick said, turning pink. "The advisors gave me orders on when to give it."

"Who delivers it to you?" Lysander asked.

"Oxley," Derrick said nervously. "The head..." Derrick's eyes shifted to me, and they widened as if he'd just realised something. "But the orders came from the queen."

Slade growled, low in his throat. "This is not medicine. It's demonic magic."

A wide gaping pit opened in the centre of my being. "And both Oxley and my stepmother have mysteriously disappeared." I choked on the words, staring at my father's moon-like face in disbelief.

"Oh no." Derrick's face twisted in despair. "I've been giving the king demon magic?"

Slade pocketed the vial, his jaw clenching and unclenching. "I'm sorry, but I know that smell from my time in the demon kingdom. It's not something I'd forget."

"You think this is what's causing my father's illness?" I asked, my heart beating against my ribs like a war drum.

Slade turned his coal-black eyes upon me and said grimly, "I have no doubt."

I should have recognised it. I should have known to stop it. But I had never seen demonic magic before, and even that one time I had looked into my father's brain, I had only seen a savage and profound warping. I hadn't even known what I was looking at. I couldn't blame myself for this. But I *did* know who was to blame.

I cast a look at Derrick. "This is my stepmother's doing. I know it."

Your stepmother is not human, the Kraasputin had said. Oxley and Stepmother had run off together. They were a part of the same group, the same team? Were they in love and run off? No, I thought. My stepmother was not capable of loving like that. She could have tricked him. She had tricked my father, after all. He had not become unwell until after my mother's death, until after Oxley took up his position as the kingdom's head advisor.

"Can it be reversed?" I asked. "The effects of the poison?"

Slade gave me a sympathetic look that told me everything I needed to know.

"I'm going to kill her," I announced. "I'm going to hunt her down like the demon she is and take her head off."

Derrick shifted uncomfortably while Lysander and Slade exchanged a glance.

"You can kill whoever you like," said Lysander apologetically. "But first, you have to get married."

That one tiny event that needed to be taken care of.

A rippling, snarling anger tore through me, violent as death, dark as Umali's blessed skin. "Let's get this over with, then."

I blinked away the tears and squared my shoulders as wedding trumpets went off, shrill and piercing. It felt like a call to arms.

The double doors were flung wide open.

A long blood-red carpet lined with pink and white roses lay before me. On either side of it, I recognised my father's liege lords and neighbouring monarchs I had not seen in months, and years in some cases. But my eyes were trained at the end of the carpet where three men stood sentinel.

King Wyxian. Prince Daxian. Drake. My father-in-law, my husband, and the commander of their special forces.

I was alone, with no mother, no sister, no cognisant father. This could not be happening.

But it was, because a piano now played to guide me in. But I couldn't move. Couldn't walk towards a fate that might very well doom me. Behind me, I heard a polite cough.

It was Uncle Osring, glancing between me and my father with a genuine sadness. I felt my face crumple. Peach Tree City had been a happy holiday spot for Altara and me as children, and I thought of Osring as family.

"It would be my honour, Saraya, in place of your father." He gently took my hand and placed it on his, leaning into me. "There are difficult things royals have to do, Saraya. Marrying to save your kingdom is one of them."

I swallowed hard and nodded. He gave me an encouraging smile. "I'm sorry for everything that has happened. You look beautiful. Your parents would be so proud."

I knew he had just said that to make me feel better. I hadn't made anyone proud because I'd failed. And each step I was now taking towards Daxian proved that. I was sinking deeper into quicksand with no way out.

You couldn't do anything.

My heart trembled in my chest, but I managed to say, "I would like my father to walk me down, Uncle. Will you drive his wheelchair?"

He gave me a smile that made my heart melt. "So proud, Saraya, So proud. I will. Of course."

I smiled back at him. I leaned down and took my father's cool hand in mine. I looked into his distant eyes. "I failed you, Father," I whispered. "But I will not fail you again." I carefully knelt down before him, the fae warriors shifting in surprise behind me. "I swear, on my mother's name. I swear on my Voltanius name. I swear by the name of the goddess Umali that I will find my stepmother, and I will kill her. I'll avenge what she's done to us. Lightning does not yield." I squeezed his hand and stood, adjusting my silk skirts. Nodding at Uncle Osring, he took Derrick's place to wheel my father's chair.

We strode down the aisle side by side, the music of the piano striking up again.

My eyes fell upon Daxian. His face was stony, resigned. Never had I ever imagined I'd be walking down the aisle to a man who didn't want to marry me. Who looked at me like I was something inconvenient. But I realised that none of that mattered. In the face of my goal, the primal roaring of my blood through my veins, this stupid marriage didn't matter.

Once we were husband and wife, I would be free to do as I pleased. There was nothing in the oath that said I had to live with him, stay by his side constantly. I had another goal now.

We reached the gathered nobles, most of whom were staring at my father with a mixture of confusion and horror. Our liege lords, the nobility of Lobrathia, were gathered at the back, closest to us. They had all suspected about my father's illness but were stony-faced as they saw him now, unable to function, his deterioration in full control. I kept my chin high for both of us. After all, lightning does not yield.

Then I reached the royals from our neighbouring kingdoms.

I walked past Queen Helena first, who gave me a nod, but no smile. Powerful King Omni gave me a grave look. Little King Junni shifted nervously, not looking at me but at Daxian.

I was two-thirds of the way down the aisle when my eyes slid from Daxian's to Drake's hazel eyes. Something in them sent a shiver down my spine as he took me in, his tattooed hands clasped firmly in front of him in a white-knuckled grip.

But as I dragged my eyes from his, a foul, creeping sensation swept over me. It was so thunderous that it made me pause. Then Osring paused, too, glancing at me in confusion.

In Ellythia, they marry in the temple of the gods, before fire and water. Nothing about this felt right, and it was like a venom in my bones. I wanted to hurl.

Something was very, very wrong. I stilled, trying to sense where the feeling was coming from. I glanced at Wyxian, who was acting as celebrant. He stared back, blue eyes furious, commanding me to come forth. But I couldn't. The air seemed to vibrate with a pregnant pause. The silence before the thunder.

The nobles around me shifted nervously.

My eyes met Drake's, standing next to the fae king. His hazel eyes were taut, shifting around the room, appraising, sensing, feeling with his supernatural instinct.

In the stained glass window behind Drake, I noticed a movement. Like a shadow underwater. I squinted at it to try and make it focus. Drake turned, following my line of sight, and I saw him stiffen. And then, every fae in the room stiffened as they sensed it. Opal began trembling on my shoulder.

Everyone in the room turned to see where Drake was looking, just as something crashed through the window.

38

SARAYA

A million pieces of coloured glass flew, and I flung myself across my father. Someone screamed.

I had never seen a flying demon before, but here was one now, leathery brown reptile skin, bat-like wings, shrieking that felt like needles in my ear.

I looked back at the window, now devoid of glass, cold night air streaming in, multi-coloured shards on the marble ballroom floor.

The demon was *physically* in the room. Everyone could see it. It was not in its astral form.

Shock whirled through me like the pale wind of death.

And then a sword hurled through the air, skewering the reptilian thing and spearing it against the ballroom wall.

I hauled myself off my father and turned to look at the source of the blade. Drake stood there, his arm reaching for another sword, his eyes darting around the room and landing on me.

I looked down at my hand and saw that I had summoned my astral sword without even noticing. My head whipped up to see both Wyxian and Daxian staring at me with an unabashed shock that I had never seen on the face of a fae.

"What's happening?" cried little King Junni.

"That was a demon, son," boomed King Omni. "But where on god's great earth did it come from?"

But before anyone could say anything, a boom shook the palace on its foundation. A roaring penetrated the air, distant and shrieking. I flew towards the broken window, sticking my head out as far as I could. Pain shot through my forearm as my skin was cut on a glass shard, but I didn't care because, in the city, people were screaming. I couldn't see properly from this side of the palace, but I sure as hell could hear my people sounding like they were fighting for their lives.

Daxian was behind me, and then Drake. I turned to give Drake a look.

The palace shook again.

"They're at the main door," Drake growled and sprinted out of the room, Slade close behind him.

Demons were trying to get into the palace, and by the sound of it, a lot of them.

"We need to find safety," King Omni said as the nobility formed a huddle.

Lysander appeared by my side. I looked up at him. "Get all the guests into my father's suite. It's the most protected, right?"

He nodded, but his blue eyes were uncertain. "Are you sure?"

I glanced at Osring, who was watching our conversation closely. He nodded at me and turned my father's wheelchair around.

"Go, Lysander, please," I said. "If they breach the castle, we're done for."

King Omni drew his sword as we all fled the ballroom. As the nobles turned left to head deeper into the castle, I made to turn right.

"Saraya!" said Helena, her face pink. "You are coming with us!"

"No," I shook my head and glanced at Daxian and Wyxian, who were now hurrying to the entrance hall. "I need to be out here. Go, Lysander."

The blond fae hesitated for a beat before he turned and led the nobles towards my father's rooms. King Omni and two of my liege lords, Farris and Lombrien, remained behind, drawing their swords. They regarded my own glowing weapon warily, but we had no time for questions with the sound of the roaring and shrieking that was now coming from outside.

I strode out into the entrance hall. First, the fae had taken the palace, but I would be damned if demons took it too. I would die protecting my city, even if it was the last thing I did.

Daxian hesitated ahead of me, pausing so that I caught up to him. "Where did you get that sword, Saraya?" he asked in a low voice.

"You don't need to know," I said, turning to give him a disgusted look. His eyes widened and flicked up to my forehead.

I realised then my skin was hot. The goddess mark was probably showing. Sighing as I strode after the human nobility, I tore off my face veil, plucked off my crown, and set it on a side table, hastily tying my hair up into a bun.

When we reached the entrance hall, Wyxian was already there, along with around twenty fae guards. Drake was talking rapidly to Slade, who nodded and ran off with a group of warriors following closely behind him.

As Drake strode up to me, I saw Wyxain casting magic over the palace doors. Navy blue magic shimmered over the entire surface. The doors shook again but remained stable. Something heavy rammed into it from the other side.

Both Daxian and Wyxian took up swords given to them by fae captains. I had a begrudging respect for that. I had half expected Wyxian to run off. But it seemed he was a warrior to the bone.

"You need to get out of here, Saraya," Drake said, standing beside me.

I held up my sword and looked at him accusingly. "You know I won't do that, Drake. This is my home. Why are they here?"

Drake sighed, unsheathing his sword and his eyes, too, flicked up to my goddess mark. "I followed a group of them the night you killed the demons on the palace grounds. I saw what they do in their astral form. They've been waiting to do this…and so have you, it seems."

I glared at him, trying to hide my confusion. "What are you saying? Are the demons not in league with your kind?"

"No, Saraya," Drake said. "They are in their own league. It's not the fae who've been stealing magic from your people but another group of beings entirely."

Shock pulsed through me. The fae were not stealing human magic? The fae were not responsible for attacking us? My mind scattered, trying to piece together what I was hearing. Drake's face was sincere, angry, furious even. And he had killed that flying demon. He wasn't lying about this. He couldn't be.

But my flurry of emotions was short-lived because I was

grabbed from behind with viciously sharp claws and pulled backwards into the air.

Drake's face contorted into a fury so animal-like it would've taken my breath away had it already not been sucked out of me by the savage sensation of being pulled backwards.

An angry scream fell from my mouth, and I looked above me to see the giant reptilian head of a flying demon, its dragon-like wings beating steadily, making us rise higher into the air. He must've come through the broken ballroom window.

But I hadn't forgotten the sword in my hands. I flipped the blade up and plunged it into the demon's neck. Blood sprayed all over my face, filling my mouth—just before the demon dropped me. I fell through the air with a scream, not realising how high we'd flown. I tried to wipe the blood from my eyes as I plummeted. But just as I anticipated meeting my death on the marble tile of my home, a warm wind enveloped me and cushioned my fall. I reeled from the change in velocity, my mind catching up to my body as I was laid gently down onto the floor. Drake's towering form stood over me, bending down to lift me up.

"Was that your magic?" I asked breathlessly, wiping my face with my sleeve. "I thought I was going to d—"

"It was me," he said quickly. "And no, you're not dying on my watch."

At that moment, the front doors were blasted open, and a stream of demons of all breeds, shapes, and sizes stampeded in. The fae warriors scrambled, but with Wyxian and Daxian in the lead, they held firm against the horde. King Omni's dark-as-night skin shone with sweat as he fought beside them —human and fae fighting side by side. My own mind couldn't compute this nightmare that was happening before my eyes. But I couldn't afford to be thinking at a time like this. Demons were in my palace, pouring in, tens by the second.

"Go back with the other nobles, Saraya," Drake said. "Please." The look in his eyes was desperate as he bid me to go.

"Please?" I repeated dumbly. But I couldn't walk away from him, from those fighting to defend my palace.

He gave me an exasperated look. "Please!"

I finally got it together and shook my head. "No." Gripping my sword, I ran alongside him. He groaned in annoyance but said nothing as we joined the fray, him slashing at demons' heads, me stabbing at their abdomens.

But there were too many of them, and the demons began slipping through our front lines.

Two blood-red demons sprinting into the palace behind me. I let out a shout and ran after them. I couldn't let them get to my father or the other nobles. I wouldn't be able to forgive myself if one or more of them died in my own palace.

I felt Drake behind me, like an icy wind on my heels, following my every turn as I sprinted after the demons, my mother's wedding silks flapping. They were splattered with blood and grime, and though I couldn't help but dismay at that, there was nothing to be done.

We caught up to the demons, who seemed to be headed straight to my father's rooms, their noses in the air as if they were tracing his scent. The cold realisation hit me in the gut. They had been sent for my father. This couldn't be happening. I didn't understand why. For what reason did they want the king?

I gained on one and leapt, slashing at its back. It shrieked, and the other turned around to attack me, but Drake was there, beheading it with an angry force. I skewered my demon through the heart, and it collapsed to the ground with a dismayed cry.

But another set came from behind us, and I turned and took their forms in with great surprise. These demons walked tall and straight like human men, with the swagger and confidence of fae males. In their pale as death, muscled hands, they both carried curved and jagged blades sparkling with green quartz crystals. This was a whole new level of demon entirely. These were warriors.

Drake swore under his breath as they came to stand before us, their fanged teeth dripping with lime-coloured venom. I noted the black scorpion insignia on their breast plates.

"I know who you are," Drake snarled. "You won't win here."

"She looks tasty," said one through a mouth full of teeth. "After we kill you, we're going to take her with us."

A chill seeped through my body. But Drake was the calm before the storm, and he chuckled darkly, taking out a second sword from the sheath that must have been strapped to his back in the entrance hall.

I stepped forward at the same time the commander did.

"You'll have to fight her first," Drake drawled. "Let's see how you do."

Unbidden, a smile crept upon my lips at Drake's confidence in me. Somehow, I was reminded of the Mountain Academy, and it felt like I was there now, under the storm clouds that followed Drake everywhere, facing an opponent who was supposed to be superior to me.

Drake stepped away from me as if to give me space. As I glanced at him, he smirked. "Do what you do best, Sara."

The cadence with which he said my name mirrored the way my long-gone parents used to say it. That's what set me off. That's who I was fighting for.

I snarled and lunged for the demon on the right. Slashing with a fury I had not quite ever tapped into before. But the demon was also fast. He met my flurry blow for blow but had to step backwards each time in the process. Left, right, left, right, with a speed that should have been impossible for me to keep up with, I chopped and slashed and stabbed. But the muscled demon snarled and swung his sword up in a blow that I only just met with my own blade, a stinging pain surging up my wrist. I swore internally, and now he struck, over and over again.

I barely registered Drake and the other demon bashing out heavy blows, grunting and snarling at each other. But I knew Drake was toying with his demon when he spat out a laugh.

I growled in frustration as my arms stung from the repeated blows. I parried and turned, but the hulking demon met me with a force I had not come against before. He nicked my cheek, then my hand, then my chest. I wasn't fast enough. Then he got a blow that slashed the muscle of my forearm, and I screamed in pain and anger.

But I knew how to fight through the pain. My stepmother had taught me that, and just when the demon lowered his sword with a smiling snarl, happy that he had finally 'got me,' I struck before he realised what I was going to do and buried my sword in his neck.

Blood spurted, and he fell to the floor with a thud.

My chest heaved as I panted and waited for Drake to dispatch his demon, which he quickly did when he saw I'd killed mine. The other fell with a killing blow, and fae commander nodded at me, scanning my body up and down as if he were assessing my injuries.

But I had already healed my forearm laceration by the time I turned and fled to my father's suite and pounded on the door. The palace was going to be overrun. I had to get my father and the other nobles out of here.

39

DRAKE

As Saraya pounded on the door of her father's room, the distant sounds of humans, fae, and demons fighting for their lives filling our ears, I wondered how to tell her what I'd learned.

Before the wedding, the fae raven had arrived from Obsidian Court with a note written by the rushed hand of Dacre Liversblood, the hundred-year-old Obsidian Court high mage who had been charged with the responsibility of monitoring demon activity.

I had sent him a raven with one question.

"Demons are astrally attacking human children, stealing their magical seed at birth. Find out more. Also, what is this symbol?"

I had sketched a rough diagram of the moon and lotus symbol I'd seen carved into Saraya's forehead by a magical hand. It was a god-mark. I knew it in my blood. Saraya had the affection of a goddess behind her, and I needed to know why.

The raven had returned with eight words in Dacre's hand.

Havrok Scorpax
Symbol for Order of Temari
Coming

HE'D NAMED A DEMON KING AND THEN AN OLD ORDER I WAS NOT familiar with. Lazy bastard could've written more. But the fact that he was coming to our aid had, at the time, placated me just a little.

But now, he would be too late. We should have known. Should have bloody well known that one of the bastards living in the underworld was going to try something. They'd been collecting magic for decades, lying low and waiting. Clearly, now whichever prince it was had gathered enough to send his forces to earth in their physical forms.

And all this time, the Order of Temari had suspected *us*.

But how the hell were they getting into the human realm? There had to be a portal somewhere around here for them to cross through. I guess it didn't matter because they were here in huge numbers, and if I wasn't careful, they were going to take over Quartz City.

I needed to get outside and assess what we were up against, but I was drawn to stay beside Saraya. As I had always been.

The human king's door swung open, and Saraya almost fell through.

"We need to get out!" she said, hastily pushing past the king regent of Serus, with his sword in hand. "The palace is overrun."

Queen Helena strode to the head of the group of royals clustered at the back of the room, obviously keen to take charge, her king husband simpering behind her. But where was Lysander? He'd probably gone outside to fight. There was no way he would've just waited in here.

"Which way out?" asked Helena.

Saraya thought for a moment before pointing to a tapestry hanging against a wall. "The servant's corridors," she said. "I'll take you—"

But at that moment, we heard a shout and the pounding of feet. It was Lysander, his face streaked with demon blood.

"Get them the fuck out of here," he cried. "They're coming!"

"Go!" Saraya shouted. "Just go!" She pointed at her father's manservant. "Lead them out, Derrick. Just leave my father here. I'll protect him."

The royals stampeded toward the servant's door, to their credit, maintaining a sense of dignity, the men letting the weaker of them go first. King Omni, god bless him, was still fighting on the front lines.

"We're overrun," Lysander muttered so only my fae ears could hear. "There's too many for our forces."

"Where the fuck are they all coming from?" I muttered. "And so quickly without our knowing?" I shook my head. "We need to get Saraya out of here. I—"

But heavy boots from the corridor outside were marching straight towards us. And they were not fae commissioned boots. Lysander and I turned to face the demon contingent as behind us, Saraya hurried the last of the royals through the servant's door.

She shut it with a definite click, her heart pounding to the beat of mine. I counted the pairs of the demonic feet by their sound and Lysander stiffened at the same time I did. There were more than thirty of them stomping in formation.

I opened my mouth to warn Saraya just as the first of them rounded the corner, but I stopped dead.

Because behind the first line of the demonic royal guard marked with scorpions, was the white face of Queen Glacine, Saraya's stepmother.

Saraya came up behind me, her body as tense as mine, her sword in hand. I knew she saw her stepmother's form when I heard her heart speed up and pound against her ribs.

Glacine saw her stepdaughter, guarded by Lysander and me, two of the best fighters of Black Court, and tilted her chin up arrogantly, her face like cold marble.

Her demon guard parted to let her pass, and it was then I saw a twisted black scorpion tattoo that was now visible on her neck. A mark that had definitely not been there when we'd come to Lobrathia for Saraya's engagement.

Saraya shouldered past Lysander and me, her sword glinting with its own blue light under the luminous yellow quartz of the hall.

"I shouldn't be surprised," said Saraya coldly. "You always *were* such a demon."

The venom in her voice made me see red. Unbidden, I growled low in my throat, the demonic guard angling their swords in what they probably thought was a menacing way, but my gaze was only for Glacine. How had I missed her demonic background the first time I'd lain eyes on her at the engagement?

"Saraya," the queen drawled. "I had hoped to never see you again."

"Likewise," the princess snarled. "And I wasn't surprised

to hear that you'd run off at the first sign of trouble. What are you doing here?"

"I am here for my *husband*," Glacine spat on the word like it was something dirty. "Get out of my way."

And then it hit me with the force of a tidal wave. Saraya's scars on her back. The Queen.

My vision narrowed onto Glacine's ice statue form, every instinct in my body screaming at me, marking her as my prey. Something to be hunted and put down. But my princess was speaking beside me, and my body obeyed the command to listen to her.

"You have no right," she said through gritted teeth. "You are no queen. You are no wife. You are nothing here. To me, or to anyone else."

Glacine rolled her eyes, sighing dramatically. "You always were an impertinent little slut. Move these people, or I will have my guards kill them."

I cracked my neck on both sides, rage boiling through me. Lysander glanced at me in warning, but my tone emerged deathly even. "Get her to shut up, Saraya, or I'll put her head on a spike."

But Saraya bristled at me. "She's *mine*, Drake, not yours."

Immediately I stood down, hating myself for it at the same time, suppressing the urge to grin at the princess' fierceness. Whatever Glacine saw in our exchange, it wiped the smirk off her face.

"Kill them!" she hissed.

They rushed at us, and gods, I relished in the murder—beheading the first, skewering the second, and slicing the third. Next to me, Lysander was doing the same thing. I'd seen these demons before, from afar. These were Scorpax Kingdom's demonic warriors who walked upright, with lean muscles bred to kill and destroy on command. They were like trained fighting dogs but with the brains for strategy.

I tasted the magic in the air, and before I could warn Saraya, going head to head with a warrior on my right, she cried out, hissing in pain. But she never faltered in her strike.

It was then that three demons came at me at once, and two swords were almost not enough.

And then something hit me with the force of a magical thunderclap. A severing, an unravelling.

An unbinding.

I reeled as a thousand memories flooded back into the crevices of my mind.

Images of Saraya. I had known her since I was a child. Through blood contract that tied my soul to hers, I had felt her every emotion from the time I was old enough to realise they were not my own. Someone else's sorrow, anger, guilt, elation.

And it was a secret someone had made me forget for seven years. My mother, my father, and Dacre Liversblood, the mage from Obsidian Court, had bound me when I had tried to escape from home to find Saraya.

Because my mother had lied about when I was born.

And there would be only one reason the memories were back. Because the person who had helped bind them was dead.

My father, King Wyxian.

My mother had told him that I was born after Daxian. And had lied about why I was so out of control. My head was pounding as it all came back to me.

But that lapse in concentration was all the demons needed to thump me across the skull. I landed on my knees, at the same time feeling Saraya next to me.

I felt her like I felt one of my own limbs. And now, I felt a stabbing pain in my thigh...in her thigh.

I roared in anger, twisting to see Saraya falling to the floor. Her brilliant green eyes found mine, and the pain in them cleaved my heart in two. With the sword in my left hand, I slashed at the demon warrior coming at my left, simultaneously bringing the sword in my right hand up to slash at the gut of the one who had stabbed Saraya.

Two more demons came at me from my left. One jumped on my back, and the other tackled me onto the floor. I looked up just in time to see Lysander being dragged down by no less than four demon warriors, each one with a limb of his in hand.

"No!" Saraya cried as two demons pinned her to the floor.

"Leave them alive." Glacine's voice cut through the air like a knife, and the six pairs of hands on me pushed me down to the cold marble floor. "Shackle them all. You have your orders."

"Whose orders?" I didn't even recognise my own voice through the rasp of anger. One of the demons savagely pressed my head into the tile, and all I could see was Saraya's face, pressed into the tile same as mine. The hem of Glacine's black gown swept between us.

"You'll find out soon enough, Commander," she said darkly before stepping away into the king's room.

"Don't you dare!" Saraya screamed into the floor. "If you fucking kill—"

"I will not!" Glacine's voice was a feral shriek. "You're no better than a common whore, Saraya. And your father is coming back with us. As are you."

I couldn't make eye contact with Lysander, couldn't make a plan to get out of this. But then someone clasped something cold around my wrists, and I knew with the magical hiss, the shackles would incapacitate me completely. They had used the obsidian quartz, usually reserved for the worst type of demon prisoners. I felt its effect immediately, the doping sensation that began climbing up from my hands. I would be limp within minutes.

I registered a scraping sound in the distance, and the smell of blood pinched the air. I sniffed, and Saraya saw my eyes widen, her face twisted into a panic.

"What is it?" she hissed.

I opened my mouth, then abruptly closed it as the smell of that blood overwhelmed me, consumed me, filled me up with a primal heartache I couldn't even register properly.

Saraya's question was answered as two demons came into view, dragging Wyxian's limp body by the hair, leaving a trail of smeared blood as they went.

The vision of it drove me near mad. It was out of my mouth before I could stop it. "Father!" I roared.

40
SARAYA

Pinned onto the floor, I froze in shock as Drake screamed at the dead form of Wyxian, being dragged along the marble tile. I didn't understand. He was the king of Black Court, undefeated in war. And where was Daxian?

I didn't even know what my stepmother was doing to my father in his room behind me. Every time I tried to twist, sharp fingered claws dug into me harder, the shackles around my wrists dampening my magic in that familiar way. Drake had used the same ones when he'd shackled me just a few days ago.

But he'd said *father*. I repeated it dumbly out loud.

"What are you saying, Drake?" I choked out.

"Saraya," his voice was a rasp, filled with rage, agony, and something else I couldn't fathom as his eyes bore into mine from where they'd pressed him to the floor, like me. Trying to send me a message. And then the words poured out of him like an opening in a dam.

"I'm Wyxian's first son. I was born two days before

Daxian, though everyone thought it was after. My mother tricked him."

His words wrapped around me like a vice.

"Your father's contract bound you to his first born son. Me. Not Daxian. And I'd known it all my life until they made me forget. I felt you then, in the Fae Realm. I feel you now."

I closed my eyes as confusion poured through me like dark, black smoke. Like something raw, pounding, and obvious. A fist knocked on a door of my mind that I had ignored. That I had shut out. That my mother had me shut out.

Build a palace. A strong one. So that no one will ever get in.

Horror tore through me as I was painfully hauled up onto my feet.

"Saraya," rasped Drake.

I looked over to Lysander, struggling against the four demons that were dragging him upright.

"Oh, you stupid girl," came my stepmother's voice. She stepped in front of me, my father being wheeled by a demon warrior behind her.

"You fucking—"

She slapped me so hard my head snapped to the side. Pain blossomed over my cheek.

Your stepmother is not human.

How could it be?

But I knew it was. Just by looking at her new, darker clothes, that tattoo on her neck, the way the demons followed her orders. I knew with every old scar on my back that she was a part of the demon kingdom. They had tricked us, using Kusha Kingdom's secretive nature as a ruse.

My stepmother took out a glass vial from her pocket, almost identical to the vials my father took his medicine in.

With a sick feeling, she uncorked it, and yet another pair of iron-strong demon hands held my head in an impossible grip.

"There are worse things than me in this world, Saraya," she said in a low, dangerous voice. "But you'll find that out soon enough in the demon realm."

Then she forced the potion down my throat. The magic was acrid and biting like a thousand bee stings down my throat. I coughed and gagged.

And then I was carried out of the corridor. Drake and Lysander were being dragged behind me, and all I could think about was Tembry and baby Delilah, Blythe and Opal. Had they gotten out? Had they been clever enough to escape out the servant's corridors? I despaired, my gut twisting as blind grief raged through me. I should have known. I should have gotten them out of here, shown them my secret tunnel. But I never had.

Carnage lay around me as they carried me through the palace, and I felt the effects of the demonic potion disabling my limbs. Demon bodies, human bodies. My eyes went blurry, and all I could see was a blur of red and black, tan and white. How many dead? How many of my people?

They carried me outside the palace and into the city, where the screams of my people were still running rampant. The cold night air cruelly stroked my skin as I strained to make sense of what I was seeing. What was happening to me.

They carried me for ages into the dark, and it was with a pang that I realised where we were headed.

The quarry.

But it didn't matter because a shadow encroached at the edges of my vision, and the last thing I saw was Drake's limp body being carried ahead of me and into the dark.

—THE END OF THE WARRIOR MIDWIFE BOOK 1—

From the bottom of my heart, I hope you enjoyed The Warrior Midwife. If you did enjoy it, pretty please leave a review at the retailer of purchase, I read every single one and it helps me make a living out of my work.

Things heat up in book two! Check out The Warrior Priestess.

Wondering where Altara is?

Well, her story is just as interesting as Saraya's! Sign up to my email newsletter to get updates about upcoming books:

www.ektaabali.com/warriormidwife

Signing up to my mailing list means that you get first peek at everything I produce, including book covers, new releases, exclusive excerpts and bonus material that I don't post anywhere else.

ACKNOWLEDGMENTS

To my dearest cover artist, Carly Diep, you know how much I appreciate your craftsmanship and infinite patience. Thank you for your tireless work and dedication to your craft, *and* for your god-level patience with me!

To Jess for your wonderful chapter heading illustrations. They really are beautiful and make the book look like an old school fairytale. And why should YA and NA readers not get that experience too?!

To Naijlka for the wonderful map. This is my first map for a series and now, I think the first of many!

Thank you to my editor Maryssa Gordon for your encouragement, suggestions and keen eyes on this manuscript.

To Sheree, thank you for your honesty about my work and also, the sharpest eyes around! Every book has errors and you always catch mine and help me look less stupid <3.

As always, mum, you know how much you mean to me, thank you for your cups of chai, your hugs and constant support. You somehow encourage me and keep me in line at the same time.

And thank **you**, dear reader, because you make this all possible. I can only continue to keep writing because of *you* and I appreciate that with all my heart.

ABOUT THE AUTHOR

Ektaa P. Bali was born in Fiji and spent most of her life in Melbourne, Australia.

After graduating Killester College in 2008, she studied nursing and midwifery at Deakin University, going on to spend eight years as a midwife in various hospitals.

She published her first novel in 2020, the beginning of a middle grade fantasy series, before going on to pursue her true passion: Young & New Adult Fantasy.

The Warrior Midwife is her third novel in the Chrysalis-verse and the first in a new trilogy.

She currently lives in Brisbane, Australia.

facebook.com/ektaabaliauthor
instagram.com/ektaabaliauthor
youtube.com/ektaabali

ALSO BY E.P. BALI

Upper YA/NA Fantasy

The Ellythian Princesses:

#1 The Warrior Midwife

#2 The Warrior Priestess

#3 The Warrior Queen

#1 The Archer Princess

#2 The Archer Witch

#3 The Archer Queen

YA Fantasy

The Travellers:

#1 The Chrysalis Key

#2 The Allure of Power

#3 The Wings of Darkness

Middle Grade Fantasy

The Pacific Princesses fantasy adventure series:

#1 The Unicorn Princess

#2 The Fae Princess

#3 The Mermaid Princess

#4 The Tale of the Three Princesses

Printed in Great Britain
by Amazon